GENA SHOWALTER

The Darkest CRAVING

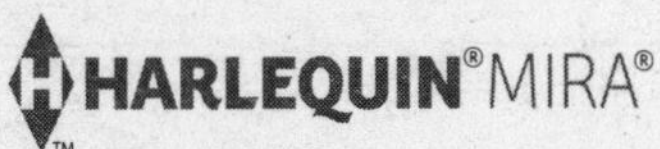

Published in Great Britain 2013
Harlequin MIRA, Eton House, 18-24 Paradise Road,
Richmond, Surrey, TW9 1SR

ISBN 978 1 848 45237 4

58-0813

Harlequin MIRA's policy is to use papers that are natural, renewable and recyclable products and made from wood grown in sustainable forests. The logging and manufacturing processes conform to the legal environmental regulations of the country of origin.

Printed and bound by
CPI Group (UK) Ltd, Croydon, CR0 4YY

Praise for *New York Times* and *USA Today* bestselling author GENA SHOWALTER'S

LORDS OF THE UNDERWORLD

The Darkest Night

'*The Darkest Night* is Showalter at her finest and a fabulous start to an imaginative new series.'

—*New York Times* bestselling author Karen Marie Moning

'Amazing! Stupendous! Extraordinary!'

—*Fallen Angels* reviews

The Darkest Kiss

'Talk about one dark read... If there is one book you must read this year, pick up *The Darkest Kiss*… a Gena Showalter book is the best of the best.'

—*Romance Junkies*

The Darkest Pleasure

'You will not be sorry if you add this to your collection.'

—*Mists and Stars*

The Darkest Whisper

'If you like your paranormal dark and passionately flavoured, this is the series for you.'

—*RT Book Reviews*, 4 stars

The Darkest Passion

'Showalter gives her fans another treat, sure to satisfy!'

—*RT Book Reviews*, 4 stars

The Darkest Secret

'It is difficult to keep a long-running series compelling, but Showalter manages it wonderfully!'

—*RT Book Reviews*, 4 stars

The Darkest Seduction

'Showalter shows her skill, and redeems the irredeemable, by crafting a beautiful love story that is both humorous and touching.'

—*RT Book Reviews*, 4 stars

ACKNOWLEDGEMENTS

First, to my editor, Emily Ohanjanians. Your insight never ceases to amaze me. Thank you so much for all your hard work and dedication.

Second, to my agent, Deidre Knight. I am so blessed to have you in my corner. No matter what I throw at you, you're always there to help me!

To Carla Gallway, for all that you do! You are generous with your time and resources and so wonderfully kind, and I'm so thankful to know you!

To the winners of the blog contest: Sabrina Collazo, Lizabel Rivera-Coriano, Charlayne Elizabeth Denney, Seemone Washington and Joni Payne. I hope you love Kane's story as much as I do.

To Michelle Renaud and Lisa Wray. You're my girls and I couldn't ask for a better team!

To my favourite restaurant, The Stuffed Olive, for feeding me while I was on deadline!

No dedication would be complete without mentioning my beloved Jill Monroe. You're stuck with me, because I won't ever let you go!

"I've been told I'm almost as dangerous as a tsunami."
—Kane, Lord of the Underworld

"I've been told I'm a tsunami."
—Josephina Aisling

CHAPTER ONE

New York City
Present day

JOSEPHINA AISLING PEERED down at the male splayed across the motel room bed. He was an immortal warrior, beautiful in a way no mortal could ever hope to be. Silky hair of jet, chestnut and flax spilled over the pillow, the multicolored strands forming a flawless tapestry, inviting the eye to linger a minute, then a minute more…sweet mercy, why not forever?

His name was Kane. He had long, boyish lashes, a strong nose and a stubborn chin. At six feet four, he was cut with the kind of muscle only earned on the bloodiest of battlefields. Though he wore stained and dirty pants, she knew a large butterfly tattoo dominated the right side of his hip, the ink thick and black, a little jagged. The tops of the wings stretched over the material and every so often tiny waves rippled through them, as though the insect struggled to lift from his skin—or burrow deeper.

Either was possible. The tattoo was a mark of absolute, utter evil, a visible sign of the demon contained inside Kane's body.

Demon...she shuddered. Rulers of hell. Liars, thieves. Murderers. They were darkness without any hint of light. They lured and tempted. They ruined, tortured and destroyed.

But Kane wasn't the demon.

Like all of her race, the mighty Fae, she had spent a good portion of her life studying Kane and his friends—the Lords of the Underworld. In fact, at the command of the Fae king, spies had spent countless centuries following the warriors, watching and reporting back. Scribes had then printed books with stories and pictures of what they'd witnessed. Mothers had bought those books and read them to their children. Then, when those children had grown up, they had made their own purchases, the need to know what happened next too strong to ignore.

The Lords of the Underworld had become the stars of the best and the worst soap opera in Séduire, the realm of the Fae.

Josephina always ate up every detail. Especially those about the ultra sexy Paris and the devastatingly lonely Torin. Kane, the beautiful tragedy, was a close third. She could probably recite his life history better than she could her own.

He was thousands of years old. He'd only had four serious girlfriends in his lifetime. Although, for a while, he'd had a string of meaningless one-night stands. He'd fought in bloody battle after bloody battle with his enemy, the Hunters. Three times, they'd managed to capture and torture him—and she'd waited, breathless, to hear of his escape.

Going back even further, to the beginning, he and his friends had stolen and opened Pandora's box, unleashing the demons from inside. The Greeks had been in power at the time, and they'd decided to punish the warriors by turning their bodies into receptacles for the very evil they'd freed. Kane carried Disaster. The others carried Promiscuity, Disease, Distrust, Violence, Death, Pain, Wrath, Doubt, Lies, Misery, Secrets and Defeat. Each creature came with a nearly debilitating curse.

Promiscuity had to sleep with a new woman every day or he weakened and died.

Disease couldn't touch another living creature without starting a plague.

Disaster caused catastrophes everywhere Kane went, a fact that sliced at Josephina's heart and resonated deep. Her entire life *was* a disaster.

"Don't touch me," he muttered, his voice a sharp, callous rasp. Powerful legs kicked the already battered sheets away. "Hands off. Stop. I said stop!"

Poor Kane. Another nightmare plagued him.

"No one's touching you," she assured him. "You're safe."

He calmed, and she released a relieved breath.

When she'd first stumbled upon him, he'd been chained to a dais in hell, his chest cavity split open, his ribs spread and exposed, his wrists and ankles hanging on by fraying tendons.

He'd looked like a slab of beef at the local butcher's.

I'll have a two-pound rump roast and a pound of ground chuck.

Gross. Just gross. I'm thoroughly disgusted with you. Over the years, she'd spent so much time alone, conversing with herself had become her only source of amusement…and sadly, companionship. *I would have ordered four pounds of pork loin.*

Despite his condition, finding him was the best thing to ever happen to her. He was her ticket to freedom. Or possibly…acceptance?

Princess Synda, her half sister and the Fae's *most bestest* female ever born, wasn't a Lord, but she carried the demon of Irresponsibility. Apparently, there had been more demons than naughty, box-stealing warriors, and the excess had been given to the inmates of Tartarus—an underground prison for immortals. Synda's first husband had been one of those inmates, and somehow, when the male had died, the demon had wormed its way inside her.

When the king of the Fae had learned of it, he'd launched a hunt for details about the cause—and the solution. So far, everyone had come up empty.

I could bring Kane to a meeting of the Fae High Court, show him off, let him answer any questions the congregation has, and my father might see me, really see me, for the first time in my life.

Her shoulders drooped. *No, I'm not ever going back.*

Josephina had always been, and would always be the royal whipping girl, there to receive the punishments Synda the Beloved was due.

Synda was always due.

Last week, in a fit of temper, the princess had burned to the ground the royal stables, and all of the animals trapped inside. Josephina's sentence? A ticket to the Never-ending—a portal leading into hell.

There, a day was like a thousand years and a thousand years like a day, so, for what had seemed like an endless eternity, she had fallen down, down, down a blackened pit. She had screamed, but no one had heard. Had begged for mercy, but no one had cared. Had cried, but had never found an anchor.

Then, she and another girl had landed in the center of hell.

How startling to realize she'd never actually been alone.

The girl had been a Phoenix, a race descended from

the Greeks. Every full-blooded warrior possessed the ability to rise from the dead, time and time again, growing stronger after every resurrection—until the final death came, and there could be no more bodily restoration.

Kane began to thrash and moan again.

"I'm not going to let anything happen to you," she told him.

Again, he stilled.

If only the Phoenix had responded to her so well. When the girl had first seen her, hatred had lanced at her, hatred going far beyond what the children of the Titans—like Josephina—and the children of the Greeks usually felt for each other. But even still, the Phoenix hadn't tried to kill her, had instead allowed her to follow her through the cave, searching for the exit, without having to exert any of her own waning energy. Like Josephina, she'd just wanted out.

They had stumbled past crimson-splattered walls, inhaling the fetid stink of sulfur. Grunts and groans had reverberated in their ears, creating a terrible symphony their deprived senses hadn't been ready for. Then they'd stumbled upon the mutilated warrior. Josephina had recognized him, despite his condition, and stopped.

Awe had filled her. There, in front of her—her!—had been one of the infamous Lords of the Underworld. She hadn't known how she could help him, when she could barely help herself, but she'd been determined to try. Whatever proved necessary.

A lot had proven necessary.

She looked at him. "You were my first and only opportunity to achieve my new greatest desire," she admitted, "something I definitely couldn't do on my own.

And as soon as you wake up, I'm going to need you to make good on your promise."

And then…

She sighed, quieted. She brushed her fingertips over his brow.

Even in his sleep, he flinched. "Don't," he snarled. "I'll *destroy* you, piece by piece. You and your entire family."

He wasn't bragging, wasn't issuing a hollow threat. He would ensure it happened, and he would probably smile the entire time.

Probably? Ha! He would. Typical Lord.

"Kane," she said, and again, he calmed. "I think maybe it's time to wake you up. My family is out there, and they want me back. While a thousand years passed for me inside that pit, only a day passed for them. Since I failed to return to Séduire, Fae soldiers are probably hunting me."

To add to her bowl of miserypuffs, *the Phoenix* was definitely hunting her, determined to enslave her and avenge the wrong Josephina had done her during their escape.

"Kane." She gently shook his shoulder. His skin was shockingly soft and exquisitely smooth, yet also feverishly hot, the muscles beneath as tight and firm as grenades. "I need you to open your eyes."

Long lashes flipped up, revealing gold-and-emerald irises glassed over and dulled. A second later, big masculine hands wrapped around her neck and tossed her to her back. The mattress bounced, even with her slight weight. She offered no resistance as Kane rolled on top of her, pinning her in place. He was heavy, his grip so tight she couldn't breathe in the rose scent she'd come to associate with him. An odd fragrance for a male, and one she didn't understand.

"Who are you?" he snarled. "Where are we?"

He's speaking directly to me. Me!

"Answer."

She tried to reply, couldn't.

He loosened his hold.

There. Better. Deep breath in. Out. "For starters, I'm your amazing and wonderful rescuer." Since receiving compliments had died with her mother, she'd decided to give them to herself at every opportunity. "Release me, and we'll work out the particulars."

"Who," he demanded, squeezing her tighter.

Black winked through her line of sight. Her lungs burned, desperate for air, but still she offered no resistance.

"Female." The pressure eased again. "Answer. Now."

"Caveman. Free. Now," she retorted as she sucked in oxygen.

Could you watch your mouth, please? You don't want to scare him away.

He jerked away from her to crouch at the end of the bed. His gaze remained on her, watching intently as she slowly sat up. A red flush colored his cheeks, and she wondered if he was embarrassed by his actions or simply struggling to hide the weakness still pumping through him.

"You have five seconds, female."

"Or what, warrior? You'll hurt me?"

"Yes." Determined. Assured.

Silly man. Would it be totally gauche of her to ask him to sign her T-shirt? "Don't you remember what you promised me?"

"I didn't promise you anything," he said, and though

his tone was confident, his features darkened with confusion.

"You did. Think back to your last day in hell. It was you, me and a couple thousand of your worst enemies."

His brows drew together, and his eyes glazed with remembrance, comprehension…then horror. He shook his head, as though desperate to dislodge the thoughts now swirling through his mind. "You weren't serious. You couldn't have been serious."

"I was."

He popped his jaw, an action of frustrated aggression. "What's your name?"

"I think it's better if you don't know. That way, there's no emotional attachment and you can more easily do what I require."

"I never actually said I'd do it," he gritted out. "And why are you looking at me like that?"

"Like what?"

"Like I'm…a giant box of chocolates."

"I've heard of you," she said, and left it at that. Truth, without explanation.

"Hardly. If you'd heard anything about me, you'd be running away in fear."

Oh, really? "I know that during the many wars you've fought, your friends often left you behind, afraid you'd cause some kind of travesty for them. I know you often keep yourself shut away from the world, terrified of the same. And yet, still you've managed to slay thousands. Dare I say bazillions?"

He ran his tongue over perfect white teeth. "How do you know that?"

"Why don't we call it…gossip."

"Gossip isn't always right," he muttered. In seconds,

he had swept his gaze through the small room and refocused on her.

She also happened to know that visual caress was a habit he'd developed through the years, one meant to take everything in. Entrances, exits, weapons that could be used against him—weapons he could use.

This time, all he would have seen was the peeling yellow wallpaper, the scarred nightstand with the chipped lamp. The sputtering air-conditioning unit. The brown shag carpet. The trash bin filled with bloody rags and emptied tubes of medicine she'd used on his abrasions.

"That day in hell," he began. "You told me what you wanted, and then you made the mistake of assuming I agreed."

That sounded like a refusal. *But...he can't refuse me. Not now.* "You gurgled your assent. Afterward, I did my part. Now you will do yours."

"No. I never asked for your help." His voice lashed like the sharpest of whips, striking at her, leaving an undeniable sting. "Never wanted it."

"You did, too! Your eyes begged me, and you can't deny it. You couldn't see your eyes, so you have no idea what they were doing."

A protracted pause. Then, quite calmly, he said, "I think that's the most illogical argument I've ever heard."

"No, it's the smartest, but your puny brain simply can't compute it."

"My eyes did not beg," he said, "and that's final."

"They did, too," she insisted. "And I did a terrible thing to get you out." Sadly, sending the Phoenix a note of apology wouldn't fix the problem.

As weak as Josephina had been in hell, she'd required help with Kane. Only, once she'd caught up to the Phoenix, still hacking her way to freedom, there'd been a slight problem. The girl had refused so vehemently—*rot in hell, Fae whore*—that Josephina had known there would be no hope of changing her mind. So, Josephina had used the ability she alone carried. A blessing in the right circumstances. A curse that had kept her locked in a world without physical contact. With only a touch, she'd stolen the strength right out of the Phoenix's body, reducing the girl to a boneless heap.

Yes, Josephina had draped the warrior woman over one shoulder and carried her out of hell, the same as she'd done for Kane, fighting demons along the way—a miracle considering she'd never fought a day in her life—eventually finding a way outside, but that wouldn't matter to the Phoenix. A crime had been committed, and a price had to be paid.

"I never asked you to do terrible things." His voice contained the darkest of warnings.

One she did not heed. "Maybe not audibly, but even still, I nearly broke my back saving you." She settled to her knees, shaking the mattress and nearly bouncing the weakened Kane to the floor. "You weigh, like, ten thousand pounds. But they're glorious pounds," she rushed to add. *Stop insulting the man!*

His slitted gaze tripped over every inch of her. The action lacked the stealth he'd used for the room, and yet, it was almost tactile, as if he'd touched her, too. Could he see the goose bumps now breaking over her skin?

"How did a girl like you manage such a feat?"

A girl like her. Did he sense her inferiority? She lifted her chin, saying, "An information exchange wasn't part of our bargain."

"For the last time, woman, there was no bargain."

Tremors of dread rocked her, overshadowing…whatever he'd previously made her feel. "If you don't do what you promised, I'll…I'll…"

"What?"

Suffer for the rest of my life. "What would it take to change your mind and make you do the right thing?"

His expression shuttered, hiding all of his thoughts. "What species are you?"

A question totally off topic, but okay, she could roll. Since the Fae were not a well-liked race, the men best known for their lack of honor in battle, as well as their insatiable need to sleep with anything that moved, and the women known for backstabbing and scandal—and okay, fine, their ability to sew a killer wardrobe—the knowledge might spur him into action.

"I'm half human, half Fae. See?" She pulled back the sides of her hair, drawing his attention to her ears and the points at the end.

His gaze locked on those points and narrowed. "Fae are descendants of Titans. Titans are children of fallen angels and humans. They are the current rulers of the lowest level of the skies." He shot out each fact as if it were a bullet.

Can't roll my eyes at a star. "Thank you for the history lesson."

He frowned. "That makes you…"

Evil in his eyes? An enemy?

He shook his head, refusing to finish the thought. Then, his nose wrinkled, as if he'd just smelled something…not unpleasant, but not welcome, either. He inhaled sharply, and his frown deepened. "You look nothing like the girl who rescued me…*girls* who rescued me…no, just one," he said with another shake of his head, as if he were trying to make sense of things that had happened. "Her face and hair kept changing, and I recall each countenance, yet what I see now I didn't see then. But your scent..."

Was the same, yes. "I possessed the ability to switch my appearance."

One of his brows arched. "Possessed. Past tense."

Even in his compromised state, he'd caught her meaning. "Correct. I no longer have the ability." The strength—and capabilities—she borrowed from others could remain with her for as little time as an hour to as long as a few weeks. She had no control over the time frame. What she'd taken from the Phoenix had faded yesterday.

"You're lying. No one has an ability one day, but not the next."

"I never lie—except for the few times I do, in fact, lie, but it's never intentional, and I'm totally telling the truth right now." She raised her right hand. "Promise."

He pursed his lips. "How long have I been here?"

"Seven days."

"Seven days," he gasped out.

"Yes. We spent most of our time playing incompetent doctor and ungrateful patient."

A dark scowl contorted his features, and oh, it was a scary thing to behold. The books hadn't done him justice. "Seven days," he repeated.

"I didn't miscount, I assure you. I've been crossing off the seconds in the calendar in my heart."

He gave her the stink eye. "You have a smart mouth, don't you?"

She brightened. "You think so? Really?" It was the first compliment she'd received from someone other than herself since her mother had died, and she would cherish it. "Thank you. Would you say my mouth is extremely intelligent or just slightly above average?"

His jaw fell, as if he meant to reply, but no sound

emerged from him. His eyelids were closing…opening…closing again, and his big body was swaying from side to side. He was about to go down, and if he hit the floor, she would never be able to lift him onto the bed.

Josephina surged forward, reaching for him with gloved hands. Though he teetered backward, he slapped her arms away, wanting no contact between them. Smart man. (As smart as he thought she was?) Down he fell, slamming into the carpet with a loud thud.

As she scrambled to her feet to rush to his side—and do what, she didn't know—the motel door burst open, shards of wood raining in every direction. A tall, thickly muscled warrior with dark hair stood in the center of the gaping hole, his features bathed in shadows. Menace lanced from him. Maybe because he gripped two daggers—and they were already stained with blood.

Another warrior moved in behind him, this one blond, with…*oh, someone save me*. Guts hung from his hair.

Her father's men had found her.

CHAPTER TWO

KANE BATTLED A tide of pain, humiliation and failure. He'd been created fully formed, a warrior to the depths of his core. Throughout the centuries, he had fought in countless wars. He had slain enemy after enemy, and had walked away with many a blood-drenched injury—but he'd walked with a smile. He'd fought, and he'd won, and others had suffered for coming after him. And yet, here he was, on the floor of a dirty motel, too weak to move, at the mercy of a beautiful, fragile female who'd seen him at his worst: chained, violated and carved open after yet another round of torture.

He wanted those images cut from her mind, even if he had to reach inside and remove them with a blade.

Then, he would cut them out of his own. The Hunters, blaming him for every disaster they'd ever faced. Their bomb. A trip into hell. A horde of demon minions attacking, killing the Hunters and secreting Kane away. Day after day of torment.

Shackles. The drip, drip of blood. Satisfied grins, bloodstained teeth. Hands, everywhere. Mouths, seeking. Tongues, licking.

A soundtrack played quietly in the background. Moans of pain—his. Moans of pleasure—none his own. The slap of flesh against flesh. The scrape of nails, digging deep. A bark of laughter.

Terrible scents filled his nose. Sulfur. Arousal. Dirt. Old copper. Sweat. The pungent sting of fear.

One brutal emotion after another bombarded him. Disgust, rage, feelings of utter violation. Sorrow, humiliation, sadness. Helplessness. Panic. More disgust.

He moaned, a tragic sound. Desperate to avoid a breakdown, he erected a brick wall around his screaming mind, blocking the worst of the emotions. *Can't deal right now. Just...can't.* He was free at least. He couldn't forget that. Rescue had come.

No, not a rescue. Not at first. Warriors had stolen him from the minions, only to tie him down for their own special brand of torture.

Then, the girl had arrived, demanding he help her with the vilest of tasks.

"What have you done to him?" a male voice roared. "Why were there Fae soldiers ready to sneak into this room?"

"Wait. You're not with the Fae?" she demanded.

"Who are you, female?"

Kane recognized the speaker. Sabin, his leader, and the keeper of the demon of Doubt. Sabin was a male who wouldn't hesitate to snap a woman's neck if he thought that woman had hurt one of his soldiers.

"Me?" the girl said. "I'm no one, and I've done nothing. Really."

"Lies will only make it worse for you."

Another speaker Kane recognized. Strider, the keeper of the demon of Defeat. Like Sabin, Strider wouldn't hesitate to harm a woman in defense of a friend.

Kane should have been comforted by their appearance. They were brothers of his heart, the family he needed, and they would protect him, whisk him to safety, and do everything within their power to ensure he healed. But he was scabbed, bruised and emotionally naked, and they were now witnesses to his shame, too.

"Oh, sweet heat. Why didn't you step into the light sooner? I know who you are," the girl gasped out. "You're…you're…*you*."

"Yes, and I'm also your doom," Sabin snapped.

The warrior assumed the black-haired girl was responsible for Kane's condition. A mistake. He tried to sit up, but the muscles in his stomach were useless, not yet completely woven back together.

"Please don't take this the wrong way," said the girl, "but that's got to be the lamest thing anyone's ever said to me, and Kane here has said some doozies. You're a magnificent warrior known throughout all the lands for your strength and cunning. I know you can issue a better threat than that."

More than once, the silly things that had come out of that candy-apple mouth had made him want to smile, despite the pain relentlessly battering him. Now was one of those times. He didn't understand it.

"There's a right way to take that?" Sabin snapped. "Guard the door," he said to Strider. "I'm going to tear her from limb to limb."

"No can do, boss. I'm calling dibs."

"Does that mean we're battling to the death?" she asked casually.

"Yes," both men replied in unison.

"Oh, well. Okay, then. Let's get started, shall we?"

Kane stiffened.

"Is she serious?" Sabin.

"No way." Strider.

"I am," she said. "I really am."

Big talk for such a tiny girl.

A girl who confused Kane in every way.

She had tended him gently, tenderly, and yet he had hurt from more than just his injuries. And not a good hurt, either, to let him know he was alive, but a sharp throb that rode the waves in his veins, reaching him at a cellular level, like a disease, a cancer, eating at him, demanding he get away from her as quickly as possible. And yet, inside, deeper still, where primal instinct jerked at a flimsy leash, a desire to grab her, to hold on and never let go, consumed him.

She was beautiful, funny and sweet, and he heard one word every time he looked at her. *Mine.*

Mine. Mine. MINE.

It was a constant stream of noise, undeniable—unstoppable. It was also wrong. His "mine" would never cause him pain. And he didn't want a "mine." Any time he'd tried to make a go of a relationship, the evil inside him swiftly destroyed it—and the female. Now, after everything that had happened to him…

A rise of the disgust, sizzling and blistering, tightened his hands into dangerous weapons. No, he didn't want a "mine."

"You eager to die?" Strider asked, stalking a circle around her.

"You stalling?" she said. "Don't think you can take me?"

The warrior sucked in a breath.

The girl had issued a challenge—intentional or unintentional?—and the warrior's demon had just accepted. Strider would do everything in his power to win, and Kane couldn't blame him. Anytime the male lost a challenge, he suffered in agonizing pain for days.

Demons always came with a curse.

Have to stop him. Whether the girl belonged to Kane

or not, she wasn't to be harmed. Seeing a single bruise on that sun-licked skin would unhinge him, he knew it, could already feel the darkness rising, his control teetering at the edge of chilling violence.

As he again struggled to sit up, multiple footsteps pounded, causing the floor to reverberate. Low growls erupted. The swish of clothing whispered past. Flesh met flesh, bone met bone. Metal clinked against metal. The males would destroy her.

"Is that all you got?" the girl taunted—a taunt undercut by her heavy panting. "Come on, fellas. Let's make this memorable, one for the history books!"

"No," Kane tried to shout, but not even his ears picked up the sound.

Strider jumped over him. Another clang of metal echoed.

"How can this be memorable?" Sabin roared. "The only thing you're doing is leaping out of the way when we strike."

"Sorry. I'm not meaning to, but instinct keeps kicking in," she said.

To anyone but Kane, who knew her secret desire, the conversation would have sounded weird.

The fight continued, the two men chasing the girl around the small room, leaping on furniture, bouncing off the walls, slashing out with hungry blades and missing as she darted out of the way.

The urge to commit violence sharpened with deadly force.

"Don't hurt her," he growled. "I'll hurt you back." He would do anything to protect her.

Even in this pitiful state?

He ignored the humiliating question.

Question. Yes. He had more questions for the girl

than he'd already asked—and this time, she would answer satisfactorily or he would…he wasn't sure what he would do. He'd lost all sense of mercy and compassion inside that cave.

The threat stopped Sabin in his tracks. The warrior lowered his weapons.

Strider refused to give up, and finally managed to grab the girl by the hair. She yelped as he jerked, tugging her into the hard line of his body.

Kane managed to get to his feet, intending to rip the two apart. *Mine.* He stalked forward, tripped over a shoe, thanks to the demon, and came crashing down. Pain consumed him.

Before the girl had a chance to scream for help, or curse Strider's very existence, he knocked her ankles together and sent her propelling to the floor. He went down with her, pinning her shoulders to the floor with his knees. Though she struggled, she couldn't work her way free.

"I said…don't hurt," Kane shouted with what little strength he had left.

"Hey. I barely touched her. I also won," the warrior announced, a huge grin lifting the corners of his mouth.

Sabin marched to Kane's side, crouched, and helped roll him to his back. Then the warrior slid gentle hands under his head and shoulders. Kane flinched from the contact, his mind blaring out a protest he refused to let his mouth deliver, but still his friend held firm, easing him into a sitting position.

"We've been looking for you, my man." Tender words meant to assure and comfort him. Too bad nothing would ever assure and comfort him again. "Weren't ever going to give up."

"How?" he managed to ask. *Let me go. Please, just let me go.*

Sabin understood his question, but not his inner plea. "There was a story in a tabloid about a superwoman in New York carrying a hulk over her shoulder. Torin worked his magic and hacked into security cameras in the area, and boom. We had you."

From her trapped position on the floor, the girl looked over at him. Panting, she said to Sabin, "Hey, can't you tell he's not liking the physical contact? Let him go."

How had she known, when one of his best friends hadn't noticed?

"He's fine," Strider said. "Why are you wearing gloves, female?"

Ignoring the question, she closed her eyes and asked, "Are you going to kill me now?"

"No!" Kane roared. *MINE! MINE!*

Strider sheathed his blades and stood. Immediately the girl climbed to her feet. Long strands of hair had fallen over her brow, onto her cheeks; she pushed the locks behind the pointed ears that had so startled him.

Most of the Fae preferred to remain in their realm. They weren't the most beloved of races, and immortals tended to attack first and ask questions later. Still, Kane had run into a few throughout the centuries. Each Fae had possessed curling white hair and skin as pale as milk. This one had a slick fall of jet-black silk, with no hint of a wave, and skin the most luscious shade of bronze. Marks of her humanity?

Her eyes belonged to the Fae, though. Large and blue, like the rarest of jewels, the color lightened and darkened with her moods. Right now they were crystalline, almost lacking any color at all. Was she frightened?

The demon of Disaster liked the thought and purred his approval.

Shut up, Kane snarled. *I'll kill you. Kill you so dead.*

The purrs became chuckles, and Kane had to force himself to breathe, in and out, in and out, slow and measured. He wanted to cut off his ears in the hopes of silencing all that sickening amusement. He wanted to tear the room apart, destroy every piece of furniture, take down every wall, rip up every inch of carpet. He wanted to…grab the girl and carry her away from this awful place.

His gaze met hers, and she offered the sweetest of smiles. A smile that said, *It's going to be okay, I promise.*

The rage dialed down to a simmer.

That. Quickly.

How had she done that?

Of all the faces she had flashed, this was by far the prettiest. She had the longest lashes he'd ever seen. Her cheekbones were high and sharp, her nose perfectly sloped and her lips heart-shaped. There was a slight point in her chin.

She was like a little girl's doll come to dazzling life, and she smelled of rosemary and spearmint—a fresh-baked bread paired with an after-dinner mint. In other words, home.

Mine.

Never, the demon snipped, and the ground began to shake.

Stupid demon. Like any other living creature, Disaster experienced hunger. Unlike others, fear and upset were his favorite foods. So when he yearned for a meal—or just wanted dessert—he caused some sort of catastrophe for Kane, as well as those around him.

Sometimes, those catastrophes were small. A light bulb would short out, or the floor would crack at his feet. Too many times, those catastrophes were large. A limb would fall from a tree. Cars would crash. Buildings would crumble.

Hatred scraped at his chest. *One day, I'll be free of you. One day, I'll destroy you.*

The shaking stopped as the demon laughed with glee. *I'm a part of you. There'll be no getting rid of me. Ever.*

Kane pounded a fist into the floor. Long ago, the Greeks had told him only death would separate him from the demon—*his* death—but that Disaster would live on forevermore. Perhaps that was true. Perhaps not. The Greeks were famous for their lies. But either way, Kane wouldn't risk death. He was twisted enough to want to witness Disaster's defeat, and just cold enough to want to be the one to deliver the final blow.

There had to be a way to have both.

"—right? Yes?" the girl was saying.

Her lilting voice brought him back to the present.

"Uh, Kane," Sabin prompted. "Did you promise to do that?"

She had been speaking to Kane, then, and he could imagine what she'd said. He shook his head, his neck almost too weak to support the action. "No. I didn't."

"But...but...his memory must be impaired." Her gaze swung to Strider, cerulean flooding her irises, becoming an ocean of anger. "What about you? Will you carry out his end of the bargain?"

"Me?" Strider thumped his chest.

"Yes, you."

"And just how do you want me to proceed, hmm?"

A violent tremor swept through her, but she said, "I

want…I want you to take your dagger and…stab me in the heart."

The warrior blinked, shook his head. "You're serious, aren't you? You actually *want* to die."

"I don't want to, no, but I need to," she whispered, the anger giving way to defeat.

Kane swallowed a roar, remembering her words in the cave.

I will take you to the human world—and in return, you will kill me. I'll have your vow first.

Maybe he hadn't believed her then. Maybe he'd been too lost to his own pain to care. But now, the fact that she wanted to die…not just no, but hell no. *He* would die first.

"Why did you dodge my blows?" Strider demanded of the girl.

"I told you. Instinct. But I'll do better next time, I promise."

Mine, Kane heard again, a deep, rumbling growl rising…rising…escaping. "Mine! Touch her and I'll kill you."

Both Sabin and Strider stared at him with astonishment. Kane had always been the calm one, and had never before raised his voice to his friends. But he wasn't the man he used to be—wouldn't ever be that man again.

"Please," she begged the warrior, those eyes swirling with flecks of baby blue. How desperate she sounded.

How much more hotly his rage burned.

Something terrible had to have happened to her to make her feel death was the only option available. Had someone…had she been forced—he couldn't finish the thought. He would erupt. Or bury his head in the hollow of her neck and sob.

He peered up at Strider. Big, blond Strider, with his navy eyes and warped sense of humor. "Bind her. Gently. Bring her with us." He would help her.

"What?" She held up her hands, palms up, and backed away from the warrior. "No way. Just no way. Unless you're planning to take me to an undisclosed location, so no one will see the blood."

He could have lied. Instead, he remained quiet as Sabin assisted him to his feet. Broken bones that had only recently been reset screamed in protest, and his knees nearly buckled, but he held steady. He wouldn't allow himself to go down. Not again. Not in front of his min—the girl.

"Sorry, honey cakes," Strider said, "but you don't get a say in what happens next. You're gonna live and not die, and that's that."

"But…but…" Her gaze found Kane and pleaded. "I've wasted so much time with you. I have no one else to ask for help."

"Good." Any man who thought to give her what she asked for would die the worst of deaths.

"Good? Good! Oh!" Anger overshadowed everything else, and she stomped her foot. "You heartless, overgrown lout!"

"Because he won't hurt you? That's a first." Strider reached out, intending to grab her.

In a snap, she kicked out her leg, nailing the male between the legs. As Strider hunched over, gasping for breath, she bolted for the door, tossing over her shoulder, "I'm so disappointed in you, Lord Kane!"

She vanished into the night.

He tried to follow after her, but curse his weakness, his knees buckled. "Come back, female! Now!"

She never reappeared.

Kane experienced a tidal wave of rage that made a mockery of what had come before. He would get her back. He would stalk through the night, grab everyone he spotted, and, if they couldn't point him in the right direction, rip their spines out of their mouths. He would leave an ocean of blood in his wake, and she would have only herself to blame. He would—

Do nothing, Disaster finished with a laugh.

It stung all the worse because Kane could only remain crumpled on the floor.

"Bring her back to me," he shouted to Strider.

Moaning in agony, the warrior toppled to the floor. He'd just been bested by a puny little girl; his demon would be throwing out pain for the next several days.

"Go!" Kane commanded Sabin.

"No. I'm not letting you out of my sight."

"Go!" he insisted. "Bring her back."

"Yelling at me isn't going to change my mind."

Kane tried to crawl to the door, but dizziness crowded into his mind, stopping him. He spit out a mouthful of curses.

Could nothing go right for him? Not even once?

Disaster started laughing all over again.

CHAPTER THREE

The Realm of Blood and Shadows
A week later

KANE ROSE FROM the king-size bed and padded to his private bathroom. Already naked, he stepped into the shower. Hot water beat against newly healed skin, all the bruises and scabs finally gone. And yet, his muscles had yet to unknot.

The fury he'd experienced at the loss of his rescuer had yet to fade, and hatred for Disaster was a constant burn in his chest. And his memories…they were the worst.

They came during the day. They came during the night. He could be lying in bed, staring up at the ceiling, and all of a sudden he would be transported back to hell, his wrists and ankles bound. He could be in the shower, like now, with the water raining over him, and all of a sudden he would see the dirt, blood and…other things once caked on his skin, and no amount of scrubbing would make him clean.

He was pretty sure the wires in his brain had gotten cut during his torture. And as he'd healed physically, those wires had been reattached in the wrong places. Darkness had become a perfume that constantly wafted from his pores. Hungry anger now simmered inside him, desperate for a target.

No one was safe.

He'd lost his appetite. He could no longer sleep. Sudden noises made him scramble for a weapon.

Once, he'd rolled with the punches life threw at him. Once, he'd been a softer, nicer guy. Now, there would be no more rolling. Now, he was a raging bull, at times too violent to contain. Any wrong was punished immediately—no one would ever think him weak enough to challenge again.

The shambles of his room proved it.

He soaped up, rinsed off and towel dried, every action stiff, forced. Standing in front of the mirror, he studied his foggy reflection. His skin was pale. Dark hair dripped water down his shoulders and chest. Because of the weight he'd lost, his cheeks had yet to fill out. His lips were compressed into a thin line, as though they'd never known a smile. Maybe they hadn't. Any memory with an accompaniment of amusement no longer seemed to belong to him. Everything positive had happened to someone else. Surely.

But the worst thing about him? His eyes were no longer a mix of brown and green. They were a mix of brown, green—and red. Demon red.

A sense of repugnance grew. Disaster was attempting to control him. And the demon was actually succeeding, whispering reminders about what had happened inside that cave.

A hand here...a mouth there...so helpless...

How dirty was Kane now? How tainted?

A whip across your legs. A dagger along your ribs.

How much of a failure was he?

Hot breath on your wounded skin...kisses...tongues...

Fighting to breathe, Kane flattened his hands on the edge of the sink. He hardly cared when the porcelain cracked. He wanted to rip Disaster out of his chest, and strangle the creature with his bare hands.

Yes. That's the way his tormentor would die.

Soon.

If he could get his mind right, at least a little, he could figure out a way to make it happen. But any time he wasn't plagued by gut-wrenching memories, he was plagued by thoughts about the girl from the motel. The Fae. He ached as he'd done when she'd touched him. He tensed. He cursed.

He yearned.

He remembered the adoration painted on her face as she looked at him, as if he were someone special. A look he still didn't understand—but wanted to experience again.

He replayed the silly words she'd spoken to him.

I never lie—except for the few times I do, in fact, lie, but it's never intentional, and I'm totally telling the truth right now, I promise.

You weigh, like, ten thousand pounds. But they're glorious pounds.

I've been crossing off the seconds in the calendar in my heart.

He wanted to know what else she would say.

Who was she? Where was she? What was she doing?

Were memories she'd rather not recall afflicting her? Was she hurt? Alone? Scared?

A few times, fear had wiped away her adoration and sass, leaving her with nothing but tremors.

He understood all too well the difficulty—the desperation—of an inescapable past.

Had she found someone to end her? Had she ended herself?

Or was she still alive?

His arms dropped to his sides as his hands fisted. She was his. She—

Wasn't his.

Still, he wasn't going to take care of his problem until he'd taken care of hers, was he? He couldn't leave her out there, desperate and afraid, possibly in danger. The girl had saved him from the most horrific situation of his life. Even though she'd run away from him, he had to step up and save her from what had to be the most horrific situation of hers.

She was right, after all. He owed her. And he would pay up. Just not the way she wished. He would fix her life the way he couldn't fix his own. Then, one of them would be happy.

She deserved to be happy.

If she still lived.

He sucked in a sharp breath. She had better still live, or he would…he would… He punched the mirror, shattering the glass. The sound of tinkling bells filled the small enclosure. Several pieces arrowed into his leg, cutting into his thigh. A gift from Disaster, he was sure. Gritting his teeth, he removed the shards.

After he helped the girl, he could concentrate on killing the demon. He wouldn't give up until he succeeded. He couldn't take this anymore, and he didn't want his friends to have to take it anymore, either. He was too much of a danger to those around him, and there were too many innocents here.

He would leave today, he decided, and he wouldn't ever come back.

Sorrow settled heavily on his shoulders, weighing him down. He couldn't talk to his friends about his decision. They wouldn't understand. They would try to talk him into taking another path. They might even lock him away for his "own good."

They'd done it once before.

Kane wouldn't sneak away, but he wouldn't admit the truth, either. He would say his goodbyes, as if he meant to return after his rescuer had been saved. Only he would know this was it. The end.

Jaw locked, Kane strapped weapons all over his body. There were multiple blades, two Sigs and several clips. He dressed in a black T-shirt and camo pants, then tugged on his favorite pair of combat boots. He stomped from the bathroom, glass crunching under his feet, his mind a field of evil laughter.

Stupid demon.

During Kane's absence, his friends had moved into a fortress in the Realm of Blood and Shadows, a kingdom hidden in a pocket between earth and the lower level of the skies. He strode down the hall, his gaze on the walls covered with pictures of a beautiful blonde female in various outfits and positions. Lounging on a velvet-lined couch, standing in a rose garden, dancing on a table. Blowing a kiss. Winking.

Her name was Viola, and she was a minor goddess of something or other, as well as the keeper of Narcissism. He couldn't help but compare her to sperm: she had about a one in three million chance of becoming a human being with actual emotions. The girl irritated the fire out of him.

He pounded down the stairs, then down another hallway, this one littered with ridiculous portraits of the warriors wearing ribbons and lace and smiles—and nothing else. They'd been painted by a dead man, if ever Kane met the guy, and had been commissioned by Lucien's fiancée, Anya, the goddess of Anarchy, without permission.

Finally Kane reached his destination. Maddox and Ashlyn's bedroom. His first stop on the Tour of Goodbyes.

Maddox was the keeper of Violence. Ashlyn was the new mother of the warrior's twin babies.

For a long while, Kane watched Ashlyn, silent. She was a delicate beauty with honey-colored hair and skin, and she swayed in a rocker, singing to the bundle of joy clutched lovingly in her arms. Beside her, Maddox swayed in a second rocker. He was a brute of a man with black hair and violet eyes, and seeing him kiss the tiny fingers wrapped around his pinky did something to Kane's insides. Twisted and knotted them, until he experienced the same lance of pain his pointy-eared rescuer had caused.

What *was* that?

William the Ever Randy—aka the Panty Melter, Kane thought with an eye-roll—sat at the edge of the king-size bed, a pink comforter plumped around his battle-honed body. Somehow, the feminine coverlet failed to diminish the savage intensity of his strength. He wasn't demon-possessed. No one knew what he was, exactly. All they knew was that he had a temper rivaled by few, and a mean streak longer than any Kane had ever before encountered. He smiled when he killed his enemies—and laughed when he stabbed his friends.

"When's it gonna be my turn?" William whined. "I want to hold my preciouses. Preciousees? Whatever. I want!"

O-kay. That was new.

"They aren't yours," Maddox snapped, doing his best to whisper for the sake of the babies.

"They kind of are. I delivered them," William pointed out.

"I conceived them."

"Big deal. Most guys can do that. Not many have the know-how to slice a woman from hip to hip and dig the little creatures out of her…uh, never mind," William said as a fierce growl rose from Maddox.

Expecting a fight, Kane stepped inside to claim the baby.

William's electric blues swung his way. "Disaster. Couldn't stay away from the most delightful darlings ever born? Oh, yes, you are," he cast at the children. "Yes, yes, you are."

Baby talk. Disgusting.

The negative reaction surprised him. Once, he would have been right there beside William, saying the same things, in the same manner. In the dark of night, he used to dream of such a happily ever after for himself. A loving wife. Adoring children. Then the minions had tried to steal his seed and he…he…

"Don't call me by the demon's name," he snarled, then realized his fervency had caused the children to jolt awake and cry. Shame coursed through him. "Sorry. But I'm not that disgusting piece of—" Yelling again. "Sorry. Just watch your mouth, okay?"

"Hush now," William said sternly, and Kane had no idea who the command was for.

Didn't matter, really. Everyone quieted.

Ashlyn glanced over at Kane, her amber eyes welcoming. She looked nothing like Kane's woman—no, not his, he quickly amended—and yet she reminded him of the girl. The delicacy of her bone structure, perhaps. Or the depth of her concern for those around her, maybe. "Do you want to hold Urban?"

"No, thank you," he replied at the same time Maddox said, "No, he doesn't."

A stilted moment of silence elapsed.

Kane ignored the hurt the words caused. The refusal was justified. He was a danger to everyone he encountered. Had his mind not been such a mess, constantly feeding the demon the tastiest of meals, light bulbs would have been shorting out and the walls and floors would have been cracking.

"I just wanted to get a look at them before… Well, I'll be leaving a little later today. I've got a female to help." He cleared the clog of emotion from his throat.

"Well, come on, then," Ashlyn said. "Sabin and Strider mentioned the pointy-eared woman from New York. I like the sound of her."

"She's…" Magnificent. Lovely. Witty. "Something." His insides tightened as he approached the rockers.

William stood to do the same, remaining by his side, stiff, his hand poised over the hilt of a dagger. To protect the babies from Kane's affliction? Yeah. Probably.

Can't blame him.

"You gettin' so close to me 'cause you're trying to taste my flavor, Willy boy?" he said to the warrior who had yet to back off. Teasing was better than raging. Or worse. Crying.

"Maybe." William allowed a few more inches of space. "But you just ruined it. Flavor? Seriously? I like my conquests with a little more maturity."

"I'm mature. I'm even old enough to plow your mom."

"Please. She would eat your liver for lunch and your kidneys for dinner."

"Could you guys be any more disgusting?" Ashlyn asked.

"Yes," they said in unison.

Urban chortled, as if he understood. The kid had a full head of black hair, and his eyes were the same shade of violet as his father's—though they were far more serious and too intelligent for a newborn. As Kane looked him over, two horns rose from the baby's skull, and black scales appeared on his hands.

"Defensive actions?" he asked.

"We think so," Ashlyn replied, sounding somewhat embarrassed. "He doesn't mean any insult."

"I know." He shifted his gaze to Maddox. The female child, Ever, had the honey-colored hair of her mother, the strands wound into tight little curls. Her eyes swam with orange and gold flames, and a mouthful of teeth peeked out from under her lips.

The twins had been born a little over a month ago, and yet they appeared quite older.

The boy stared at Kane as if plotting his murder.

The girl looked him over and dismissed him, concentrating on William and holding out her arms. Grinning, William claimed her from her father. She nuzzled against the warrior's neck, resting her head on his shoulder and sighing with contentment.

"Isn't she the best?" William said, his grin widening. "She used to have claws, but they shrank. Didn't they, princess? Oh, yes, they did, but they'll come out to play if some dumb loser ever tries to take what you don't want to give, won't they?"

Another sharp pain tore through Kane's chest. "The children are beautiful," he told the beaming parents, and he meant it. He removed a bejeweled dagger from the sheath at his side, and handed it hilt first to Maddox. "This is for Ever, from her uncle Kane."

Maddox nodded his head in acceptance.

He palmed the matching dagger, and placed it on the small table beside Ashlyn. "This is for Urban."

She offered a soft, sweet smile in thanks. "How wonderfully thoughtful. The children will love them, I know it."

"Well, I don't. Put those dangerous things away," William chided. "My darlings can't play with knives for another couple of months. And why are you giving them presents now? Why can't you wait until the appropriate time and—" His gaze zeroed in on Kane, and he pressed his lips together.

Did he suspect the truth—that Kane was leaving for good?

Whatever. Kane ignored him, slapping Maddox on the shoulder. "I want to thank you for everything you've done for me. Words cannot express what you mean to me." He didn't wait around for the warrior's reply; he couldn't. The backs of his eyes were burning. He must have gotten dust in them.

He strode from the room, intending to hunt down the remaining warriors he loved more than life. Torin, Lucien, Reyes, Paris, Aeron, Gideon, Amun, Sabin, Strider and Cameo. Over the centuries, they'd fought together, avenged each other, saved each other. Yes, for many years they'd been split into two different groups, one determined to battle the Hunters, the other determined to exist in peace. But at heart, they'd always been together. And in the end, the war had boiled over, bringing them back to the same purpose. Survival.

Each warrior would be devastated by his departure. He knew that for a fact—because they'd once lost another of their brethren. Baden, the keeper of Distrust. They had mourned for centuries, and still hadn't truly recovered. But Kane didn't have a chance to hunt down a single person. William swept up to his side, keeping pace.

"You're leaving," the warrior said.

"Yes." He'd already admitted that much.

"Forever." A statement, not a question.

He wanted to lie. William could try to stop him. William could tell the others, and *they* could try to stop him. Still he said, "Yes." Demons loved lies, and while there wasn't much Kane could do to deny Disaster pleasure, telling the truth was one of them.

"Well, I'm going with you," William announced.

Kane stopped and faced the male, irritation hanging in the air as heavily as shackles.

Shackles.

Breathe. "Why?" His tone lashed with more force than he'd intended. "You don't even know where I'm going or what I'm planning."

A shrug of those wide shoulders. "Maybe I could use a distraction. I've been hunting a Sent One, some punk kid named Axel, but he's proven to be wily and it's starting to annoy me."

Sent Ones policed the skies, killing demons. They were winged, like angels, but as vulnerable to their emotions as humans. Right now, the Lords and the Sent Ones were on the same team.

Everyone knew that could change at any moment.

Kane narrowed his eyes. "Maybe you think I need a babysitter."

"That, too." As always, William was utterly unabashed.

"Well, no thanks. I don't need you, and I certainly don't want you nearby, bugging me all the time."

William clutched his heart, as though offended. "What's wrong with you? You used to be so sweet."

"People change."

"Not me. I've never been sweet, and I never will be. Your needs and wants don't matter to me. I'm more concerned with saving my babies. I have to make sure you live up to your word and stay away from the fortress. Have you forgotten you're destined to start an apocalypse?"

CHAPTER FOUR

Los Angeles

APOCALYPSE. THE WORD echoed in Kane's mind for days. No matter what he tried, he couldn't escape it.

Right before he was captured by the Hunters and escorted into hell, the Moirai had summoned him to their realm in the lowest level of the skies.

The three keepers of fate were neither Greek nor Titan. He thought they might be witches, but he wasn't sure. They'd told him three things—one for every witch. He could marry the keeper of Irresponsibility. He could marry another female—William's daughter. And lastly, he would cause an apocalypse.

He believed them. To his knowledge, their predictions had never been wrong.

He knew there were two definitions for the word he would love to forget. The first: to uncover or reveal. More specifically, to give revelation, especially concerning a cataclysm in which the forces of good permanently triumphed over the forces of evil.

That, he liked.

The second? Not so much. Universal or widespread devastation.

With the demon of Disaster living inside him, he had to assume he would be responsible for widespread devastation.

"You won't regret a pit stop like this," William said, pushing his way through the crowded nightclub. He had to yell to be heard over the erratic pulse of rock screaming from large speakers. "It's just what the doctor ordered—that, and a pair of testicles, but I can only deliver on the first."

"I'll see what I can do," he said drily.

Kane had made the mistake of sharing a motel room with William, and apparently he'd thrashed and moaned in his sleep, giving Detective William a few hints about what had happened in hell. Now the warrior was convinced a night with a woman of Kane's choosing was the only way to ever really heal.

"By the way," William added, "you can call me Dr. Love."

"I'd stab you in the heart before I called you that." He stayed on William's tail, already wishing he'd said no to this. He should be hunting his Fae. And he would have been, if he weren't just desperate enough to try anything.

What William told him this morning made sense, in a sick, twisted way. If Kane could be with a woman of his choosing…if he could control how things went down…if he could use someone the way he'd been used…maybe the dark cloud of his memories would finally dissipate. Maybe he would stop hurting when he neared the Fae. Without the pain, he would be stronger, more alert. He would have a better chance of helping her with her problems.

At least, for tonight, he didn't have to worry about her. She was alive, holed up, and safe. With some fancy computer work, illegally tapping into satellite feed, Torin had found her in Montana. Kane had only to swoop in and grab her.

Soon I'll be ready.

Disaster banged against his skull. A second later, the floor cracked at Kane's feet.

Apparently, the mire of Kane's emotions no longer satisfied the demon. Since leaving the fortress, any time Kane even considered helping the Fae, Disaster worked himself into a frenzy.

Hate her, the demon snarled.

The person passing by him tripped and fell, and bone snapped. A howl of agony blended with the pulse of music.

Grinding his teeth, Kane followed William up a flight of stairs, thankfully leaving the bar and dance area behind. Almost to the top, the step under his boot broke, and he fell to his knees.

Disaster laughed, proud of himself.

Kane blanked his mind before he erupted, stood and stomped the rest of the way up. He spotted a big red door at the end of a long hallway, with an armed guard posted in front. The male was tall and muscled, but human. Hardly a threat, even with a weapon.

The guard grinned with genuine happiness when he spotted William. "Willy! Our best money-maker is back."

William grinned, saying to Kane, "Sometimes, when I'm bored, I do a little Magic Mike show for the ladies. Very tasteful. I'll get you tickets." He returned his attention to the guard. "My boy here needs the private room."

"Sure, sure. Anything for you." The guy opened the door, but Kane couldn't see past the thick cloud of shadows. He heard gasping, the slap of skin against skin, moans and groans, and then curses as the guard "helped" the couple stop and dress. A moment later, the pair was tripping past the entrance, red-faced as they pulled on their clothes.

The guard reappeared, his grin wider than before. "All yours, Willy."

William pushed Kane inside. "Did you see anyone you wanted on the way up here?"

"Anyone will do." A woman was a woman, as far as he was concerned.

Just as soon as the thought registered, some part of his mind spit and hissed at it. The Fae wasn't just—whatever. No thinking about her. Anyone was better than a demon minion, and that's all his sense of choice cared about.

"Give me five minutes," William said. "I know the working girls. I'll find you someone who will let you take her any way you want her."

Crude, but necessary.

The door shut, sealing Kane inside. The pungent smell of sex thickened the air and his stomach filled with acid. He hated the dark, and quickly flipped on the light. In front of him was a wet bar, and beside it a couch, the cushions askew. On the coffee table was a box of condoms. At the other end of the room was a small bathroom with only a toilet and a sink, and beside it a queen-size bed with the covers tangled in a heap at the end. There was a condom stuck to the top.

After pouring himself a shot of whiskey—then another and another and another, then deciding to take the entire bottle with him—Kane settled on the couch.

By the time the door opened a short while later, the bottle was empty. Alcohol never affected him as strongly as it did a human, and only served to dull out the fiercest of his emotions. That dullness was desperately needed now. His limbs were trembling, and sweat had beaded over every inch of his skin. He expected to melt—or shatter—at any moment.

William walked in with a pretty blonde tucked into his side. She wore a short red dress and lipstick to match, and she was smiling at something the warrior had said.

"This is my friend." William motioned to Kane with a tilt of his chin. "The guy I was telling you about. He'll pay you whatever you want. Just make sure you *do* whatever he wants."

Kane set the bottle on the ground, pretending he wasn't about to vomit.

"Of course." She bit her lip as she studied Kane. Interest lit her dark eyes. "It'll be my pleasure."

"Good," William said, chucking her under the chin. "You have nothing to worry about. He won't bite—unless you ask him real nice." With that, the warrior took off, leaving Kane alone with the girl. The stranger.

His lungs constricted, nearly blocking his airways.

A moment of silence passed as she shifted from one high-heeled foot to the other. "You're even more gorgeous than William promised." There was a bead of excitement in her tone.

She was talking. Why was she talking? He didn't want to have a conversation with her. He would begin to wonder what kind of life she'd led, what had brought her to this point, and he would feel sorry for her. He didn't want to feel sorry for her.

Disaster hummed with contentment.

Contentment? Why?

Just get this over with. "Come here," Kane said.

The female obeyed, slipping into the spot beside him. Her scent hit him, and he wrinkled his nose in distaste. A cloying perfume, laced with the scent of cigarette smoke. Nothing like the Fae, who had smelled as though she'd spent the day in the kitchen. Like a wife.

Maybe he shouldn't do this.

A gust of wind burst through the room, lifting the bottle of whiskey off the ground and slamming it into the woman's chest.

"Ow!" she cried.

Kane cursed the day he'd stolen Pandora's box.

She rubbed her chest, saying, "What just happened?"

"Could have been an air vent." It was possible.

"Why don't you kiss me better?" She inched closer to him.

"No kissing." Harsh words. Even harsher tone.

"What about sucking? I'm really good at sucking." She leaned over to unfasten his pants, but Kane flipped her over. He pressed her stomach into the cushions of the couch, holding her down. He didn't want anyone's lips on him.

"We do this my way." Bile rose as he lifted the hem of her dress and tugged down her panties. Though he would have rather sawed off one of his limbs, he unbuttoned his pants, undid the zipper. The trembling of his hands magnified. Acid rose from his stomach and collected in his throat, scorching him. He paused.

What was the problem? He'd done this before. When he'd realized relationships weren't feasible, he'd lived off one-night stands. At least for a little while. But none of them had ever broken him down like this….

"Am I doing something wrong?" she asked.

Gritting his teeth, he sheathed himself in a condom and…and…

Do it! Disaster commanded.

He took her.

He was rough, ragged, utterly without sensuality and

carnal ambition. He had no focus, no desire to watch her reach climax. His mind despised this. And yet, his body liked it. But then, his body was a traitor. It had liked what the minions had done, too, and that's what haunted him most. That a part of him had enjoyed his own violation.

This had been a mistake.

He didn't want this woman, didn't know her, might not even like her if he did. She wasn't…*her,* the Fae his instincts craved so desperately.

Disaster cursed at the direction of his thoughts.

And as the female groaned to encourage him, images began to fill his head. *Hands here...mouths there... minions everywhere...*

Nearing panic, Kane somehow, some way, managed to finish. He wasn't sure whether or not he'd gotten her off, and at the moment, he didn't care.

The demon's curses tapered into statements of approval.

Fighting a tide of self-disgust, Kane discarded the condom and fixed his clothing, then threw a few hundreds on the couch cushions beside her. He walked to the door, and motioned her out. First thing he saw was William taking a woman against the wall. The guard was nowhere to be seen.

"But…don't you want my number?" asked the blonde. "In case the urge strikes again? I'll make myself available to you any day, any time."

"No," he said, being blunt to be kind. He would never call her, and he didn't want her hoping for the impossible.

"Was I not what you were looking for?"

"No. You weren't. Now leave."

Sighing, she straightened her dress and strode out of the room, the hall.

"All done?" William called. He hadn't pulled from the woman, but he'd stopped moving at least.

More, Disaster said.

As much as Kane hated the words brewing at the back of his tongue, he said, "Bring me another one." The sex hadn't done what he'd wanted. The memories and all that came with them were still knocking at the door of his mind, ready to pounce. But Disaster was happy. So, Kane would take a second woman. And a third. However many proved necessary, until the demon was so saturated with satisfaction, *he* forgot what had happened.

Kane received an unapologetic and shameless thumbs-up before he shut the door, stalked to the bathroom and vomited. When he finished, he cleaned his mouth with the contents of another bottle of whiskey.

And not a second too soon.

A knock sounded at the door. William and a brunette strutted inside.

"How about this one?" the warrior asked.

"Whatever," Kane said. "She'll do."

Before the night was over, Kane took twelve women. He used different positions, and different types of females. Girls in their twenties, women in their forties, more blondes, more brunettes and even two redheads. He hated every second, even hated himself. He vomited every time.

Disaster loved it all, and yet he never stopped tossing out images of Kane's torture.

He hated the demon a thousand times more.

His time's coming...soon...

The mountains of Montana

KANE HACKED THROUGH the foliage in front of him. Branches continually slapped at him, courtesy of Disaster. The satisfaction the creature had experienced during the sexual marathon hadn't lasted long. Now, rocks rolled in his way, tripping him. Insects snapped at him.

He had to reach the Fae before the demon did any major damage…or Kane's mind finally snapped. Whichever came first.

His head was even more unfamiliar terrain, with dark valleys and impossibly high mountains he could never hope to climb. Or maybe he could. When he'd left the club, he'd realized the Fae had become a source of light to him. His only source of light. She had made him want to smile during the worst period of his life. For that alone, she was a miracle.

He could really use a miracle.

Perhaps she could do what the parade of women had not: wash away the worst of his memories. Bring peace, if only for a little while.

Perhaps. But perhaps not.

Either way, he had to know. Had to see her, talk to her. *Save* her.

Deep inside, where instinct still demanded she belonged to him, he suspected she was his only hope of survival.

So, he would find her.

Would she smell the stale cigarettes and old perfume he hadn't been able to wash from his skin? Would she demand he leave her alone?

Probably.

Would he obey?

No.

I'm disgusting. Cruel. A user and a whore.

I didn't used to be this way, he wanted to shout.

What was the Fae's name? The fact that he didn't know was starting to irritate him. He would call her… Kewpie? No. Those big, gorgeous eyes fit, but nothing else. Tinker Bell, then. Yeah. Tinker Bell worked. She was such a delicate little thing, with her pointy ears and sharp little chin, and she flittered from here to there, always out of reach.

According to Torin's surveillance, she was staying in a cabin in these woods. About an hour ago, Kane had found the cabin but not the girl. However, he *had* discovered fresh tracks. Human. Female. Size six feet. She couldn't have much of a head start on him, and she couldn't be moving very fast. As deep as her prints were, she was carrying a heavy load. Plus, night had fallen.

The half-moon lacked its usual glow, allowing an almost suffocating darkness to reign. The air was cold, the breeze wafting from the snow-capped mountains and chasing away any hint of warmth. Trees knifed toward the blackened sky.

"What's got your panties in such a twist?" William asked from behind him. "It's not my fault the pleasure train failed to work for you. You must not have done it right."

Kane ignored him.

"What's so important about this girl, anyway? I mean, really."

Again silence.

"Does she have a magic pu—"

Kane spun around and punched him in the jaw. "Enough!" Fury bubbled in his blood, molten, acidic—

poisonous. "Don't go there. Don't ever go there. Not with her."

William rubbed the wound. "So why are we hunting her?" he asked as if Kane hadn't just resorted to violence.

Could nothing shut the warrior up? Kane jolted back into motion. "She says I owe her." And it was true…if not the full truth.

"And you always pay your debts? What kind of craziness is that?"

"Some people would say it's honorable." Maybe the only honor Kane had left.

"Some people are stupid."

"And there's the number-one reason I'll never do anything for you."

"Because you're stupid like everyone else? That's being a little harsh on yourself, don't you think? I mean, sure, if you ever entertained a bright idea I'd have to say it was beginners' luck, but you have your moments."

I can act like I'm a calm, rational being. Kane stalked past a wall of green and entered a clearing. He stopped and breathed deeply. The air was clean here. Pure and untouched. Also kind of annoying. He wanted to catch a hint of rosemary, mint and maybe even smoke, indicating Tinker Bell was still here and warming herself in front of a fire.

He could swoop in and grab her. She would probably fight him, but he wasn't worried. She lacked skill. And strength. Was probably fatigued. *But she's got heart,* he thought, a now familiar ache lancing through his chest.

"Well?" William prompted.

"We set up camp." Not because they'd been on the move since leaving the club and needed to rest—though they had and they did—but because he could tell they were being followed and he didn't want to lead his shadow to Tinker Bell.

He doubted the Hunters were after him. Apparently, during Kane's forced stay in hell, a battle had been waged in the skies, Hunters against Lords, Titans against Sent Ones.

The Lords and Sent Ones had won, utterly destroying the Hunters and severely weakening the Titans.

Kane gathered stones, twigs and dried leaves to build a fire. He cared little about warmth. He wanted the one following him to see the smoke and assume he was relaxed, unprepared. Was the culprit immortal? If so, what race? And why was he after Kane?

Doesn't matter. He withdrew a dagger and sharpened it against one of the stones he'd set aside. His reflection caught on the silver metal, and firelight illuminated the image. The red in his eyes had intensified.

Disaster had grown stronger, Kane far weaker. Disgusted, he set the weapon away.

"You know we've got a female Phoenix on our tail, right?" William asked.

A Phoenix? He'd never messed with the fire-happy race. "I do. Of course I do." Now. "How did you know?"

"I can smell her. How else?"

"Right."

"The plan?"

"To wait."

"And slaughter her on our own turf," William said with a nod, black hair shagging around his supermodel face—or whatever he insisted on calling that ugly mug. "I like it. Simple, yet elegant." He eased onto the only rock in front of the fire he hadn't helped build, and dug through his backpack. He withdrew a pistachio nutrition bar he'd stolen from Kane, tore off the wrapper—and ate every bite, never offering Kane a taste.

Typical.

"That was good. You should have brought one." William brushed his hands together. He wore a T-shirt that read *I'm a Jenius,* and that pretty much encapsulated the male's entire personality. Silly, unconcerned, irreverent. Misleading.

Kane dug through his own pack. He withdrew three daggers, two Sigs and the parts to his long-range rifle. What could a female Phoenix want with him? He knew the race lived for the enslavement of others. He knew they were nearing extinction, many having met their final end. Like cats with nine lives. He knew they were bloodthirsty and war-hungry…but they usually only picked battles they could win.

So confident. Disaster chuckled with evil glee. *So wrong.*

Kane ignored him. He'd tried engaging the fiend, snapping retorts, issuing threats, but look where that had gotten him. Now, he wasn't going to waste his time or energy. And why should he? This was a full-on case of dead demon talking.

Suddenly sparks flew from the fire, shooting out white-hot streams in every direction. Grass sizzled, and black smoke billowed. Heat licked over Kane's pants, blistering his calves.

William scrambled around, patting out the flames. "You're a menace. You know that, right? Everywhere we go, something terrible happens."

"I know." And the worst was yet to come. "To your knowledge, have the Moirai ever had a wrong prediction?"

"Oh, yes," William said. "Definitely."

Hope bloomed. "When?" He fit the rifle's barrel on top of the frame, and the scope on top of that. He inserted the screws and gently tightened. "How?"

"When—too many times to count. How—free will. Our choices dictate our future, nothing else."

Intelligent words from a Jenius. Go figure. "They think I'm destined to marry the keeper of Irresponsibility."

"So do it. Hunt her down and marry her."

William made it sound so easy. Just snap his fingers, and boom. Done. Only one little problem. He had yet to meet the keeper of Irresponsibility.

"I'm not sentencing a woman to an eternity with me." He attached the bipod and rested the entire weapon on a thick stump.

"What about White?" William grumbled. "I happen to think you'll end up with her, whether I like it or not."

White was William's only daughter, and, if Kane had to take a guess, one of the reasons William had followed him out here. William wanted Kane to stay away from the girl.

"I know you do," he said. "What I don't know is why."

"Simple. *I* was once told her husband would cause an apocalypse."

"By the Moirai?"

"One of the Moirai. I slept with Klotho. And both of her sisters."

"I *so* did not need to hear that. Dude, they're *ancient*."

"They weren't at the time," William said with his classic wanton grin.

"Whatever. What about your whole free-will over fate spiel?"

"I believe you'll choose her."

"I hate her." He remembered how, in hell, she had stood over his bound and mutilated form. Silent. Uncaring. Then, she'd left him to his suffering.

Actually, *hate* was too soft a word for what he felt for her.

"Maybe I'll just avoid both women," he added, "and save myself the trouble."

"You? Avoid trouble? Ha!"

He gnashed his molars. "I can try. And what will you do if White and I do end up together, huh? You don't think I'm good enough for her."

"I certainly don't. You just slept your way through a baker's dozen."

"At *your* urging."

"And your point? I didn't hold a gun to your head."

In some ways, Disaster had.

"If you two hook up, I'm moving back to hell. I don't want to clean up her mess," William said. "And I know she'll make one. She won't be able to help herself. It's her nature."

William, the adopted brother of the underworld's king, Lucifer, had once lived in hell. Eventually, the hate, greed, envy and wickedness living in his soul had mated with the vengeance living in his heart. White, as well as her brothers, Red, Black and Green, had spewed from him.

He'd heard demons call them the four horsemen of the apocalypse. But these four were not, not really; they were more like shadows of the originals.

Actually, that's exactly what they were. Shadow warriors.

They had been birthed in evil, and prophecy claimed they had futures to match. White was to conquer anyone she encountered, before somehow enslaving herself. Red was to bring war, Black famine, and Green death.

Little wonder Kane wanted nothing to do with White. He had enough problems, thanks.

And yes, he knew being conceived in evil had no bearing on the girl herself. He knew those in darkness could find their way to the light. He knew something beautiful could come out of something terrible. After all, diamonds were formed in the mantle of the earth, with horrendous heat and bone-crushing pressure.

He knew. But he didn't care.

It wasn't White he longed to see. It wasn't White he yearned to scent.

It wasn't White his mind pictured and his treacherous body suddenly responded to, shimmering need flash-flooding him, riding on bolts of lightning. It was Tinker Bell. Sweet, sexy Tinker Bell, with her—

Hands wandering...hot breath fanning over him... moans, groans...

Scowling, he tossed a handful of dirt into the fire. The flames sputtered and died. "You don't need to worry about me. Like I said, I don't want to marry anyone."

"You would be lucky to win White!" William huffed.

The words penetrated Kane's blooming rage and actually calmed him. One of his brows arched. "Now you *want* me to make a play for her?"

"No. But you should want me to want you to make a play for her. She's highly desirable."

"Well, I don't want and I won't ever want."

"Why? Are your ovaries swollen?"

A bead of amusement rose in his chest, surprising him. "How has no one ever killed you?"

There was a pause as William opened another stolen nutrition bar, stuffed half into his mouth and swallowed. "Like anyone would want to see me dead. I'm too pretty."

Pretty could only aid a person so long. "How many women have you been with?"

"Countless. You?"

"Not so many I can't count them."

"That's because you lack skill."

"Maybe, but at least I can control my desires. Your lust is too strong and your willpower too weak to allow you to resist anyone with a pulse."

"Don't be ridiculous. I've been with plenty of people without a pulse. More than that, I say no to Gilly every day."

Gilly, his best friend. A human girl Reyes, the keeper of Pain, had rescued. She was only seventeen years old, and for some reason, she'd developed a crush on William. A crush that had deepened every time the warrior had come to visit the Lords, whom she lived with. She'd doctored him every time he'd gotten hurt in battle, and he'd comforted her every time she'd cried out from bad dreams, the horrors of an abusive stepfather rising to haunt her.

Now, she called the male every morning at 8:00 a.m. to make sure he was "all right." Translation: alone.

He always was.

William might take a new woman—or ten—whenever the mood stuck, but he never let the females stay the night with him. Not anymore. He didn't want to hurt his precious Little Gilly Gumdrop's feelings.

Kane wasn't sure why William took such care with the girl, when he'd never done anything sexual with her. At least, Kane didn't think he had.

He better not have.

Eyes narrowed, William threw the rest of the food into the ashes. "Just remembered something. As I was packing, Danika showed up and asked me to give you the most important painting of your life." He dug through his pack and withdrew a small, wrapped canvas.

Danika, Reyes's woman, possessed the ability to see into heaven and hell, past, present and future, and paint the images. Like the Moirai, her predictions had never been wrong—that he could prove.

About ten yards away, a twig snapped.

The Phoenix had decided to close in, he realized.

Kane grabbed the canvas from William and stuffed it inside his own pack, then swung the whole thing over his back, using it as a shield, and lay flat on his belly. Closing one eye, he pressed the other against the night-vision scope on the rifle. In an instant, the world around him became painted with bright green.

The Phoenix was…there. She had climbed one of the taller trees and was currently walking across one of the thicker limbs…nope, she was hopping to another limb on another tree, coming closer and closer, clearly trying to sneak up on him.

Mine, Disaster said with a possessive growl, and Kane frowned.

Another mine?

The female looked to be five foot nine and scantily dressed, considering the weather. She wore a bralike top and tiny shorts, and there were two daggers tied to her calves, two sheathed in her combat boots.

Kane tracked her for a moment, watched as she paused and reached for one of the hilts. *Never bring a knife to a gun fight, sweetness. You'll lose every time.* He squeezed the trigger.

Boom!

He was a great shot and knew he'd grazed her thigh before he even heard her shriek of pain. He leaped up and started running. By the time she hit the ground, gasping for breath, he was there, in her face. She was pretty. Blonde. Bold. Though he would have rather bathed in acid, he pressed his arm into her throat, making it even more difficult for her to take in any air, and patted her down to discard all of her weapons.

There were more than he'd realized. Eleven daggers. Two guns. Three throwing stars. Two vials of poison. A bag of pills. Detachable metal claws. And the makings of a bomb hidden in the soles of her shoes.

He tried not to be impressed.

Working quickly, he bound her wrists with a rope of chain he'd been using as a belt and tied her to the base of the tree. The moment he finished, he jolted away from her, severing contact. Already his stomach was churning, sickness brewing. But at least he didn't experience the pain Tinker Bell caused.

A swarm of bees darted from the trees, circling Kane's head. Disaster laughed.

"Who are you?" he demanded.

The girl kicked out her uninjured leg, swiped only at air. "Let me go!"

"I doubt that's your name. Try again."

"I had no plans to hurt you," she snarled, her struggles increasing. Heat radiated from her, such intense heat, and it was only getting stronger. Any moment now, she would catch fire with flames as hot as those in hell and melt the metal links. "I only want to hurt Josephina. Now, I'll kill you *and* enslave the girl."

"Josephina?" A sting in his neck. He slapped at the wound, and a bee stung him on the wrist.

"As if you don't know the girl you're following. The Fae."

His rescuer's name was Josephina. Pretty. But he liked Tinker Bell better. "You want to enslave her, do you?" Was that why the girl had a death wish? She feared what the Phoenix would do to her?

Buzz, buzz.

Sting. Sting.

"Argh!" Again she kicked out. Again she missed. "I refuse to answer any more of your questions. Let me go or I'll make you regret it before I slay you!"

"Did someone mention a lay? For the right price, I'm willing to make myself available." William strolled into the area, chewing *another* nutrition bar. "And do you think she's talking about the Fae female who just raced through our camp?"

"What!" Kane got in the warrior's face. "When?"

"Just now."

"And you let her go?" he roared.

Buzz. Sting.

"Well, yeah. Our chase would have ended, and I'm not ready to go home. She told me to tell you hi, though. Or maybe she said to tell you to do what you promised or leave her alone since you're drawing the wrong attention to her. It's so hard to tell when you're not really listening."

Battling an urge to slice the warrior to ribbons, and waste time, Kane gritted out, "Don't let this one escape," and bolted into action.

CHAPTER FIVE

JOSEPHINA SPRINTED THROUGH the forest, twigs beating at her, leaves sticking to her. She pumped her arms and legs with all her might and began to pant, the night air burning her nose and throat. In one terrible swoop, all of her enemies had found her—yet none of them wanted to kill her.

A Fae army was here, determined to escort her home.

The Phoenix was here, determined to enslave her.

Kane was here, determined to…finally do as he'd promised? Or did he plan to hand her over to her family and collect a reward?

Probably the reward. Some of the Lords were wily like that.

What had she done wrong? How had she been spotted? She'd been so careful, sneaking here, hiding there. Only twice had she spoken to a human, and only to ask the males to run her over with their cars.

Both men had looked at her as if she were insane.

Maybe she was.

All she knew was that death—any death—was preferable to life with her family. The pain and suffering that came with Synda's punishments was bad, but the agony of not knowing what the next punishment would be was far, far worse.

Her own father hated her, and rejected her at every

turn. For centuries, she'd just wanted someone to love her. To see value in her.

Of course, then there was Leopold. Her own half brother wanted her in his bed, and wouldn't stop pressing until he got her there.

Every day was a new stress. Josephina would wake up feeling as if she were standing on top of a mountain, screaming for help, but no one cared enough to listen. Tension never left her. And by the end of each day, her nerves were so frayed she feared she would have a nervous breakdown.

It was too much. She was tired, so very tired. She craved an end. *Needed* an end. Finally.

Sadly, she couldn't kill herself—and how morbid was a thought like that? Other Fae could end their own lives, but not her. To purposely injure herself was to suffer with that injury, no matter how severe, for weeks, sometimes months. Eventually, she would heal. Even from a beheading. Yes, her body would grow back. Her father had made sure of it, using an ability she would love to steal, but couldn't. The guards protected him too diligently.

Something hard slammed into her back, tossing her down. She hit the dirt and twig-laden ground with a loud crash, her lungs momentarily deflating. As she struggled to breathe, she was flipped over. Panic overwhelmed her, heating and freezing her at the same time. Tiny black dots winked through her vision, yet she managed to make out the shape of a man looming over her.

"Josephina," he gritted out.

Kane. She recognized the low, gruff quality of his voice, and the panic receded. "Jerk! Just because you're a star doesn't mean you can act that way. A simple 'stop' would have sufficed."

"I did say stop. You ignored me." The weight of him lifted from her, allowing her to pull herself into a sitting position. She drank in as much oxygen as possible, and her eyesight finally cleared.

The warrior crouched in front of her, slivers of moonlight dancing over him. His hair was disheveled, but that hardly mattered. The strands of flax glowed as if they'd been sprinkled with stardust, reminding her of gorgeous ribbons of gold only the Opulens—the Fae upper class—could afford. The darker strands blended into the night. Red eyes watched her intently, angrily… with the barest glimpse of sizzle?

"Your eyes," she said, unsure whether she shivered or shuddered. She recognized that bloodlike color, had seen it glowing from Synda's gaze too many times to count. But the princess had never caused her every pulse point to flutter wildly.

He looked away, as though shamed. "They're red. I know."

Poor Kane. "What happened?" What had caused the demon to become so strong?

Without thought, she reached out to brush her gloved fingers against the skin underneath. He caught the motion and stiffened, reminding her of his dislike of contact; his air of anger intensified. But he didn't flinch, as he'd done with Sabin.

"Is this okay?" she whispered.

He gave a stiff nod.

Gulping, she continued reaching.

At contact, his pupils expanded, gobbling up every bit of color. Even the red. His breathing changed, from slow and even to deep and shallow. The very air around them seemed to charge with electrical impulses, little sparks dancing over every inch of her.

I...like him?

No. Surely not. She'd had crushes before, but this was something else entirely. More intense. Almost overwhelming.

"That's enough." He grabbed her by the wrist, moving with lightning-fast reflexes, and she realized he was trembling. "Forget my eyes," he bit out, setting her hand away from him. "Every time I'm near you, I hurt. Why?"

Deep down, part of her mourned the separation with him. The other part of her wanted to cry over this brand-new rejection.

You're angry with him. This is silly.

"How should I know? You're the first person ever to complain."

"You're not doing anything to me?"

"Of course not. Now, how did you find me? How do you know my name?"

"The answers don't matter. I came to help you."

"Help me?" Hope opened as sweetly as a rose in sunlight, bright and beautiful. "Really?"

He nodded.

"Oh, Kane. Thank you!" He planned to kill her, the darling man. No longer would fear be her constant companion. No longer would she have to endure her half sister's punishments. No longer would she have to avoid Leopold's advances. "How do you want to do it? A dagger? Your bare hands? Poison? My vote is quick and painless, but I'll be satisfied with whatever you choose. Really. You won't hear a single complaint out of me."

Kane flashed his perfect white teeth in a scowl. "I'm not going to kill you, Tinker Bell."

Wait. What? "But you just said you'd help me." And had he really just called her freaking Tinker Bell? *I'm not a thumb-sized sprite, dang it!*

"I will. I'll take care of your problems. That way, you'll want to live."

Every ounce of the hope withered. He had no idea what he was saying, or how impossible such a task would be.

"Where have you been?" she asked, ignoring his offer. Had he gone home to a girlfriend? The last story she'd read about him had claimed he was single, but a year had passed since then. Or, in her case, a thousand and one years. Had he pampered this nameless, faceless female?

I'm the one who saved him. I *deserve to be pampered.*

"Respond to my promise," he growled.

She sighed. "Why do you want to help me, Kane?" Beautiful Kane, with his rainbow of colors.

"I can't *not* help you."

"But…why?"

"You're min—" A muscle ticked below his eye. "I owe you."

He'd only get himself killed, and she didn't want that. "Well, I release you from your debt. How's that?"

He shook his head. "I'm your new constant companion, Tinker Bell. It'll be better for both of us if you get used to the idea."

Kane…with her every second…

A blessing and a curse, just like her strength-stealing ability. "Either kill me, get me out of the forest, or get lost. Those are your three choices."

"I'll get you out of the forest," he said, standing, circling her with all the predatory intent of a ravenous beast, "and while I'm doing it, you'll tell me how many people I need to kill to make you feel like your life is worth saving."

She wrapped her arms around her middle lest she be tempted to reach out again. "Too many."

"So the problem *is* people." He stopped in front of her.

"Yes, but did you hear me? There are too many of them."

"Too many is my specialty." Hesitant, he held out his hand to help her up.

More contact? Freely offered this time?

She licked her lips and stretched out her hand.

He recoiled, as though startled, even though he'd been the instigator, and his arm dropped to his side. He made a fist, a dark, frightening need springing to life in his eyes. But…a need for what?

Trembling, she labored to her feet under her own steam. Which, to be honest, wasn't much. Her adrenaline must have crashed. Her knees knocked together, struggling to hold her up.

"I'm sorry," Kane said, his voice low and quiet, yet somehow far more undisciplined than she knew him to be. "I should have helped you."

Clearly, he hadn't gotten over his aversion to touch. *Especially hers.* "Yes, well, I'm not going with you, and I don't want my problems murdered. An attempt would only create *more* problems."

"I'm afraid your days of making your own decisions are over. I've got problems of my own, and I can't see to them until I've seen to yours."

She backed away from him.

He shook his head. "Don't you dare run, Tinker Bell. I'm strong enough to chase, and I don't think you'll like the results."

Her stupid body tingled, a clear disagreement. Did

he wield some strange ability she'd never before encountered?

Stop thinking and move! She faked a pass to the right. He followed, and she darted to the left. Then, she ran at full steam.

He slammed into her, knocking her down. He wasn't even winded when he said, "Consider this your final warning," his warm breath caressing the back of her neck.

Oh my…. His weight was as heavy as before, pressing her into the ground, but this time, because she knew the culprit, she didn't feel threatened. She felt…achy, her nerve endings sizzling with undeniable awareness.

"Let me go. I'll hurt you if you don't."

He stood, dragging her with him. He held on tightly, surprising her, his arms steel bands she couldn't break—didn't want to break. But he was still shaking, as if touching her was somehow more painful to him than he'd claimed her nearness was. It shouldn't be. Not yet.

"Kane," she said. "I'm serious. I don't want to hurt you."

"Sweetheart," he replied, practically breaking her heart with the sudden thread of gentle kindness in his tone, "this is for your own good. I promise."

No, it wasn't. He simply didn't understand. She tugged off one of her gloves. Her hands were her only weapons; he would hate her for what she was about to do to him, would never again come near her, but he'd left her with no other option. "Last chance."

"I told you. I'm not letting you go." He hefted her over his shoulder and trudged forward, shouldering his way through tree limbs determined to slap him. "I'm saving you."

"You can't save me." Fighting wave after wave of

guilt, Josephina reached out and gripped his forearm. "Please don't make me do this."

"And just what is it you think you're doing, hmm?"

Leaving you helpless. Tears welled in her eyes. *No other choice.* She tightened her grip on him. Instantly, her pores became tiny vacuums, sucking the strength out of him and into her.

He stilled, gasping. "What are you doing, Tinker Bell? Stop that."

"I'm sorry." Warmth flooded her; warmth and the fizz of energy…so much energy, lighting her up. No, not lighting, she realized a second later, but darkening. Then, utter blackness gobbled up the light, cloaking her, sending her tumbling straight into a spiraling pit of despair.

Kane set her on her feet.

A terrible scream cut its way through her throat. Her knees buckled, but he was no longer able to hold her up. She slammed into the ground, contact finally severed. What was happening? What was wrong with her? And the screams—hers, and someone else's, someone sinister—argh! Growing louder and louder.

And yet, through it all, a single whisper managed to claim her attention. *I hate you. Hate you so much. Want to kill you.* Will *kill you. Soon, soon, so very soon.*

I don't understand, she thought, panicked.

You deserve pain, and I'll make sure you get it if you go near him again. He's mine. Mine. I won't share him with you. Never you.

Nearing hysteria, she drew on every reservoir of strength she possessed, lumbered to her knees and crawled forward, away from Kane. Yes, she had to escape Kane. All of this had come from him. Belonged to him. The more distance, the better. *Please.*

Rocks sliced at her palms and knees, but she didn't care. In the distance, she heard the snap of breaking wood. The whoosh of air. Something hard slammed into her, knocking her feet out from under her and planting her face first in the dirt.

When the daze cleared, she realized the culprit wasn't Kane this time, but a tree.

She fought her way free, tears streaming down her cheeks, and continued her journey forward.

"Josephina," Kane called. "Tinker Bell…what did…you do? To me?" His voice was weak, rasping.

A spark of light dashed across her small line of vision, followed by another. Soon, colors formed, taking shape. Bushes, tree roots and trunks, piles of leaves, a coyote stalking past—only to stop and bare its teeth, as if preparing to attack her. But another tree fell, slamming against her and scaring the animal away.

Hate you. Hate you, hate you, hate you.

Pain momentarily stunned her, her abused back threatening to shatter.

Before she could fight her way free, a pair of boots appeared in front of her. Boots she recognized.

Josephina swallowed a groan. No. No! Anyone but him.

"Well, well," the owner of those boots said. "What do we have here?"

She recognized the voice, as well. Leopold, her half brother, had found her. He would ensure she returned home…back to her own personal hell.

KANE HEARD TINKER Bell screaming, and battled a rage unlike any other.

Mine, he thought. No one was allowed to hurt her,

not even him, not even as angry as he was with her for what she'd done to him.

What had she done to him?

He wanted to stand and help her, whatever was wrong with her. He did. Yet, his body was too weak.

He'd vowed never to be weak again. Or, barring that, to kill the cause.

Tinker Bell was the cause, somehow, but he wouldn't be killing her. He would be…he wasn't sure, and didn't like that he couldn't decide.

One second he'd been as normal as a man like him could be, carrying her over his shoulder. The next, he'd felt warm silk pressed against his arm, and he'd begun to weaken. He'd set her down as his limbs began to tremble. Then, he'd crumbled.

But then, so had she.

The darkness he'd carried for so long had thinned, but instead of strength taking its place, he'd experienced extreme fatigue.

He'd watched, helpless, as Tinker Bell curled into herself. Her skin had gone pallid, and horror had consumed her features. She'd looked…haunted. He'd reached for her, but she'd managed to crawl away. He hadn't managed to follow. Soon she'd disappeared beyond the line of trees.

Must help her.

"So, it's safe to say this night isn't going according to plan."

William's voice hit him, and he struggled to sit up. "The girl."

"Escaped. Burned me, too, the little—"

"Not the Phoenix. The Fae. Go get her."

"I'm too hungry to run."

Rage gave him enough strength to hurl a rock at the warrior's fat, ugly head. "Go!"

"Fine." Footsteps echoed. "But you'll owe me." Swaying limbs, swishing leaves, then…nothing.

In and out Kane breathed. There was something else happening inside him, something stranger than the sudden weakness, and he needed to figure out what it was. And it should be easy. For the first time in centuries, his mind was silent. Thoughts were easy, without any kind of dark filter. Emotions were pure, without any kind of terrible guidance. He was—

Alone, he realized.

Realization knocked him flat on his back. In that moment, there was no hint of the demon's presence. No sickness in the pit of his stomach. No icy fingers of dread crawling all over his skin. No terrible whispers in the back of his mind.

But…how could that be? Kane was alive. And if he was alive, the demon was with him. Right?

Or, had the Greeks lied to him and his friends the first day of their possession, as he'd hoped? Gideon had once survived several minutes without his demon. Of course, the creature had still been tethered to him, and had returned.

Kane thought back. He'd never actually seen a possessed warrior killed simply because the demon had left his body. His friend Baden had died from a beheading. Cronus and Rhea, former king and queen of the Titans, had been demon possessed and had died from a beheading, too.

What if Disaster *was* gone? Permanently? But where could the demon have gone? With Tinker Bell?

Was Disaster the reason she'd screamed?

Or had she somehow killed the creature?

Had Kane finally experienced something good?

He rolled his shoulders, the muscles knotted and protesting as if he'd never really used them. He and Tinker Bell were going to have a long talk. He would ask questions and she would supply answers. If she hesitated, he would spank her. Yes. That's what he'd do to her, he decided.

Part of him wanted her to hesitate.

He'd never thought to experience sexual desire again—not true desire—and yet, when he'd tackled her, her softness beneath him, and he'd had her scent in his nose, and her panting breaths in his ears, he'd yearned to strip her, to see her, all of her, and take everything she had to give.

She might have let him. But just how would his body, and his mind, have reacted?

Now, the need for her was still there, a thorn in his side. He didn't like it, had to get rid of it.

A frowning William returned—without the girl.

Kane growled low in his throat. "What happened?"

"There was no sign of her," the warrior said. "And don't get your panties in a twist, but, uh, there *was* evidence of a struggle."

CHAPTER SIX

The Realm of Blood and Shadows

LONG AGO, CAMEO had been cursed to host the demon of Misery and oh, the creature's presence had never been more apparent than now. A deep sense of sorrow pressed heavily against her. Despair burned the center of her chest. Corrosive whispers drifted through her mind.

There's no hope...

Life will never get better.

You'll never succeed at anything. Might as well give up now.

She hated the demon of Misery with every fiber of her being. He was the essence of evil, darkness without any hint of light, yet she couldn't survive without him. Problem was, she knew she couldn't survive *with* him, either.

But what could she do?

Nothing, that's what. Always nothing. Forever nothing.

And so, for the rest of her existence, tears would always burn at the backs of her eyes. If ever she laughed, she wouldn't remember it. Her friends claimed she had, upon occasion, smiled, but she couldn't recall a single instance—and never would.

But. Yes, but. While she couldn't make *her* life better, she could make Kane's better. Surely. Hopefully.

A few days ago, she'd visited him in his room. He'd worn anguish like a second skin, though he'd tried to mask it. He probably would have succeeded with anyone but Cameo. The misery of others delighted her demon.

For a moment, only a moment, she had felt better. Lighter. Finally free. Then, she had felt a thousand times worse as her own misery had merged with Kane's.

Kane hadn't seemed to notice. Distracted, he had played with the ends of her hair, the dark strands pretty against the bronze of his skin. "Silver Eyes," he'd said, using his favorite nickname for her. "I missed you more than I can say."

Lovely words. True words. They always missed each other when they were parted. But then he'd stood, not giving her a chance to reply, and padded to the bathroom, shutting himself inside. He hadn't looked back.

He always looked back when he walked away from her.

He always winked at her.

She always blew him a kiss. Sometimes, when she was mad at him, with bite. He always chuckled.

Then, he'd left the fortress without saying goodbye to her. He always said goodbye.

They'd fought together for centuries, and never once had they deviated from their traditions. Traditions that had started because, after they'd first met, they had briefly dated. But his demon, Disaster, and her demon, Misery, had caused far too many problems and they'd eventually broken up. He'd become her best friend. Her confidant. Their traditions were all they had.

Since his return, something had changed.

He had changed.

She should have expected it. He'd spent several weeks in hell, bound and chained and tortured. He hadn't spilled the details, and she hadn't needed them. She could guess—and knew the worst of her imaginings wouldn't even come close to what he'd suffered. She'd wanted only to make him feel better, at least for a little while.

As if you can do anything to help anyone.

Gritting her teeth, she blocked her mind to the demon's manipulations. *I can help him, and I will.*

Cameo stood in the center of a bedroom emptied of all furniture. The walls were made of crumbling stone, and peppered with cameras. Torin was fierce about security. The marble floor was cracked—Kane had been here, and recently. The air was cool, but dry, and coated with dust.

She studied the four artifacts in front of her. Wars had been fought for them. People had killed to find them, to protect them, to steal them. She and her friends had done all of that and more to obtain them.

Somehow, some way, these seemingly useless things would lead the way to Pandora's box. To the Lords' freedom. And their ultimate doom.

The Cage of Compulsion was a rusted four-by-four cell. However, when trapped inside, a person was compelled to do whatever the owner commanded.

Then there was the Cloak of Invisibility. A simple piece of fabric. However, when a person draped the material over their shoulders, no one could see them.

Then there was the Paring Rod, a long, thin spear with a glittering crystal rounding out the top end. When touched, it could steal a spirit from a body, leaving only an empty shell.

Finally, there was a painting from the All-Seeing Eye, given to Cameo only this morning.

Danika, the Eye, could sometimes see into the skies and sometimes the abyss. Sometimes the past. Sometimes, as a gift from the Most High, the future. In this painting, Danika had obviously seen into a man's office—in the present? At the far right wall, there were treasures locked inside a glass case, and one of those treasures was a small box made of bones.

Could it be Pandora's box? A container hidden for centuries. A dangerous weapon supposedly constructed from the bones of the female incarnation of oppression. When opened, the box would suck the demons from Cameo and the other Lords, trapping the evil inside.

Ending their lives.

Cameo had sensed Kane's hatred for Disaster. She had sensed his desire to rid himself of the creature's influence, in any way necessary—she had sensed, because it was a mirror of her own yearnings. If he couldn't find a way, he might decide to hunt down the box and use it.

She couldn't let him die.

So, she would just have to eliminate this method of deliverance. She nodded. Yes. That's how she would help him.

But…how was she supposed to put each of the artifacts to use at the same time? Because that was the key to finding the box. Should she climb into the cage while wearing the Cloak and holding the painting and the Rod?

"What'cha doing?"

The voice came from beside her. Cameo cut off a groan as she turned to face Viola, the keeper of Narcissism and the newest bane of her existence. Seriously. Dealing with a pack of rabid wolves on a steady diet of dark-haired, silver-eyed females would have been way easier.

Curling blond hair cascaded over Viola's dainty shoulder, and eyes the color of cinnamon twinkled. She wore a skimpy, skintight dress with enough ruffles and bows to put Christmas morning to shame, and she held her pet Tasmanian devil in her arms. Princess Fluffy… something was his name.

Yes. The princess was a he.

"I'm spending time alone," Cameo finally replied. Hint, hint.

"Well, I hate being the bearer of bad news almost as much as I love it, but spending time alone isn't a good look for you. Your face is all scrunchy. It's quite frightening. You should try to be more like me and look good no matter who you're with. Or not with."

"Thanks for the tip."

"I know! I'm so smart it should be criminal."

Gotta find that box. Cameo wouldn't destroy it right away. She would run a test, just one, and shove Viola near it. Then, she would find out exactly what happened when a demon-possessed immortal approached it. Maybe Viola would survive. Fingers crossed she wouldn't.

As if he sensed the direction of her thoughts, Princess Fluffywhatever lunged out and sank his fangs into Cameo's wrist, a quick in-and-out job that left her bleeding. Viola continued chatting about nothing, unconcerned.

Cameo bent down, doing as Super Nanny had taught her, and as she'd often had to do with the men in her life, looking the little cretin in the eye. "If you do that again, I'm going to have he-princess for breakfast. I doubt you'll taste very good, you're too bitter, but that's what mustard is for."

The devil-dog yelped, jumped from his mistress's arms, and raced out of the room.

"I wonder what's wrong with him," Viola said.

Talk about having a megawatt attention filter. If something didn't revolve around Viola, the female never noticed.

"Do you recognize any of these artifacts?" Cameo asked her. Might as well make use of her while she was here.

"Of course I do. I can recognize anything. I'm quite gifted."

Gotta find it real soon. "Tell me what you know."

Viola puffed up, saying, "Well, the pieces are quite old. And ugly. Except for the painting. It's new and ugly." She traced a fingertip along the canvas and her expression of self-love melted away. "Be very careful." How serious she suddenly sounded. How dire. "If you fail to use each artifact properly, you'll find yourself trapped. Forever." Then she traced her finger over the Cloak, grimaced, and returned to her old, annoying self. "It's not very soft, is it? I prefer soft. My skin is very delicate. And perfect."

"How do I use each artifact properly?" Cameo insisted.

"What are you talking about? How should I know? I've never used them. And besides, while I know everything, I sometimes like to be appreciated for more than my magnificent brain." As she spoke, she bent down to peer into the crystal at the end of the Rod. "Oh, a pretty," she breathed, appearing entranced by her own reflection.

She reached out. Made contact.

One second she stood beside Cameo, the next she was gone.

Silence filled the room.

"Viola," Cameo said, spinning, but there was no sign of the girl.

Heartbeat picking up speed, Cameo focused on the camera in the far right corner. "Did you see that? Did what I think just happened really happen?"

There was a crackle of static before Torin's voice flowed from strategically placed speakers. "Yeah. The moment she made contact with the Rod, she was adiosed."

"What should I do?" she demanded.

"Nothing. I'm going to do a search for info and see what I can find."

No. She wasn't content to do nothing. Besides, he'd been searching for info since they'd gotten the thing, and hadn't found anything.

Moving swiftly, Cameo unfolded the Cloak.

"Hey! What are you doing?" Torin demanded. "Stop that right now."

"Make me." He was the keeper of Disease. One touch of his skin against another's and a plague would start. The poor guy spent most of his time alone in his bedroom, watching the world from a distance.

In a moment of weakness, they had begun a hands-off relationship, but just like with Kane, the sparks had quickly fizzled and they'd realized they were better off as friends.

"Cameo. Don't."

He was concerned for her. She knew that. She also knew he liked to think before acting. To plan. To test. Most of the warriors living in the fortress were like that. Not Cameo. The longer she waited to do something, the more useless she became, the demon's misery filling her, consuming her.

More than that, Viola could be in pain. Cameo didn't like the girl, but she wasn't going to let her suffer—no matter what she'd planned to do to her. She had to try to extract her.

Cameo reached out with a shaky hand.

"Don't you dare do what she did," Torin shouted over the speakers.

She paused. Maybe there was another way. Maybe—

"Maddox!" Torin's voice boomed. "You're needed in the artifact room. Now! Reyes, you, too. Anyone. Cameo's about to make a huge and possibly fatal mistake."

No time to reason things out.

Trembling, Cameo set the painting in the cage, grabbed the Cloak, and entered. She shut the door, and the lock automatically engaged. The moment she heard the soft click, she felt as though a heavy ring of metal had wrapped around her neck, wrists and ankles. But when she looked, she saw only the tan of her skin.

"I'm commanding you to stop, Cameo," Torin said.

The Cage clearly didn't consider him its owner, because she felt no compulsion to obey him.

She wrapped the Cloak around her shoulders and reached through the bars, intending to latch onto the Rod. Just before contact, her gaze locked on the painting. She froze. In an instant, insignificant details were wiped away. She saw the box, and in the shadows behind it, a man. He was of average height, with a thin build.

She couldn't make out his features, could only see the red glow of his eyes. Who was he? *What* was he? Would he be friend or foe? Was he guarding Pandora's box? Trying to prevent her from destroying it?

With so little muscle mass, he'd never stand a chance.

Find Viola. Find him.

Footsteps echoed inside the room. Hinges on the door creaked.

Maddox stormed inside, violent anger radiating from him. "Don't you dare—"

She grabbed the Rod before he could finish his sentence, just in case, and felt the coldness of the crystal against her skin.

And then she knew nothing more.

CHAPTER SEVEN

Séduire

CURRENTLY, JOSEPHINA WAS the ketchup in a beefcake sandwich. Two palace guards held her in a viselike grip, preventing her from running away. They were beautiful men, tall and strong—though not as tall and strong as Kane—with looks typical of the Fae. Each had white hair, blue eyes, pale skin and red lips. They wore fitted violet overcoats, and had several medals pinned along their shoulders. Their pants were white, without a speck of dirt, and practically painted on. Black boots stretched to their knees.

Oh, yes. They were beautiful men, but they were the proud owners of cold, dead hearts. They knew what would happen to her, but wouldn't let her go. They held her all the tighter.

So close to freedom, she thought, fighting a wave of despair. *And yet here I am.*

At least the hatred and evil she'd borrowed from Kane had left her and returned to him.

The royal dais loomed in front of her. King Tiberius sat upon a lavish throne carved from a single block of the purest gold, his hand curled around the center of a bejeweled scepter. On his right was a smaller throne, and perched there was the elegant Queen Penelope. On his left was yet another throne, this one for the flawless Princess Synda.

Behind the trio was a higher tier. Higher, yet still it seemed the area was nothing more than an afterthought. There sat Prince Leopold. Even as much as he claimed to want her, he'd wasted no time escorting Josephina to the guards and abandoning her to their "care."

The Opulens stood behind her. Dressed in their finest, they had gathered here to watch her newest chastisement. The women wore elaborate gowns with fitted bodices and wide, flaring skirts. Bold makeup decorated their faces, the colors dusted with diamond powder. Their hair was partially hidden by large, bejeweled headdresses that fanned out to form half-moons. Metal necklaces circled their throats and dripped beads down their shoulders and cleavage.

The men wore velvet jackets in every color imaginable, metal pieces sewn into the shoulders, elbows and hem. Their trousers were looser than what the guards wore, but still managed to mold to hard-won strength.

In Séduire, beauty mattered more than brains and clothing mattered more than food. Political intrigues were always in full swing. An open mouth was a lying mouth. Power was just as valuable as cash. Lust, greed and torture were always on the menu.

Josephina hated it here.

Every Fae wielded some type of extraordinary ability—though she actually wielded *two*—but some were better than others. The king was doubly gifted, like Josephina, able to bequeath abilities to others, as well as form a protective shield around his body. The queen had the power to touch an object and know its complete history. Leopold could cause pain in others with a single spoken word.

Any ability Synda possessed had been buried when she'd obtained the demon. Josephina had heard stories, though, and thought her half sister had once been able to turn any inanimate object into gold.

The king looked Josephina over with those eyes of crystal blue. Oh, how she despised the color. She much preferred Kane's eyes, jade and amber—and she had to stop thinking about him, didn't she? Their association was over. She wouldn't be seeing him again. He wouldn't *want* to see her. Not after what she'd done to him.

Regret clawed at her. Already she mourned the loss of him. The strong, beautiful warrior who'd come to save her.

A small cry parted her lips.

"Have you nothing to say for yourself, Servant Josephina?" King Tiberius demanded. "You caused us all kinds of trouble."

"Yes, you should be on your knees right now," Queen Penelope said, flicking an invisible piece of lint from the skirt of her dress. "Begging for our forgiveness."

Ignoring the burn of rejection accompanying those words, Josephina kept her gaze on her father. Though he was hundreds of years old, he looked almost as young as she was. He had silver-white hair, unblemished skin, and enough muscle to snap the bones of any man.

"I'm angry with you, girl. You didn't return on your own. You had to be hunted, wasting time, energy and resources."

"I was being chased by demons." It was the truth.

He flicked his tongue over an incisor. "Excuses aren't to be tolerated."

She gulped, and wisely kept her mouth shut.

"However, I am feeling benevolent, and will not punish you. This time. But if you ever again try to deprive my precious daughter of her blood rights, whatever the reason, I'll be forced to hobble you for the rest of your life."

I'm your precious daughter, too, her heart cried. The only difference was, the queen wasn't her mother.

Murmurs of excitement erupted behind her. The people wanted to see her hobbled.

The queen petted the ribbon of fur hanging from the collar of her gown. "We sent guards to await you at the exit to hell. Did you kill them?"

"No. The demons must have done it, because there was no one waiting for me."

"Ugh. Demons," said Princess Synda.

Josephina met her sister's gaze.

The girl blinked. All innocence. Zero remorse.

A quintessential Fae, Synda had her white curls twined with a wide, arching headdress of crystal spears. Her luminous eyes were framed by sharp sweeps of sapphire shadow, and currently without any hint of the red the demon caused when it acted up. Her cheeks were brushed with the dust of rubies, and her lips with the flakes of diamonds.

She displayed moments of utter sweetness, like now, followed by *looong* stretches of utter nastiness. She obeyed no rules, not even her own, and always acted without thought or concern for anything or anyone.

Josephina was younger by several hundred years, and at the time of her birth, Synda already contained the demon. The stories she'd heard about the princess's past, about what the female had been like before the possession, had shocked her. Apparently, there had been no one more kind, concerned and happy.

How much had Disaster changed Kane?

You're thinking about him again.

Tiberius slammed the scepter into the floor, a loud boom shaking the entire room. "You will concentrate on the proceedings, Servant Josephina, or I'll have to make an example out of you."

"Maybe she likes it when you punish her," the queen said with an evil grin. "Maybe that's why she tempts you to give her more."

Josephina shuddered. "Just…let me go. Please."

The king leaned forward, placing his elbows on his knees. "Have I not been good to you? Have I not given you a home? A worthy purpose?"

The queen smirked.

Synda selected a pastry from the tray beside her.

Leopold shook his head in regret.

I won't cry. Not again.

Tiberius sighed. "Take her to the dungeon. I can see the desire to run in your eyes, girl. You will be locked away until you've realized how well I've treated you—and how much worse it can be for you."

The Opulens cheered.

She opened her mouth to protest, but closed it with a snap. Speaking after judgment had been handed down would only earn her further chastisement.

As she was dragged away, she heard another guard say to the king, "Two immortal warriors were following Servant Josephina. We left them in the forest, but placed a tracker on their equipment. What would you have us do with them?"

Though she didn't hear the king's answer, Josephina mewled with dismay.

THE WHOOSH OF a whip sounded, followed by screams of pain. Josephina flinched as every blow landed on the man on the other side of the crumbling stone wall.

Her poor arms were chained over her head, her fingers ice-cold from pitiable circulation. Once again she was sandwiched between two men. Only, these two weren't guards. They were prisoners, like her, and they'd made the grievous mistake of owning land the king wanted for himself.

They, too, had their arms chained over their heads, but they were either unconscious or dead. They had been deprived of food for so long, their bodies were emaciated. And they had gone unwashed for years. Oh, the stench…

Footsteps pounded, and the dungeon master stalked around the corner. Prince Leopold smiled at her, genuine affection gleaming in his crystalline eyes. Like Princess Synda, he had curling white hair. Unlike Synda, he was tall, taller than their father, and leanly toned. Eligible Opulens were always drooling and panting for him.

He stopped in front of Josephina and pinched a lock of her hair between his blood-splattered fingers. "Did you miss me, little flower?" he asked, warm breath fanning over her face.

"Not even a bit," she replied truthfully. "If you want the brutal truth of the matter, it was my hope we'd never see each other again."

A muscle ticked in his jaw, a testament of his anger. First point, Servant Josephina. "Give yourself to me, and the king will no longer use you as Synda's substitute."

I'd rather die—obviously. "Even if that were true, which it's not, my answer would be the same—never. Does that work for you?"

His lashes fused together, leaving only tiny slits. "Why don't you want me? I'm desirable."

Where to begin? Oh, yeah. "You're my brother."

"Only by blood."

Was that all? "Well, you disgust me. How about that?"

He leaned in. "I would be good to you. Very, very good."

She stiffened, gritting out, "Stop. I'm not interested."

"Just give me a chance."

Josephina turned her head away. Her body ached in the worst way. Her mind was foggy from hunger. She couldn't deal with him right now.

He took her chin in a firm grip and returned her attention to him. "I could force you. You know that, don't you?"

If he'd wanted her that way, he would have taken her years ago.

She remembered the first day they'd come into contact outside the throne room. She'd been walking through the royal garden, plucking the prettiest of the flowers for her mother. Back then, her mother had been the king's favored concubine and Josephina had been free to do as she pleased—when she wasn't being punished for Synda's crimes, of course.

Yes, the king had used her that way even then, despite her mother's protests.

Leopold had just achieved his immortality, never to physically age again, and he had been celebrating in the garden with two female slaves. Josephina had stumbled upon the group, seen them doing things that still made her blush; he'd heard her startled gasp and looked up. She'd backed away, afraid he would tell his mother she was a spy, and the queen would have her whipped. Again.

But Leopold had smiled, commanded Josephina to stay where she was, then righted his clothing and sent the females on their way. He'd gently teased her about her blush, picked up the flowers she'd dropped and gallantly presented them to her, as if she were an Eligible and worthy of his attention.

For the next few years, he'd met with her often, purposely, talking with her, laughing with her, and for the first time in her life, Josephina had felt a kinship with someone other than her mother.

But the day Josephina had achieved her own immortality, though so much more fragile than those of full blood, the focus of Leopold's attention had changed. He'd gone from brotherly to amorous, charming to persistent, and had even tried to kiss her. At the time, she'd run away from him.

He'd been chasing her ever since.

Things had never been the same between them, and never would.

"You won't," she said, confident.

The prisoner across from her snickered over her continued rejection.

Leopold's cheeks reddened the slightest degree. He released her and stomped over to the offender. Rather than rain his fists in a fury of punishment, he tilted his head to the side and said, "Agony."

The man screamed in sudden anguish, his entire body shaking. Blood soon leaked from his eyes, his nose, and the corners of his mouth.

"Stop!" Josephina cried. "Stop it, Leopold! Please."

He did. When the man was dead.

Bile burned her chest, and collected in her throat.

Leopold spun to eye every male in chains. "Anyone else have anything to say?"

Only the rattle of chains could be heard.

The scowling prince locked gazes with Josephina,

spit on the ground at her feet. “It’s only a matter of time before Princess Synda commits another crime. You’ll be whipped in her place. Or worse. Let me protect you.”

“Even if you could save me, I’d never consider you the better choice,” she replied raggedly.

“We’ll see about that. I leave to capture the men hunting you. One of the imperial guards will be in charge of your care. I doubt he’ll be as gentle.” With that, he stalked from the dungeon.

A bitter laugh escaped her. Kane had wondered why she wanted to die. Kane had wanted to know what he could do to help her. Well, here was why. And clearly, there was nothing he could do. Just as she’d known.

There was nothing anyone could do.

But I can help him, she thought. She could use the second ability she possessed and warn Kane about the tracker the guards had placed in his equipment. That way, when they found him, he wouldn’t be caught unaware. He could fight. And he could win. Or run.

It was the least she could do, and had nothing to do with the fact that she wanted to see him again. Really.

CHAPTER EIGHT

Texas
The Teaze

ROCK MUSIC POUNDED through the nightclub, shaking the floor, rattling the walls. Strobe lights flashed all the colors of the rainbow and spun, creating a dizzying kaleidoscope that somehow lowered inhibitions. Immortal men and women flailed on the dance floor, walked the aisles in search of fresh prey, or sat at the tables, flirting in between throwing back shots of the beauty maker.

The world might be ugly before you drank a glass of ambrosia-laced whiskey, but it sure was beautiful afterwards. At least for a little while.

Kane wanted to leave, memories of the last time he'd been inside a nightclub playing through his mind, sickening him, but he'd texted Torin for information about Tinker Bell, and for some reason, the warrior had sent him here.

As usual, William was off trolling for women.

Kane pushed a vampire out of the chair he wanted, and claimed a place at the bar. The guy didn't protest, just took one look at him and rushed away. Kane ordered a shot of the beauty maker. Anything to dull his riotous emotions.

Where was Tinker Bell?

Was she okay? Safe?

She no longer had custody of Disaster—if that's what had happened, and he suspected it was. There was no other explanation. The demon had come roaring back to Kane a few hours after he'd left the forest. He'd been disappointed for himself, but relieved for her. He didn't like the thought of such a delicate half immortal going against such evil.

But at least he had an answer to one of his questions now. The Greeks had indeed lied. The demon wasn't as much a part of him as his lungs and his heart. Kane couldn't survive a single moment without the organs, but he *could* survive a few hours without Disaster. Maybe more.

Hate you, Disaster growled.

Assure you, the feeling's mutual.

One of the legs on his chair snapped, and he nearly hit the floor. He brutally kicked the broken stool out of the way, and decided to stand.

"About time you got here," a female said.

His gaze snapped to the left, where a tall, lithe blonde stood. She was exquisite, with long hair that tumbled to a perfectly curved waist and snow-white skin covered in makeup to mute its luminous power. Blue eyes held his stare without wavering or fear.

She's mine, Disaster shouted. *All mine.*

Kane ground his molars together. Just how many "mines" were they supposed to have?

"Taliyah Skyhawk," he acknowledged. She was Sabin and Strider's sister-in-law, as well as a Harpy known for her cold-as-ice demeanor. "You knew I was coming?"

"Torin gave me a heads-up."

His focus sharpened on her. Well, okay, then. "You got info for me?"

She motioned to the bartender, and waited, silent, for a bottle of vodka to be slid in front of her, as if Kane weren't suddenly vibrating with impatience. "This belongs to him," she said, hitching her thumb in his direction.

Knowing Harpies couldn't eat or drink anything without stealing or earning it, he threw a few bills on the counter without complaint. "Anytime would be great, Tal."

She drank straight from the bottle, wiped her mouth with the back of her hand and faced him, her expression impassive. "There's a Phoenix chasing your Fae. Her name's Petra, and she's a vicious little troll."

Not exactly a news flash. "So, how did you know that?"

"You remember when my friend Neeka the Unwanted was given to the Phoenix, even though she's a Harpy, to save my sister? Well, little Neeka keeps getting stolen from different clans—everyone wants a piece of her, which is so wonderfully ironic, considering her name. She gets bored between travels and spies for me. I knew the stuff about Petra would be important to you because my sisters told me about your encounter with the Fae."

Sabin and Strider were such pansy blabbermouths.

"Anyway," Taliyah continued. "The rest of the information is going to cost you."

He arched a brow, saying, "How much?" Whatever the price, he'd pay it.

"I want the fortress in the Realm of Blood and Shadows."

A thirty-thousand-square-foot monstrosity for a few words? A fair exchange, in his opinion. He wasn't sure his friends would agree. "There's a problem. The place isn't mine to give."

Taliyah drained the rest of the bottle with a grace matched by few. "Too bad. It would have been nice doing business with you, Kane. See you." She walked away from him without another word.

Coldhearted. As always.

Kane leaped into action, dragging her back to the bar—and she let him. She had more at stake than she wanted him to believe, then. "It's yours," he said to her. "The fortress is yours. When do you want it?"

Winter-blue eyes sparkled triumphantly. "Three months and two days from now. No sooner, no later."

"Fine. I'll kick my friends out myself."

"Even my sisters?"

"No," he said, thinking that was what she'd want to hear. "They can—"

"Deal's off. Sorry." Once again she walked away, and once again he had to drag her back.

"Fine," he rushed out. "I'll kick them out, too." They'd want to stay with their husbands, anyway.

She nodded, satisfied.

"Why can't you stay there with everyone else?" he grumbled. She had before.

"You're not going to tell anyone I'm there. You do, and I'll hunt you down. Immortal races will be talking about the things I did to your entrails for centuries."

Harpies, man. They actually had the strength and stomach to back up their threats, and that was a serious downer when the women weren't on your side. "What do you need the fortress for?"

"None of your business. Now, do you want the information I've got or not?"

"I do."

"Okay, so, apparently, a Sent One—Thane, I think his name is—suddenly appeared in one of the Phoenix camps a few weeks ago. He threw a big fit, and killed lots of the warriors. One of them was the king. The Sent One was eventually subdued, and a new king took the throne. This new king was finally able to claim the woman he's been craving for centuries—the dead king's wife."

"What's this got to do with anything?"

"I'm getting there. The new king took the widow as his concubine, but only a few days later, this Petra girl killed her. As punishment, she was cast into the Never-ending. And now that Petra's on the loose, the new king wants her back. Like, bad. The things he'll do to her when he finds her…it's going to be legend—wait for it—dary. Oh, and the concubine was Petra's sister. Meaning, there's no line this troll won't cross. If your Fae is on her radar, she's in trouble."

He would get to her first.

The glass shattered in his hand, cutting his skin.

Stupid demon.

He dabbed at the wounds with a napkin.

He waited, but Taliyah said nothing more. "That's all you have for me?"

"As if Neeka is that poor of a spy. I was just waiting for you to digest. So get this. Petra was seen buying a key to Séduire."

Séduire. The kingdom of the Fae, though many humans lived there, located in a realm between realms. Some immortals could flash there, moving from one space to another with only a thought. Most could not. Kane was among the could-nots, so, for people like him, a special key was needed to open one of the invisible doorways.

"If this Petra is following Tinker Bell's scent, and she bought a key, Tinker Bell must have returned to Séduire," Kane said, thinking out loud. Finally, he had a location.

"Tinker Bell?"

Disaster growled.

William scooted into the seat beside him, saving him from having to answer. The warrior was without his usual random woman (or six) and scowling. "What are you doing here, Ice Witch, and how did you find us? We're on a boys-only vacay."

Taliyah rolled her eyes. "I just answered those questions for Kane and won't do it again for the likes of you. And what a way to say hello, Man Whore."

So. The two hated each other now. Interesting.

William looked at him, and Kane could see the excitement banked in his eyes. "You're just going to let her talk to me like that? I should pack my bags and leave you."

"I should be so lucky." Kane signaled for another whiskey. The glass shattered as he downed the liquid inside it, and he choked on a shard. Coughing blood, he stood. "I've got to find a key. Don't call me if you need me."

What are you doing? Disaster demanded. *Don't leave the Harpy. She's mine. I want her.*

Taliyah reached out and grabbed his wrist. He…felt no pain, he realized, and no desire, either. Apparently no one's touch affected him like Tinker Bell's. "Remember what I told you."

Yeah. He remembered. No one could know she wanted the fortress.

"What did you tell him?" William demanded. "You

might as well confess. I'll just bug the answer out of him if you don't."

Kane rolled his eyes, knowing he'd be dodging William's annoying prods for weeks, but walked away before the Harpy could respond and never looked back.

THE MOMENT HE was outside, Kane whipped out his cell phone. Yesterday, he'd taken a snapshot of Danika's painting and saved the image as wallpaper.

In it, he was on his knees, tears streaming down his face, hands lifted toward the heavens. A blonde female lay in front of him, a hole the size of his fist burned into her chest. Her face was turned away from him, so he had no idea who she was—and wasn't sure he wanted to know.

The painting was a problem that would have to wait.

He called every black market contact he had, looking to buy a key to Séduire. He would also need a guide, since he had no idea where to find a doorway. But one call after another proved unfruitful. No one was able to help him.

A sense of urgency drove him, and he paced toward the darkened alleys about a mile from the club. There, immortals would be peddling their wares. Drugs. Sex. Anything and everything. Even if he couldn't find a key, he could find someone who knew someone else with the contacts to help him.

A thick white fog suddenly rolled in, and he paused. Through the density, he could just make out the shape of a…woman? Oh, yes, definitely a woman. She glided toward him, and he could see she was wearing a glowing white dress. Long, dark hair fell over one delicate shoulder, reminding him of…

"Tinker Bell?" he asked, shocked to his core.

Disaster banged against his skull.

Kane raced to her, tried to grab her despite the pain it might cause him, the unwanted desire, and whatever she'd done to him in the forest, but his hands ghosted through her.

Her eyes were as white as the fog and as luminous as the most expensive diamonds. "Would you please stop calling me that?" she said, exasperated. As freaky as she looked, the normalcy of her voice surprised him.

"What's going on? Are you…dead?" Even uttering the question made him want to kill someone.

"I'm not dead. I'm simply projecting my image into your mind."

Relief was like a gentle rain, dousing the budding rage—and the overwhelming sorrow he didn't want to explore. "Exactly how many abilities do you possess, woman? And what exactly did you do to me in that forest?"

"There's no time for that. I'm weakening, and must hurry."

Weakening? In a snap, the rage returned. "Why?"

"Doesn't matter. Listen, Lord Kane. I know I'm not your favorite person right now, and you probably don't trust me, but please believe me when I say you're in grave danger."

Him. Not her. Better. "More danger than usual? And don't call me Lord Kane. I don't need a title." Not from her. "I'm just a man." *Your man*.

The thought hit him with the force of a tsunami, and he fisted his hands. His body was suddenly rock-hard, ready to prove the claim, to strip her and take her as he'd longed to do in the forest. A temptation he found as exhilarating as it was frightening.

Can't touch her.

But if he could…

What would she do? How would she react?

How would he?

Would her skin be as soft as it appeared? Would her curves create the perfect cradle for him?

A few feet away, the lid to a trash bin flew open. As the wind picked up, debris propelled toward Kane, most assuredly courtesy of Disaster.

Tinker Bell stomped her foot. "I can't concentrate when you look at me like that," she said.

"Like what?"

"Like I don't know how to describe it. It's like you want to strangle me or something."

Or just wanted to get his hands on her. But he got what she was saying, knew his desire was tangled with darkness.

He nodded, ashamed of himself. "I'll stop."

She licked her lips, and said, "My people know you're looking for me, and now they're hunting you."

"Your Fae family or your human one?"

"Fae."

"And that's who you're with right now?" he asked, wanting to verify the information Taliyah had given him.

"Yes. I don't know what you've heard about the race, but the Fae can be brutal, bloodthirsty and without a shred of compassion. They'll haul you before the king and he'll sentence you to death just for looking at me. No matter how star-struck he is by you!"

He wasn't sure what the star-struck comment meant, and wasn't going to waste time finding out. "Why would he want to kill me?" The only viable answer slammed into him, and the patent stillness of a predator came over him. "Are you his lover?"

She gave another stomp of her foot. "Would you be serious?"

"Answer me." The words were nothing more than a hiss.

"Of course I'm not his lover! What a disgusting prospect!"

He relaxed—and he had no desire to ponder why he'd reacted so fervently to the thought of her with another man when he wouldn't be taking her for himself. "I've been hunted by brutal, bloodthirsty people before."

"Yes, I know, but the Fae are gifted with special abilities. Like, say, causing you pain with only a word."

Like the pain she caused him? But then, she'd never needed to speak for him to feel it. "Can you do that?"

"No, but my brother can," she said.

"You can project your image, as well as rip the demons out of people."

Her jaw dropped. "So that's what happened. I took your demon?"

"You mean you didn't know?"

She hooked several tendrils of hair behind her ear, the action feminine and sweet and somehow more erotic than a striptease from another woman, and if he didn't get his thoughts and his body under control right now, he would self-destruct.

"I take abilities and strength for a few hours, maybe a few days or weeks," she said, "but not…*that*. Never anything like that."

"You can. You did. You must take weaknesses, too." And that's exactly what the demon was. "Don't do it again," he stated flatly. Already her life was so miserable she wanted to die. How much worse would it be for her with Disaster hanging around? And what if she got stuck with the creature forever, rather than temporarily? Was that possible?

Kane didn't want her to risk it. This girl, she was… he didn't know what she was to him. He only knew he couldn't bear the thought of her suffering.

Her nose went into the air, making her look sullen and defiant and utterly adorable. "Don't get any ideas about rescuing me. I'll do what I want, when I want."

Want me.

The ground cracked beneath his feet. He didn't care.

"Can you control the ability?" The words croaked from him.

"I don't know," she admitted softly. "I've never gotten to test my limits with people I didn't want to borrow from." Her gaze lowered to his lips, and she shifted from one foot to the other.

She's not thinking about kissing me. She can't be thinking about kissing me. "You need skin-to-skin contact?"

"Yes."

"I'll help you with that, too."

Her eyes brightened, the clouds rolling out to reveal endless oceans backed by glorious sunlight. The brightness didn't last long, however. She glowered, and the clouds returned. "You can't help me, Kane, not without putting yourself in danger. So will you listen to me and either prepare for battle or run for your life?"

"No to both. Why would the king of the Fae want to kill me for looking at you?"

She was desperate to argue; he could see it in those narrowed eyes. But she must have realized he was stubborn enough to wait all night for the answers, and just messed up enough to get physical with her the next time they were truly together.

No telling what would happen then.

"He feels he must dispose of anyone who threatens to take me away from the kingdom."

"Does he plan to have me brought into the kingdom or have me executed on sight wherever I'm found?"

"The kingdom. He likes to watch."

Good. "I'm glad they're coming."

"You're glad?" she choked out.

"They'll do the work for me."

She sputtered for a moment before finally deciding on a verbal path. "What work?"

"Finding you. I will, you know." A promise.

One that came with razor-sharp desire.

The crack in the ground widened, dropping Kane several feet.

"I just told you not to—argh! Kane, don't be foolish! Please."

The sound of pounding footsteps caught his attention. On alert, he palmed a dagger and looked around, but all he saw was more fog and trash. Then, three…no, five…no, eight bodies broke through, stopping a few feet away from him.

"I found him," a hard male voice called.

If anyone could see Tinker Bell, they gave no indication.

"But…this is Lord Kane, a warrior of the Underworld," someone else gasped.

Murmurs of awe arose. "I can't believe this. I can't believe I'm standing in the presence of Lord Kane."

Questions were thrown at him.

"Will you tell us about the battle that took place in the skies? Our men weren't able to attend, so details are sparse."

"Did you really chop off a Hunter's foot and stuff it

in his mouth, just because he called Cameo an abomination?"

Tinker Bell paled, backed away. "Oh, Kane. They found you. I'm sorry." She vanished.

CHAPTER NINE

BRUTAL? KANE THOUGHT. Bloodthirsty? Hardly.

"I'm sorry for the need for this, Lord Kane, but I must bind you, as ordered." The soldier appeared grief-stricken by the thought. "I'll be slain if I refuse."

"Do it, and don't even think about being gentle about it," snapped the tallest of the bunch. "And you," he said to Kane. "Where's the other man? The one traveling with you."

"There's a good chance I killed him."

The guards nodded their agreement, as if they knew him and expected nothing less. All but the one who'd asked the question. He had to be the leader. Nothing else would explain the great waves of entitlement bouncing off him. *I'll call him Evil Overlord.*

"The shackles!" Evil Overlord proclaimed, and the soldier raced to obey.

Kane hated being bound, would rather die than endure it again. And yet he allowed the Fae to cuff his hands behind his back without protest.

Hands...all over him...

Mouths...biting at him...

Nails...scraping at him...

As the memories took center stage, he felt as if thousands of tiny needles were being injected into his skin. A loud ring erupted in his ears, and his heart kicked into a dangerously fast rhythm. His lungs constricted, the tissues burning.

Breathe. Nice and slow. In. Out. Good. That was good. And this was necessary. He had to get to Tinker Bell, and this was the fastest way.

Evil Overlord stepped to the side and waved a hand through the air.

That was it, a wave, and yet a doorway from one realm to another appeared. At the edges of the opening was the red brick of the club, the trash bin and cardboard boxes. Through the narrow opening, Kane saw a darkened landscape with multiple torches lining a cobbled pathway. That pathway led to a wide, towering palace comprised of gold-veined marble and bright, sparkly diamonds.

The soldiers formed a circle around Kane and urged him to march forward. One second he was in the city of cowboys, the next the land of the Fae. The night was crisp and damp, the torches giving off little heat. The scent of a thousand floral perfumes saturated the air, and he gagged. Sweat beaded over his skin. More fireflies than he'd ever seen in one place twirled and danced through the sky, creating what appeared to be a shower of glowing raindrops.

Playing his part, he snapped, "Where am I? Who are you?"

"Silence, Lord Kane." Evil Overlord wasn't as tall as Kane, nor was he as muscled. None of them were. "What were your plans toward Servant Josephina?"

Servant? For some reason, that irritated him. "Would you like me to be silent or give you the answer? I'm happy to give both a try, but I don't think you'll like the results."

The male scowled at him.

Disaster growled inside his mind. *Leave this place.*

Screw you.

Hate the girl, Josephina. Want to kill her.

You touch her, and I'll...

What? One of his daggers fell from his boot, and the demon laughed. *You want to stay here? Fine. But you'll do it without your weapons.* Even as the creature spoke, another dagger fell away.

"You guys seem to know a lot about me, considering we've never met," Kane said, ignoring the demon. His hands were weapons enough.

Evil Overlord smirked. "We do. You're Kane, a Lord of the Underworld. Disaster. Supposedly undefeatable. Wicked. The worst of the worst enemy to ever have."

"And I touched him," said the guy behind him, his tone overjoyed. "My wife won't be able to get enough of me tonight."

"Then your wife is a fool. This man is nothing. A no one. Look at how easily we were able to subdue him."

Evil Overlord thought he had Kane beat, and that's what Kane had wanted, but hearing that sneer really irked him. How many times had he been left behind during the war with the Hunters because his friends couldn't risk the damage Disaster would cause? Countless.

Kane had always felt like the weak link—had always *been* the weak link—and he was tired of it.

He jumped up, swinging his feet through the circle his arms provided, placing his arms in front of him. The moment he landed, he elbowed the leader in the face, breaking the guy's nose. He threw the weight of his skull into the Fae next to him, knocking the warrior to the side. He kicked out a leg and nailed the male on his other side. As the soldiers stumbled for purchase, he reached out and grabbed the hair of the male in front of him, jerking backward.

The male hit the ground and Kane stomped on his face to get to the guy in front of the line, wrapping his bound hands around the guy's neck and choking. Everything had happened so quickly, no one had realized what was going on—until then. The others sprang into action, leaping at Kane, but he kicked out one leg and then the other, sending two warriors rearing backward. He spun the guy in the chokehold, knocking his body into the others and sending them flying backward.

"Pain," he heard.

Just like that, the sharpest of pains tore through him. From the top of his head to the soles of his feet. His knees buckled, and he hit the ground with a heavy thud.

Tinker Bell's brother? he wondered, remembering what she'd said.

"That all you got?" he gritted.

That earned him a meet-and-greet with the hilt of Evil Overlord's dagger.

Two soldiers grabbed him by the armpits and dragged him forward.

"Lord Kane beat me up," one said with a grin. There was blood on his teeth. "Did you see?"

"Best. Night. Ever."

Evil Overlord—definitely Tinker Bell's brother—glared at Kane through eyes a slightly darker shade of blue than his sister's. "The king will order your death, despite who you are, and I'll take great pleasure in delivering it."

"Now why would your king want to kill me, hmm?"

"Because you dared lust after the princess's blood slave."

Tinker Bell was a blood slave on top of being a servant? What exactly did that mean?

Kane was hauled up a wide set of ivory steps, the railing shaped like a winged dragon. At the top, the guards passed through open double doors of dark wood and twisted iron. And then, Kane was inside the palace. The spacious foyer had a floor of mosaic tiles and was surrounded by life-size statues. Velvet-lined walls were covered by paintings of elaborately dressed Fae.

There was another staircase, and past it, a long, narrow hallway. Chamber after chamber whizzed by. The guards entered the last—what had to be the throne room.

Other guards milled about, interspersed with young girls and older gentlemen. Every person present had white hair and blue eyes, and every one of those eyes landed on Kane. Jaws dropped. Both men and women gasped with a sound he hadn't heard since his weeks in hell. Rapture.

A few of the braver ladies approached him. Arms reached out. Fingers brushed against him.

Hands, roaming. Tongues, licking. Teeth, biting.

His stomach lurched, and he barely bit back a grunt of distress.

Mine, the demon said.

Die.

Yet another blade fell from his body.

He snapped his teeth in warning at the women, and they twittered with excitement.

"Lord Kane almost bit me!"

"You're so lucky."

"He's even more handsome than the scribes claimed."

Scribes?

Evil Overlord shoved past anyone foolish enough to

get in his way and motioned for his comrades to do the same. They tugged Kane along for the ride, stopping in front of the crowd.

Kane studied the area, taking everything in. There were veins of gold running through the walls, the doors, and on the windows were fabrics that appeared to be woven from rose petals. The ceiling arched in the center, and vines teeming with golden flowers grew from the edges.

Below, there was a tiered dais covered in purple ivy, with the smallest throne situated on the highest level, and the three larger thrones centered on the next one down.

Evil Overlord abandoned his men to pound to the top of that dais. He turned with a graceful flourish and eased into the smallest throne, and it took a moment for Kane to compute the reason why the guy would be allowed to sit there.

He was the prince.

So…he couldn't be Tinker Bell's brother. Could he?

Dude. This doesn't change my feelings for you. Kane flipped him off.

The male displayed a smug smile. He thought he had Kane by the short hairs.

He was wrong.

Kane dismissed him, catching sight of a male and two females sweeping into the room from a side door. They eased into the remaining thrones, and it didn't take a Jenius to know the king, queen and princess had just arrived.

The king was a brute of a man, and surprisingly young. The queen was small and delicate, but appeared to be a few years older than her husband. The princess had the quintessential Fae hair, all-white, with no hint of color, and those endless eyes of blue. Her small, fragile body was squeezed into a bold red gown. The bodice dipped low enough to reveal the tattoo between her breasts, a—he sucked in a breath.

A butterfly. A match to his.

She was...*you've got to be kidding me. How?*

She was possessed by one of Pandora's demons. But which one? And how had she come to acquire it?

He had a very bad feeling.

Before his possession, Kane had been a soldier in King Zeus's army, and he'd locked many of the inmates of Tartarus away; he'd butted heads with the rest. There was no way the princess had been inside the prison when the demons of Pandora's box had been unleashed, and the leftovers distributed among the inmates. So, how had she come to be possessed? And which demon afflicted her?

The same door the royal family had used was opened again, and this time a dark-haired girl was escorted inside. Part of Kane wanted to continue staring at the princess, trying to unravel the mystery of her, but the scent of rosemary and mint wafted to him and his body reacted as if he'd just been stripped and caressed.

Only one female had that scent—and that effect.

He returned his attention to the newcomer with laser focus. She was dirty, bruised and worn down—and his heart almost stopped. She *was* Tinker Bell.

The urge to go to her consumed him, and he stepped forward. A guard caught him, stopping him from going any farther. He could have broken free of the hold, but didn't.

She was here. She was alive. Fighting now, before he'd gathered all the necessary information, could get her hurt far more severely.

He took in the rest of her. Her hair was tangled around her arms, all the way to her waist. Grime streaked her reddened cheeks. An apron hung around her neck, and it was in the same shape as her gown. She kept her eyes downcast, fear radiating from her.

Someone would pay for this.

He had to lock his knees to prevent another surge forward. Had to grip his pants to stop himself from throwing punches.

When the males released her, she tumbled to the ground, unable to sustain her own weight, slight though it was. Her knees hit the floor, and as she whimpered in pain, she braced herself with her hands, causing the fabric of her gown to rise, revealing her wrists. Angry red welts marred her skin. She'd been chained.

Tinker Bell. Chained.

Someone would pay *severely.*

Forget information. He stepped toward the dais, going for the king. This time, he was whacked in the back of the head.

He heard a muttered, "I'm so sorry, Lord Kane."

Growling, he spun and slammed his joined hands into the culprit's jaw. Bone snapped—and not Kane's.

A yowl of agony split the air.

The rest of the regiment spurred into action. *Bring it.* He had enough violence pooling in his veins to take down a pack of rabid animals.

"Enough!" a voice thundered.

Everyone stilled and quieted.

"Tell me what's going on."

Kane's gaze landed on the speaker. The king. Anger contorted features that promised to unleash death and destruction.

Whatever. Kane would get his information, after all.

The guard on his left bowed low. "My liege, this is Kane, a Lord of the Underworld, and the host to Disaster. He was the one chasing Servant Josephina."

Behind him, wild murmurings arose. Tinker Bell's gaze shot up, and landed on him. Her eyes widened, and she shook her head, mouthing, "Run."

He popped his jaw. *I'm here, honey, and I'm not going anywhere without you. Get used to it.*

Excitement danced in the king's eyes. "How we've longed to meet you, Lord Kane." To the guard, he said, "Release our honored guest. Now."

The bonds were instantly cut away. Kane rubbed his wrists.

"I must ask what you want with Servant Josephina, Lord Kane," the king continued more warily. "She is a…special charge of ours."

"Perhaps I wish to buy her." If she was a slave, she was for sale, special or not. And if he had to go that route to get her out of here and started on her new life, well, he'd consider it a blessing.

"We will give you anything you desire—except her," the king said. "I would never sell my own daughter."

The queen *hmphed* with disdain. "Only a fool would want such an ugly, wretched female."

Kane scowled at her.

Disaster was quick with an agreement.

Wait. Back up. Tinker Bell was the king's daughter? A princess? But why was she dressed like, treated like—

Blood. Slave. The words rolled through his mind, and more pieces of the puzzle finally slid into place, little tidbits of information he'd picked up over the centuries drawing together. Tinker Bell was of royal blood, but only partway. Therefore, she qualified to bear the punishment meted out to those in her family.

Anytime the "real" princess had committed a crime, Josephina had been the one punished for it. She would have endured whippings, beatings, stonings and probably a thousand other things he couldn't bring himself to consider. That's why she'd ended up in hell.

Oh, Tinker Bell. Poor, sweet Tinker Bell. The very things he'd endured during the worst weeks of his life, she had endured for a lifetime. No wonder she wanted to die.

Kane's jaw clenched, the only reason he was able to silence the spew of curses brewing at the back of his throat. No, the king would never let her go. Not for any price. Not for any reason.

I won't let her go for any price or any reason, either.

Oh, really? asked Disaster.

The Fae next to Kane tripped, falling into him, knocking him to the side. "I'm so sorry. I don't know what happened," the man babbled.

Kane straightened.

"He's so beautiful. More so than I ever imagined. And he's just like me!" The princess clapped her hands, exclaiming, "I want him, Daddy. Please? Please! Give him to me."

The king stiffened, only to relax a moment later. He eyed Kane with intrigue, the cogs in his brain clearly churning in a direction Kane wouldn't like. "I do find the thought of our family being joined to that of Lord Kane's intriguing."

No. He didn't like it. In any other situation, the threat would have enraged him. A rampage would have ensued.

"You will do us the great honor of wedding our

daughter, Princess Synda," the king said, a statement rather than a question.

He liked that even less.

But okay. All right. Kane needed to stay in this realm long enough to plan an escape for Tinker Bell. If he agreed to a wedding, he might be allowed free run of the palace. If he didn't, he would have to fight the army every second of his stay.

"Sure," he said with a nod. "Fine. Whatever. I'll wed your daughter." He wasn't wedding anyone. "But Tink—Josephina can't be harmed while I'm here."

More murmurs slithered through the room. He tried to make sense of the words, couldn't.

The king drummed his fingers against the shaft of his scepter. "We would love nothing more than to accommodate your request, Lord Kane, but a crime was committed last night, and a price must be paid. That's why Servant Josephina is here."

"What crime?"

"Princess Synda was caught with the butcher's son, a male far below her station. Worse, a human."

"Then punish Princess Synda." Problem? Meet solution.

A shake of the king's head, firm and sure. "That's not how we do things around here, Lord Kane. Since the spawning of our race, blood slaves have helped ensure the well-being of the royal family."

"I see." The blood slaves had also helped ensure the maliciousness of the royal family. "And what's to be Josephina's punishment for Synda's crime?"

"Servant Josephina will be shunned for one month. Anyone who speaks to her will be killed."

Better than he could have hoped. Still, Kane squared his shoulders and braced his legs apart, preparing for battle. "Well, then, we've got our first real problem. I'm going to talk to her, and that's non-negotiable."

Crystal eyes narrowed. "Very well," the king said after a few moments of thought, "but you will be lashed for every word."

"What?" someone in the crowd gasped out.

"No. Not Lord Kane!" another cried.

"No," Tinker Bell croaked.

Kane cut her a sharp glance. *Silence.*

She shook her head, dark hair wisping over her shoulders, saying, "Don't do this."

Still looking out for him, even after he'd failed her so miserably. His determination intensified. To the king, he said, "I will never willingly submit to such a punishment." It would weaken him, and he needed every bit of strength he could summon. "I doubt you can force me—" except for Evil Overload, and his ability, but then, Kane could remove his tongue and that problem would be settled, too "—and the men that try will pay a very dear price."

Behind him, a female fainted.

The princess flattened her hand over her heart and grinned. "He's so wonderfully fierce. How soon can the wedding be planned?"

"Excellent question. We'll make sure it's done by the end of the month. That gives us ten days." The king slammed his scepter into the marble floor so forcefully cracks formed in both. "Now. Everyone will return to their duties. And you," he snarled at Kane. "You will join me in my chambers."

CHAPTER TEN

JOSEPHINA SCRUBBED A rag back and forth over the already-clean upper staircase banister, surprised she hadn't dimmed…whatever the material was. It looked like starlight and clouds. A chandelier hovered just above her, the rotating streams of opals, sapphires and emeralds attached to nothing but air, casting rainbow flecks in every direction, even the floor many stories below.

I wish I could jump.

Stupid Kane. He should have killed her when he'd had the chance. Now, she was going to make him wish he had. Yes. She liked that plan.

How dare he agree to wed Princess Synda?

Synda would lie to him, and cheat on him. The girl's desire always burned white-hot, but died quickly. She would chew Kane up and spit him out, and there would be nothing left of him but bones. Bones Josephina had risked her life to save.

How could he want that girl? How could he not see beyond her pretty face?

Stupid, stupid, *stupid* man! Josephina stomped her foot. Anger was easier than hurt over yet another rejection.

The moment he'd agreed to the wedding, something inside her had cracked. Dark emotions had spilled out.

She'd nearly broken down and sobbed. She'd nearly shouted, "He's mine! All mine!"

But he wasn't hers, and he never would be.

She, however, might become his.

Would Tiberius give her to Kane, thinking the warrior would punish her rather than his beautiful new wife when she misbehaved? Would Kane actually punish her? If he did…her nails scraped against the rag.

I won't just make him wish I'd died. I'll make him wish he *had.*

Her chin trembled, and she sniffled.

"I want to talk to you, Tinker Bell," a masculine voice announced.

Jolting out of her wrathful thoughts, Josephina realized Kane stood just beside her. There were two guards behind him, careful to look away from her, shunning her properly, all while keeping watch over their charge and listening unabashedly.

Kane had just spoken eight words to her. Meaning, he'd just bought himself eight lashes of the whip. Josephina wanted him to suffer, but not that way.

"Go away," she said, wiping at her eyes with the back of her hand, just in case.

"Give us some privacy," he said to the guards.

"Anything for you, Lord Kane." The pair raced to the other side of the hallway.

"You know you're not allowed to talk to me," she said. "No one is."

"You want me to waste a few words telling you I do what I want, when I want? Because I will. I don't mind."

Thirty-two lashes. All for nothing! "Shut up, you stupid man."

His lips twitched at the corners, the bout of amusement confusing her. She'd just insulted him, yet he was battling a laugh? *I'll never understand him.*

"Your eyes are back to normal, at least," she said.

He patted the skin underneath. "They are?"

Thirty-four. She nodded, hoping her silence would encourage his own.

That hazel gaze raked the length of her body, burning her everywhere it touched. Whatever he saw must have angered him, because he ran his tongue over his teeth. "The blood slave thing is the reason you want to die, isn't it?"

She gave up trying to count his words, and simply replied. It was his back, his agonizing pain; if he wasn't going to help himself, she wasn't going to try and do it for him. "Yeah. So? Why do you care?" *You're an engaged man!*

"I have no desire to see you hurt."

And yet, in the past few hours, he'd managed to hurt her worse than all of her whippings combined. "Just leave me alone, all right? You're not the rock star I thought you were."

He flinched. "I'm sorry I disappointed you, but everything I've done since finding you in the forest, I've done for you."

Pretty words, nothing more. He'd seen Synda and wanted her, just like every other man, and it had had nothing to do with Josephina.

They stared at each other, quiet. He towered over her, as intense and savage as a man could be, and she felt small in comparison…surrounded by his utter maleness. Trapped.

But what a beautiful cage.

Her limbs began to tremble. Her breathing quickened, and she noticed he smelled of the forest he'd found her in. Pine and dewdrops, clean and untainted by the cloying fragrances the Opulens preferred. There was no longer any hint of the roses she'd scented in the motel room.

While on the run, she'd done a little research. Apparently, when an immortal closed in on death, he began to smell like roses.

How close had Kane come?

And why did she long to reach out, to flatten her palms on his chest, to feel his warmth and his strength, to assure herself he was here and he was real and oh, sweet mercy, her blood was heating, and her lips tingling, as if preparing for his seduction. He wasn't her friend or her boyfriend or even a suitor.

Tensing, he crossed his arms over his chest, clearly expecting her to…what?

"I don't know what you want from me, Kane."

"That makes two of us," he replied darkly, anger firing up his eyes. Frustration tightened the skin underneath, and determination pulled at his lips. He stepped forward, and she stepped back, until the banister stopped any further retreat. "Do you know what *you* want from *me?*"

"Yes," she whispered. "Your absence." *Before I crack.*

"I don't believe you. I think you want something… I think you want me. The way you look at me sometimes…"

"No," she said with a shake of her head.

"I believe we've talked about that look."

"I don't want you," she croaked.

"There's a difference between not wanting a man,

and not wanting to want a man. Which is it for you, Tinker Bell?"

She gulped. There was no way she would answer that.

Kane placed a hand at her left and a hand at her right, holding her captive. Tremors nearly rocked her off her feet.

"You make me feel…*you make me feel,*" he said quietly, fiercely, "and I don't like it. I want it to stop. Now."

For the first time in their acquaintance, he frightened her. There was an intensity to him she'd never noticed before, a vibe of uncontrolled danger. "I don't know what you're talking about."

His gaze locked with hers, snaring her, drawing her in even while pushing her away. "Don't you?" A thousand caresses in the dark waited in the softness of his voice.

"I…I…"

A second passed. Another and another. Neither of them moved. They didn't speak. Just stared. Somehow, those suspended seconds were more intimate than anything else she'd ever experienced. More…electrically charged.

She flattened her hands on his rock-solid chest, marveled at the strength he contained. "S-stay back." His heartbeat was a wild tumult, just like hers. It was a shock. A revelation.

A pleasure.

He stumbled away from her, breaking the connection, destroying the electrical charge.

It was what she'd wanted. But she hated being without it, she realized.

"What did you and the king discuss?" she asked, trying not to care—but caring anyway.

"You mean your father?"

Her shoulders lifted in the most casual shrug she could manage. "I am what he says I am."

Kane reached out, as if to caress her cheek. His hand fisted just before contact, and fell away. "We drank some whiskey, smoked some cigars and discussed a few details for an engagement ball to be held in my honor. We played some chess. I won. He pouted."

A ball. A ball Josephina would have to labor over. She would be forced to set up, then serve the guests food and drinks. The women would put their noses in the air and ignore her, and the men would forget their distaste for her, pat her on the bottom and maybe even try to pull her into shadowed corners. She would have to paste a grin on her face, and pretend all was well in her very dark world.

Meanwhile, Kane would be pampering the already pampered Princess Synda. The unfairness of it clogged her throat, making breathing difficult.

"You're lucky to be alive," she said stiffly. "Tiberius is the worst loser of all time."

He waved her words away. "Let's talk about your sister."

Already he was obsessed. Jealousy hit her. Jealousy, and so much hurt she wasn't sure how she was still standing. "What do you want to know?"

"She's possessed, yes?"

"Yes. Her husband was the keeper of Irresponsibility and after he died—"

Kane's lips pulled back from his teeth and a hissing sound left him.

"What's wrong?" she asked, annoyed by an overwhelming surge of concern for him.

"Her husband was possessed by…Irresponsibility, you said?"

"That's right. For several centuries, he was a prisoner of Tartarus. He died while…you-knowing Synda, and somehow she ended up with the demon. That's why our race has studied you and your friends so intently. Well, one of the reasons."

He scrubbed a hand through his hair. "This couldn't get any worse. William tried to warn me, said I'd have to make choices, but I thought…hoped…and she's blonde, just like the girl in the painting, and…well, it doesn't matter. It's happened. She is who she is. I'll deal. I'll figure things out. Somehow."

Babbling she had no idea how to decipher. "What are you talking about?"

Again, he waved her words away. "You studied us, you said?"

"Well, yeah."

"Us, meaning me and my friends?"

"Who else?"

"How?"

"Are you sure you want the truth?"

"I am."

"Fae spies have followed you guys for centuries. They report back and books are published and sold all over the realm."

"Spies," he said flatly. "Books."

"Pictures are drawn. Discussions take place. Fan clubs meet."

Though his gaze remained on her, his head dropped, his chin nearly hitting his sternum. "Are you a member of a fan club?"

"Of course I am."

He arched a brow, a command for her to offer more details.

She did. Happily. "I belong to Touch Me Torin." She sighed dreamily. "He's so kind and caring, always protecting those around him."

Kane grabbed her by the upper arms, jerking her into the hard line of his body. The moment he realized what he'd done, he set her back in place, away from him, and lowered his hands, mumbling, "Sorry."

I'm not. All that strength…

Stop enjoying his touch. Stop craving it. He's not for you.

"You will stay away from Torin," he said.

"But meeting him is the one and only thing I wanted to do before I died."

He closed his eyes, as if praying for patience, and inhaled sharply.

One of the jewels hanging from the chandelier detached and plunged down, shattering on Kane's head. Cringing, he brushed the pieces out of his hair.

"Okay, that's never happened before. Are you all right?"

"Fine," he gritted.

Feeling generous, she said, "Do you want to know the name of *your* fan club?"

"Not if you're not part of it," he said, an edge to his tone.

She wasn't an *official* member, no. "Just so you know, Synda's hobbies include backstabbing, causing trouble and ruining lives. You'll never be happy with her."

"She got you sentenced to the Never-ending, didn't she?" he said. "You. Not her, the keeper of Irresponsibility." He rubbed at his temples. "That's how you ended up in hell."

He seemed to be talking to himself as much as he was talking to her. "Yes. There are many openings to the Never-ending, and one is actually in Séduire. I was pushed inside, fell down the pit for a thousand years, yet only a day passed here. The bottom is the center of hell, and I finally reached it."

"A thousand years," he rasped. "Another reason you want to die. You don't want to endure such torture again."

Torture. Such a mild word for what had happened. "We've all heard the stories about it, but none of them do it justice. In that pit, it's dark, with no hint of light. Soundless. You can't even hear yourself scream and beg for help. It's empty. There's nothing to anchor you." She shook her head to dislodge the memories. "No, I don't want to endure it again."

A strange vibration moved through him, as if he were barely holding himself back from an act of violence. He paled.

"Kane?"

"I'm fine," he rasped. And then he shocked her, taking her hand, twining their fingers, holding on to her as if she were a lifeline. The contact only lasted a few seconds, but it was enough to make her reel.

To hide her confusion…and her sudden inability to breathe…she returned her attention to her rag, rubbing at the banister. "I've got tons of work to do, Kane. I'm sorry, but I have to ask you to leave."

"Why not kill yourself?" he continued, ignoring her. "Not that I'm suggesting you do such a thing. I'm not, and I'll make you regret it if you try. I'm just curious."

"I can't."

"Explain."

She sighed. "Whatever I do to myself brings only suffering, never death."

His brow furrowed. "What if you managed to remove your head?"

"My body would grow back."

"No way. One of my friends was beheaded, and there was nothing we could do to save him."

"That doesn't change the fact that I'll recover."

"Impossible."

Josephina peered over the edge of the railing, and gave another sigh. "I'll prove it." And in the process, escape the sensations he awoke in her.

Trying to mask her fear, she climbed up the railing.

Behind her, she could hear the stomp of the guards.

Kane grabbed her by the arms, and forced her back to the ground. He was even warmer than before, his grip so deliciously firm. Her skin was suddenly more sensitive, tingling and aching. Her ears picked up every rasp of his breath, and heated. Her eyes drank in the purity of his features, and her nostrils became saturated with the decadence of his scent. Her mouth watered for a taste of…of…him?

"Stay back," he called. "I've got her."

The men retreated.

"I don't need a demonstration," he said to her, his voice tight. "I'll believe you, whether it sounds far-fetched or not. Okay?"

The crystals in the chandelier rattled powerfully—a second later, the entire thing dropped from the top level and fell down, down, down, crashing into the floor at the bottom. Shards of glass shot in every direction. Screaming people raced out of the way.

Kane cursed under his breath. "Pay no attention to what just happened. Tell me about your problem."

She nodded, because she didn't *want* to think about the mess she would be forced to clean. "However I try to kill myself, I suffer with the pain for weeks, months, even if my organs go splat on the ground. Everything eventually grows back or heals."

"How is that possible?"

Easy. "You know how I can absorb the abilities of others with a simple touch? Well, Tiberius can *impart* abilities to others. He imparted this one to me."

"But what you absorb doesn't last."

"What he imparts does," she replied simply.

He tapped his temples. "What about your ability to invade my head?"

Turning back to her rag so that he wouldn't see the sudden bead of tears in her eyes, she said softly, "It was my mother's ability, and she gave it to me right before she died. I guess it stayed with me because it had nowhere else to go."

"But she was human. How did she possess an ability of a Fae?"

A pang in her heart as she said, "I probably should have qualified my description of her. One of her ancestors was Fae, but the line had become so diluted she was considered human."

A pause. Then, "You have too much to live for, Tinker Bell, and I don't want you to seek a killer while I'm here. Got it?"

She would vow no such thing and told him so with her silence.

He leaned down and whispered, "I'll kill anyone you ask, and I won't be nice about it. They'll hurt, and they'll beg, and they'll scream, just like you said you did in the Never-ending. Only, their suffering won't end as quickly as yours did. A thousand years? Try ten thousand."

Trembling, she gripped the railing. "You have to let me do what I think is right."

"When what you think is right is actually wrong? No. You're mine, and I'll see to you."

Her gaze jerked up.

His cheeks reddened. The cascade of his warm breath stopped abruptly as he straightened. "I mean, you're my responsibility now. I want you alive and well."

You're mine. Her body had come alive with those words. Her pulse had quickened. Her stomach had quivered. Every inch of her had heated. But the sensations had fled with his addition. She was a responsibility, nothing more.

"What's wrong?" He pinched a lock of her hair between his fingers, tickling her scalp.

"Nothing." She batted his arm away. One second he ran hot, the next cold. The next hot. He was twisting her into terrible knots, and she didn't like it.

He frowned. "Tell me you won't do anything foolish."

"I can't do that. I consider this conversation foolish, and yet I'm still participating."

He took no offense. "There's got to be a few things you want to do before you die. Besides meeting Torin." With the dryness of his tone, he might as well have rolled his eyes.

There *was* something she wanted to do…. Her gaze fell to his lips. She wanted to kiss him. So bad. She gulped and croaked, "Like what?" *Now who's running hot and cold?*

"Like…fall in love."

Love. Yes. Something she'd craved, especially in the dark of the night, when men came knocking at the door of the room she shared with seven other servants. The women always giggled, thrilled to be summoned, to be kissed and touched and maybe even held afterward.

"Have you ever fallen in love?" she asked.

"No," he said.

"You've had sex, though. A lot." And she suddenly wasn't happy by the thought.

He nodded stiffly. "You heard stories about that, too, I guess."

"A few." But the spies had only witnessed his public encounters. She wondered what happened when he was behind closed doors, and shivered.

"When was the last?"

The sharpness of the question surprised her. "Story?"

He nodded.

"A year ago. We were told you had a one-night stand."

He relaxed. "If you're hoping for an exclusive packed with details, you're not going to get it."

"I'm not. If you were Paris, though, I might beg for it." She smiled with fond remembrance. "Sweet, beautiful Paris."

"You are really trying my patience, woman. Paris already has a female, one who is very powerful and would not find your yearning amusing." Kane leaned down, putting them nose-to-nose. "Even if he didn't, you're mine. Don't ever forget."

This time, he offered no addition, and the warmth returned to her body, speeding through her veins, and oh, sweet heat, suddenly her heart was racing faster than ever before, her bones melting, the rest of her liquefying.

"Your responsibility?" she asked with a tremor.

He tapped her on the nose, irritating her, and said, "I have a lot to think about. I'll find you later and let you know what I've decided."

"Decided?" She grabbed the sides of his shirt. "About what?"

"You'll know when I know." He tugged from her hold and walked away, never looking back.

The guards leaped into action, probably intending to escort him to the king for his whipping. She almost opened her mouth to say she would take the punishment for him. She'd been whipped before, and she could survive being whipped again. But in the end, she let him go. He was Synda's fiancé now, and Josephina couldn't allow herself to forget.

Not even when the words *you're mine* were echoing in her mind.

So. Many. Problems.

Kane's mind whirled. Synda was possessed by the demon of Irresponsibility, but Tinker Bell had spent time in the Never-ending. Synda was blonde, and could very well be the girl in Danika's painting. But, his pose seemed to suggest he cared about the girl, and it was Tinker Bell, a brunette, his mind and body craved.

Her sad crystalline gaze tore him up inside. Her lips were so lush and red and...*lickable.* Yeah, that was the perfect word to describe them. Her body was curved in all the right ways—dangerous.

And she wanted Torin. Or Paris.

Once upon a time, he would have been fine with that. She wasn't the kind of woman he would have wanted. He would have considered her too sweet, too innocent, and no match for Disaster. But Kane would have been wrong. He would have missed out on a very good thing. Yes, Tinker Bell was sweet. Yes, she was innocent. But she was also strong. Resilient.

Perfect.

What Kane felt for her was different than what he'd ever felt for another. It was more intense. Intense enough to overshadow self-disgust and tainted memories, and utterly consume him. He was beginning to like touching her, despite the pain she elicited. But the thought of having sex with her…no.

He would only disappoint her. Memories would overtake him, and he would humiliate himself by vomiting. He wouldn't be able to please her, but he would have no problem disappointing her. She had lived with enough disappointment. Enough humiliation—she didn't need his.

He wouldn't be able to treat her as he'd treated the girls at the club, and just go through the motions. She deserved more. Better. But he wouldn't be able to give her more and better.

And what would Disaster do if Kane ever got her into bed?

Being so near her, putting his hands on her time and time again, and wanting so badly to kiss her, had finally driven the demon over the edge. Disaster had erupted, roaring with upset, banging against Kane's skull in an effort to drive him away from her. He'd stayed put, desperate for one more second of her time, her scent, her gaze…the possibility of more contact. And that's when the chandelier had come crashing down.

Now, he stomped to the bedroom he'd been given, and shut the door in his companions' faces. He halfway expected the pair to burst inside and ask for his autograph, but they opted to survive the rest of their day.

They didn't know the king had changed his mind about the whipping. That Kane had won their chess game, and the prize had been the freedom to speak with Tinker Bell anytime, anywhere.

He could have told Tinker Bell the truth, but he had liked her concern for him too much. As mad as she'd been at him, she hadn't wanted him to suffer.

Did she have any idea what that did to him?

No. Probably not.

What was he going to do with that girl?

What was he going to do about the princess?

And, curse it all, why was he even wondering about this? He wasn't here to find a mate, had even thought to avoid the one the Moirai predicted was his. He leaned against the door, and pushed out a heavy breath. He was here to save Tinker Bell. Afterward, he would kill Disaster. Then, and only then, would he figure out what to do about his future.

So. Just how was he going to save Tinker Bell? If he took her out of Séduire, she would be hunted for the rest of her life. If he killed her royal family, the Fae would strike back at him. They might try and return the favor by killing *his* family, the Lords. A long, bloody war could erupt, and his friends had enough to deal with.

Frustrated, he stalked forward and slammed his fist into the poster at the end of the bed. Solid gold met bone, and bone lost, splitting in several places. Pain radiated up his arm, and he grinned without humor. The wound would heal. His fury wouldn't.

Too often lately he'd been without answers, without direction, unsure of what to do or how to proceed. Confusion was a toxic sludge inside him, rising and rising, and he needed to get rid of it.

Hinges on the bathroom door creaked. Kane straightened, assuming a battle stance. Only, it wasn't an enemy here to attack. It was Synda—utterly naked.

She leaned against the door frame and toyed with the ends of her hair. Short, delicate of bone structure and yet plump of flesh, she presented the perfect picture of feminine carnality. Add a little muscle tone to her, and *she* was the kind of woman he had once enjoyed.

Mine, Disaster purred.

"What are you doing?" he demanded. This was to be his private room, and that's the way he wanted it to stay. Private.

"I'm seducing you, of course." A soft smile lifted the corners of her lips, inviting him to join in her amusement and arousal. There was no red in her eyes, no hint of her demon. "I took one look at you, and knew we were destined to be together. You're everything I've ever wanted in a man."

Destined, she'd said. "Have you spoken to the Moirai?"

"I've never had the privilege, no."

He wasn't sure what to think about that. "And just what is it you've wanted in a man, hmm?"

"Strength. Fierce ability. A streak of viciousness when needed. Someone possessed, like me. Someone beautiful."

Yeah, but she had no idea the price she'd have to pay to be with him, if ever he were interested in her.

He stalked toward her. Her smile grew wider. No question, she expected him to toss her on the bed and ravish her. Instead, he picked her up and unceremoniously hauled her to the door, surprised to find contact with her was not accompanied by pain.

Surprised and irritated. Why couldn't contact with Tinker Bell be this easy?

"Wait," she cried. "You just passed the bed."

He said nothing.

"I don't mind doing it in public, warrior, but I was hoping to have you all to myself for a while."

He twisted the knob and pushed at the seam in the wood with his shoulder. The guards were still there, probably commanded to remain all night. They snapped to attention.

"Is there anything we can get you, Lord Kane?"

"Anything at all?"

Tinker Bell stood in front of them, a fact that startled—and delighted—him. Her eyes locked on him, and relief bathed her expression. "Kane, I—" Her gaze fell to Synda, her lips pressing together. The relief faded, leaving the same resentment and hurt he'd experienced himself. "Never mind."

The princess was her enemy. He got that. But he couldn't explain himself, couldn't tell her that he was only using his promise to wed Synda to help her. If the princess learned of his plan, it would fail. She would tell her father, and the king would do as he'd threatened during their game and target Kane for elimination.

"Is something wrong?" he demanded.

Up went Tinker Bell's chin. "Nope. I'm fine."

She wasn't fine. He set Synda on her feet and pushed her forward. "I'm taking you to your room, Princess. And I'm leaving you there. Alone."

She twisted to face him, flames of red erupting in her eyes. "You're rejecting me?"

"For now," he said.

"Oh!" She beat at his chest. "Fetch me a robe, then. This instant!"

And take his eyes off Tinker Bell? No. She would run.

Kane whipped off his shirt and tugged the material over the girl's head. "There. You're covered. Let's go."

The red disappeared as Synda gaped at him, practically drooling. "So. Many. Muscles." She reached, intending to brush her fingertips over the ropes in his stomach, but he stepped backward, avoiding any further contact.

Tinker Bell peered down at the floor, refusing to look at him.

"Your room, Princess," he prompted.

Synda turned with a flourish, ignoring Tinker Bell, and marched away. "Come on. This way."

He followed, dragging Tinker Bell with him. "You're not leaving my sight until I know why you came to see me."

"It doesn't matter why. I've changed my mind," she snipped.

"Well, change it back."

She hmphed. "Make me"

Dangerous words. He could already think of several ways to do it.

Synda led them to the top floor of the palace, to a suite of rooms with more riches than a sultan's treasury. Antique furniture, diamond vases, marble, onyx, every portrait framed in gold, Persian rugs, a table made only of rubies and a massive bed capable of sleeping twelve.

The princess stripped out of the shirt as she strolled to her bathroom. "Bath time," she called, stopping to look over her shoulder at Kane. "There's still time to join me."

"No, thanks."

The flickers of red returned to her eyes. "I'll make sure you enjoy yourself."

Doubtful. "Why don't you save it for the wedding

night instead?" Kane stared down at Tinker Bell, who still wouldn't meet his gaze yet somehow managed to radiate animosity. "Where's your room? We'll talk there."

Pale, she muttered, "I'm not taking you to my room."

"I'll find it with or without your help. It'll just be better for you if that happens sooner rather than later."

Her eyes narrowed as she huffed out a breath. "Fine. This way," and tugged him out of the suite.

Synda called out. He didn't hear what she said, and didn't care.

Tinker Bell ushered him down several flights of stairs, into a darker, dank area of the palace. The servants' quarters, he would bet, and the knowledge angered him. How could the daughter of a king be treated so shabbily?

She stopped in front of an open door, and he peeked inside. Through the darkness, he could see cot after cot, sleeping body after sleeping body, but that was all. There were no luxuries of any kind.

"You're not staying in there," he gritted out.

"Uh, yes, I am."

And know she was uncomfortable while he slept on something as soft as clouds? Never. But he wasn't going to take the time to argue with her. Once again, he hefted a woman over his shoulder. Unlike the princess, Tinker Bell protested, beating her fists against his back, pounding her knees into his stomach.

"Is that the best you've got? If so, you don't deserve the name Tinker Bell. It's too masculine for you. From now on, all you're getting is Tink."

"Tink! I'm no Tink! I'm more ferocious than a wild animal!"

"A newborn kitten, maybe."

"Argh!" She bit him on the butt.

For just a moment, the action dropped him straight into hell, and he tripped over his own feet. He caught himself before he hit the ground, and as he fought for breath, he managed to straighten. *You're with Tinker Bell. Your Fae. You're safe.*

"Scratch that," he said, picking up their conversation as if it had never lapsed, hoping she wouldn't notice the change in his tone. From teasing to tense. "You're as gentle as a little puppy. I'll call you Yappydoodle."

"You…you…slime! I'll call you Jackhole! Because that's what you are!"

Jackhole?

He barked out a laugh and then blinked in surprise. How did she always pull him from the brink of despair so quickly? "Now, now. No reason to dirty your tongue with name-calling. I'll just have to wash your mouth out with—"

My tongue, he silently finished. He was flirting with her, acting as if he was normal. As if he could do normal things.

"Forget it," he muttered.

She remained quiet, and he remained in this sudden foul mood.

When he came to his chamber, he wasn't surprised to find the guards were still at their posts.

"Nice to see you again, Lord Kane."

"Can I get you anything? It would be my pleasure."

Without a word, he shoved past them and shut the door. Then, he tossed Tink on the mattress. She bounced up and down, and when she stopped, glared over at him.

Leave her! Disaster commanded.

One by one, he discarded the weapons he'd stolen from the king. As the floor cracked beneath his feet, he made sure the blades were within quick reach of the bed.

"What are you doing?" Tink gasped out.

"Getting ready for sleepy night-night time. You should try it." He was too stressed and tired to find her a room of her own. At least, that's what he told himself. He wouldn't consider his inability to part with the girl.

Her mouth formed a small O and, seeing it, he was struck by the desire to kiss it right off her face—to taste her and learn her and *brand* her. The desires angered him. He was all emotion, no action, and he knew it.

He kicked off his boots, but left on his pants, and climbed onto the mattress.

"We can't sleep together," she said with a tremor. "It's highly improper."

And probably dangerous. For both of them. "Will you be punished?"

A heavy pause before she said, "For spending private time with precious Princess Synda's betrothed? What do you think?"

He sighed. "I won't let anything happen to you."

"We'll see" was all she said.

"You guys seem pretty accepting when it comes to sex. Why was Synda punished for sleeping with the butcher's son?"

"She's Fae. He was human. Such unions are prohibited, since they lead to a dilution of the bloodlines."

"I'm not Fae, yet the king will allow me to wed his precious daughter."

"You're a Lord of the Underworld. You're a celebrity. Rules don't apply to you."

Good to know. "Your mother was considered human, which means the king—"

"Yes. It does. So?"

"So. Was he punished?"

"What do you think? He's the king." She ran her tongue over her lips, leaving a sheen of moisture behind. *Gorgeous. Down, boy.* "And you, well, you can have anyone you want without worry, too. Tiberius never chastises upper-class males for their extracurricular activities. They can have who they want, when they want. They just have to be careful."

He caught the tinge of bitterness in her tone. "Has anyone ever…" *Forced you.* He couldn't ask her. He wasn't sure how he would react if the same question were presented to him.

"No," she answered, anyway. "I'm only viewed as a sexual object at parties, when men have been drinking, but the most they ever do is pat my bottom."

"Uh, yeah. Sure. I'm certain you're right. That it takes alcohol to find you attractive."

"It's a blessing and curse, I know. But then, I'm a blood slave, and nothing more."

So innocent. She hadn't even caught his sarcasm. "What about being amazing and wonderful? I believe you once described yourself that way."

She flicked her hair over her shoulder, the picture of feminine pique. "I'm a person, too, you know. I deserve compliments every now and then, and since I'm the only one willing to give them to myself, I do."

That might have been one of the saddest things he'd ever heard. "I think you're beautiful," he admitted softly. "And smart. And brave." And so sexy he would have killed a thousand men and thrown them at her feet just for the chance to woo her…if only he'd been the man he used to be.

Her eyes widened. "You do?"

"Am I in the habit of lying to you?"

"No."

"So there you go." He forced himself to relax against the softness of the mattress.

She scooted away, as if she feared what would happen next.

"I'm not going to force myself on you, you have my word." *Gentle. Easy.* "You stay on your side of the bed, and I'll stay on mine, and you'll leave in the same condition you entered." And she would be the first.

"It's still improper," she grumbled.

"And that argument still isn't going to sway me. Good night, Tink." He reached over and extinguished the lamp. Darkness flooded the room.

At first, she did nothing. Then she fluffed her pillow and settled under the covers.

A breath he hadn't known he'd been holding slipped free.

He peered up at the darkened ceiling, inhaling the sweetness of her scent, holding it, holding it as long as he could, unwilling to give it up until the last possible second. For the first time in weeks, his muscles began to unknot. He thought he might actually be able to fall asleep, to actually rest, and yet, he resisted. Tink would never be witness to his nightmares.

He could lash out. She could try to comfort him. In a dazed state, he could hurt her.

He would rather die than hurt her.

Annnd…his muscles were knotting up again, though it had nothing to do with the past. Tink was here, in his bed. Within reach. All he had to do was stretch out his arm, and his hand could cup the fullness of her breast. Then, slide lower. Lower still. Surely he would not have an adverse reaction to such innocuous contact. She was dressed, after all.

Still. She might respond. Might encourage him.

Might actually ask for more.

He pressed his tongue to the roof of his mouth.

Time for a distraction. “So…what’s the name of my fan club?”

“I thought you didn’t want to know.”

“I changed my mind. Apparently that’s allowed in our relationship.”

The sheets rustled as she turned. “Cataclysmic for Kane.”

He told himself to hush. He asked, “You ever been to one of the meetings?”

“I might have stumbled into one…by accident.”

“How many times?”

“Six…teen. Girls get lost very easily sometimes.”

He fought a grin. “So, what were you going to tell me when you reached my room?”

A weary sigh left her. “It doesn’t matter now.”

“It does. By the way, nothing happened between Synda and me.”

“A naked Synda,” she muttered.

He wanted to tell her the truth. But what would happen if he had to do something he didn’t like in order to reach his goal? The truth would then become a lie. He’d be better off keeping all his options open. But the nail in the coffin? A part of him needed to preserve some distance between them, and the engagement created it.

“Maybe, when I came to your room, I was going to tell you I’ve never met anyone as dumb as you,” she said, and he imagined her features scrunched up in what she probably hoped was a snobby expression. “You’re going to hurt so bad when you’re whipped for talking to me.”

Can't laugh. "I won't be whipped. The king and I came to an arrangement."

"What! Why didn't you tell me?"

"You were having too much fun counting my words."

She muttered a few more choice names for him. "Yeah, well, Synda will be punishment enough, I suppose. She lives for the moment and nothing more. She forgets her every promise. In a few weeks, another man will catch her attention and you'll be left with a broken heart."

Resentment blasted from her, and he had to tighten his grip on the pillow to stop from reaching for her. "I may be dumb, but my Spidey-senses are telling me she broke your heart, too."

She hmphed, as if he were crazy.

"Well?"

She must have been tracing circles on the sheet, because her knuckles brushed against one of his nipples. The contact electrified him, and he nearly shot off the bed.

"Maybe she did," Tink said, unaware. "Long ago she promised to protect me from our father. Then, the very next day, she was caught stealing horses from visiting Harpies. It started a war, and punishment was decreed, but she said nothing as I was dragged away to be whipped."

The story doused his lust. "I'm sorry," he replied, hurting for her. "I really am."

"Thank you."

Did she look as sad and exhausted as she had sounded? "I'm going to make things better for you, Tink," he vowed. Somehow, some way.

She sighed. “I’ll believe it when I see it.”

“No faith in me?”

“No faith in anyone.”

CHAPTER ELEVEN

KANE STOOD BESIDE the bed and peered down at Tink. Sunlight streamed in from the window, and, as if drawn to her, enveloped her and her alone. Spotlighting her. Highlighting every luscious nuance. She exuded peace to an astonishing degree. A peace he craved for himself.

She was Sleeping Beauty. Or, more accurately, Cinderella, complete with an evil stepmother and half sister.

Too bad for her, Kane was to be her Prince Charming.

He hadn't meant to, but at some point, he'd fallen asleep. A nightmare had awoken him—and he'd found Tinker Bell asleep on his chest.

Had she rolled there on her own, or had he pulled her over?

The contact had hurt him in more ways than one. His lust had returned full force.

After he'd eased her aside, he'd been more diligent, and remained awake, listening to her every breath, waiting for her every movement, remembering the way she'd made him smile, dying inside because he'd still wanted to roll over, on top of her, and strip her, and touch her, and do things to her, even though the very thoughts had him fighting back an all-consuming panic.

He didn't deserve her. His moods were too mercurial. He was happy one minute, ticked off the next. He was decided on a course one minute, confused the next. She needed someone solid. Dependable. Like Torin.

She had no faith in anyone, she'd said, and that was downright sad. Whether Kane deserved her or not, he wasn't going to let her down.

Kill her, Disaster said. *It's what she wants.*

What she wanted wasn't what she needed.

Tink's lips parted on a breathy sigh, and his chest constricted. How innocent she was.

Kill her!

Kane turned and stalked from the room, the demon cursing him with every step.

JOSEPHINA HAD MANY duties, and serving breakfast to the royal family was one of them. A decree straight from Queen Penelope, meant to humiliate her at the start of her day, every day.

Waiting to begin, Josephina pressed against the far wall in the dining room, holding a pitcher of freshly made pomegranate juice. She should have been finished already, should have returned to her housecleaning, but no one had arrived. Everyone was probably busy congratulating Kane and Synda on their upcoming nuptials and the happy couple was probably gorging on the compliments.

Oh, Kane. Everyone's right. We're so beautiful together, Synda was probably saying. *So perfect together.*

I'm perfect for everyone, Kane was probably replying. *But I'm glad I ended up with you.*

The pitcher shattered in Josephina's hands.

Cold liquid seeping through the fabric of her gloves and making her gasp, she rushed to the kitchen and gathered the rags she needed, trying to evade Cook's eye. He welcomed any chance to lash out at her.

Once, as a means of punishment for one of Synda's crimes, Josephina was starved for a week. Three days in, the hunger pangs had become so severe she'd snuck into the kitchen and stolen a hunk of bread.

Cook had caught her, but had vowed to remain silent if she would spend the night in his bed. She'd turned herself in instead, and he'd never forgiven her.

So, maybe she hadn't been entirely honest with Kane. Maybe some of the men—other than her brother—*did* see her as more than a blood slave.

Annnd…Cook cleared his throat, and she glanced over.

"What did you do now? What new problem have you caused me?" He stomped over to her. He grabbed her by the wrist, only to rear backward with a wheeze. "You're wet."

"And your cooking sucks. So?"

"How dare you! I don't care who you are, you will not insult my divine cuisine."

"I just did."

"Do it again. I dare you."

Okay. "Your pies are flavorless, and your cakes are hard as rocks."

His palm flew up and out, swiping over her cheek. Her skin instantly flamed, stinging. Josephina slapped him back. As he gurgled his outrage, she blew him a kiss and flounced away.

Maintaining a brave face, she cleaned the mess in the dining room and donned a fresh pair of gloves. Only after she had made a new pitcher of juice, with Cook avoiding her, did she return to her post.

The royal family still hadn't arrived.

Inconsiderate toads!

She flinched at the uncharacteristic outburst. The

ache in her cheek must be making her cranky. And, well, Kane had no business marrying Synda after he'd forced Josephina to spend the night in his room. He should have called off the nuptials with the rising of the sun!

And I never should have gone to him. Never should have thought to take him up on his offer, hoping to get him away from Synda.

Josephina had been mad about his engagement before, but standing there, thinking about last night, she became enraged. Kane probably didn't remember, but he'd suffered from terribly violent nightmares last night. He'd cried out and he'd thrashed, but she had managed to calm him.

She had. Not Synda.

He'd held her for a long moment, his arms tight around her, as if he couldn't bear to let her go, then he'd rolled her to her side of the bed. Obviously, he'd gotten over his aversion to touch somewhat—and yet, he hadn't tried to kiss or touch her.

He must be saving that kind of thing for the princess.

Why did that tear her into so many ragged pieces?

An engaged man shouldn't share a bed with anyone but his intended, and anyone that did should be… should be…castrated!

I could help him with that, she thought. *I have no experience with knives, but a quick slice and dice shouldn't be a problem.*

Contemplating mutilation? I don't know who you are anymore.

I'm you, *dummy.*

What if Kane was already in love with Synda?

Why do you care?

I don't. Okay, fine. I do.

She had lain awake for hours, trying not to enjoy her first taste of luxury, all the while hoping to sneak out of the bedroom the moment Kane fell asleep. But *he'd* lain awake for hours, too, and her eyelids had eventually become too heavy to hold up. Then, his thrashing had woken her, and she'd cuddled him, and she'd liked it far more than she should have. Had even been tempted to ask for more.

If Synda found out…

She raised her chin and focused on the here and now. Four small chandeliers dripped with hundreds of opals and hung over a long, square table hewn from gold, diamonds and sapphires. The chairs were carved in the shape of dragons, with cobalt velvet lining the seats. Colorful murals of naked, frolicking Fae decorated the walls, and a soft white rug lined the floor.

There were three windows, each overlooking the flower garden out back. She adored that garden, and allowed herself a peek outside—wait. Armed guards were running toward the gate.

Something was happening. What—

King Tiberius strolled inside the room at long last, his latest mistress on his arm. Josephina snapped to attention. The mistress was lovely, to be sure, but only seventeen years old. She'd had a bright future before the king had taken notice of her, and most likely would have married the richest of the Opulens; she would have had a family and never would she have wanted for anything.

Except, perhaps, love and fidelity.

But now, no man would have her, not even the lowest of the servants. When the king discarded her, and he would, no one would want to risk his ire by pursuing what he suddenly deemed "unworthy."

The king's expression was troubled as he claimed the

seat at the head of the table. He motioned for the scantily clad female to take the seat at his left—the queen's seat. Josephina groaned. Queen Penelope knew of the king's affairs, of course she did, everyone knew; in public, she simply pretended not to care. But in private, when only Josephina was around, she ranted and raged.

"—not sure why an army of Phoenix warriors are attacking us," the king was saying. "Do they really want to start another war? They have brute force, but they haven't the numbers."

Oh, no, no, no. If the Phoenix were here, they were here for Josephina. And if her father found out she was the reason, he would unleash a torrent of wrath upon her.

A tremor rocked her, and liquid sloshed over the sides of the pitcher.

Tiberius cast her a reproachful glance.

"You have nothing to fear, my darling," he continued, patting his mistress's delicate hand. "The soldiers will be dead by the end of the day, their heads sent back to their people."

"Thank you, Majesty" was the soft reply. The girl kept her gaze downcast. "You're so strong. Utterly undefeatable."

Kane strolled inside, and Josephina quivered with the memory of his embrace. His savage beauty had never been more apparent than at that moment, as morning light streamed over him. The two guards were stationed at his back. His gaze swept the area, and Josephina was certain he'd somehow managed to catalog every detail at once, though she fought a wave of disappointment when he simply skimmed over her.

Good morning to you, too, she thought, trying to ignore a fresh tide of hurt and resentment.

"Lord Kane. We're pleased you've joined us." The king motioned for Kane to take the chair at his right. Synda's chair.

Kane sat, putting his back to Josephina. He held up his arm and cocked two fingers. Was he…summoning her over?

Those fingers moved again, more adamantly this time.

He was. He really was. *I'm going to smash his face!*

Teeth grinding, she moved forward and poured three drops of juice into his goblet.

When she tried to move away, Kane grabbed hold of her wrist. Startled, she almost dropped the pitcher. His grip was strong, his skin white-hot.

"There's a mark on your cheek," he said with the stillness she'd come to recognize as dangerous. He looked up at her, the thick shield of his lashes hiding whatever emotion gleamed in his eyes. His lips pressed into a thin, hard line.

"Well, yeah," she replied.

"From?"

"A hand."

"I get that. Whose?"

She licked her lips, and his gaze followed the motion. "Doesn't matter. I took care of it."

He squeezed her wrist harder. "Whose?"

"Why?"

"So I can kill him—or her."

She had no loyalty to Cook, but she wouldn't allow the man to be put to death for so minor an offense. So, she remained silent.

Kane released her and glared at the king. "If she's hurt again, I'll make sure everyone in this palace regrets it."

Unused to such irreverence, Tiberius blustered for a moment. “My admiration for you won’t save you from my wrath, Lord Kane. Tread carefully.”

“Do you want an enemy you can’t afford to have? Because you’re walking the line with me,” Kane snapped. “You’ve got Phoenix running wild out there, and your men will never be able to take them down. You’ve allowed the army to become lazy, living off of the triumph of past conquests.”

“How dare you! My men are as strong as ever.”

Kane smiled, but it wasn’t a nice one. “If I were to walk out there right now, I could slay every single male under your command and not break a sweat. Want me to prove it?”

What was he *doing?* She wanted to jump in front of him and shield him from the curses and punishments about to start flying, but it was no longer her place to protect him. She returned to her spot against the wall.

Tiberius leaped to his feet, planted his palms on the tabletop and peered down at Kane with undiluted rage. “A dead man can’t prove anything.”

Kane stood, too, refusing to back down from the mighty king of the Fae—something very few had tried and none had survived. His chair toppled over, one of the legs poking him in the back of the knee. He didn’t seem to notice.

“I have some experience with the Phoenix, and I know they’ll play with your men these next few weeks, testing their abilities. Then, the Phoenix will seem to vanish for a few weeks more and you’ll relax. *Then,* the warriors will return with a vengeance and torch the palace and everyone in it.”

Crystal eyes narrowed. “If that’s the case, the problem will be yours as much as mine. Your engagement ball is set for eight days from now, and your wedding nine days from now."

Just enough time to plan a feast but not so long the bulk of Synda's personality flaws couldn't be hidden.

I can't watch their courtship. I just can't. And she couldn't allow herself to be drawn in and spit out by Kane anymore. From now on, it would be better for her if she kept her distance from him.

Maybe she should run away. She'd done it before. Of course, she'd been captured swiftly and disciplined severely, and had later vowed never to take such a risk again.

A silly vow, she realized now.

Leopold strolled into the room, and Synda skipped in behind him, branching off to close in on Kane.

Tiberius sat. Kane righted his chair and settled down.

"Good morning, warrior." The princess tried to kiss him on the cheek, but he reared back, stopping her.

Perhaps he hadn't gotten over his aversion, after all.

"What are you doing?" he gritted.

"Making your morning even better, of course," she said, unperturbed as she smoothed her skirt around her chair.

Gag.

"Next time wait for permission."

The queen was the last to enter. She spotted the king's mistress and stiffened.

Trembling, Josephina filled her goblet with juice.

The queen sipped—and spit the liquid out on Josephina's shoes. "This is horrid swill. How dare you ruin the start of my day with it!"

"I'll get you something else," she muttered, her cheeks burning hotly.

"You'll stay here," Kane growled. "The juice is fine."

Penelope looked to the king, expecting him to side with her. Tiberius nodded to Josephina to continue with her duties.

Josephina's stomach threatened to rebel. The queen would make her suffer for this.

Her trembling increased as she moved to Leopold's side and poured his measure of juice. He pressed his hand against the small of her back, as if holding her steady. Meanwhile, he spread his fingers to cover as much ground as possible, even daring to delve between the cheeks of her bottom.

She tried to shift out of the way.

Kane unleashed a stream of dark curses, and all eyes swung to him.

His gaze was locked on Leopold, and slitted.

Her brother shifted uncomfortably, lowered his arm.

What had *that* been about? Kane hadn't been able to see her brother's hand, had he? And if he had, he hadn't cared about it. Had he? He'd simply wanted to…what? Confused, she flittered away to the kitchen to gather the food.

"Hurry up, you lazy cow," Cook snipped.

She stuck her tongue out at him before returning to the dining room.

"—take me shopping tomorrow? Please!" Synda was saying to Kane.

"An excellent idea," King Tiberius replied, as if the question had been directed at him.

"Josephina will go with us," Kane said firmly.

Her birth name on his lips just seemed wrong. She wasn't fond of Tinker Bell or Tink, but she also kind of loved them. They were special, meant just for her. He'd never used a nickname with Synda.

The king opened his mouth to reply—probably a

refusal, considering the glint of anger in his eyes. But Synda clapped happily, and said, "Of course she can come. We're going to have the best time ever!" so he remained quiet.

"What about the Phoenix?" Leopold asked tightly. "A woman of royal blood shouldn't be wandering about town with such a threat on the loose."

"The king has assured me your men can contain the threat. Besides, the ladies will be with me," Kane said. "They'll be protected."

Tiberius thought for a moment, nodded. "You will accompany the pair, Prince Leopold, and ensure nothing happens to Warrior Kane and Princess Synda."

The pair, he'd said, rather than the threesome. As if Josephina didn't count.

The truth was, she didn't.

The prince looked ready to argue, but quickly thought better of it. "As you wish, Majesty."

Kane grinned without humor. "Until tomorrow."

KANE SPENT THE rest of the day doing a bit of investigative work, questioning every servant he came across. The moment he learned the cook had been the one to put the mark on Tink's cheek, he locked the kitchen, preventing anyone from escaping, and beat the man senseless.

He whistled with satisfaction as he went in search of Tink.

CHAPTER TWELVE

A HAZE OF early-morning sunlight filled Kane's bedroom, chasing away the shadows.

As he shook off the horrors of another nightmare, a sense of excitement rose.

Last night, his attempts to talk to Tink had failed. He'd spied her in the throne room—but she'd disappeared behind a door the moment he'd approached her. He'd found her in the weaving room—but she'd pulled another disappearing act. He'd snuck up on her in the garden—but she'd wiggled from his hold and run away.

Today, though, she couldn't do any running. According to the king, she had to stay by her sister's side. Which meant she would be within Kane's reach at all times.

A lamp toppled from the nightstand and smashed into his skull.

He scowled.

A knock sounded at the bedroom door.

Kane rose from the bed, stalked over and, with a dagger in hand, opened the obstruction. Prince Leopold stood before him, relaxed, utterly confident Kane would behave himself.

Foolish prince. Kane had a serious beef with the male. Not because of his taunts the day they'd met, but because he'd flattened his hand against Tink's lower back while gazing at her with desire in his eyes. It had startled Kane. He'd thought he was misreading. But Disaster had snickered, seeing something Kane could not, something in the spirit realm in which he existed, perhaps. A dark cloud of lust? Another demon, sitting on Leopold's shoulder, driving his actions? Kane had heard the Sent Ones talking about such an occurrence.

In the end, the reason didn't matter. Results did.

"What?" Kane snapped, fingers tightening on the hilt.

Regal features darkened. "The princess is ready for your excursion. I'll escort you to her, and accompany you into town, keeping everyone safe."

Kane knew the Phoenix had taken off for the forest; he'd seen the little fires they'd left here and there. So far, though, the Fae had had no luck catching one or even engaging in any kind of battle.

Petra had to be the leader. She wanted Tink, and would stop at nothing to have her.

Well, Kane would stop at nothing to protect her.

"And the servant?" he asked.

"You'll ignore."

So not happening, dude.

"Or you'll suffer," the prince added. "The things I'll do to you…"

"Understood." Kane forced a smile. "Lead the way."

The prince turned his back, just as confident as before, and Kane sheathed the blade. He stayed close to the male's heels, conscious of his every step.

"You don't think you'll need guards while you're with me?" Kane asked.

A smug laugh rolled from him—the same one Kane had heard at their first meeting. "Hardly. One word, and I can have you on your knees."

They pounded down a winding flight of stairs, then

another and another. When they reached the bottom floor, and neared a door leading into a storage closet, Kane forcibly bumped the man in the shoulder, sending him crashing into the wall.

Before the prince had time to react, Kane punched him in the throat, cutting off his airway, and pinched his carotid, stopping the flow of blood to his brain. In seconds, the prince was crumpled on the floor, unconscious.

"Got anything to say now?" he muttered.

A maid turned the corner, spotted them and ground to a halt. She gasped, her hand fluttering to her heart.

"He's fine. Just napping," Kane said. "He'll wake up." Eventually. "Don't disturb him. You know how cranky he can get when he goes without his beauty Z's."

She nodded, wide-eyed, and hurried away.

He opened the storage closet, and dragged the prince to the center. Then, he rigged the lock, ensuring no one would be able to enter without force.

Mission accomplished.

Kane kicked back into gear. He'd memorized the layout of the entire palace, had secretly peeked through every door, and knew the front entrance was just around the corner. As promised, the princess and Tink were waiting.

Anger returned full force as he looked them over. Synda was decked out in a crimson-colored velvet ball gown, the material feminine and flattering. Tink was stuck wearing some kind of cheap, ill-fitting dress that left pink scratches on her beautiful skin.

A frilly hat with ribbons perched on Synda's head.

Tink was without a hat, her hair pulled into a severe bun at the back of her neck.

Synda smelled of floral perfume.

Tink smelled of pungent floor cleaner.

His hands fisted. He wanted to kill someone. He wanted to hug Tink and never let go.

Synda smiled when she spotted him, skipped over and planted a kiss directly on his lips. He stood still and stiff, not wanting to deal with another outburst. His gaze immediately sought Tink. Her eyes were downcast.

"Where's Prince Leopold?" Synda asked, oblivious.

"He's sleeping. We should go."

"Sleeping? Even though he was awake five minutes ago?" Tink asked. Then she looked at Synda, and pressed her lips together.

What? She wasn't allowed to talk on this little excursion?

His knuckles nearly burst out of his skin, so tightly did he squeeze his fingers into a fist. "Yes. Sleeping."

A dog came racing around the corner. The creature made a beeline for Tink, and the demon laughed, assuring Kane he was responsible. Kane jolted forward, sticking his leg in the path of wrath. Sharp teeth sank into his ankle, stinging.

"I'm so sorry," a servant said, chasing after the dog. "I don't know how he got away from me."

With as gentle a tug as he could manage, Kane ripped the creature's canines from his bone and handed him over.

"Come on, everyone," Synda said cheerfully, skipping through the double doors held open by two guards. "I've been waiting days and days for this."

Days. When it had only been mentioned yesterday.

Tink followed after her, and Kane followed after Tink. The sun was shining, though it was a muted and murky version of the one he was used to, the sky gray with threads of black rather than blue, as if a storm brewed. There was a high, transparent wall surrounding the palace, glittering brightly, and behind it, a lush green forest. Much of the military forces were still out there, chasing the Phoenix.

A cobblestone path led to a horse-drawn carriage. And there were other carriages on the road, he saw. Three that he could see up-close, and two in the distance, slowly closing in. In the three up-close perched females dressed as fancily as Synda, each peering at him with abject longing.

"Isn't he gorgeous?" Synda called with pride. "He's mine."

Kane almost snapped a denial. He reached the carriage first, and hefted the princess inside. She braced her hands on his shoulders, and he had to grit his teeth against the horror of the contact.

Hands…all over him. Caressing him, scratching him.

Breathe. He had to breathe.

A punishment for his distaste of the girl, he supposed, the demon lashing out.

Next was Tink. He unfolded his fingers, revealing his palm. She hesitated a moment before placing her gloved fingers against his. As expected, there was a lance of pain, though it was lighter than usual, but…his mind was fine. The terrible memories retreated, Disaster unable to drudge them back up. Why?

Because, as Kane had realized in the forest, she was his light? Maybe. The memories were his darkness, and darkness had to flee in the presence of light.

Even after she'd sat down, he maintained contact, lingering, marveling, once again fighting an inexplicable need only she was able to stir.

"Kane," she said, her voice taut, and he forced himself to release her. He climbed inside the carriage. One girl was on the left, one on the right. Embracing the chance to touch Tink again, he picked her up by the waist. So delicate. So feminine. Her gasp of surprise fanned over his skin as he set her beside her sister. Then, he settled into the other bench on his own, now able to watch both females.

"You look pretty today," Synda said to Tink. And astonishingly enough, she sounded sincere.

This must be one of her sweet moments. Never had he met a person who could change moods so quickly—and he was counting himself. But then, Synda hadn't yet learned to fight the demon inside her. Darkness drove her. Urges came, and she gave in without stopping to analyze the wisdom of her actions. Emotions came, and she never tried to look past them to the reasons behind them.

She needed help, but she didn't want it—last night, at dinner, he'd offered and she'd declined.

"I want your body, Lord Kane, not your mind," she'd said.

He'd shrugged. And yeah, he felt a little guilty about his lack of concern for her. She might just be his destined mate.

No. Impossible. Kane must have misunderstood what the Moirai had said. And what about the prediction William had mentioned? His daughter, White, wedding the man destined to start an apocalypse.

Kane didn't even want a mate. He wanted…he needed…yeah, some part of him wanted and needed a mate.

For the first time in centuries, he had a reason to hope. He'd watched his friends fall in love, and that love had strengthened them. They'd overcome centuries-old rages and self-loathing simply to become the men their women needed. What if Kane's mate could help him defeat Disaster? What if she was the key?

The right girl could calm him, soothe him. The right girl mattered. But again, who was the right girl?

The princess, who carried Irresponsibility? Tink, who had spent time in the Never-ending? Or White? The wrong choice could torment him as much as the demon.

What he felt toward Synda was anger and pity.

She didn't make him want to live, just to be with her.

She didn't make him forget the trials of his past.

She didn't make him long for something better.

What he felt toward Tink was…powerful.

She made him eager to achieve his goals.

She made him ache, in body and in soul.

She made him smile.

So, yeah, when he next had sex, it would be with Tink.

When? Whoa.

Had he seriously just thought the word *when* in conjunction with sex? He'd promised himself he wouldn't go there with Tink. He would only disappoint her. He would ruin her innocence. Now, he considered her a foregone conclusion?

"You can speak," Synda was saying to her. "I won't tell Daddy. Swear."

"You had better speak," Kane reiterated. He wouldn't be able to endure this little jaunt otherwise. "I'll make sure no blame is cast your way."

The buggy jolted forward, but Tink remained quiet.

A few minutes later, Synda stood up and said, "Oh, look. There's the Twenty-fifth," nearly tumbling out the side of the vehicle. "Hey, Aos Sí Caroline! Look at—hmph."

Kane grabbed her hand and forced her back into her seat. "Stay," he commanded. "Don't move."

The princess crossed her arms over her middle and pouted. "You're no fun."

"I'm devastated you think so. Now, tell me why you called that woman by a number, and what ees-shee means."

Upset forgotten, Synda giggled like a schoolgirl. "Twenty-five is her number, silly, and Aos Sí is her title."

Vapid does not even begin to describe. He looked to Tink.

After a lengthy pause, she drew in a deep breath and said, "Every Opulen outside the royal family bears a number. Caroline is twenty-fifth in line for the throne, meaning, she's the twenty-fifth member of the high court. There are fifty members. All others are part of the lower court, and without a number."

Was nothing more important than status to the Fae? "And the title?"

"The literal translation of Aos Sí is *her people*. Every female in the upper class bears such a title. The males are referred to as Daoine Sídhe."

Good to know. "What's your number and title?"

Red stained her cheeks; she clamped her lips shut.

"She isn't an Opulen," Synda said matter-of-factly.

So...she didn't have a number or a title. He didn't like that.

He spent the rest of the fifteen-minute ride drilling the girls with questions. How often had the throne changed hands? Answer: eight times in the history of the Fae. How had the past kings died? Answer: murdered by their successors. Had the race ever been without a king? Answer: never.

The exchange ended when the carriage stopped in front of the first shop in a row of shops. The buildings were comprised of dark stone and some kind of glittery material, with crystal roofs and windows surrounded by ivy, reminding him of something out of a fairy tale.

And…was that William the Panty Melter entering the shop at the end of the street? The…Devil's Punchbowl, was the name, and it was clearly a tavern.

Kane popped to his feet. "I've spotted our first stop," he said.

He helped the women exit the buggy, cringed against the memories Synda's touch caused, marveled anew at the mental peace Tink's wrought, and surged forward. When Synda tried to enter a shoe store, he dragged her away.

"But…" she began.

"The tavern first," he said, and Synda stopped fighting.

"Why didn't you say so? I'm always up for a good drink or twelve."

"You can't be serious, Kane," Tink said with a groan. "It's early morning and you want to get trashed? With the darling of the Fae? I'm going to be blamed for this, I just know it."

"You're not going to be blamed," Kane said. He wouldn't allow it. Not ever again.

He shouldered the doors open, and scanned the area. He spotted a dark-haired warrior sliding into a seat, claiming a handful of cards, and knew beyond any doubt. Yes, that was indeed William the Ever Randy.

Had he talked to Taliyah and followed Kane here?

One female and three males formed a circle around William. Kane recognized each. White, the female, and her brothers, Red, Black and Green. In hell, Red and

Black had rescued him from Disaster's minions, but rather than setting him free, they'd bound him, hoping to learn his secrets—whatever those were—then kill him to prevent him from hooking up with their sister. As long as they'd lived in hell, as many horrors as they'd seen, they'd come to hate demons with every fiber of their beings. It was a sentiment Kane shared. But they'd made the mistake of lumping him in the same category as Disaster and *that* he resented.

Then, of course, Green and White had found him and walked away, leaving him to his agony until Tink had found him.

He owed all four a little payback. With knives.

The five-person gang smoked cigars and drained shots of whiskey as they studied their cards. Synda tugged from Kane's hold and skipped to the bar, where she ordered "my regular." Tink remained by his side, unsure.

"What are you doing here?" Kane demanded.

"What else? You forced me!" she snapped.

"Not you, sweetheart."

William glanced up, grinned and waved him over, not the least surprised to see him. "Kane, my boy. We're playing hard. But not as hard as you, it seems. Two women? Really? I'm shocked Kanie the Prude can manage so much estrogen at the same time."

White and her brothers looked over at him. In unison, the three guys pushed back their chairs and stood, glaring at him with murderous rage. White went back to studying her cards.

"Down," William commanded easily. "Now isn't the time for a battle royale."

"When?" Red insisted.

"When I say so. I feel like finishing our game first."

Though William wore a T-shirt that read DADD: Dudes Against Daughters Dating, and it was difficult to take him seriously, the three obeyed without protest. But even still, Kane was never taken out of their cross hairs.

Black cracked his knuckles. "Today, demon, you die."

He couldn't help but grumble, "I wish you had rotted in hell, I really do."

"I'm getting the impression he doesn't like us," White said, blowing out a puff of smoke. She flipped her cascade of pale hair over her shoulder. "I'm very okay with that."

"What are you playing?" Synda asked, closing the distance and, without waiting for an invitation, plopping herself on Red's lap.

Uncharacteristically patient, the dark-haired male with eyes of the cruelest blue settled her more comfortably against him and began to explain the game.

In that moment, Kane knew she couldn't be the female for him, no matter that she was the keeper of Irresponsibility, and no matter what the Moirai had meant. He felt no sense of jealousy or possession.

Would there be consequences if she was the one and he blew her off? Maybe.

Did he care? No.

The woman in Danika's painting had been blonde. White was also blonde, but while William's daughter was lovely and strong, Kane absolutely despised her and that wasn't going to change.

Tink, however, continued to interest him greatly. But if she was the one for him, why did he continue to ache when he neared her? And who was the blonde in the painting? What did she mean to him?

Kane pulled up a chair beside William, and forced

Tink to sit in his lap. He wanted her nearby, wanted his hands on her to prevent her from running, and wanted to ensure every man knew to keep his grubby paws off her. The action ensured Kane received all three at once. Screw the pain, he thought. Yeah, it had bothered him less today, but now, he just flat-out didn't care.

"How'd they get free of hell?" he asked, even as Disaster screamed a protest about the seating arrangement.

William shrugged his massive shoulders before tossing his cards on the table. He faced Kane. "I thought you could use a bit of help. You didn't want your friends knowing what you were up to, so my own brood of vipers was my only option."

"That tells me nothing."

"Nor was it meant to. I sprang them early, and that's all you need to know."

"Fair enough. But answer me this. Why are you playing cards with them instead of helping me?"

Another shrug. "We heard about your engagement, and figured all was well."

"You could have checked in."

"Yeah. I could have, and I even thought about it. And it's the thought that counts, right?"

"No. No, it's not."

William claimed a cigar from White, and took a drag. Smoke puffed around him as he said, "Clearly I have more faith in you than you have in yourself. You're welcome."

Ashes drifted from the cigar and should have fallen to the floor. Disaster ensured they fell on Kane's arm and leg, burning little holes in his clothing and singeing his skin.

Tink pressed a hand against her heart. "That's so sweet of you to say, sir. What a kind man you are."

Kane looked at her and did a double take. She was serious, he realized, and she was gazing at William as if he were everything she'd ever wanted but had never really thought she could have. Razors of jealousy cut through Kane and calmed the demon.

"Did you hear stories about him, too?" he demanded.

"No. I can just tell you're lucky to have a friend like him."

"William's not sweet," he gritted. "I've seen the bloody results of his temper tantrums."

"And I've heard of the bloody results of yours," she quipped.

William beamed up at her. "I like you."

"I'm glad, because I have a proposition for you," she said to him.

"No, she doesn't." Kane squeezed her tight, silencing her.

"Go on. I'm listening," William prompted.

"The night I left you in that club, I went looking for a key into Séduire," Kane said before Tink could decide to talk over him. She was stubborn like that. "All the while, you clearly already had one."

"Nah. I would have flashed here, but I had to buy one for my kiddies," the warrior said.

"By *buy* he means *steal,*" Red said, not even bothering to look over at them. "And by *steal* I mean *kill for.*"

Stated so simply, it was a testament to the hardness of the warrior's heart. To the savage lengths these men would go to get what they wanted. *Bring it.*

"Your kids—" even saying the word in conjunction with the powerful warrior felt odd "—were okay with coming here and helping me?"

"Don't be ridiculous." Grinning all over again, William waved the question away. "You heard the part about the battle royale, right? No, they weren't okay with helping you. I had to promise they could have a real down and dirty brawl with you, with blood and broken bones and maybe missing body parts. It's going to be great!"

Tink melted against Kane, as if trying to use her body as a shield to protect him. The scratchy material of her uniform irritated his exposed skin. How could she stand wearing that thing?

Every glass on the table shattered, liquid spilling, warriors cursing.

"When is this fight to take place?" Kane asked, unperturbed.

"Have you not been listening to anything I've said?" William dabbed at the wet stain on his leg. "After the game."

He thought for a moment. "I would love nothing more than to engage your spawn in a showdown. Tink—uh, I mean, Josephina—and I will be back by the time your game is through." He actually wanted to take her shopping more than he wanted his revenge. She wasn't going to wear rags while everyone around her wore riches.

Anyone who didn't know Kane might have thought he planned to run away. But William knew him better than that. "And Tink is what you call her? Really? I would have chosen Ivanna B. Withwilly. What? It's a good, solid name."

Can't respond to that. Will just encourage him. "Meanwhile," Kane gritted, "the princess is your responsibility. Don't let her get into any trouble."

William thought for a moment, nodded. "You do remember that I like to sleep with my responsibilities, right?"

Yeah. He did. "I also know you'll be tempted to

throw her to the wolves once you get to know her, but don't harm her or let anyone else do so, either." The king would protest, and Tink would be liable.

"So…you're saying you won't mind if I seduce your future wife?"

"I wouldn't mind, but I don't want you to go that far. She could get in trouble, and they'll try to make Tink bear the punishment. So, feel free to flirt with her, even make out a little, if she wants, but no more than that." Synda would be amused, and stay out of trouble.

Two birds, one kinky stone.

William placed a hand over his heart. "I think you just moved to the top of my best-friend-forever list."

Kane rolled his eyes, stood, and held out his hand. "You got a revolver or semi I can borrow?"

"Borrow? No. Pay to use for a short time? Yes." The warrior slapped a .44 in his hand. "I'll let you know the price tag later."

"Thanks." Kane stashed the weapon at the back of his waist and ushered Tink out of the bar. Chairs scraped the ground, and he knew the three males, and maybe even White, had just stood, intending to come after him.

He heard William say, "Settle down. He's coming back, and then he's yours."

CHAPTER THIRTEEN

JOSEPHINA HAD NO idea what was going on. "Where are you taking me?"

"Shopping."

"Shopping? Without Synda?"

"And then the fight," he continued, as if she hadn't spoken.

"But it'll be three against one," she squeaked.

"I know. It's hardly fair for William's kids, but they're insisting so what can I do?"

They walked away from the black-haired devil with eyes so cold and Fae-like she'd known he would deliver a deathblow to a female without pausing to ask questions. He was the answer to her problems. Now, however, she looked back at him with dismay.

He winked at her.

She scowled at him. He was okay with Kane getting hurt, and that made him unacceptable on every level.

Kane forced her to clear the door of the tavern and enter the daylight. The streets were a little more congested with horse-drawn carriages, and the pathways littered with chattering Opulens and the servants trailing a few feet behind them. The moment a gaze landed on Josephina, any gaze, it darted away. Voices tapered to quiet, and bodies inched out of reach, as if touching her would cause some kind of disease.

"What is such a magnificent man doing with *her?*" one of the Opulens said to her friend.

"Males do like to slum it upon occasion."

Josephina tugged against Kane's grip, a puny motion, really, but one he allowed to slow him nonetheless.

"Shut your mouths before I do it for you," Kane snapped.

They shrieked at his vehemence and ran away.

Josephina blinked with surprise. "*Why* are we shopping without Synda?" she asked, trying again.

Again he ignored the question. "They're treating you like a whore, and it's going to get them killed."

"To them, I'm a human servant without a mistress in sight. I have no business being in this part of town, alone with a man, unless I'm getting boned by him on a daily basis."

One of his brows arched. "Boned. Who taught you to talk like that?"

"You! I studied you and your friends for years, remember, and picked up on your verbal cues."

He massaged the back of his neck, and she wasn't sure whether he was fighting a smile or a scowl. "I hate the double standard here. Those same women would have stripped for me just last night, and I wouldn't have had to speak a word."

She gaped at him. "Uh, maybe we should get a bag for your ego. That might make it easier for you to carry it around."

His lips twitched for several seconds—definitely fighting a smile. "Let's get you out of sight before I gouge out a few eyes and dangle them from a necklace I'll be presenting to you as a gift."

I would totally wear that.

They leaped back into motion. He bypassed the shoe

shop, the ribbon store, the millinery and stopped in front of one of the dressmakers.

With his hand on the doorknob, he said, "What do the Fae use as money?"

"You might find this hard to believe, but…money."

Another twitch, before his frown returned. "What happens if someone touches the skin on your face or your shoulders?" As he spoke, his gaze traced the areas in question—and glinted with hunger. "The same thing that happens when they touch your hands?"

Her ability to breathe abandoned her. Was he thinking about touching her here, now? Her blood heated, and her knees almost buckled. "No. My hands are the only problem."

Did that needy voice belong to her?

"And you know this because…"

"Because I had a mother, and she told me so. Back then, I couldn't control what happened with my hands—" and still might not be able to "—but nothing ever happened when she helped me dress."

He lifted his hand, his fingers closing in on her face. A tremor shook her. Any second now…

Two giggling girls walked past them.

Cursing, he dropped his arm to his side. "Okay, then." He stalked into the small building, tugging her behind him. A bell tinkled overhead. The scent of floral perfume hit her first, the preferred fragrance of the Opulens and one she despised. Kane clearly felt the same. He wrinkled his nose and pursed his lips—and he looked utterly adorable doing it.

I've got to get this...whatever it is under control.

An older woman with silver hair and typical Fae eyes sauntered out from the back. She wore the current fashion, an elaborate gown of yellow silk, material twisted along the belled skirt to form a bouquet of roses. Her skin was lined from a life of hard work. Like Josephina, she was half Fae, half human, but unlike Josephina, she would age to her death. The human part of her was clearly stronger than the Fae.

"I'm Rhoda, the owner," she said, the words slow and precise. Her expression brightened. "And you're… you're…*you*. How may I help you, Lord Kane? Anything you desire is yours."

"I want her," Kane said, dragging Josephina forward and forcing her to stand in front of him. He placed his hands on her shoulders to ensure she wouldn't bolt, a tremble spilling from him and into her. "Better dressed."

Maybe it was irrational, but once the initial shock wore off, she experienced a sudden urge to cry. She wasn't good enough as she was. Her father had told her. The queen had told her. Now, Kane's actions told her. The mighty Lord of the Underworld beloved by all didn't want to be seen with a servant wearing rags.

Her gaze met his in the mirror across the room, and he frowned.

"What's wrong?" he demanded.

I can hold it together. At least for a little while. Later, she would probably hide under her covers. "Don't worry. I'll walk behind you from now on. You won't have to be seen with me."

His fingers dug into her. "Sweetheart, I don't like the way this material chafes your skin. It's too pretty to be streaked with red."

Oh. My.

KANE TIGHTENED HIS grip on Tink, and the trembling in his hands increased.

He wanted this woman. *So bad.*

He wished he were the man he used to be. He would have laughed and flirted with her, relaxing her. He would have charmed her, delighted her. She would have welcomed his attentions—would have even begged for them. Instead, he'd hurt her feelings in the worst way.

"Please, let me do this for you," he said.

She turned and faced him, peering up at him with those electric blues he should have found as unappealing as all the others, but...hers were different.

He liked that they changed colors with her moods. Liked that right now they were laced with multiple shades of blue. A mix of light blue, dark blue and something in between, creating a sort of poetry, a kaleidoscope of loveliness no one would ever be able to re-create.

"It's a wonderful gesture, and I am beyond grateful, but you can't. I can't wear anything but my uniform. If I do, everyone will have permission to tear the clothing off me—no matter where I am or who I'm with."

And she would end up naked. As beautiful and naturally sensual as she was, the men around her would gawk, possibly reach out and touch her. Possibly even try to do more.

A bead of rage rolled through him, growing larger the deeper it reached.

He looked to Rhoda. "Make her a new uniform, just in softer, better quality material. And add pockets. Lots of pockets." He wanted her armed and at the ready at all times. Prepared—as he hadn't been. "Can you finish it within a couple hours? I want her to leave wearing it."

"Of course, of course, that's what I'm known for" was the reply. "I hate to bring this up to so distinguished a customer, but...how will you pay, my lord?"

"With this." He withdrew the wad of cash he'd stuffed in his boot before beginning this journey.

Rhoda nodded. "Very good. I'll take her back and—"

"No. She stays within my sight at all times."

Tink flattened her gloved hands on his chest, and he responded instantly. His heart sped into a now familiar beat, and the increased flow of blood caused his body to ready for her. For all the things he wanted to do to her.

It was painful. Far more than before. It was pleasurable. Far more than he was willing to admit.

The need he felt for her…the edge of it sharpened daily, hourly, and if he wasn't careful, it would soon cut through him, severing the ties of his good sense, his better intentions, and his concern for the complications.

Disaster roared with fury. *Hate her! Leave her!*

Kill you, Kane roared back.

Rolls of fabric tumbled from a table to the floor, the heavy spools hitting Kane's feet with a surprisingly harsh thud.

"I'm so sorry," Rhoda said, rushing to clean up the mess. "I'm not sure what happened."

Adamant, Josephina shook her head. "I can't disrobe in front of you."

"Why not?" But he already knew the answer. They weren't lovers. They weren't even friends, not really. She would be vulnerable. He couldn't promise not to look. Like the men he'd just disdained, he would look.

He should be ashamed. He'd picked up on a bit of palace gossip and knew her mother, who'd been considered a lowly human, had been the king's mistress. He knew her mother had been taunted, and suspected she had even been shunned. Any hint of impropriety had to remind Tink of her mother's anguish. Perhaps even make her feel she deserved the cruel words the two Opulens had uttered outside.

But she didn't. That kind of thinking had to stop—now.

"I just can't," she insisted.

"You can. You will. Like I said, I don't want you out of my sight, even for a second."

"Kane..."

A pleading tone. One he might have heeded if she had been underneath him—*have to get her underneath me*. He gritted his teeth. "Keep arguing with me. I'll find another way to change your mind. A far more intimate way."

Her eyes widened. "You can't."

He leaned down until his lips hovered just over hers. "Try me. Please."

Red infused her cheeks and she glanced back at the shop owner.

How could he have forgotten about Rhoda?

Straightening, he met the older woman's shrewd stare. "Where she goes, I go, and that's non-negotiable."

A nod, and the woman turned away, saying, "Please, follow me."

Kane peered down at Tink. "This is for your own good, I promise you. I can't take the chance you'll leave, and I won't allow anyone to hurt you."

"That's great, wonderful, but this is going to ruin my reputation," she muttered. "Worse than it already has."

"I'm sorry for that." But it had to be done. "I'll think of something to fix it."

"Before or after men start seeing me as more than a blood slave?"

A direct hit. Jealousy bloomed, hot and razor-sharp. "That happens, and men will start dying."

"But—"

"Sweetheart, I need you to stop stalling." He gave her a little push, forcing her to move forward. He trailed behind her. They entered a small room in back, where another girl bustled about, moving drapes of fabric out of the way, revealing a chair for Kane and a stepstool for Josephina.

A stepstool perched in front of a three-sided mirror.

He eased into the cushioned seat. A pin stuck him in the back, and he grimaced.

In record time, Tink was stripped to bra and panties, and he noticed both garments were woven from plain white cotton. Molding to her. Hiding the details of her femininity from him…begging him to seek. He was unable to cloak his reaction, every inch of him hardening. Her body was a work of art, slender, yet so beautifully curved. Bronzed to perfection, without any kind of tan line. Toned from the amount of work she was forced to do every day.

He gripped the edges of his chair to keep from reaching for her.

He could help himself. He could.

The seamstress attempted to remove Tink's gloves, but she shook her head.

"They stay."

Rhoda looked to him for confirmation.

He nodded. Maybe Tink could control her ability to absorb another person's strength and abilities, maybe she couldn't, but they wouldn't be taking any chances until he found out.

Tonight, he would find out.

She would have to put her hands on him. On his skin.

The arms of the chair cracked.

Tink was measured and fitted with different fabrics

to discover which one felt the best to her. Once the decision was made, the two seamstresses began the arduous process of cutting and sewing the dress.

Toward the end, Tink's stomach began to growl.

"Hungry?" he asked, with a tinge of guilt. He should have fed her before bringing her here. Being classified as a servant, she probably wasn't given proper meals.

Disaster chuckled with delight.

Never again, Kane thought.

"I'm starved," she replied, still not daring to meet his gaze.

"I have food," Rhoda said, and waved her assistant away.

The girl puttered from the room, returning several minutes later with a rolling cart piled with sandwiches, cookies and a pitcher of tea.

Tink appeared dazed. "For me? Really?"

How eager she sounded, when such treatment should have been an everyday occurrence for her.

Should, should, should. He was already sick of the word. From now on, he was going to take such good care of her.

"For you," he said.

Holding the new, as yet unfinished dress to her chest with one hand, she reached out with the other and claimed a sandwich. He watched her as she ate, the way her eyes closed in surrender, the way a smile curled the corners of her lips, the way she chewed and savored.

So lovely. So sensual, even without meaning to be. *So mine...*

His skin prickled, and maybe he moved. Maybe he spoke. Her gaze lifted to meet his. Her lips parted on a startled exhalation. Could she see the rawness of his need?

"Kane." A breathy entreaty.

In that moment, the cry of the demon ceased to matter. The past faded, leaving only the present…the future, and the unstoppable tide of the pleasure to come. Every bone vibrated. He needed to get inside her. Here. Now.

It would be agony.

It would be ecstasy.

Tension coiled low in his gut, only to spring apart and jolt him into a stand. "Leave us," he said, his voice a broken rasp.

No questions. No protests. The two seamstresses flittered from the room, shutting the door behind them.

The teapot shattered on the tray, dark liquid spilling everywhere.

Tink didn't seem to notice, was too busy watching him. "I-is something wrong?"

Silent, he stalked toward her. A predator with a purpose. He was done resisting. Done thinking about all the reasons why not. Today, he was taking something.

Perhaps sensing the dark, greedy urges driving him, she straightened with a snap. Her breathing quickened. "Kane," she said.

"Tell me to stop." He stood a mere heartbeat away, their gazes locked together, trapped. Nothing else would halt the madness.

"I…I can't."

He breathed her in. The scent of cleaning supplies had faded, and she smelled of rosemary and mint again, sweet and innocent. Perhaps she could finally wash away the taint inside him. Or burn it away with passion—he could feel the intense heat radiating off her body. Perhaps she could melt the ice that had taken residence inside him.

Perhaps she could save him.

She swallowed, licked her lips. "Wait. I think you're right. I think I should tell you to stop. This isn't right."

"No. It's not. It's necessary."

I'll hurt her, I swear I will.

Kane ignored the demon, pressing ever closer to Tink.

"Stop?" she said, a question when she'd probably meant it to be a statement.

"Too late." Unless… "Have you ever been with a man?"

She gave a slow shake of her head.

That answer should have ended this.

It didn't.

He should walk away.

He didn't.

Possessiveness clawed at him, so sharp, so deep, he knew he would feel the wounds for the rest of eternity and be glad for it. He brushed his fingertips along her jawbone, and oh, she was just as soft and electrifying as he'd imagined. She nearly unmanned him when she leaned into the touch, seeking more intimate contact. He gave it to her, cupping the back of her neck, fisting her glorious hair, and forcing her gaze to stay with his.

"I won't let myself take you—" not here, not now "—but I want something from you. Need it."

A tremor swept through her. "What do you want?"

Disaster banged against the sides of Kane's skull. *I'll hurt her. I will. Hate her so much.*

He gnashed his teeth. *Shut up! You hate her because she's the only relationship I can have that won't end in disaster, and that—*

There it was. The answer. The reason the demon hurt him whenever Tink neared. She was a blessing and not a curse. *Of course* the demon wanted to be rid of her.

She really was Kane's "mine," just as his instincts had screamed.

His. And not the demon's.

He looked into her mesmerizing eyes, and felt a swell in his heart. His fingers hadn't abandoned the silkiness of her hair, and were now holding on to her as if she were a lifeline, causing her neck to arch. He should probably loosen his grip. He didn't. He couldn't. He wanted to own her, even in the smallest way, whatever the future held, and this was how he'd go about it.

"Let me kiss you, Tinker Bell."

She wet her lips, and whispered, "What about Synda?"

"I don't want Synda."

And now, he was done talking. He swooped in, not bothering with preliminaries or gentleness, but thrusting his tongue inside her mouth, then against hers, unleashing all the intensity of the need driving him. She softened against him despite the ferocity of his claiming, and welcomed him fully. The utter sweetness of her taste stoked the fire inside him from a blaze to an inferno.

She held nothing back, leaning into him, wrapping her arms around his neck and giving herself up to his total domination.

And dominate he did.

Taking. Giving. What he wanted was too powerful to contain. It was overwhelming. Shattering. A connection more binding than flesh and bone. Undeniable. Uncontrollable. He crackled with new life as he fed her one frantic kiss after the other.

And still he yearned to give her more. He jerked her so firmly against him, not even air separated them. His passion was insatiable, demanding her total acceptance, and an unending obsession. More than she was probably willing to give, more than she'd probably ever expected to give. But he demanded without mercy, forcing her tongue to keep pace, and her body to grind against his.

He would meld her to his soul.

One of his hands slid down the bare skin of her upper arm, then down her side, to the sumptuous curve of her waist, then hooked beneath her thighs and lifted her. He spun her and strode forward, until her back pressed against the wall. Hands now free to roam, he jerked at the hem of her gown, untangling the material from her legs. Automatically she wound herself around him, his body becoming an anchor for hers.

It nearly slayed him.

He'd never had more reason to despise intimacy, and yet he'd never craved it more.

The harder he kissed her, the more she rubbed against him, his own little kitty, and the more she rubbed against him, the more he wanted their clothing out of his way. Every hated piece. Her skin was like heated silk, and he was desperate for more. All. Her taste and scent were his dream of home…his…yes, yes. His, and no one else's. He needed to put his mark on every inch of her.

She moaned, and he lifted his head long enough to peer down at her passion-hazed features. Her beauty was a fantasy he'd never dared have. Her lips were swollen and red. Moist. Perfect.

Her eyelids slowly parted. "Kane?"

She was panting just as forcefully as he was.

He had to have this woman. And he would. He dove back down for another taste. He would rip away her new dress, and the underclothing. He would toss her on the floor. He wouldn't bother removing all of his clothing.

He would just undo his pants. He wanted her too badly to waste time stripping—no matter how badly he craved the skin-to-skin contact. That would come later. After the burn of the first time had been extinguished.

Now, he would spread her legs, and bury himself so deep inside her.

—no, no!

Disaster's piercing shriek claimed his attention for one poisoned second.

That was enough. He stilled, tried to catch his breath.

"Kane." A moan escaped Tink as her glove-covered fingertips scraped against his back.

Hands...all over him...

Suddenly feeling like a caged animal, he straightened. He set her back on her feet, his head swimming. She had no idea how close she'd come to losing her virginity in a dress shop.

The demon had somehow broken past whatever barriers Tink had built, intending to taunt Kane with the reminder. Instead, the creature had done him a favor.

Tink traced the seam of her lips with trembling fingers. "I'm sorry. Did I do something wrong?"

He didn't want to explain and have to deal with the humiliation, but he owed her, and he would pay. Whatever the cost. He tried to get his breathing under control. "In hell…the demons…forced me to…"

Her lashes fused, but not before he caught a glimpse of her pity.

Pity.

He hated pity.

This was what he'd feared, however. Making a fool of himself sexually. Dealing with the aftermath.

"I'm sorry for what happened to you," she said. "I wouldn't wish such a fate on my worst enemy."

He nodded to let her know he'd heard her, but offered no more than that.

"But…about the kiss. We can't do that again," she said with a tremor. "Whether you want Synda or not, you're engaged to her, and I won't be the other woman. Ever. Not for anyone, not even for you."

"You're right." Not because of his supposed engagement—but because he had nothing to offer her. As he'd known, but ignored. As he'd just proven.

He hated this situation, too. Hated his mind, and his emotions, and yes, the weakness he would have denied with his dying breath.

"No, really, we have to—wait. I'm right?" She shook her head, as if to dislodge the thoughts, dark locks of hair dancing over her shoulders. "Never mind. I only ever want to kiss *my* man, and that's not you, so…"

"You're right. I'm not."

Cheeks reddening, she said, "Besides, I don't want a man. We would…you know, and I would have children, and the king would want to use them the way he uses me, and I would *never* allow my own flesh and blood to suffer in such a way."

"I may be a warrior, and cruel to my bones, but I understand." She was protective of what she considered hers. Fiercely so. It was admirable. But hope had been stolen from her, exactly as it had been stolen from him. She couldn't see herself in the future. Couldn't see herself happy or content—or even safe.

Every day, she broke his heart a little more.

Disaster gave up screaming and began growling. Overhead, a light bulb shorted. The crack in the floor widened to such an astonishing degree it could no longer be ignored. The entire building shook. Kane stepped away from Tink and the temptation she presented.

"What's happening?" she asked, glancing around.

"A revolt."

She stumbled, creating even more distance between them, and the commotion died down. "That was you, wasn't it?" she asked.

He could have lied. He wanted to lie. But he said, "Yeah. That was me."

"The demon?"

"Yes."

"Then not really you," she said, baffling him. She understood the difference between the man and the evil. "He's acting up."

"Yes," Kane repeated.

"And that's all he's got?" She laughed, a sound as pure as Christmas bells. "How pathetic."

Disaster snarled inside his head, and Kane grinned. The woman dreaded the things her family could do to her, and yet she was fearless in the face of a demon.

Desire stormed through him all over again.

"Let's have the seamstresses finish your dress so we can return to the bar," he said, turning away from her. "I have a fight to attend."

"I'm still not on board with that fight."

"It's gotta happen eventually. The guys want to stop me from dating their sister."

All of her humor drained, leaving her features pinched. "Well, by all means. Let's get you to that fight so you can date whoever you wish."

CHAPTER FOURTEEN

THE NEW UNIFORM fit Josephina perfectly, the material soft against her skin, a divine caress rather than an irritating scratch. She loved it. But she had no idea what to think about the man responsible.

He was cold. But he was kind.

He was fierce. But he was tender.

He was cruel. But he was sweet.

If she weren't careful, she would become smitten with him—and end up heartbroken. He couldn't be trusted. He'd kissed her, but he had no plans to break his engagement to Synda. He'd kissed her, but he was thinking about dating another woman, the blonde from the tavern.

How many females did he have dangling at the end of his beautiful rope?

Too many. Obviously.

And Josephina had almost become one of them.

I'm going to have to erect a wall of ice against him.

She'd expected her first experience with passion to be gentle—if ever she'd weakened enough to succumb to a male's charm. She'd expected a hesitant exploration, cool, a little tame, and yet there'd been unbearable heat, necessary heat, and her every pulse point had turned into a wild drum. A frightening beat, but oh, so thrilling.

Kane had *owned* her mouth, had staked a claim and

demanded a response, and she had been unable to deny him, unable to hold back, not wanting to hold back. He'd tasted of whiskey she hadn't seen him drink, and he'd intoxicated her. His hands…in her hair…on her arms… her waist…he'd caressed and he'd squeezed and he'd left a white-hot trail of need in his wake.

For the first time in her life, she'd felt alive. She'd had something to look forward to, something worth the hardships she faced. But then he'd pulled away, as if she had disgusted him, and yes, she'd wanted to cry.

Knowing the disgust had nothing to do with her assuaged her. But it also made her want to cry. What he'd endured in hell had left him scarred, and he needed to move slowly, to wrap his head around the things his body was feeling, but he didn't want to move more slowly *with her*. So, fine. Whatever. The other two women were welcome to him.

Squaring her shoulders, Josephina kept pace beside him. He stopped in front of the Devil's Punchbowl and met her gaze. "The Fae can pretend they're better than you, but that's all they're doing. Pretending. There's *no one* better than you."

He didn't wait for her response, but shoved his way inside the building.

Reeling, she followed after him. What had…why… Surely her translation from English to…uh, English had screwed with the essence of his meaning. He'd just lavishly praised her, even though he didn't want her? Something had to be off with her thinking.

"Maybe you should forget the fight and we should go somewhere to talk about our—" *My poor eyes.* Wearing only her undergarments, Synda was dancing on top of a table, her gown swinging from her upraised hand.

The men hoping to pummel Kane into blood and pulp circled her, cheering and clapping.

At least the rest of the patrons had cleared out, leaving no other witnesses to the princess's behavior. Still. Josephina would be penalized for this. Lewd acts among the Opulens were encouraged, often rewarded, but this was a common bar and these men were…she wasn't sure what they were.

The blonde—the one Kane wasn't supposed to date—sat in the back corner, eating grapes, unconcerned by the chaos around her.

Josephina disliked her immediately.

"Gentlemen," Kane said, sounding calm.

All four males looked over at him. Three lost their smiles. The other—William—just grinned wider.

Silence reigned…until Synda spotted him and sighed. "Is the fun over?" she asked with a pout.

The grinning warrior stalked forward. He had dark hair and the electric blue eyes of the Fae, though he clearly wasn't Fae. The power humming from him was too…unique. It was also the strongest she'd ever encountered. One touch, and she suspected the man's energy would cause her body to combust.

"Candy Kane," William said. "You're back."

Kane nodded in greeting. "I like it."

"And there's Ivanna B.," William said to Josephina. He held out his hand, intending to clasp hers and perhaps bring it to his lips for a kiss.

What did that name even mean?

Before she could reach out, Kane batted the man's arm away with enough force to crack bone. "No touching." The fierce warning in his tone echoed from the walls.

"I'm wearing my gloves," she said. "I wouldn't have hurt him."

"It's not him I'm worried about."

Her?

"You'll share your soon-to-be bride, but not her servant," the other man said good-naturedly. "That's not weird at all." To the others, he called, "Clear a space. The battle is about to begin."

The men rushed to obey. Soon the tables and chairs were pushed against the walls, leaving a circular clearing. Synda was escorted to the grape-eating female. Facing Kane, the man with pale hair cracked his knuckles. The bald one leaned his head left, right, aligning his spine. The dark-haired one withdrew two hooked blades.

Trembling, Josephina fisted the skirt of her soft new gown.

William paced in front of the eager combatants, saying, "First rule of Teach Kane a Lesson: you don't talk about Teach Kane a Lesson. Second rule of Teach Kane a Lesson: you don't talk about Teach Kane a Lesson. Third rule of Teach Kane a Lesson: if someone taps out, you just keep fighting. Fourth rule of Teach Kane a Lesson: there are no rules. Got it?"

Kane cleared his throat, gaining William's attention. "Is it okay to kill them, or would you rather they survive?"

The man tilted his head to the side, as if he were actually pondering the question.

"Alive," finally came the response. "But close to dying wouldn't be a terrible thing."

Uh…hello, confusion. Whose side was he on?

The males were confused, too, and hurtled curses at William.

The warrior shrugged, unaffected, saying to Kane, "I love them and I hate them. They're a joy and a pain. I can't ever decide if I want to hug them or choke them. Right now, they're in need of an attitude adjustment, and I think you're the man for the job."

Kane led Josephina to the table where the blonde woman and Synda waited. "White," he said, a warning. He gently pushed Josephina into a chair. "What I said to your dad goes for you. Don't touch her."

"Kane," the woman—White—said. "Who is this girl to you?"

Josephina's ears twitched, as she waited to hear his answer.

"That's none of your concern," he finally replied, disappointing her. "Just keep your hands to yourself or bad things will happen."

The woman shrugged. "Very well. My problem is with you, not her." She traced a grape over her mouth, licked away the juice. "I won't allow the supposed fates to dictate my future, and if that means getting rid of you, I'm fine with that."

The fates—the Moirai. Three women with an eternal case of verbal diarrhea. Josephina hated the hobags with every fiber of her being. Because of them, she had helped destroy her mother.

And they thought Kane and this White person would end up together?

Josephina pressed her tongue to the roof of her mouth. *I won't say a word.*

Hitting doesn't involve words.

"So kind of you, White," Kane finally said, his tone cutting. His gaze moved to Josephina and stayed. He leaned over and planted his hands on the arms of her chair, caging her, surrounding her. "You are to stay put. Understand?"

She lifted her chin. "What reason do I have to do what you say? You and your hot-and-cold attitude are nothing to me."

He rubbed his nose against hers. "I'm something all right, but I respect your fight against it."

She…had no reply.

"Candy Kane," William called, as she tried not to shiver. Kane's nearness was addling her brain. "The clock's ticking."

Kane stayed just where he was. "You were right before, you know. We do need to talk, iron some things out."

A lump grew in her throat, and she nodded. She found herself saying, "Be careful, okay?"

"Now that I've got something to look forward to?" His gaze dropped to her lips, lingered. "Definitely." He straightened, ending the comfort—and sensuality—of the contact.

What did he have to look forward to? Their talk? Or, as that parting look had hinted at, another kiss?

Melting...

"What about me?" Synda asked, squirming in her seat. "What should I do?"

Kane flicked her an impatient glance. "You'll behave for the first time in your life. After the fight, I might do the world a favor and put you over my knee to spank the poor judgment right out of you. I guess we'll find out together."

Red sprang into the princess's eyes, her expression hardening. "Say something like that again, and I'll cut out your tongue while you're sleeping."

No longer peering at her, Kane reached out blindly

and patted her on top of the head. "I'd probably be scared if you actually knew how to keep your promises."

A rumble rose from Synda's chest, and spewed out her mouth, the sound more animal than Fae. Josephina had heard the sound before—right before the princess had set the stable on fire.

"Kane!" William snapped. "Sometime today."

"No, wait." The moisture in Josephina's mouth dried as she held up her gloved hands and wiggled her fingers to gain his attention. "Don't be so hasty to count me out. I could…you know."

"No." He turned to her, adamant. "None of that."

"But—"

Once again he got in her face. Only this time, he wasn't gentle about it. "Don't push on this. I will never willingly put you in harm's way. Plus, I don't know what you'd end up with."

Their powers, he meant. "Whatever I take, it'll be temporary." More than that, the men might do what Kane had refused to do: kill her.

She would die. Finally. Never again would she have to deal with her father or the queen or her brother or her sister. There would be no more whippings, no more shunnings, no more punishments of any kind. But… but…

I don't want to die.

The realization shocked her to her bones. Knowing the bliss of Kane's kiss, she only wanted more. Like, his hands on her bare skin next time, touching her…everywhere. Like, his voice in her ear, whispering all the things he planned to do to her. Like, his body delivering on every single promise. She wanted…

Everything he had to give.

"I want you safe," he said. "Whatever the cost."

Melting faster…

He straightened and faced the men. "Everyone clear on the rules?"

"We've been clear for hours now." From the blond.

"Definitely." From the dark-haired one. "You should have stayed in hell. You would've had an easier life—and death."

A nod from the bald one.

Kane grinned without a shred of humor. "I can't wait to prove you wrong."

"Ding, ding," William said.

And just like that, the battle was on. The males converged on each other, becoming a tangle of fists and legs and weapons.

Synda cheered, "Go, Kane, go!" as if the two hadn't almost come to blows seconds before.

White snapped her teeth at the girl. "You should cheer for my brothers. You just had sex with two of them in the bathroom."

"Oh, that. It meant nothing."

Josephina cringed, knowing she would be punished for this transgression, as well. But okay, all right, she would deal. Right now, Kane was more important—and he'd just vanished from her sight, a black cloud appearing and surrounding the men. Her hand covered her mouth to silence her cry of dismay. Grunts and groans and the click of metal against metal filled the air. Her blood chilled. What was happening in there?

She pushed to shaky legs, took a step forward.

"I wouldn't do that." William joined the women at the table. He grabbed one of White's grapes and tossed the little fruit in his mouth.

"Do what?" Josephina croaked, unable to pull her attention away from the battle.

"Whatever you're planning. The boys will attack anyone inside their force field, and Kane will punish them for it. They may not survive, and like I told Kane, a part of me wants them to survive."

That "force field" raised the fine hairs on the back of her neck. It possessed some sort of electrical charge, attempting to pull the energy out of her the way she often pulled the energy out of others.

Was it draining Kane?

"Let her join," White said. "She'll die, and I'll have an open playing field."

"You wouldn't have an open playing field if you were the last woman on earth," Josephina snapped.

"An open playing field?" William growled. "I thought you wanted Kane dead."

"I did."

"And now?"

"Supposedly Kane is my destined mate, and my destined mate has no business lusting after another woman."

"You said you cared nothing about destiny," William roared.

Josephina didn't hear White's reply, didn't care to; she was too busy marching forward. Whether Kane realized it or not, he needed her. He could take those men, but she doubted he could take the cloud. Look how easily he'd fallen when pitted against *her.*

When she reached the darkened dome, she removed her gloves and reached out. Lightning jolted through her, startling her. Her bones throbbed, and her blood fizzed, but she pushed through. The darkness soon cleared, and she realized she was standing in the midst of a raging battle. Blood was splattered across the floor. And Kane's opponents…they'd become monsters.

One had horns. Or rather, what should have been horns. They were shredded and bleeding.

One had wings. Or rather, what used to be wings. They were misshapen and bleeding.

One had scales. Or rather, what were probably scales. They were ripped out in patches and bleeding.

All had fangs and claws.

What…how…

Kane stood in place, wielding two daggers with perfect precision. He contorted his body left and right, forward and backward, avoiding impact with his enemies. He was…winning, despite the cloud and…and…despite the fact that the floor was cracking beneath his feet?

The demon was acting up again. Why? So he'd lose?

Oh, yes. Defeat would be considered a disaster, after all.

Thank goodness Kane knew what he was doing. When his feet caught on one of the cracks, he tilted forward, going with it, rolling into the motion, allowing his weapons to slash against his opponents with more force.

Relief speared her. She backed away.

He must have sensed her, though, because his gaze found her across the distance. His eyes widened, and a roar split his lips. He gave up his offensive stance to stalk toward her. A mistake. One of the monsters nailed him in the chin, a brutal slash of claws, slicing his skin and leaving *him* bleeding.

Josephina didn't think about her next actions. She launched into motion, throwing herself into the monster closest to her. He went down with a moan the moment she touched him. A shocking amount of strength poured through her, more than her little body had ever had to hold, but she twisted to reach the second one… the third one…

On the heels of the strength came darkness, such terrible darkness. Worse than what had come with Kane. Then silence. Josephina stumbled. *What's happening?* She was falling…falling… *No, no, no! I'm back inside the Never-ending.*

A sharp pain tore through her head before blackness took over.

CHAPTER FIFTEEN

TORIN, KEEPER OF Disease, paced the floor of the room where he'd last seen Cameo. Days had passed since she'd vanished, leaving all of the artifacts behind, but he couldn't stop thinking about what had happened here. Her gaze had locked with Maddox's. She had reached out. Then, she had been gone, with no trace of her remaining. Where was she? What had happened?

The other warriors had come and gone, inspecting the room before stalking out to hunt down anyone who might know how to save a woman Torin loved with all of his heart. Not as a lover, though they had once tried to go that route, but as his best friend.

If he would die for his friends, he would kill for his best friend.

And yet, Torin was stuck here. He could do nothing but wait. He'd already checked online, but the information he desired wasn't out there. Or, if it was, he hadn't yet found it.

He couldn't leave the fortress, because he couldn't risk touching anyone. Were his skin to accidentally brush against the skin of another immortal, that immortal would then carry the taint of Torin's curse, infecting anyone *they* touched with disease. Were his skin to brush against the skin of a human, that human would sicken and die—but not before passing the disease on to others. A plague would erupt. Again.

Yeah. He'd once lusted after a woman he hadn't been meant to have. He'd rescued her from the hands of his enemy—they'd noticed his interest in her. Then, he'd removed his gloves and touched her, desperate for contact. Skin-to-skin. Warmth to warmth. He'd thought she would be the exception, that his yearning for her would somehow overcome his handicap.

Her eyes had closed, and her lips had curled into a small grin, and pleasure had overwhelmed him. But then she'd sickened. Then her family and friends had sickened. Then they had all died—along with thousands of others.

Now, when Cameo needed him…

He was worse than useless. He was a failure. He hadn't gotten here soon enough to save her, and he couldn't race to her rescue. Frustration and fury burned in his chest, a toxic combination adding to the poison in his blood.

He stopped in front of the Cage of Compulsion. Two of the artifacts were inside, exactly where they'd fallen when Cameo vanished. The Rod was propped outside, against the corner. If he did what Cameo had done, could he get to where she was? To where Viola was?

Maybe.

Probably.

Worth the risk, he thought.

He stepped forward and curled his fingers over the edge of the cage.

"Hey! What do you think you're doing?" a voice said from behind him.

He stiffened. "What do you think I'm doing?"

Anya, the incarnation of Anarchy and girlfriend of the keeper of Death, leaned against the door frame, her arms crossed over her middle. She was tall and blonde and one of the most beautiful females ever created; she was also one of the most troublesome, preferring chaos over calm. Today she wore a skintight blue minidress that looked—wait, it *was* painted on.

Sweet heaven.

"Better question. Are you going to tell Lucien?"

"When he took off this morning to escort a few souls to the hereafter, he failed to wake me with a kiss and tell me he loved me. Therefore, I'm currently giving him the silent treatment."

And Lucien was probably loving it. Not that Torin would ever say such a thing aloud.

He changed the subject, saying, "New look?"

"New form of torture for Lucien. He'll never not kiss me again!"

"He probably thought you'd demand more than a kiss from him, when he wouldn't have the time to give it to you."

"There's *always* time to give it to me."

He wanted to smile, and the thread of humor, even as small as it was, surprised him. But then, Anya had that effect on people. "Want to try and talk me out of this?" he said, motioning to the artifacts.

"Nah. I want Cameo brought back as much as you do. But if you die, well, I call dibs on your room. I'm thinking about getting a pet that will eat Viola's devil, and my baby will need a place all her own."

"It's yours."

She nodded, as if she'd expected nothing less. "Just know that I've always enjoyed looking at you. I'll miss your sexy face."

The smile bloomed to full wattage, unstoppable. "I've always enjoyed looking at you, too."

She blew him a kiss.

Because he carried the All-key inside his body, he was able to unlock anything with only a touch. The cage was no exception. He entered. The door slammed shut behind him.

"I feel like this is the perfect time to admit I'm the Cage's owner," Anya said, tapping her chin and eyeing him thoughtfully. "Cronus gave it to me. I could command you to strip and you'd have to obey."

Torin ignored her, looking over the painting. A man's office. A glass display case. Artifacts. One of them was a small box made of bones. Pandora's box? Maybe. Why had he not noticed it before? He picked up the Cloak and draped the material over his shoulders, just as he'd watched Cameo do. Then, he took off his glove, reached out and gripped the Rod. But…

Nothing happened.

"Well, that wasn't disappointing," Anya said drily. "See you later, Disease."

She left him alone in the room, and he cursed. "You don't want my disease inside you?" he growled at the Rod. "Huh? Is that it? Do you get to pick and choose the ones you accept?"

He tossed the artifact on the floor, exited the Cage, and, disgusted, followed the path Anya had taken.

CAMEO FELT AS though she was trapped inside a washing machine, being swirled and churned this way and that, round and round, never pausing. How many days… months…years…had passed since she'd climbed inside the Cage of Compulsion and touched the Paring Rod? She wasn't sure. Time had ceased to exit.

"Viola!" she shouted.

She bumped into something solid—something that grunted and cursed. Definitely not Viola. Someone other than the goddess was with her in this dark, winding pit?

Hard bands shackled her waist, jerking her against a male…yes…and he had to be eight feet tall, and as wide as a building. He surrounded her with his heat and his scent…sandalwood and peat smoke…and even stopped her from spinning.

"Who are you?" he demanded in a deep, rumbling voice she didn't recognize.

"Cameo," she managed to grit out. She wished she could see him, but was kind of glad she couldn't. He couldn't see her, either, so he couldn't know how close she was to vomiting. Her stomach *hurt*. "You?"

"Lazarus." Warm breath caressed the top of her head, ruffling strands of her hair.

"Where?"

He knew what she meant. "The Paring Rod. We're trapped inside it. You were hurtling through it—and you're still being pulled toward something." His tone was strained, as if all of his strength was needed to hold on to her. "I'm trying to keep you in place, and believe me, I'm as tough as they come, but whatever's got you wants you desperately, because I'm being dragged with you."

"Well, then, let go." Translation: save yourself.

"Uh, that would be a no. If you're being pulled out, I'd kill my own kin to go with you."

"Could be…dangerous," she said. *Breathe. Just breathe.*

"There are hundreds of people trapped in here and no one has ever escaped. If there's a chance that is what's happening with you, I'm going to take it."

No. Not yet. She hadn't had a chance to search. "I

can't leave without a little blonde who's in love with herself."

"Sorry, female, but you don't get a choice in the matter."

"But—"

He tightened his hold, practically flattening her lungs.

"Air…need…"

"That's not me," he gritted, sounding just as winded as she was. "Walls…closing in."

Suddenly, the pressure eased. Cameo slammed into something solid—a floor, maybe…yes, a floor, she thought, patting the area around her. It was cold, solid.

"The bottom of the Rod?" she panted. That would mean the Rod had shrunk her to thimble size, and she wasn't okay with that.

Lazarus released her and rolled away. "I've been all over the confines of the Rod, and this isn't part of it. I think we did the impossible and escaped."

His excitement was contagious. Maybe Viola had escaped, too.

Blinking to clear her line of vision, Cameo clambered to her hands and knees. With the action, the urge to vomit increased, the dizziness careened out of control *annnd*—yes, she spewed the contents of her stomach all over the man's shoes.

"Nice," she thought she heard him say.

At least he hadn't batted her away.

"I need you to move now," he said. "I want these shoes *off*."

Inhale. Good. Now exhale. Several minutes passed before she was able to lift her head enough to see what was around her. An office. The one from the painting, she realized. There was a desk piled high with papers.

There was a glass display case brimming with artifacts. And there was Pandora's box.

So close.

For the moment, Viola was forgotten. Cameo pushed to a stand and wiped her mouth with the back of her hand.

"How did the Rod send us here?" She took a step forward. And where was here, exactly?

Lazarus chucked his shoes. He moved beside her and latched onto her arm, his grip strong, unbreakable. She turned to face him—and gaped. He wasn't as tall as she'd imagined, but he was still a giant. He had a muscle mass even the biggest of her friends had yet to achieve. But it was his face that truly arrested her attention.

He. Was. Gorgeous. He wouldn't have to speak to a woman to gain her interest. He'd just have to look at her. He had black hair, black eyes. Fathomless eyes, really. A proud nose, a stubbornly square chin. Lips the color of rubies, and the perfect contrast to all that dark. His skin was bronzed to perfection.

"You okay?" he asked.

"Yes." *You're a warrior. Act like one.* She tugged from his hold, and the only reason she succeeded was because he let her; she knew it. "I've seen you before."

Strider was dating, or whatever, Kaia the Wing Shredder, and Strider had beheaded Lazarus to protect her. He was the consort of another Harpy, one even more annoying than Kaia, who was desperate to avenge his death.

"How are you alive?" she demanded.

"My body was destroyed, but not my spirit. It was trapped inside the Rod all this time."

Trapped. Past tense. They'd really gotten out? "If your body was destroyed, why are you solid to me?"

"Your body was destroyed as well, the moment you entered the Rod."

"No."

"Don't worry. I can make us both another one, just as soon as I get home."

She wouldn't panic. She would believe him. She didn't like the alternative.

"You have a weapon?" he asked.

Did she? She patted herself down and came up with…nothing. Silent, refusing to admit the lack, she raised her chin. "You want to fight me or something? Before you answer that, you should probably know I lack any sort of softer emotions and I'll do things to you that you wouldn't wish on your worst enemy."

"Yes, I want to fight, but you're not the opponent I'm jonesing for—even though I'm intrigued by the things you say you can do. I want to fight him." Lazarus nodded to a place behind her. "We'll need to work together to defeat him. I'm good, probably the best and strongest warrior you'll never have the pleasure to meet, but we just happen to be in the same room as the only male ever to beat me."

Him, he'd said. The skinny red-eyed male she'd seen after draping the Cloak over her head and peering at the painting? And the guy had once beaten Lazarus? He must have powers the painting hadn't revealed. Dread washed through her as she turned, but…she couldn't see him.

"He's here?" she demanded. "Who is he?"

"You can't see him?"

She licked her lips, once again refusing to admit to a lack.

"He has the ability to reveal himself—or not. He must have decided you're not worth playing with." He sighed angrily. "I guess it's up to me to save the day, then."

CHAPTER SIXTEEN

DISASTER LAUGHED WITH diabolical glee. Laughed harder than he'd laughed when Kane had been tied down, raped, beaten and humiliated. All because Tink had collapsed to the floor, her body contorting into the most painful positions, her features screwing up tight. Moan after moan escaped her. The kind he'd only ever heard in battle, after the last sword had been swung, the only enemy left standing finally defeated.

Red wheeled away from her, the horns on his head shrinking…vanishing. "What's happened to me? I'm so weak, and yet…yet…"

Black dropped to his knees, his wings snapping into his back and vanishing.

"Weak yet…at peace."

Green stood frozen, his eyes wide with shock, the scales falling from his skin.

The cloak of mist surrounding them split at the sides, like a veil torn asunder. Suddenly Kane could see William, Synda and White, and when the three spotted the remnants of the battle scene, they stood in unison, chairs skidding backward.

"I told her not to do it," William said, hands going up in a display of innocence.

"Are you ready to leave now?" Synda asked, studying her nails. "I've been waiting forever."

White nodded with satisfaction—until she saw the

state of her brothers. Angry eyes locked on Tink's writhing body. "What did she do?"

Ignoring everyone, Kane rushed over to Tink and scooped her up in his arms. Her presence barely registered, she was so light, but her scent was there, sweet and strong, wonderfully familiar, and he found comfort in it. He had her close. She would be okay. He would make sure she was okay.

"She draws other people's abilities inside herself." The secret was out now. He needed answers. "What'd she get from your boys?" he demanded of William. "They're not demons."

There was a heavy pause, then a shrug. "No, they're not, but as you know, they carry the essence of war, famine and death. She's probably swarming with all three."

His heart slammed against his ribs. "Get the princess to the palace." He didn't wait for a reply, but raced from the bar. The sun had dimmed, casting an eerie sort of darkness over the land. How long had he been fighting? The princess's carriage was gone, probably driving around the area to keep people from knowing exactly where the princess was and what she was doing. Taking the time to look for it wasn't an option.

People now littered the sidewalks. Men in suits. Women in fancy dresses. Every eye found him and remained locked on him. Hands brushed against him, pulled at his clothing.

"Come home with me," a woman said.

"I want to have your baby," another intoned. "Please, Lord Kane!"

He shoved his way through the crowd. He had to get Tink to the palace as quickly as possible. Had to summon the best physician in the realm. And he wasn't moving fast enough, he thought, his jaw locked in irritation and frustration. He scanned the area. There was a carriage winding down the street at a slow pace—slow, but unencumbered.

Kane picked up speed. Though Tink was cradled in his arms, her head tucked securely in the hollow of his neck, her arms and legs flopped with the force of his motions. Finally he caught up to the carriage and jumped through the opening in the side.

Two females were seated inside; they gasped at his sudden appearance. Both women wore the same type of ruffled, lacy gown as Synda, taking up too much space, so he knew they were part of the upper class.

"Either watch over the girl while I take over the driving, or get out of the vehicle," he said. "But you should know that if you harm her, I'll kill you."

The two leaned toward him, pressing against him. "You're Lord Kane! I've been so desperate to meet you."

"Say you'll come to my party tonight," the other pleaded.

They weren't going to cooperate. Fine. He grabbed the female closest to him and "helped" her out of the vehicle. She rolled on the ground, screaming in shock and anger, dust flying all around her.

He turned to the other girl and reached.

She blew him a kiss and jumped.

Casting a final glance to Tink—nothing had changed; she was in the same condition—Kane swung out the door, holding on to the roof. He had to kick up his leg to crawl to the top of the vehicle, then slide down to the driver's seat. The scent of animal and sweat immediately assaulted him.

The driver jolted, startled by his sudden presence, and tried to seize a weapon. Kane kicked him off the ledge and confiscated the reins. He whipped at the horses, and the carriage picked up speed. Once Tink was healed, he would leave this land, he thought. From the beginning, she'd been right. He couldn't help her. If not for him, she wouldn't be in this situation. He'd only made things worse for her.

In fact, he'd made things worse for everyone.

Once Disaster was taken care of, he would come back for her.

While he was gone, a man might come along and fall in love with her. A man worthy of her, good for her. That man would move heaven and earth to save her; he would do whatever she needed done. Wage war on her family. Yes. Romance her. Absolutely. Delight her, thrill her. Definitely. Sweep her away to another land, somewhere safe. The two would marry, and they would make love, have the children Tink was too afraid to have now, and she would be happy. Finally, blissfully happy.

Yes, one day.

And then I'll kill the male for daring to take what's mine.

The horses suddenly whinnied and stopped, raising their front legs and kicking in protest.

"Whoa, whoa," Kane said. When they settled, he saw the blonde from the forest—Petra—standing in the road, her hands anchored on her hips.

"You shot me, and I assure you I'll have my vengeance. But we'll deal with that later," she announced. "Right now, I want the girl."

Get in line, female. "Too bad. She's mine."

Little golden flames exploded in her eyes. "Why don't we bargain? You give her to me now. I'll enslave her in the way of my people, and consider us even, then I'll give her back in a few thousand years. How's that?"

Kane would die first. "I hurt you once. Don't make me do it again."

She chuckled with genuine amusement. "I'd love to see you try, warrior. You won't catch me by surprise a second time."

Mine, Disaster said.

Kane snapped the reins, forcing the horses to plow ahead. The girl had to jump out of the way to avoid impact, but she waited until the very last second, grabbing onto the back wheel to be dragged along. Dust sprayed the air, probably choking her.

Silly girl. What did she think she would accomplish—

Tendrils of smoke wafted to his nose, and he coughed. Stiffening, he glanced back. The Phoenix had fallen away from the carriage, but she'd left one of the wheels engulfed by flames. That. Quickly. He grabbed the dagger hidden in his boot and cut the horses loose. As the carriage teetered to one side, Kane scrambled toward the doorway…teetered more wildly…and fell through the center door as the entire vehicle slammed into the ground.

Impact was brutal, but he managed to wrap his arms around Tink and absorb most of the shock. And when the carriage finally settled, smoke forming an impenetrable cloud, he realized Tink had gone quiet. Too quiet.

Extreme heat licked at him as he pressed two fingers into the pulse at her neck. A faint thump, thump greeted him, and he could have wailed with relief. Coughing, he lifted her and draped her limp body through the door frame. He pulled himself out, gaze scanning as he hefted her over his shoulder. Through the thickening smoke he saw the Phoenix racing toward them, her body a living flame, fully engulfed, just like the wheel—no, the whole bottom half of the carriage now—and crackling with menace.

He expected to see her fellow warriors, but there were none. He made a split-second decision.

He had to kill her, if only for a little while. As with all Phoenix, she would die and her body would burn to ash. But there was a very real possibility she would rise again, more powerful than before.

Whatever. Kane threw the blade still clutched in his hand, and it soared toward her, flipping end over end. She jumped up and to the side, attempting to move out of harm's way, but the dagger he'd taken from the Fae king possessed an ability she hadn't anticipated, switching course and following her, amazing him. As high as she was, the blade found a home in her belly, rather than her spinal cord.

She grunted, hit the ground without any grace.

He tossed a second dagger, but didn't stick around to make sure it succeeded where the first one had failed. He hopped to the ground, ran off the road and into the forest with Tink bouncing on his shoulder. He tried to be gentle, but gentle wasn't possible. Thick trees surrounded him, but he pushed through the leaves and limbs, determined and angry and already planning his next move.

"I'll take care of the Phoenix," he vowed to Tink. While he might not be able to do much for her before he left Séduire, he could do that.

He found tracks created by the palace guard, the imprint of their boots giving them away. They'd clearly stopped and checked out all the singed places where the Phoenix had burned a bush or a plant or a patch of grass. But what he didn't see were imprints of more than one Phoenix. Only the girl.

Could she be on her own? Simply making it seem like others were with her?

That…made sense, he realized. She had to think an army of Phoenix would intimidate the Fae, make them more likely to give up Tink to save their land from war.

Not on my watch. He burst from the shield of the forest, turned a corner and made it to the cobbled path that led to the palace. Of course, the first person Kane spotted was Leopold, leading a contingent of armed guards out the front doors.

"You're going to pay," the prince vowed.

"You can try to hurt me later," Kane replied, never slowing.

Blue eyes fell on Tink and flared with concern, the rage completely obliterated. "What happened? What did you do to her?" The prince waved the guards away. The moment Kane was within reach, he snapped, "Give her to me."

"Get out of my way!" There was enough crazed fury in Kane's tone to startle the man. Wisely, the prince backed off. Kane barreled past him, past the double doors, and shouted, "I want a doctor sent to my room. Now!"

Leopold rushed to his side, keeping pace. "She absorbed the abilities of someone, didn't she? No, no need to deny it. I know her. She did. I also know one of our doctors wouldn't be able to help her. Not with something like that. Take her to my room and I'll—"

Kane ignored him, stomping up the steps and into his own bedroom. He kicked the fancy, impractical cover away and eased her atop the mattress. She was still too quiet.

His hand trembled as he smoothed the hair from her

face. Beads of sweat dotted her brow, causing several of the strands to stick. Her cheeks were fever-bright.

The prince approached the other side of the bed. "I could have you arrested for what you did to me, and what you allowed to happen to the princess's blood slave."

"I plan to leave as soon as she's healed. If you want me to spend my remaining days here wedding Synda, killing your father, taking over the kingdom and ordering your torture, you'll threaten me again." Actually, that wasn't a bad plan. It was quick and easy and effective—but it meant being with someone other than Tink. "If not, you'll shut your mouth."

The prince shut his mouth.

Kane hated that a doctor couldn't help her, hated that only time would heal this woman who'd snuck past his defenses—if there was even a cure. But he hated the feeling of helplessness more, of doing nothing but waiting for her to awaken…or die.

CHAPTER SEVENTEEN

JOSEPHINA TUMBLED THROUGH a world of darkness, every corner offering a new chamber of horrors. Screams of agony here. The worst kind of silence there. Big, fat insects everywhere, buzzing around her, biting at her. Pangs of the most intense, bone-deep hunger she'd ever experienced, burning, gnawing at her insides. And rage, so much rage filled her; she wanted to fight someone, anyone. Wanted to conquer and destroy. But how could she do either? She was conquered herself, already destroyed.

Her blood was molten, liquid flame. Her throat hurt, as if it had been scraped raw with a blade. Did she have any skin left? She felt peeled…exposed to the world.

"Kane," she tried to shout, but no sound emerged.

Where was he? Where was *she?* What had happened to her?

Memories of a life she hadn't lived bombarded her. She swung a sword, beheading a demon. She stood over the dying body of a human soul, laughing. She watched a winged female with desire building in her veins. Death…death…all around her. Pain, suffering, regret. More than even a legion could bear.

Something soft brushed against her cheek, trailed along her jaw. "I'm here, Tink. I'm not going anywhere."

His voice. Soothing, beseeching. Pulling her out of the darkness, out of the horror, and into a light…a growing light…brighter and brighter. A moan left her as she struggled to rise.

"That's the way, beautiful girl. Come on, sweetheart. You can do it."

Her eyelids pried apart, and in the next instant she was peering into Kane's handsome face. *I'm safe now. He'll keep me safe.*

Their gazes got tangled up, neither of them able to look away, and relief softened his expression. Yet, despite the relief, lines of tension bracketed his eyes and mouth. His skin was pallid, and his clothing wrinkled. His hair was spiked, as if he'd stuck his finger into a light socket.

"You're back."

"Where'd I go?" Her voice was a mere croak. She tried to reach up to massage the soreness out of her throat, but her arm proved too heavy to lift. "Where am I?"

His lashes fused, hiding whatever emotion her words had elicited. "I brought you to my bedroom."

Her gaze, the only thing she could currently move, swept around to find…yes, Kane's bedroom. She recognized it immediately—while hers was small, plain and filled with eight cots and seven other females, his was total luxury. A gold-and-crystal chandelier hung overhead. The walls were splashed with gold-framed paintings by famous Fae artists who had died throughout the centuries.

Josephina sprawled across the huge, ultra-soft four-poster bed, wearing a T-shirt far too big for her, as well as her gloves, with a velvet blanket covering the lower half of her body.

"Do you remember the bar?" Kane asked. "The fight? The three warriors you touched?"

Remember…yes. She'd touched one, then the other, and the other, and a surge of strength had overcome her, such beautiful strength. But then…oh, then, the darkness had enclosed her, dragging her down, down, down, into a cavern of despair and helplessness.

"You drew the evil out of them and into yourself. I carried you to the palace," Kane continued. He removed his hand from her face, becoming her anchor, the only thing holding her here. "You've been in bed for four days."

Four days!

The realization sickened her. Her father would be angry with her—had probably even tried to force her out of bed at some point. She had duties, and she would be punished for failing them. But the real reason she panicked? Kane's wedding was now that much closer.

"Don't worry," he said. "I dealt with your father."

His gorgeous hazels were still glued to her, seeming to drink her in and memorize every feature. She could barely blink, caught up in the intensity of him, captivated by the majesty of him…confused by the number of injuries on him.

"What happened to you?" she asked. "My father? Brother?"

He rubbed the angry cuts on his forehead. "Disaster."

She'd always hated Synda's demon, and she'd always hated the Lords' demons. They wreaked havoc on their keepers and ruined…everything. But what she'd felt then could not compare to what she felt now. She wanted Disaster dead. "Well, thank you for taking care of me." Besides her mother, he was the first to ever do so.

He smiled softly…tenderly. "I thought you'd curse at me."

For a lot of things, yes. But that? Never. "Why?"

"I haven't forgotten your desire to die, Tink," he said, his voice a low, menacing scrape.

"Not that way," she whispered. Never that way. The evil she'd housed would have dragged her straight into hell, condemning her to a worse fate than the one she now lived.

Kane toyed with the ends of her hair, and the contact, slight though it was, awakened the very pangs she'd battled at the dressmaker's shop. Hunger—for him. Need—for his touch. Desire—for so much more.

"Have you ever spoken to the Moirai?" he asked.

Even the name tainted the atmosphere around her. "No."

"Have you heard of them?"

"Of course. They claim to weave the fates."

"Claim?" He released her to lift a cup of water from the nightstand. "You think it's a lie?"

"Absolutely." Until that moment, Josephina hadn't realized how thirsty she was. Everything else was forgotten.

He placed a straw at her lips, and she sucked and sucked and sucked, the cool liquid soothing her throat.

Kane watched her mouth…her throat.

When the cup was empty, she leaned back, licked her lips.

He watched that, too.

"More?" he asked, heat darkening his eyes.

"Yes, please." But she wasn't sure what she wanted—more water, or more Kane.

He lifted a pitcher and poured more heavenly water into the cup. The moment the straw returned to her lips, the bottom of the cup broke. Cold liquid splashed over her, and she gasped.

"I'm so sorry," Kane mumbled, hopping up to gather

something to help. He started to dry her off, cursed, then handed her the rags.

When she finished, he hesitantly offered her another cup.

"Don't worry about it," she said. "I probably needed a bath."

His lips twitched with the barest thread of amusement. "I made sure you stayed clean."

Cheeks heating, she drained the water. At last, strength began to return to her, running through her veins, sparking her organs to life.

"Why do you think the Moirai are liars?" Kane asked.

"Well, to start, people have free will. Fate doesn't decide what direction they ultimately go."

His fingers returned to her hair, as if drawn by an invisible string. "William said something similar."

"William is quite wise."

He rolled his eyes. "Continue."

"Fate says everything is *meant to be*. But I can't believe my mother was meant to endure such hardships. I can't believe I was meant to be a slave."

"Explain."

One-word demands had never been so…sexy. Shivering, she said, "My father decided he wanted my mother, so, he took her. It was her decision to stay here. I was born and told I had a purpose, and it was my choice to believe it or reject it."

He peered at her, silent…thinking? "What about marriages? Do you believe there's someone destined for everyone?"

"Oh, yes, but not everyone follows that destiny." She hoped he heard what she wasn't saying—he needed to be careful about Synda and White. "Hence, free will can get in the way."

"So, you're saying choices *and* destiny shape the course of our lives?"

"I think so, yes. It's just easier to blame fate for all of the mistakes."

He ghosted his thumb along the curve of her jaw, drawing goose bumps to the surface. "You've been hurt by other people's choices."

Caught up in the intimacy of the moment, she leaned into the touch. "So have you."

"Yes." A pause, as if he struggled with his next words. "The Moirai say I'm destined to start an apocalypse."

On top of wedding the girl, White? Did he believe them?

The spell was broken. "Those hobags aren't all-powerful, Kane."

"Hobags?" He grinned.

How could she make him understand? "They simply thrive on chaos, planting their ideas into our heads. *We* think about it, *we* obsess about it, ultimately acting in a manner befitting what was said, thereby *causing* what was said to happen."

"Like a self-fulfilling prophecy." He arched a brow. "You know all of this, and yet you've never spoken to them?"

Touch me again. Gather me in your arms. Tell me you don't desire White. "Well, I never said they hadn't spoken to me."

He stiffened. "So you've actually met with them?"

"Yes." And the meeting had enraged her.

Years ago, the three hags told her she was destined to cause her mother's death. All she'd managed was a few gasps before they'd shooed her away, but from that moment on, Josephina had begun to fear hurting her beloved mother in any way, and had overanalyzed her every word and action.

Josephina had stopped eating, stopped sleeping. She'd stopped visiting her mother, too afraid of what damage she might cause. After a while, the fear had become infectious. Her mother had begun to worry over Josephina's health, and had mourned over Josephina's perceived defection. Glorika had lost weight, energy and vitality—and soon, the king's favor. She was cast out of his bedroom and back to the servant quarters.

There, she was treated more shamefully than ever. She was shunned by the women and secretly harassed by many of the men. The queen had taken great pleasure in humiliating her at every turn.

In the end, Glorika had killed herself. All because Josephina had stayed away from her. So, yes. Josephina had helped destroy her. Had she never worried, nothing bad would have happened to either of them. Her mother would still be alive.

"The best decision you'll ever make is to forget what the Moirai told you," she said.

He shook his head, dark locks of hair falling over his brow. "I carry the demon of Disaster. How could I *not* cause an apocalypse?"

She heard the dread in his voice, the torment. "Think about it. You're doing everything in your power to stop yourself from causing an apocalypse, aren't you? And yet everything you've done has only exacerbated the problem."

"So I should do nothing?"

"No. You should live. Truly live. Stop looking over

your shoulder, expecting disaster. Stop planning your next step based on the demon's actions."

He pushed out an angry breath. "I'm not sure whether you're wise, as I first assumed, or the dumbest woman on the planet."

Dumb? Dumb! "Well, you're definitely *not* the sweetest man."

"I never claimed to be."

"Because no one would have believed you!" Surely that wasn't *her* shrieking at him?

He massaged the back of his neck, not seeming to notice her outburst. "The Moirai told me something else. They said I'm destined to marry the keeper of Irresponsibility…or White, the girl you met in the club."

What he didn't say, but she heard: he was to stay away from a Fae blood slave. "Don't let the hags decide your bride, Kane. You decide. Wed for love, or don't wed at all."

Kane leaned down, putting them nose-to-nose. He whispered, "I used to be, you know."

He was so close, his clean, soapy scent thick in her nose. Heat radiated from him, enveloping her, and the tremors within her increased. "Used to be what?"

"Sweet."

She reached up, shifted the strands of his hair through her gloved fingers. How badly she wanted skin-to-skin. "You still have your moments. But what changed?"

"Me. Everything." His gaze dropped to her lips, and lingered, his pupils expanding. "I shouldn't want to kiss you again, but I do. I want it. Not because of the Moirai but because of you. What are you doing to me?"

Her heart skipped a treacherous beat. "I'm not doing anything."

"Oh, you're doing something." Slowly he lowered his head…coming closer…closer still. "I already stole your first kiss, and I shouldn't steal the second."

What if I give it away? "Are you afraid?"

"Yes," he admitted. "I've never wanted a woman the way I want you."

"Not even Synda?" she managed to respond, breathless.

"I understand why you're so insecure about her. Your family has always picked her over you. But that isn't the case with me. I have wanted you since moment one. I have never actually wanted Synda. She's a means to an end, nothing more."

A means to an end—not a bride. He *wouldn't* wed the girl. And he'd wanted Josephina since moment one.

Her.

Overcome, Josephina threw her arms around him, and pressed her lips against his. He moaned, his tongue thrusting into her mouth, demanding the very response she yearned to give. He was a master, sublimely skilled, every stroke propelling her need higher, and maybe she gave as good as she got, because his control seemed to be fraying at the edges, little growls rising from him, his tongue thrusting harder, faster.

Then he straightened, a funny look on his face as he traced a fingertip over lips now swollen and tingling from his possession. "You make me burn, Tinker Bell."

"Kane," she said, then gulped.

"Yes."

"That's not me. You're actually on fire."

Frowning, he glanced down at his shoulder. The ends of his hair were tipped with flames that had jumped from the lamp on the nightstand.

Josephina patted the strands, dousing the fire.

"Stupid Disaster."

"I'm not afraid of him."

He toyed with the collar of her shirt, making her skin tingle. "Still want me?"

"More than anything," she admitted softly.

Tentative, he licked the seam of her lips. When nothing terrible happened, he gave her a wicked grin.

"Gonna make you so happy you said that."

He tugged at the cover, pulling it down, down, down her body, baring her legs, his heated eyes never straying from hers…even as he reached for the hem of the shirt. He crawled onto the bed, graceful as a panther, and straddled her waist.

Breathing was impossible, her insides so keyed and ready for whatever he planned, she could only pant as he continued lifting her shirt, baring her breasts to his view.

He paused to look his fill, his pupils so large his irises were devoid of color.

"You are so beautiful."

She trembled as he reached out and cupped her, kneaded her.

"So perfect."

She was shaking too badly to reply.

His fingers slid down her belly, stopped at the top of her panties. He traced the band, and she quivered.

He stilled, frowned. His ears twitched. "Someone's coming."

No! It was just getting good!

Kane jackknifed to his feet, and Josephina sat up, smoothing her clothes in place, trying not to huff her disappointment. No longer was her warrior vibrating with arousal. He was eerily still, a living blade, ready to slash.

Four guards burst into the room, Leopold at the helm.

The prince scowled when he spotted them. “Josephina Aisling. The princess has been charged with baring her body to outsiders. Now that you’re awake, you are to be taken to the throne room to hear your punishment.”

CHAPTER EIGHTEEN

As the guards approached the bed, Kane growled from deep within his chest. A feral sound. A primitive warning—uncontrolled danger awaited. The males weren't getting near the girl. If they insisted, they would die. He'd taken care of her all four days. He'd left her side only once, to visit the king. He had bathed her. Had poured water down her throat. He and he alone had done everything that needed doing to ensure she survived.

She belonged to him, and he took care of what was his. Even though he'd decided to leave her to save her from Disaster.

That was still the plan. *Had* to be the plan. But she'd woken up, looked at him with those haunting crystal eyes, her cheeks hollowed, the fever-flush finally gone from her skin, that mass of dark hair tangled around her delicate shoulders, and all of his possessive instincts had risen with undeniable fury.

Mine, he'd thought, even as Disaster had screamed in denial.

Kane withdrew a bloodstained dagger.

The guards stopped to eye the prince, silently asking for direction.

The prince watched him, daring him to act. With only a word, the man could have Kane on his knees, pain consuming him, leaving him helpless. Exactly what the male had to want. Kane could be carted to the dungeon, leaving Tink to face the punishment alone.

The only recourse was to take this matter to the king. Together.

The last time he'd visited the king, he'd requested permission to doctor Tink. Tiberius had reluctantly agreed, but in exchange, Kane had had to promise his friends would attend the wedding.

"I'll escort her," Kane said as calmly as he was able. He would fix this situation, and then he would leave. The time had come. "Tell me, though. How did you know she had awakened?"

"Voices were heard."

"I'm not going anywhere," Tink said, fear glazing eyes that had been filled with passion only a few minutes ago. "I'm staying here."

"Josephina," the prince began, his features softening with a desire he had no right to feel. "I'm sorry, I am, but I have to do this."

Kane offered Tink his hand. "Trust me, sweetheart. I won't let anything happen to you."

Her shudder rocked the entire bed. She closed her eyes, breathed in…held it, held it…then exhaled. When she faced him, he could tell she was battling tears. Yet still she bravely placed her hand in his, the thickness of her glove hiding the temperature of her skin.

"I need to change into my uniform," she said.

He'd had it cleaned. It was folded and waiting on the nightstand for her. He pulled the garment over her head, fitting it over the T-shirt he'd dressed her in, never letting anyone see anything they shouldn't.

He tugged her to her feet, and she hmphed as she tumbled into his side. He snaked his arm around her waist, holding her up.

"Follow me." Back ramrod-straight, Leopold turned on his heel and marched from the room. The guards were quick to pursue.

Kane practically had to carry the weakened Tink. He wondered where William had gone. Was he still in town? Kane could have used his help right now.

Synda had come to see Kane to ask his opinion about patterns and fabrics and other things he couldn't remember, and he'd asked her how William had gotten her home, what the warrior had said, but she'd claimed to have forgotten.

As he stalked down the hallway, he noticed the maids were pressed against the walls. They smiled and waved when they spotted him, some even coyly twirling the ends of their hair.

Drop the girl, and pick one of these, Disaster commanded.

Die, Kane shot back.

His boot untied, and he tripped.

He straightened, stopping in his tracks when he spotted a portrait of—no way, just no way—but it *was* of him and it *was* hanging next to one of Synda.

"What are you—" Tink's gaze followed the line of his and she nearly choked on a sudden giggle. "Oh, wow. You look so…"

"Don't say it," he gritted.

"Don't say that you look *happy?*"

If the situation hadn't been so dire, Kane would have taken a moment to gouge out the eyes of everyone who'd walked through this hallway. Apparently, William had stuck around the palace after dropping off the princess. There was no other way the Fae royal family could have gotten one of the monstrosities Anya had commissioned.

He bit the side of his cheek. He wanted the people of this realm to respect his strength; they would be less likely to act against him. But anyone peering at the canvas with him bent over a zebra-print lounge chair, wearing only a blue feather boa while holding a rose between his teeth, would assume he was…

Steam had to be curling from his nose.

No wonder Leopold hadn't minded the king's directive to leave Tink in Kane's care. No wonder the prince hadn't sought secret vengeance for being chopped in the throat and threatened. *This* was punishment enough.

I'm gonna tear William a new one.

By the time the group reached the throne room, the air was thick with flowery scents and as cloying as usual. His nose wrinkled in disgust; he hadn't gotten used to the smell, and he doubted he ever would.

The king perched upon his golden throne, and just as before, Synda occupied the throne at his left. The queen was nowhere to be seen.

"Lord Kane," the princess said with a nod of greeting. "Servant Josephina. So good to see you're up and about."

Tink stiffened, remained quiet.

Synda never ceased to amaze Kane. Her grip on reality was nonexistent, as was her ability to pick up on emotional cues or comprehend why a person would be angry with her.

"Lord Kane," the king acknowledged. "Before the proceedings begin, we must say how thrilled we were to meet your PMS."

Uh… "My what?"

"Your personal male secretary. He escorted the princess home the day of your shopping trip. We gave him a room in the same hall as yours."

Well, that answered that. "Very…generous of you."

"We want you happy here, Lord Kane."

"Then make a decree that Josephina isn't to be hurt."

The king pressed his lips into a stubborn line. "As *you* know, you were granted custody of Servant Josephina for the duration of her illness. Since she has recovered, we must now see to her duties."

Tink trembled, and he tightened his hold. He cataloged the rest of the room and everyone in it, planning for every eventuality. Escape. A mob. Battle.

He found Red, Black and Green standing on the sidelines, in front of the growing crowd of Fae upper class. Ice chips crystallized in his veins, giving new meaning to cold-blooded. Were they here for revenge against Tink? Or Kane?

"Do you know who those men are?" he asked, motioning to the warriors.

"Of course," the king replied. "They are your servants. They arrived this morning."

They did, did they? "My servants have a little problem with thieving. Make sure your guards accompany them wherever they go."

The king snapped, and guards rushed to take up new posts behind the warriors.

None of the three seemed to notice or care. They kept their gazes on Tink, their expressions bright with fascination. Kane suddenly realized why—and it had nothing to do with revenge. They wanted her to pull the darkness out of them once more and forever. They wanted to feel whole, untainted. Normal. She was the only way to accomplish such a feat.

Rage liquefied the ice. Rage directed at the warriors—and himself. He'd brought this on Tink. Him. No one else. Now, she had to face yet another disaster.

"It is time for Servant Josephina's sentence to be revealed," the king announced. *Bang, bang, bang,* he slammed his scepter on the ground.

Kane focused. One battle at a time, he thought.

"Because Princess Synda was caught undressing in public, Servant Josephina will be forced to undress here, to be branded on the chest with a mark of shame."

Tink cried out with alarm.

Kane roared a curse.

"But—" Leopold began, only to go silent when Tiberius shot him a narrowed look.

Four guards reached for her. Kane threw her behind him, using his body as a shield, and withdrew two daggers. The men paused, unsure how to proceed and survive.

William's boys stiffened, as if preparing to stomp to Kane's side and help him help Tink; but they remained in place, and he knew why. The three needed Tink alive and unharmed to get what they wanted from her and figured Kane wouldn't allow anything bad to happen to her. They expected him to fight for her, even though the outcome of that fight was unimportant to them. Amid the chaos, they could sweep Tink away. He wouldn't even be surprised if they'd been the ones to tattle to the king about what Synda had done in the tavern, just to set up this little scenario.

"I'll take the punishment," Kane called. A fight would be avoided, and he could force Tink to stay by his side.

The warriors would never try and take her so openly.

"He's going to remove his shirt," a female twittered.

"I know! It's going to be glorious!"

Tink's hands flattened on his back. "No, Kane. You can't." Her voice trembled with fear and upset. Ignoring her, the king pondered the suggestion for a moment. "You aren't blood of Princess Synda's blood," he said to Kane. "Therefore, the exchange would not be acceptable."

"Give Josephina to me, then. All of her. Now and forever. That kind of bond is as strong as blood, if not stronger."

Blue eyes lasered at him, direct and piercing. "You are to have my daughter and none other. She is the only female worthy of you."

One day, I'll cut out his tongue. "If the princess is my female, she is my responsibility. Therefore *I* am to decide her punishments, correct? *I* am to see them through."

The king stiffened. He knew he'd been caught in the web of his own rules. "Very well," he finally said. "You may have the blood slave as well, and use her as she is meant."

Knowing Tink was being placed in his care filled him with the greatest satisfaction he'd ever known. Enough to overshadow the only problem: he couldn't save Tink from further abuse without wedding Synda.

"Thank you," he said.

A nod of agreement. "I know better than most the power of an attraction for the wrong female—and that's what you feel for Servant Josephina, isn't it? If I take the girl away from you, you will want her even more. If I harm her, you will blame me. But if I give her to you, the yearning will quickly die."

Kane held back a humorless laugh at the king's ignorance. A yearning this strong *couldn't* die.

"He wants a servant? A servant?" Scowling, eyes glowing bright red, Synda removed one of her shoes and chucked the thing at Kane's head. He ducked just before contact. "You don't deserve me!"

"Now, now, darling," the king soothed. "Did you not hear me? The yearning will die."

He could stay long enough to wed the princess, Kane thought, then place Tink in the care of his friends. They would protect her as fiercely as he would, knowing what she meant to him. The Fae would leave her alone. The Phoenix would leave her alone just as soon as Kane took care of her—which he still planned to do—and all of Tink's problems would be solved now rather than later.

After the wedding, Tink would want nothing to do with him, of course, and he wouldn't be able to blame her. But she would be safe, he reminded himself.

She would also be in confined quarters with Torin. And Paris.

Dark fury scraped at his chest.

And what about Synda? What was he supposed to do with her? He loved his friends too much to make them responsible for such a mercurial brat. But he definitely had no desire to keep her with him, wherever he went.

"Please, don't do this," Tink whispered to him. Her fingers clutched at his shirt in an effort to pull him down to her height. "I don't want you harmed on my behalf."

Her concern touched him deeply, placed him that much further under her spell. "I told you I wouldn't allow you to be hurt, and I meant it."

"Kane," she said, sounding desperate now. "If you do this, I'll be angry with you."

"But you'll still kiss me better." He wasn't married yet.

Kane stepped forward, and tugged his shirt over his head. Feminine twitters rose throughout the room, and he rolled his eyes. He reached back and pulled Tink as close to him as possible. A portable fire pit was wheeled in from the side door and left in the center of the room. In strode a male holding a branding iron. He stuck the rod into the burning coals, allowing the metal to heat. Guards approached Kane's sides, intending to lock him in place. He shook them off and extended his arms.

"I won't budge," he proclaimed.

A nod from the king had the males backing down. Tiberius, Synda and Leopold leaned forward, each watching him, perhaps curious to know if he would keep his word.

"Kane," Tink said, quivering palms pressing on his shoulder blades. Fear radiated from her. "Please don't."

Silent, he reached behind and wrapped his arms around her, twining his fingers together, caging her against his hard back. She rested her forehead against him, and he thought he felt the wet warmth of a tear trickle down his spine.

The suspicion rocked him. Undid him. Because it meant she cared for him. A care that went deeper than desire.

Don't know if I can ever let her go.

The man lifted the rod, and steam curled from its end—a very large end shaped like a dragon. He approached Kane with hesitant steps.

"Do it," Kane commanded.

"No," Tink cried, violently shaking her head.

After a slight pause, the man jabbed the dragon into the center of Kane's chest and held it steady. Flesh instantly sizzled and melted away. Far more pain than he'd expected slashed through him, the scent of overcooked meat overshadowed the fragrance of flowers. He wanted to gag. Instead, he seethed. These people had thought to do this to Tink's delicate, beautiful body. *Would* have done it to her.

Disaster laughed as the man tried to remove the poker—and failed.

The metal had fused to Kane's sternum.

As hard as the man continued to pull, the dragon refused to budge,

Gritting his teeth, Kane gripped the shaft of the rod and jerked with all of his might. Separation was finally achieved—but the rod took some of his bone with it. He dropped the thing with a *thud*. In and out he breathed, trying to regain his bearings. First thing he noticed—utter silence filled the throne room. Everyone was waiting for his reaction.

Used to pain, he lifted his chin and said, "Next order of business. I wish to spend time with the princess, getting to know my future…bride." He had to keep her out of trouble. Had to do something to ensure she was tucked into bed without any more punishments thrown Tink's—or his—way.

"Oh, Daddy, you were right!" A grinning Synda stood up before her father could reply, and skipped to Kane's side, as if she'd never been angry, never tossed her shoe.

Tink ripped away from his hold.

He spun, tried to grab her. "You're coming with us."

Their gazes tangled in a heated clash. Hurt blazed from her, and he felt branded by the rod all over again.

"Tink…"

"Absolutely not. Excuse me, please," she said, pushing her way through the crowd, leaving the room.

He moved to follow her, but Synda clutched him by the wrist. "Let her go. She's nothing to us."

Rage had him spinning toward her, his teeth bared.

"You will not ever speak like that again. Do you understand me?"

She blanched under the ferocity of his attention.

King Tiberius pushed to his feet.

And Kane realized he had to play nice. He softened his voice, saying, "I don't want my…servants anywhere near Josephina."

The king's nod was stiff. He snapped his fingers and guards surrounded the three warriors, impeding any moves they might have made. "Your turn, Lord Kane. *I* don't want my daughter upset."

To Synda, Kane gritted, "Let's take a walk through the gardens. No…servant."

She gave a little pout. "You don't want to go back to my room?"

"No." He realized how insulting that probably sounded, considering everything else he'd done and said this day. "Like I said, I want to get to know you better first."

Synda beamed and Kane did his best not to grimace.

"Go with them," the king said to one of the guards. "See to their protection."

The only one in need of protection was Synda. From Kane. She'd unwittingly helped Tink get away. A killing offense.

Just get through the next few hours, and you can hunt your Fae down.

Once he found her, he wasn't going to let her out of his sight. He wasn't going to leave her, either, he realized. He couldn't. Not while William's kids were here.

Besides, Kane might be a magnet for disaster, but to him, there was nothing more magnetic than Tink, and he couldn't bear the thought of letting her go.

CHAPTER NINETEEN

JOSEPHINA RACED DOWN the hall, tears burning the backs of her eyes. Kane wanted to spend more time with Synda, a supposed means to an end. What end, exactly? Allegedly, his goal for being here was saving Josephina from—yes, okay, there was a good possibility he was catering to the princess for Josephina's sake.

Perhaps she shouldn't have let a sudden burst of jealousy and hurt send her fleeing Kane's side. The man had just suffered horrendous pain on her behalf, taking a punishment meant for her. But…if he would suffer through something like that, just to keep his word and prevent Josephina from being injured, he would be willing to wed Synda to keep her safe, too.

Another blessing. Another curse.

He might even desire such an outcome, at least on some level. After all, the Moirai had told him Synda could very well be the girl for him.

A choked sound escaped her. Kane was hers. Hers! And she didn't want to share him. His dark, tantalizing kisses had done something to her. Changed her. Now, she craved the heat and ache and crazed need only he could bring forth. She craved…more.

A hard hand latched onto her upper arm, stopping her progress and swinging her around. She came face-to-face with Leopold and experienced a sharp pang of dread.

When he noticed the wetness on her cheeks, he scowled. "What's wrong with you? You just escaped punishment."

"Let me go, *brother*." A shaming reminder for him.

One he failed to heed. "Me, you deny. Him, you cry for. Your demon-possessed beast is going to wed the princess and make you his mistress. You realize that, don't you?"

I will be no one's mistress. Not even Kane's. "Who are you to cast stones?"

The prince studied her for a long while, probing her features for any sign of weakness. "No matter what I say, you'll still want him. I can tell." He hauled her to the window and flicked the curtains apart. "Look out there. See him for what he truly is."

Kane and Synda were in the garden Josephina and her mother had once tended. He was still shirtless, his gorgeous, muscled chest a mess, the wound in the center open and raw. He bent down and picked up a rock, then threw it a good distance away. Synda took off in a run, searching for the rock. When she found it, she picked it up and skipped back to Kane.

He threw it again.

She chased it again.

He was…playing fetch with her?

Oh, yes, she thought. He was definitely doing this for Josephina's benefit. A smile lifted the corners of her lips, only to fall a second later. The revelation didn't change the course he'd set.

Leopold crowded behind her, pressing her against the glass—pressing hardness to softness. She tried to squirm away from him, but he planted his hands beside her, caging her in, holding her captive. Fear sparked to sickening life.

"I'll treat you better than he ever could," he whispered.

"Let me go, Leopold. Now."

"I shouldn't want you," he continued as if she hadn't spoken. "Everyone would be horrified if they knew. But I look at you, and I can't help myself. The desire is there."

"Resist it."

"You don't think I've tried?"

"Keep trying."

He laughed without humor, and it was a tortured sound. "No, I'm done trying. I'm done waiting. You're everything I need. I know you understand me in a way no one else can. You're lonely, admit it. You need someone to lean and rely on, just like I do. I know you'll finally be the one to satisfy me…the way I'll satisfy you."

"No. No!" she said, intensifying her struggles.

"Be still. I only plan to take a little, to show you how good it can be."

A little was far too much. Though she had no kind of training, instinct kicked in and she elbowed him in the stomach, stomped on his foot and head-butted his chin. As powerful as he was, he gave no reaction.

He kissed the side of her neck. "Settle down and accept it. It's going to happen."

Don't do this. Please, don't do this...

As if he'd heard her silent plea from the garden, Kane stiffened and looked up. His gaze found the window and narrowed. Rage darkened his features, and he jolted into a dead sprint, blasting past the guard, knocking him to the ground. Synda tried to follow after him, but he was too fast for her. The princess stopped and hunched over, struggling for breath.

If Leopold had noticed the activities below, he gave

no reaction. He nibbled on Josephina's earlobe. "You're going to like what I do to you. I promise," he said, then spun her around.

He tried to mesh his lips against hers. She turned her head away, tried to push him. He grabbed her wrists and pinned her arms at her sides.

Panic choked the air from her lungs, but she managed to jerk up her knee, aiming for his groin. But he'd angled his lower body, as if he'd expected such a move, and she ended up rubbing herself against him.

He moaned with pleasure, and she mewled with distress.

Kane flew around the corner and tackled the prince to the ground. Leopold was too stunned to fight or use his ability as Kane hammered fist after fist into his face.

"You don't touch her! Ever! Do you hear me?" Kane spit the words between punches. Blood sprayed in every direction, raining over the walls. The sound of breaking bones echoed. A tooth skidded across the floor. "You don't touch her, and you don't touch me, you don't touch anyone. Understand? *You don't touch!*"

Leopold's body began to flop with the force of the blows, but not once did he try and shield himself—he couldn't. He was too busy being unconscious…maybe dying.

Shaking, Josephina drew her arms around her middle. "Kane!"

As quickly as the one-sided battle had started, it stopped. Kane swung around, his narrowed gaze landing on her. His irises were bright red, glowing. He was panting. "Are you all right?"

She nodded, bit her lip. "You have to stop." As upset as she'd been with him, she couldn't stand the thought of Kane bearing any further pain. "Any wrongdoing against the prince will be punished, and your only blood slave is—"

"No. Never."

Me, she silently finished.

He straightened and closed the distance between them. His hands dripped with crimson as he reached up and cupped her cheeks. He flushed the moment he noticed the wet streaks he'd left behind, and released her to lift the hem of her skirt and wipe her clean.

"Sorry," he muttered, clearly shamed. Then he flushed again, and cursed. "Your new dress is ruined."

"That's okay. I can—"

"I ruined it," he continued hollowly.

"Really, Kane, it's no big deal. I don't care about the dress."

"I'm buying you a hundred more. Nicer ones, no more uniforms. You belong to me now. I get to decide."

"Listen to me. You have to leave the palace before anyone sees what you did. All right? Okay?"

His gaze found hers, searched deeply. Whatever he saw caused the red to fade from his eyes, and his expression to soften. "Neither of us will be punished. The prince isn't going to admit what happened. Are you?" he shouted down at the now-writhing male, who was in the process of coming to. "Because you know this was only the appetizer. I'm capable of worse."

An agonized moan was the only response.

Booted footsteps filled the little alcove, and the guard Kane had knocked down in the garden came racing around the corner. He spotted the prince on the ground and stopped to reach for a weapon.

Josephina threw a protective arm in front of Kane and rushed out, "He totally could have been like this when we got here," at the same time Kane said, "He fell."

Neither one of them had lied.

"Get him to his room and call a doctor," Kane added. "And tell Prince Leopold to be more careful from now on. The next incident might kill him."

The guard gulped, nodded.

Kane scooped Josephina into his arms and stomped off. She offered no protest.

"Lord Kane," the guard called. "I think I'm supposed to follow you."

"No need. I'm headed to my room." A few minutes later, they arrived at their destination. Kane stopped in the private bathroom and eased her onto the toilet lid.

"Stay," he commanded.

She raised a brow. "Treating *me* like a dog now?"

His smile was sweet and kind and even a little sad. "That's probably better than the alternative."

"Which is?"

He flicked her the barest of glances. "A lover."

The very heat Leopold had tried—and failed—to attain now fanned to life. Just like that. With only two words.

"I have to get this blood off me," he said, "and I want you within reach. So. Like I told you, stay. Please." He messed with the knobs on the shower until water began to spew. Then he placed his fingers at the waist of his pants, paused, as if trying to decide what to do next. Finally, he exhaled heavily and unfastened the material.

The pants hit the floor and he stepped out of the pool of material.

His beauty stole her breath. His legs were long, muscular and sinewy, with the lightest dusting of hair. Sexy…perfect.

He watched her as he hooked his thumb in the waist of his underwear.

Sweet mercy, I'm finally going to die. I'll have a heart attack. Surely. "So, uh, how did you know to look at the window?" *Good. Keep it casual. Maybe he won't realize you're staring.*

He paused, saying, "It's strange. I felt like there was a string attached to my gaze, tugging it up."

She gulped. Why was he stalling? "Has anything like that ever happened to you before?"

"No."

Were they...connected somehow?

At last, he pushed the underwear down his legs.

Oh.

Oh, my.

Kane, keeper of Disaster, was utterly *magnificent.* He was sun-worshipped, and chiseled with strength from head to toe. The wings of the butterfly tattoo appeared more jagged than before, stretching closer and closer to his...his...*there.*

Oh, my, oh, my, oh, my.

The heat in her cheeks intensified, and her mouth went dry. He wasn't a man, but a warrior. Built for battle, honed by fire and steel. Powerful in a way so few would ever know or understand.

"Do I want to know what you're thinking?" he asked, his deep voice sounding hoarse.

She forced her gaze to lift, and met his stare. The air around them instantly sizzled with the awareness she couldn't ever seem to escape. They were alone. He was naked.

Oh, the things I want to do to him...

"I don't know," she said, the huskiness of her voice surprising her. "Do you?"

His heated stare bore into her. "It'll be safer for us both if I deny the truth."

Clang. Clang. Clang.

Weapon after weapon hit the floor. Soon there was a pile of daggers, guns and throwing stars at her feet.

"Give me your dress. I'm going to wash it."

"I—*hmph*."

He'd closed the distance and forced her to stand, reaching around her to unzip the back of her dress. He had the material shoved down her arms, past her waist and to her feet before she realized what was happening.

As close as he was, as naked as he was, as aroused as *she* was…sweet mercy, her blood heated to a dangerous degree, and every inch of her skin tingled, craving more of him. Only, ever him. Her limbs began to tremble. And his…his…his tattoo was getting larger, because one of the butterfly's wings rode the length of his…

Seriously dying, she thought.

It grew, and it thickened, and it hardened, and it mesmerized her.

"Oh, my goodness," she said on a moan.

"Step out of the gown, sweetheart."

Yes.

For balance, she put her hands on his shoulders before doing as he'd commanded. Contact had her gasping. Even as warm as she already was, he was hot enough to burn her—and she found that she liked being burned. His muscles were hard and intractable, yet covered by silk.

He straightened, but didn't move out of reach right away. He peered down at her, his breathing fast and shallow, a match to hers. The still-sizzling air thickened with steam from the tub…with desire…with a thousand other things she couldn't name.

"I…you…" she whispered. *Do something.*

He blinked, shook his head. Stiffening, he turned and entered the shower, then jerked the curtain across the rod, blocking her view. Within seconds, the rod was bending in the middle, nearly collapsing. She heard the whoosh of skin against porcelain, as if Kane had slipped. He cursed.

Her knees gave out, and she fell back onto the toilet lid. Soon, the scent of soap wafted to her. She breathed deeply, letting it wash through her, subdue her trembling. "Kane?"

Only the slightest pause before he said, "Yes, Tink."

"Thank you." They weren't the words she'd wanted to say, but for now, they would do. "For everything. I mean it."

There was a bang, as if he'd just thrown his fist into the tile. "I shouldn't have left you alone."

She heard the self-castigation in his tone, and sighed. "I ran away from you, remember? And besides, you can't be with me every second of every day."

"Want to bet?"

Don't tempt me. "So…how many fights have you been in?"

"You mean your storybooks haven't given an exact tally?"

"No. And I wish they had. You're quite good."

"You will be, too. I'm going to train you."

"Really?"

"Yes, really."

"But other men will make fun of you if they find out."

"Why would they care?"

"Women aren't supposed to learn how to fight," she said, "and anyone who dares to teach us is shunned."

"That's dumb."

Agreed. In the Fae realm, men were supposed to be their protectors, but as Leopold had proven, protection was often overlooked in favor of lust and greed. "You don't care about being shunned?"

"By these people? I'd consider it a blessing."

She twirled a strand of hair around her finger. "I have to ask you a question."

"Anything."

"Are you seriously going to marry Synda?" She'd meant to ask as matter-of-factly as she'd asked everything else, but that hadn't exactly happened. She'd whispered, instead, all of her hopes seeping from her voice.

And rather than answer, he began whistling.

Well, that was answer enough, wasn't it?

Disappointment, frustration and anger pooled in the pit of her stomach. She'd been right. His feelings wouldn't change his course.

"On days like this, I wish I had Dear Heloise on speed dial. There's blood on my girl's dress," he muttered. "Should I use club soda or vinegar?"

My girl's dress, he'd said. My girl. Josephina.

Argh! *You can't have more than one, Kane,* she nearly shouted.

The water shut off. "Throw me a towel."

Josephina pulled a white cloth from the cabinet, then volleyed the material over the rod.

"Thanks."

"Welcome," she said with more sharpness than she'd intended.

The curtain was brushed aside, and she had a brief realization that there was no steam—why?—before her mind…completely…derailed. Kane was still naked, of course he was, but now he was glistening. His hair was darker when it was wet, and dripping water down his face. The dragon brand on his chest was no longer red, but already scabbed and black. The towel was draped around his hips, hiding his butterfly tattoo—and other things.

Breath caught in her throat as he hooked her dress to the bar. The soaked ends of the cotton smacked together.

"I need something to wear. I need to leave the room," she managed to say. "I have duties." *And I need to get away from you. Before I forget I don't like to share.*

"I'll see to the duties. You're going to stay in here and rest."

Her eyes widened with bafflement. "You can't. I can't."

"I'd love to see you try and stop me. Or leave this room. Now make a list of what you have to do."

If he wanted to do her chores, fine. Opulens would see him and laugh. Even the servants would snicker. Josephina would finally have time away from him—time of peace. The feelings he stirred…she was beginning to hate them. Their intensity.

Grinning with sugary sweetness, she stalked into the bedroom and dug a pen and pad of paper from the nightstand. Then she wrote. And wrote. And wrote. He used the silent minutes to strap on his weapons, rifle through the contents of the closet and dress in the clothes the king had provided for him. Her wrist was aching by the time she finished the list.

He approached her, wearing a black shirt and black pants, and looking absolutely edible despite having covered up his magnificent body. She handed over the paper.

He gazed at it, scowled. "You do all of this?"

"Almost every day."

He read over the list a second time. "I should just kill your father and brother right now."

"And be hunted by the Fae for the rest of your life?"

"That doesn't worry me," he said, and he sounded sincere.

"It should. I know Tiberius has allowed you many liberties, and you probably think my entire race is a joke—otherwise you wouldn't be so cavalier—but you haven't seen everyone revved up for a blood vendetta. I have."

"I'm still not worried."

She anchored her hands on her hips. "If the Fae want you dead and fail to find you, they'll find your closest friends and torture them to force you out of hiding. Even the famed Lords of the Underworld."

"And if I'm already dead?"

"They'll do it just for fun."

CHAPTER TWENTY

In seconds, Kane had the lock on his bedroom door rigged, keeping Tink in and everyone else out. Ropes of guilt threatened to jerk him under a river of shame, which was ridiculous. He was doing her a favor. She needed rest and he needed to make sure she was safe and, prisoner or not, this was the only way to ensure those things. Maybe one day she'd even thank him.

Battling a sense of urgency, he hustled together a handful of the servants and issued a round of orders. The humans rushed around to take care of the twenty-nine items on Tink's list—and avoid the consequences of failure. Soon, the wrinkles were being steamed out of curtains, the floors were being scrubbed, the banisters were being polished, and the queen's bathroom was being cleaned.

The last was a chore meant to humiliate Tink, nothing more, he would bet. At breakfast, he'd witnessed the way the queen watched her, with resentment in those royal blue eyes. And he didn't have to guess why. Tink was living proof the king had cheated, and Queen Penelope was lashing out in the only way she could. But that crap ended today. No longer would Tink serve a single member of the royal family.

She'd been placed in Kane's care. She would serve him, and no one else.

He smiled. Tink would have balked if she'd heard his thoughts.

After speaking with one of the guards, he'd learned that Synda, his other responsibility, had decided to go for another walk in the garden, without protection and despite the Phoenix infestation.

As he stomped outside, a brutal wind suddenly kicked up, causing a hoe to lift from the ground and slam into him. When Kane failed to find the girl in the garden, he prowled into the forest. One hour passed, then two, but he found no tracks to suggest Synda—or even Petra—was out there. He would bet Synda had met someone, had sex, and returned to the palace. *Sounds about right.* As for Petra…he wasn't sure. He only knew she wasn't the type to give up.

Frustrated, he returned to the palace.

What a mess.

Disaster released a maniacal laugh.

Kane moved through the corridors, staying in the shadows, watching, listening. This had become his nightly ritual. He liked to make sure everyone was where they were supposed to be, staying out of trouble, and making no plans to come after Tink. The king snaked around the far corner, leading his new mistress toward his suite of rooms. The man was huffing and puffing with eagerness, his hands already roaming under the girl's dress. The girl muttered an encouragement, with zero inflection in her voice. She sounded dead.

They disappeared through the door, and Kane moved on. Synda was now in her bedroom, playing strip poker with Red, Green and Black. No surprises there, though Kane was relieved she was back at the palace at least. Where was White? In the billiards room, he discovered a surprisingly healthy Leopold playing with three human maids. All three had long, black hair.

Like Tink.

Kane pressed his heels more firmly into the floor. *Can't kill him without causing Tink problems.*

"You missed your shot," Leopold said to the one holding the cue. "You'll have to pay the penalty."

The girl crooked her finger at him. "I'm more than willing."

Leopold advanced on her, bending her over the table as he smashed his lips into hers. The other females watched, giggling.

Kane had heard the gossip. He knew the king had despised his son since his birth, yet Synda, the eldest, the one with the freaking mental disorder, he adored. What Kane didn't know was why.

He backed out of the room. In the hallway he paused, booted footsteps claiming his attention.

"—must have chased the Phoenix horde out of the realm," a guard said as he marched past.

Neither he nor his companion noticed Kane in the shadows.

"Cowards," the other spat.

In the next room over, a group of servants were dusting and straightening a sitting room with a pink couch, pink loveseat, and multiple pink chairs.

"—just like her mother."

"I know! I hear she's sleeping in his room."

A dreamy sigh wafted through the air. "I'd love to sleep in his room."

A muscle twitched below his eye. They were talking about Tink, insinuating she was a…that she was his… He couldn't even think the word anymore without wanting to kill someone. Painfully. He left the room—and ran into White.

"Are you following me?" he demanded.

She shrugged, unabashed.

He stepped around her, but she grabbed onto his wrist. He jerked from the contact, while Disaster purred.

"I'm confused about you, Kane, and I don't like being confused."

"That's not my problem."

A grinning William stumbled from the queen's bedroom, and White rushed away down the hall.

"Hurry back, my darkling," the queen called, oblivious to her audience.

"As if anything could keep me away for long, my pet," the warrior twittered.

Kane stopped, waiting, his hands fisted.

The moment William shut the door, Kane was in his face, demanding softly, "What do you think you're doing?"

The grin fell away, revealing a scowl of irritation. "Besides fighting a gag reflex? I'm getting answers. Why? You think I was betraying you?"

"You say that like I'd be crazy to think so, but we both know you once stabbed Lucien in the chest."

"Ah, memories," the warrior said with a grin. "But you aren't trying to steal from me the way Lucien was. And by the way, I never do cougars free of charge. You so owe me for this."

He eased off, but only slightly. "What have you learned?"

"I'll tell you when I'm sure we're alone. Wouldn't want anyone to hear and think I actually enjoy helping my friends." William led him down the hall and around the corner, then shouldered a portion of the wall—it opened, revealing a secret passage Kane hadn't yet discovered. They entered the torch-lit space and pounded up a flight of creaking steps.

"Well," the warrior began, as promised, "the king recently found out our good friend Paris is screwing Sienna, the new ruler of the Titans. He also learned Sabin and Strider are whipped by Harpies, and that Lucien had his balls removed by Anarchy. He fears your family and wants to be a part of it, whatever the cost."

"Wow, so informative. Thanks for the old news."

But, hearing the facts stated so plainly, he had to wonder how deeply the king's desire ran. Enough to finally claim a connection to Tink, allowing Kane to wed her rather than the princess?

Wed…Tink, he thought. Tink. His bride. His wife.

His. Forever.

Happiness bloomed, as warm and bright as a ray of sunshine.

No! Disaster screamed, and the floor beneath Kane's feet cracked. *I'll kill her! Kill her so dead!*

Kane tripped, hit his knees on one of the steps. Could he really subject Tink to the demon's rages *forever?*

No. He couldn't.

But could he really wed Synda?

Maybe he should call his friends. They would come. Sienna commanded a legion of immortal soldiers. Harpies could chew through an army with both hands tied behind their backs and their legs hobbled. Anarchy could destroy the world and laugh while doing it. War could be waged against the Fae, and Kane would be able to free Tink without having to wed anyone.

But what if someone he loved was hurt? How would he be able to live with himself? Worse, he would once again prove himself to be a failure, unable to achieve success on his own.

So, no. He had so little pride left. He wouldn't go that route unless absolutely necessary.

"Okay, you've gone from turned on to pissed to dejected in three seconds. It's quite entertaining, and I'm flattered—I've always known you were crushing on me—but now I want in. What are you planning?" William asked.

"I wish I knew."

"Well, figure it out. The sooner you do, the sooner we can leave. If I have to go down on the queen one more time..." He shuddered. "Don't get me wrong, it's usually one of my favorite pastimes, but she's given my tongue frostbite."

"You think I'm not trying to figure this out?" he snapped. Whatever road he chose came with terrible consequences, and he was getting whiplash from deciding on one route, then changing his mind, then changing his mind again.

"You don't want to know what I think."

"You're right. If you aren't thinking about having sex, you're thinking about getting sex."

"I like that you know me so well. By the way, the queen and princess are playing some kind of game in the gardens tomorrow morning, and your Tinker Hell will be involved somehow. I suggest you make an appearance."

Another attempt to humiliate Servant Josephina—and if he heard that title again he was going to erupt. "I will. And you do me a solid and keep your kids out of my way. They claimed to be my assistants, just to get close to Tink."

"Well, yeah. It was my idea. They liked what she did for them and want more."

Kane shoved William against the wall, his hand wrapping around the male's windpipe and squeezing. "Your idea?"

Electric blues gleamed with amusement. "Yes, and this is the thanks I get? I did you a favor. You should appreciate having your enemy within reach. I would."

Bit by bit Kane eased his hold. "They can't have her. I'll kill them if they try." He might, anyway.

"Were you hit in the head? Of course I know that. Which is why I warned the boys about Lords of Pussy-whip Manor and their women." William motioned to the closed door in front. "And now, our little convo is over. This is a door to your hallway. Off you go, Candy Kane."

Kane left him without another word. Thankfully, there were no guards in the area, saving him the complication of sneaking. Everyone assumed he was inside—with his mistress.

As quietly as possible, he fixed his lock and entered his room. He wondered what Tink was doing, if she was mad at him. He didn't like the thought of her angry; he wanted her relaxed, happy.

He found her on the bed, buried under the covers. As he tiptoed forward, something in his chest softened. He reached the side of the mattress and gently pushed back the covers, desperate to see her face, perhaps brush his knuckles along her cheekbone. He saw…a bunched-up pillow?

As his mind sputtered to compute what this meant—had Tink done this or had someone done it for her? Was she safe?—he heard the rustle of clothing behind him. At his side, a shadow moved. Next, a quiet whistle caught his attention—glass being brandished through the air. Kane spun, and grabbed his would-be assailant.

A delicate bone structure registered first, followed by the heartwarming scent of rosemary and mint. Warm, soft skin. A feminine gasp. He realized it was Tink *after* he'd thrown her on the bed. She bounced up and down, and when she stilled she scrambled to press against the headboard, disheveled hair tumbling down her shoulders.

The vase she'd held shattered on the floor. Several pieces found their way into his shin.

He stood there, glaring down at her. "I could have killed you."

"Well, what do you know? You almost kept the first promise you ever made me." Eyes as dark as sapphires threw daggers at him.

Daggers that pierced him soul deep. He'd always experienced some kind of ache around her, but this was different. This affected every cell in his body, tearing him apart. "Is that what you still want? To die?"

"Right now I want *you* to die!" she huffed.

"Is that so?" he asked quietly.

The anger drained from her, and her gaze fell to the floor. "No. Okay. No. I'm sorry I said it. But I do think you need to learn a lesson. You trapped me in here, you…you…argh! I don't know a name terrible enough."

"I did you a favor. Seeing you in my clothes would have verified what everyone already thinks."

"What does everyone think?"

He arched a brow.

"I knew it! They don't just think I'm your property, they think I'm your slut!" She beat her little fists against the covers. When calm, she said, "But it doesn't matter. It *wouldn't have* mattered. No one would have seen me. I could have snuck to my room and stayed there."

"You're not exactly a girl who can be overlooked, Tink." And he would have utterly destroyed any man who *had* gotten a glimpse of her. Like, body parts and organs would have littered the floor.

"Don't be ridiculous. I've been overlooked all my life."

"Not by Leopold."

"Yes, well, he's out of commission right now, isn't he?"

"Actually, no. He's already healed." Kane eased onto the side of the bed, trying not to allow her nearness to affect his body this time—failing, as always. "Don't tell me you're upset about what I did to your brother."

"I'm not. I'm grateful. It's just that I had—"

"Chores. I know. They've been outsourced."

She blinked with incredulity. "You told the other servants to do them, and they obeyed you?"

"Yes." Drily, he added, "Some people actually fear my wrath."

Her lips turned down at the corners. Such lush, pretty lips, even when she was frowning. "Are you saying I should?"

Lord, save me. "No, Tink. You never should." He clasped her wrist and lifted her arm, knowing what he was about to do was dangerous, especially now, as the adrenaline of their clash burned the leash holding on to his desire. "Now that we've gotten the pleasantries out of the way, we're going to test out what you can do with your hands."

She tried to tug from his grip. "No way. I might hurt you."

"That should thrill you."

"Well, it doesn't."

"You don't have to sound so defeated about it." He removed one glove, then the other.

He'd never seen her hands before, he realized. They should have been soft, but they were bruised and scarred. Despite the barrier she always wore, calluses littered her palm and her nails were chipped.

Again she tried to tug away.

Again he held firm.

"Stop staring," she said, shifting uncomfortably.

"Why? I like what I'm looking at."

"Right, because they're so beautiful."

"They are. Actually, they're beyond beautiful." And that was the truth. Her hands spoke of hard work and a strength of character possessed by few. He placed a kiss on each of her knuckles, realized he should have waited until he knew whether or not she'd drain him, then released her.

She watched him through widening eyes.

"Touch me," he commanded.

"You…you trust me not to purposely take from you, just to escape your room?"

"I do."

"But why? I just tried to bash your skull with a vase. And what if I take from you accidentally, huh? What then?"

He shrugged. "What happens will happen. We have to know what we're dealing with."

Even more adamant, she shook her head. "No. I'm not going to risk you."

Did she have any idea how telling those words were? "Either touch me, or I'll leave you in this room and go find Synda. I'm sure she wouldn't mind—"

With a shriek of anger, Tink jumped to her knees and slapped her hands against his cheeks. "You are *such* a jerk, and you deserve whatever happens."

He wanted to laugh. But he couldn't. They were skin-to-skin, heat-to-heat, and all he had to do to get her underneath him was lean forward. She'd fall back, unable to maintain her balance, and he'd stretch out. It would take him two seconds to strip her. Two more to strip himself.

One more to get inside her.

The painting hanging over the headboard shook, fell. Its frame broke.

"Are you good?" Tink asked, too intent to notice the destruction.

Disaster spewed a stream of hateful curses, as loud as ever.

"I am."

"You're sure?"

"I am," he repeated. "You can stop now."

Relieved, she lowered her arms—but the relief didn't last long. He tore his shirt over his head. "What are you doing?" she demanded, her eyes instantly riveted to his chest.

"Now let's see what happens when you're distracted."

"What? No! Put your shirt back on. You're…you're… so sexy." The last ended with a dreamy sigh. "Uh, I mean…uh…"

"No take-backs." He smirked as he took her hands and placed them on his pecs. The sensation was almost too much. He groaned. She moaned. "Ready for stage two?"

"There's more?" she breathed.

"Oh, yes." So much more.

He should resist, but he wasn't going to. Every second in her presence was a torture with only one cure. Here, now, with her scent in his nose, an obvious hunger for him in her eyes, she could give it to him.

Mine. He lowered his head slowly, taking his time, savoring every moment, before pressing his lips into hers. Her mouth opened immediately, welcoming him, and he swept his tongue inside. Her intoxicating taste invaded his senses, and all thoughts of leisure were abandoned. Need he'd denied far too long roared to the surface. He was a starving man, desperate to devour.

Driven by instinct, he leaned and she fell back on the mattress, just as he'd imagined. He pressed his weight into the softness of her sweet little body, and pinned her down. In this position, no part of them remained disconnected from the other.

"Kane," she gasped out.

"Tinker Bell."

He forced her head to tilt, taking more. Giving more. This time, bad memories were kept at bay. And there was no pain in the action—no pain at all, he realized, not that he would have cared. This woman… she chased the darkness away, showed him pleasure and light. Beauty.

Mine. She's mine. I keep what's mine.

They'd started this for a reason—why had they started this?

Her fingertips glided down the length of his spine; her nails scraped back up, sending waves of pleasure through—wait, yes, her hands. "You must have instinctively built mental barriers. You're not draining me."

"Keep checking. Just to be sure." Distracted words. She opened her legs to him, providing a cradle for his aching shaft—*want her, want her so bad*—and he fell into it, pressing intimately against her. Hissing at the utter pleasure. So perfect. He couldn't stay still, was already moving against her, rubbing, seeking.

She moaned with breathless excitement and clutched at him. Innocent, he reminded himself. She'd never had this. He had to be careful with her.

But he wasn't careful as he kneaded her breasts, or

when he reached between their bodies to cup her between the legs and rub, hard, harder, because she didn't seem to want careful. The more demanding his touch, the louder her cries of abandon. He lost his finesse, was nothing more than an animal nipping and pawing at her.

He bit the cord at her neck, and she shuddered.

"Yes! Again," she demanded.

He obeyed. Every nerve in his body cried for satisfaction—to give her satisfaction. This woman…oh, this woman. She'd been made for him, only him.

She arched against him. She scratched at his back all over again. She squeezed his hips with her knees. Then…she palmed his length.

Going to lose something else...

"This all right?" she asked.

"Better than."

This should stop, before he pushed them both past the point of no return.

Stop.

No, he still couldn't stop.

He'd wanted this for so long…too long. To walk away now…no, he would rather die.

"Please," she rasped. "Do more to me."

"Yes." His fingers trembled as he jerked at the hem of her shirt. He had to strip her. Had to taste every inch of her. Had to prove she belonged to him, that they belonged together, and no one and nothing could ever tear them apart.

The hollow of her stomach…perfection. Her breasts… exquisite, just as he remembered. He was utterly snared, couldn't tear his gaze away.

Then she moved her legs, planting her feet at his sides and bending her knees.

The panties had to go.

Disaster shook the walls of the bedroom, maybe the entire palace. Suddenly furniture was rattling, and a chair was toppling over. Kane was too lost to care. *Such a lush, ripe female. Perfect in every way.*

And if you take her, then marry her sister?

The thought swept through his mind, springing from a conscience he'd thought had been murdered. He brushed it aside. He would make sure she liked everything that happened, that she never had any regrets, that she—

Suffers with shame and guilt.

That thought was too shattering to ignore. He couldn't take her, he realized like a harsh slap in the face. Not here. Not now. Not like this, with things left unsaid and unplanned.

Frustrated, he smoothed down her shirt and jolted upright. His body screamed a protest, his every cell rejecting the separation from her. He punched the headboard. Wood shards rained.

Tink gasped with surprise. "K-Kane? What's wrong?"

His shame rose. "Sorry. I didn't mean to scare you."

At least the shaking had stopped, Disaster calming.

"Did I drain you and not realize?" she asked.

"No." Remaining on his side, facing her, he lay down. "The demon was acting up." Despite the pain of unsatisfied lust, there was no underlying ache—but there *was* a surprising underlying wave of contentment.

"I want to go to my room now," she said hollowly.

Or maybe not. "You're staying here. You're sleeping here. That's not up for discussion."

"You don't get to decide what's up for discussion and what's not." Her voice had a bite to it.

"I do get to tie you to the bed if you even think about leaving."

She closed her eyes, hiding the anguish he'd just glimpsed inside their depths. "You are so confusing! One second you're all over me, the next you're pulling away. I shouldn't have kissed you, I admit that. Ultimately, your circumstances haven't changed. In fact, they're worse. I asked if you planned to marry Synda and you refused to answer."

If the situation had been different—if he planned to marry Synda for any reason other than to save Tink—he would have agreed. "I thought it might prove necessary." Yes, he'd entertained the notion of going through with the marriage to Synda, and yes, it was still an option, but just then, with Tink's taste in his mouth and her warmth enveloping him, he knew it wasn't an option he would ever be able to take. "I was wrong."

He would think of something else. He would.

One of the wood shards had caught on the bed railing and now fell into his eye. He hissed.

Kane tilted back his head and poked around until he found and removed the tiny sliver.

Hatred for Disaster burned that much deeper.

"Is there anything you're sure of?" Tink asked quietly.

He was sure he was tired of pretending. Tired of thoughts and memories and fears and indecision and… everything but this girl. "I'm sure we both need some rest." Before Disaster caused *her* harm. "We'll talk about this later."

CHAPTER TWENTY-ONE

"GUESS WHAT? IT'S LATER."

Kane looked around. Josephina stood at the side of the bed, surrounded by the same glittering white mist he'd seen in the dark alley beside the club. "Did you project yourself into my mind again? Even though you're right next to me?"

Wait. She was next to him, wasn't she?

He patted the space beside him, and sure enough, the heat of her caressed his hands.

She raised her chin, probably trying for haughty but only managing adorable. "Would you be angry if I pleaded guilty?"

"You'd already be over my knee if I were angry."

An amused gleam danced in her eyes. "You would *not* spank me."

"Are you sure you want to challenge me on this topic?"

She held up her palms and backed away from him. "No, no. Not me. I'd never do something like that."

He laughed and waved her back, the sense of being carefree astonishing him. "Why not just talk to me in person?"

"Three reasons. I'm impatient. Our real bodies are clearly exhausted right now. And Disaster can't hurt me here."

"Way to bury the lead," he said with a smile. "Who else have you invaded like this?"

"My mother." She offered him a sad little smile. "Before she gave me the ability forever, I accidentally took it a few times."

Curious, he said, "Why not use it with others?"

"There's no one in this realm I want to talk to, and no one who wants to talk to me."

Always breaking my heart. "Well, don't invade anyone else." He didn't like the idea of her being this intimately involved with another.

She stuck out her tongue. "Whatever you say, Dad."

He tsked, sitting up. "Careful. That's an invitation to a guy like me."

"What is? The action or the insult?"

"Both."

She opened her mouth, and he suspected—hoped—she meant to issue a verbal invitation. But all she said was "Kane?"

The muscles in his stomach jumped as if she'd caressed him. "Yes." He threw his legs over the side of the bed.

"There's something I've been wanting to ask you." She paced in front of him. "It's kind of personal."

Dread rolled through him. "I told you, you can ask me anything."

She stopped, motioned to his hip. "Why a butterfly?"

Okay, that one was easy. He stood—but somehow left his body behind.

He frowned. "What just happened?"

"Uh, I think you just projected your image. Like I'm doing."

"How?"

"I don't know."

Were they bonded on some deep, primal level? Her abilities becoming his? Or, had she left a piece of herself behind when she'd taken Disaster from him?

She reached out, tracing her fingers along the curve of the wing stretching above the waist of his pants. "Like this, I can *feeeel* you."

Instant. Hard-on. "And I can feel you," he croaked.

"The butterfly…" she prompted with a shiver.

Right. "My friends and I have our theories, and none are the same."

"I want to hear yours." Her knuckles brushed against his navel, and he had to fight the urge to grab her hand… to force it to go lower.

"Inside a chrysalis, a caterpillar breaks down into imaginal cells. Those cells put themselves back together in a new shape and the creature emerges as a butterfly. Once, I was a warrior. Then the demon came, and I was broken down and reshaped into something else. Something dark and twisted."

Her gaze found his. "But you and the demon aren't one being. You're separate."

"Not yet, but we will be," he said, unable to hide his determination. Before she could question him further, he offered his hand to her.

"What?" she asked, confused.

"Take it."

A moment passed before she twined their fingers.

He remained quiet, easing forward into a slow walk around the room. She kept pace beside him, the mist constantly swirling and dancing with their motions. He enjoyed the peace and tranquility. "How does this ability of yours work? You projected your image into my mind, but do you control everything I see?"

"For the most part, yes."

"Show me."

"What would you like to see?"

"The best you've got."

She cut him a look of determined delight. "Prepare to be amazed by my amazingness." Rubbing her hands together, she closed her eyes. A moment later, a forest of lush green trees took the place of the room. A mutant dog-monkey hybrid materialized on one of the branches, swinging toward him and throwing an apple at his head.

He dodged, but not quickly enough. The red fruit hit his shoulder, causing Tink to chuckle.

"You're in trouble now," he said.

"Oh, dear, oh, no. Are you going to give me that spanking?" she gasped out with mock fear—and another apple slammed into his shoulder. "Or is the mean warrior going to give me a very stern lecture?"

Kane released a low snarl, as fake as her fear. "I'll give you a lecture all right."

She giggled as she raced forward, throwing over her shoulder, "You'll have to catch me first."

That giggle…as much as he wanted to kiss and touch her again, he wanted to hear that giggle more. He darted after her, chasing her around thick trunks and other mutant animals she'd thought up. The cat-deer. The squirrel-wasp. The elephant-zebra. He almost caught her, and she giggled again; he laughed.

He wasn't sure whether or not they were ghosting through walls, or still inside his bedroom, and he didn't care. He'd never acted like a child. He'd never *been* a child. He'd come into this world fully formed, a vessel meant for war and vengeance. Then, after the Pandora's box debacle, he'd become a container for evil—and his weeks in hell had only increased the darkness inside him. Until Tink, he'd never been anything more; he'd never known light.

"You can't catch me I'm the muffin man," she called.

"Gingerbread."

"Are we saying random foods now? Cupcakes."

He was shaking with laughter when next he caught her, and she managed to slip away.

"Poor Kane," she called, and he could tell she was struggling not to pant from exertion. "Too old to keep up with such a young Fae?"

Pumping his arms and legs faster, he increased his pace until he was practically breathing down her neck. She released a laughing scream when he grabbed her by the waist and spun her around.

"Think I'm too old now?" he asked.

"You're thousands of years old. Of course you're too old."

"Yeah, but am I too old for *you?*"

"I have daddy issues. No one's too old for me."

He choked on another laugh. "You are the oddest mix of innocence and modern sass."

A pause as insecurity filled her eyes, then, "Too odd for you?" she asked hesitantly.

"Absolutely perfect for me," he admitted. A man could get used to this. A man could get *addicted* to this.

Too bad it wouldn't last. Not for Kane.

He settled her on the ground and stretched out beside her, wondering if the pain would make another appearance. He knew Disaster hadn't given up, so why the lack?

"Thank you, Tinker Bell," he said.

"For what?"

"For…being you."

KANE WOKE UP gradually, his mind coming to the slow realization that there was something soft and warm intertwined with his limbs—and he hadn't been plagued by nightmares, but had actually slept. The scent of rosemary enveloped him. He blinked open his eyes, disrupting the haze, and spied the culprit. His mouth lifted in a leisurely grin.

This was the life he craved for himself. A beautiful woman he admired, respected—*hungered for*—wrapped around him, her head resting on his arm, her bare hands on his chest, and one of her legs propped on his hip.

Tink's features were stunningly relaxed, and there was a soft, pink color in her cheeks. He wasn't sure how she kept ending up in his arms, but he would have loved to know.

He smoothed the hair from her face. She leaned into the touch and smacked her lips. Lips he'd tasted last night.

Lips he wanted to taste again…

He leaned into her, preparing to do just that. The moment he realized where this was headed, he froze. Yesterday he'd stopped, knowing Tink would hate herself if she had sex with a man currently engaged to another woman.

But he'd since realized the truth. He couldn't marry Synda. Not for any reason.

He was going to have Tink.

He might regret it. She would definitely regret it. A sweet man would walk away now.

He wasn't a sweet man.

He closed the rest of the distance. At the moment of contact, a moan escaped him. Her lips…so wonderfully soft. The women from the club had wanted his kisses, but he'd refused. The thought had even disgusted him. But with Tink, things had always been different. He wanted more from her than he'd ever wanted from another—and he would have it.

Her lashes fluttered open. Cobalt met his penetrating stare, and he waited for the confusion to evaporate—and realization to take its place.

"More?" he said, a question and a demand. Desire burned white-hot, sizzling through his veins.

She arched, rubbing her needy little body against him, creating the most delicious friction. "Absolutely."

He dived down for another taste. His tongue licked into her mouth and she moaned, already as lost as he was, in a place where nothing mattered but the pleasure. He was tentative at first, as gentle as he was capable of being. She was hesitant, unsure this early in the morning, with the room teeming with sunlight, but the more time he took with her, the deeper she allowed him to take possession of her mouth. The deeper his possession, the more she melted against him. Soon, their tongues were meeting thrust for heated thrust.

The bed shook. A growl sounded in his head.

Kane slid his hand under her shirt and palmed her breast. Her back arched, and he began kneading. Such a delicious fit. She mewled, a decadent noise that drove him wild. "You like when I touch you this way?"

"Yes."

"I can do more." He slid his fingers down her stomach, to the apex of her thighs. "And I can do it here."

"Please."

One-word responses, as if she couldn't focus on his voice, only his touch.

"I want your clothes out of the way. All of them."

"Yesss."

He ripped the collar of her shirt, and put his mouth where his hands had been. While he sucked her, he worked at the zipper of his pants. Then, finally *then*—

"Wait," she said, seeming to blink through a sensual fog. "Wait. Maybe we should think about this."

He wouldn't curse. "We can think later."

"But…I'm not sure…maybe this is a mistake…"

He heard footsteps and a male's whistle beyond the door.

Not. Happening. Not again. Especially now, when he was desperate to find out why Tink thought they were making a mistake.

A knock sounded at the door. "Yo. Warrior. It's garden time," William called. "You don't want to leave her queenliness waiting. She's already sent a guard to hunt your Tinker Hell down."

He roared, "Go away."

A pause was followed by a laugh. "Bad time?"

"It's okay," Tink said, breathless but unsure. "If the queen wants me in the garden, she has a game of cricket lined up. I need to go."

He. Hated. William.

At least the bed stopped shaking.

"Get dressed," he said. "I'm going with you."

"IT'S SIMPLE," THE QUEEN explained, using her snobbiest tone. "Servant Josephina will tie her drab little—"

"That's not her title anymore," Kane roared, making Josephina gasp.

The queen blanched. "Well, she must stand with her hussy's legs apart…I mean her legs," she corrected when Kane took a menacing step toward her, "and we will each take turns knocking our balls through the gap with our mallets."

Heat filled Josephina's cheeks as she latched onto Kane's wrist to hold him in place. As soon as she knew he wouldn't attack the woman, she released him with every intention of entering the clearing to assume her position.

He was the one to grab her by the arm this time, stopping her. He snapped, "She won't be doing that."

The queen huffed and puffed, and Josephina listened as the two sped into a heated argument about her purpose in the game.

"I'll go get the king and allow him to settle this," Kane said. "The girl is mine, and I decide what she does and does not do."

Penelope's gaze strayed to William.

"The disagreement is a waste of time. Give him what he wants," the warrior said. "And later, I'll do the same to you."

There was a strange mix of boredom and huskiness in his tone.

"Fine," the queen huffed, either too afraid to go against the king or too eager to have whatever William was offering. "We'll play without Servant—I mean, the girl."

"Better." Kane patted Josephina on the butt before joining the group in the clearing. She had to press her lips together to keep from laughing.

Next time, I'm going to stand up for myself. Kane had once called her brave, and he wasn't a liar, so, it was time to act the part. There would be consequences, consequences she'd once feared more than anything. But she wasn't a slave, that wasn't her lot in life, wasn't something she would tolerate any longer, she thought.

Choices. They were hers to make. Hers to see through.

The sun was brighter than usual, casting golden rays

over the rows of multicolored flowers and alabaster statues Tiberius had commissioned of himself, Synda, Queen Penelope and Leopold. Though the one of Leopold had been battered by weather, but never fixed. The air was warm, and it was a good thing, too. Her dress was still a little damp from the washing Kane had given it.

Synda skipped to her ball, looked to Kane and nibbled on her lower lip. "Will you come help me, Lord Kane? I'm far too weak to hit my ball very far."

Was that…flirting?

Kane paused only a moment before stomping over to her.

Yeah. That was flirting.

Synda fluttered her lashes at him and preened as he positioned her hands on her mallet. Rage stewed, bubbling up. Josephina hated seeing the warrior—her warrior—anywhere near the princess.

"This is still proving tedious," William said to the queen, in a stage whisper everyone could hear. "Why don't you go upstairs and wait for me? In a few minutes, I'll follow, so no one will suspect we're together, and we'll play a game of a different sort."

"Well…" Queen Penelope peered at her daughter, her mind clearly whirling. Then, she nodded.

"That's a good girl."

Off she raced, without a goodbye, heading toward the palace as if her feet were on fire.

They were lovers?

Josephina knew the queen had taken other men to her bed. Men the king had killed, though Tiberius had never admitted that was the reason why.

Poor William. He wouldn't survive, either.

He sidled up to her as if he hadn't a care.

"Your friendship with Kane won't save you," she told him. "If the king finds out what you're doing with the queen, and he will, he'll—"

"Trying to save me, female?" He flashed a perfect, white smile. "How adorable is that? But you're wasting your time. Your father is nothing more than a fly."

"Why don't you challenge him, then?"

"And steal Kane's moment?"

She rolled her eyes. "Excuses, excuses."

He shrugged. "By the way, your step momma is a terrible lay. Seriously, I've been with dead girls who have more life."

Okay. Too much information. She covered her ears.

William forced her hands to her sides. "I'm distracting her, and look, it's working."

"Well, then, why don't you distract the princess, too?"

"I only have one Big Willy, and he's currently on loan to the queen."

Synda gave a tinkling laugh, and Josephina looked over. The princess was now smashed against Kane, her arms wrapped around his neck. She was tiny and delicate in comparison, peering up at him with expectation of a kiss, and though he was stiff, he wasn't exactly fighting her off. Josephina's hands fisted tightly. If he did it, if he allowed his lips to meet the princess's, she would…she would…oh! There was no action violent enough.

"He's got a lot of darkness inside him, you know," William said. "You're helping, I'll give you that, but if you can't stick around until it's all gone, back off. You'll both be better off."

Her shoulders straightened in a snap. "How about you back off? I'm dealing, but that doesn't mean he can do whatever he wants with whomever he wants anytime he wants."

"And here I thought you were intelligent. He doesn't want that girl in any way."

"I know, he told me, but that doesn't mean he won't marry her if he thinks that's the best course of action." And if he didn't? If he chose Josephina, as he'd seemed to do this morning? What then?

The answer was simple: war.

William reached over, plucked an ice-blue rose from the bushes, and tucked the bud behind her ear. "I'm surprised he told you that much. You can't be mad at him for his plan, though. The only reason he'd ever marry such a shrew would be to save you. Hopefully, though, it won't come to that."

Hopefully, he'd said, as if there was a greater chance Kane would have to do it. "Are you trying to help his chances with me or torch them?"

He ignored her, saying, "Listen up, and listen well. What Kane has gone through would have killed most people. He thinks I'm staying with him to keep him away from White, but he's wrong. I'm trying to help him heal. I can tell you being with him isn't going to be easy."

Was he referring to Kane's time in hell? "I know what he went through," she said.

William anchored two fingers under her chin and forced her to look up at him. "He told you?"

"Some of it, yes. I also saw him right after it had happened."

"Surprising. On both counts. He talked, and he let you live with the knowledge." He shrugged, and said, "Give him time. He'll figure out the best course of action, it'll please you, things will smooth out, and you'll live happily ever after. I'll be quite disgusted, I'm sure."

Time? Was he serious? "The ball is tomorrow, and the wedding is the day after that. How much time do you think I should give him?" And how selfish was she, to actually have put Kane in such a position? To marry her horrible sister, just to save her, or to marry her, and live with the ensuing bloodshed?

William smiled, and it wasn't a nice smile. "Are you planning to run away if things don't go your way, little fairy? I'd rethink that if I were you. He'll track you down. He may not punish you when he finds you, but I will. I'll do things to you you've only read about in horror stories. I don't like to be inconvenienced, and I don't like to see my friends suffer. Combine the two, and I'm afraid I get a little cranky."

"Save your threats. I'm not—" A waft of smoke sent her into a coughing fit. She searched the area, and found a raging fire spreading through the flowers.

She heard Kane curse under his breath. "The Phoenix is here," he threw at William before taking off in a run. Only, he stopped after just a few feet and turned. His narrowed gaze locked on the warrior, who still had his fingers under Josephina's chin, then he started running again—in the opposite direction, flying straight toward the two of them.

He launched himself at William, shouting, "No one touches her but me!"

CHAPTER TWENTY-TWO

HE HAD TO get himself under control.

Kane had tackled his only ally, just for touching his chosen female, allowing a mortal enemy to escape.

Now, that chosen female was nowhere to be found. She'd run into the palace during his fight with William, and he hadn't been able to find her since. He was forced to sleep alone—not that he did much sleeping. Without Tink in his bed, he couldn't relax.

By morning, the palace was a flurry of activity. Servants rushed here and there, cleaning and moving furniture around to accommodate three long buffet tables.

He caught one of those servants by the arm, stopping her. "Where's Josephina?"

The female grinned up at him, delighted by his attention. "I last saw her in the kitchen, Lord Kane. I'll fetch her, if you like. I'll do anything you ask." She stepped closer to him. "Anything."

Mine, Disaster said.

"Thanks, but I'll fetch her myself." He stalked to the kitchen—and missed her by less than a handful of seconds.

He picked up a bowl, his grip so tight the crystal instantly shattered. He didn't want Tink working. He wanted her out of harm's way. He wanted to kiss her and finish what they'd started yesterday morning.

Then, when his body was calm—finally, blissfully satiated—he could figure out his next move.

He left the kitchen and ran into Synda. "Lord Kane!"

Mine, Disaster shouted.

Her smile of greeting slowly faded. "Tell me you're not wearing those hideous clothes to the ball."

He was wearing the clothes he'd come here in, but they were clean. "Will you cancel if I do?"

She patted his cheek, and he stepped out of reach. "You're so cute when you expect the worst, but you're even cuter in the proper attire, so make sure you change, or I'll be very unhappy." With that, she skipped away.

Whatever. With Tink avoiding him, he might as well try to take care of her Phoenix problem. He slipped out of the palace and into the forest, pleased to find Petra had left tracks today. Ridiculously obvious tracks, he realized with a frown. Did she *want* to be captured?

Yeah, he thought a moment later. She did.

A long time ago, he'd done something similar. He'd planted tracks, allowing his enemy to find him and escort him into their camp. Once there, he'd rained absolute and total destruction.

"—will suffer for what your people have done," a male voice said.

Kane pushed through a veil of bushes and found four Fae soldiers pinning Petra to the ground and tying her hands behind her back. She was struggling, but her efforts were puny at best.

"Let her go, and stand back," Kane commanded, pulling the gun he hadn't given back to William and aiming at her head.

All eyes whipped to him.

The men frowned. Petra cursed.

"But Lord Kane, the other Phoenix have fled. When

they return we can use this girl to threaten them," the shortest exclaimed.

Kane bared his teeth in a scowl. "I said, let her go."

The four instantly stepped away from her. She popped to her feet, and the rope they'd used fell away, the ends singed.

"You always ruin everything!" she screeched with a stomp of her foot.

Mine, Disaster purred.

Shut it!

"Let's have this out," Kane said. "Me and you. Winner gets the girl."

She stilled, studied him with intrigue. "You'd fight a female?"

"I'd do worse than that." Hadn't he proven it already?

She gloated, saying, "Kill me, and you'll only strengthen me. I'll rise from the ashes and enslave you."

"Maybe. Maybe not."

She paled at the reminder that no Phoenix was guaranteed an eternity. At some point they all died for good.

"To be honest," he said, "I don't really want to kill you. I want to give you back to your people. After all, I was told your king would like to…speak with you."

Fear darkened her eyes, and she backed a step away. Kane smiled—and squeezed the trigger once, twice. Screaming with pain and surprise, she collapsed. Blood leaked from both of her thighs.

"However," he said, "I'll do what I have to do."

"So will I." Cringing, she reached for one of the gaping soldiers. The moment her fingers touched the male, he burst into flames, flailing about, screaming with agony. Kane lost sight of the girl as he patted the man down. By the time the flames had been doused, Petra was gone.

He hunted for one hour…two…six…determination driving his every movement. He found multiple trails of her blood, but no more than that. She remained expertly hidden.

His mood was black and stormy by the time he returned to the palace. He could hear the murmurings of the crowd, and remembered the party. Tink would be serving. Still in his "hideous" clothes, he snuck in through one of the secret passageways and, after claiming a glass of whiskey, camped in a shadowed corner.

The ballroom had been decked out. The chandeliers dripped with diamonds as big as his fist, and dragon-shaped pillars had been wheeled inside. The heads moved, ruby eyes scanning the room, forked tongues darting from between blackened lips, and releasing smoke.

Fae males were dressed in weird, girly suits with lace and bows, and the women in big, puffy gowns, with their hair styled bizarrely, with knots and spikes shaped to look like animal heads. There was a lion. An eagle. An antelope. The atmosphere was very…Victorian era meets *The Hunger Games* in Wonderland, with an R rating. The men were feeding the women by hand, then going in for a taste themselves. On the dance floor, bodies gyrated together, hands roaming, clothing being shoved aside.

Kane watched as Synda fluttered from one group to another, sipping champagne and laughing gaily. The king had left his throne and now "graced" the assembly with a dance. Leopold waited at the entrance, greeting guests as they arrived. The queen was perched on a settee in back, ten of her friends sitting at her feet, watching the proceedings with hawk eyes.

William—*my PMS*—had gotten his stupid kids an invitation, and the group had taken up residence in the corner across from Kane. They watched him watching them, trying to intimidate him. All they did was irritate him.

Ignoring them, he searched for Tink. She had to be here. She—

Had just entered the room.

Breath caught in his throat. Her fall of black hair was tied in a simple bun at her nape, yet several tendrils had escaped confinement and framed the incomparable elegance of her face. She was captivating, and maddening, and utterly enchanting.

She was…everything.

He finished off his whiskey and dropped the glass in a potted plant. His blood heated, practically boiling in his veins as he pushed from the wall and stalked across the room. His gaze remained on her, studying her more intently. She wore the now-clean uniform he'd bought for her, managing to outshine every other woman in the room.

She carried a tray and gathered empty glasses, stealthily looking this way and that, searching for someone. For him?

A female stepped in his path and he ground to a halt to avoid plowing into her. "You're Lord Kane." A giggle filled the minute portion of air between them, overshadowing the soft hum of music in the background. She traced her fingertips along the center of his chest. "I've been so eager to meet you."

He bit back an angry retort and set her aside.

Another girl moved into his path, and this one had

brought a few of her friends. The females circled him, wolves intent on their prey, and rapid-fired comments at him.

"Ask me to dance, Lord Kane. Please."

"Let's adjourn to the balcony. I have a present I'd love for you to unwrap. Hint—it's me."

"My husband is spending the night with his mistress. I would love it if you kept me company tonight. I promise not to wear any clothes."

"The only thing I'd be willing to do is spank the living hell out of you for accosting a stranger," he said. "This is my *engagement ball,* and you think it's okay to come on to me?"

Just like he thought it was okay to chase down Tink?

Whatever.

He barreled past the floundering females. Finally he reached Tink and the tension inside him eased. "Need help?"

She gave him the swiftest of glances. "You shouldn't be talking to me." Her hands trembled as she gathered the glasses the guests had discarded in the oddest places—and he cursed himself for what he'd done with his own.

"When have I ever done what I'm supposed to do?" he asked.

"Point taken. Now leave."

Disaster purred his approval.

Anger sparked. "Why are you acting like this?"

"Why are you still here?"

He gnashed his teeth. "You want me, Tink. Don't try to pretend otherwise."

"Are you so desperate for compliments?" She tried to maneuver away from him, but he herded her in the other direction, away from the crowd and into the shadows. "What are you doing? Stop. I'm not giving you one."

"It's not a compliment I want from you, Tink. It's information. Why have you run from me today?"

She wiped a few droplets of liquid from the wall before pressing her forehead into her hand. "Because! Whatever you want from me, Kane, I can't give it to you."

Because of Synda. Because he hadn't yet broken things off. Guilt had him looking away. He spotted Red's determined approach and realized it was just a matter of time before Green and Black decided to tag along. Kane latched onto Tink's arm and hauled her toward the secret doorway he'd used.

He had her inside in less than a blink. Anyone watching would have had trouble tracking the movement.

"What are you doing?" she demanded. "I have a job to do."

He scrubbed a hand through his hair. A two-way mirror covered the wall, allowing them to peer inside the ballroom. "Do you see the warriors standing where we just were?" He pointed. "The ones from the bar?"

She looked, groaned. "Yes. I see them."

"They want you for their own. They want to use your ability to remove the war, famine and death from their bodies."

"More enemies," she muttered. "Great. Just great!" She whirled on him, eyes narrowed but no less ablaze. "Do you know what this means?"

"Yes. I'm a disaster," he said hollowly. "I know."

She peered at him for a long while, and whatever she saw in his expression calmed her down. Her shoulders stooped. "No, that wasn't what I was going to say."

"Why not? It's true."

She shook her head. "They're trouble. Another threat against you."

"And you." He stepped closer to her. She stepped back, widening the distance. He took another step, and another, and she did the same, until she had nowhere else to go. The wall behind her stopped her retreat.

He leaned down and rubbed his nose against hers. Contact with her was as necessary as breathing.

She closed her eyes, as if pained. "How do you do this to me, Kane?" she whispered.

"Do what?"

"Make me want you, despite everything."

He heard only two words—*want you*. He moved swiftly, fitting his mouth over hers. Though she remained closed to him, he could already taste her, and desire rushed through him, drowning him.

Mine, he thought.

Never, Disaster spat.

"Let me in," Kane said, ignoring the beast. This close, he could see each individual lash framing her crystalline eyes, and they were long and gorgeous, badges of innocence blended with wanton need.

"No, I—"

This time, when he dove in for a taste, her mouth was already open. He took full advantage, thrusting his tongue against hers.

Moaning, she gave up the pretense of resistance. Her arms wrapped around him as she kissed him back with the fervency of a starving woman.

He tried to slow things down, but she began to writhe against him, lost to the sensations, all inhibitions forgotten. He nipped at her mouth, and she nipped at his, and that was it. They became animals.

He growled, and she growled, and they ate at each other. He kneaded her breast with one hand, his grip strong, too strong, but just like before, she didn't seem to mind. He caged her wrists with the other and locked her arms above her head.

Her back arched, pressing her body more firmly against his.

"More?"

"Please," she rasped.

"I like that word on your lips." Blood aflame, he lifted the hem of her dress. His knuckles brushed against the warm, tender skin on her inner thigh and he shuddered with the intensity of the pleasure. Then he hefted her up, anchored her, forcing her to wrap her legs around him, like she'd done inside the dress shop, finding a measure of release and deeper need with his erection pressed against her.

His fingers curled around her backside, past the edge of her panties, seeking more intimate contact.

"Ow!" she said, suddenly fighting to get away from him.

Concern instantly replaced desire as he set her on her feet. "What's wrong?"

She patted at the sleeve of her dress. Flames from one of the torches had showered over her.

Scowling, he backed away from her. As he tried to tamp down his raging need, he made sure to keep a safe distance. Disaster would flip his lid if Kane continued what he'd started.

It wouldn't always be this way, he reminded himself.

She sighed, gave him a pained look. "Just proves we shouldn't be doing this."

"We're meant for each other, and you know it."

She raised her arm with the charred sleeve. “Kane, did you see what just—”

“Did you think about me today?” he interjected, needing her to affirm that there *were* feelings there, no matter what she was saying. “Did you wish I was with you?”

She lowered her arm. “More times than I liked.”

“I thought about you, too,” he said.

“Why?” she whispered, her head down but her gaze remaining on him. “Why are we thinking about each other? It would be so much better for both of us if we walked away from each other.”

“I’ve tried. I can’t.” His gaze was piercing. “I could marry you,” he said softly.

She closed her eyes for a moment, looking as if she could burst into tears. Then, she closed the distance, expression more determined with every step. Before he could move away, she rested her hands on his shoulders. He stiffened, afraid for her, for what Disaster would do, but he didn’t dissuade her. He yearned so badly for some kind of contact with her, even this.

“I like your kisses,” she said. “I do. *So* much.”

“Like is too weak a word for how I feel about yours.”

“And I like when you touch me. And I like you, snarly beast that you can sometimes be.” Her chin trembled. “That’s why it pains me to say…no. No, I…don’t want to marry you.”

He reared back as if she’d nailed him with a hammer. “Because the demon burned you?” he croaked. “I won’t always have him. I plan to kill him.”

“I could lie and tell you that’s why. I could tell you I want someone else and you’re in the way. But the truth is, I don’t think you can help me. Not without getting hurt.”

He felt as if he'd just been punched in the stomach. Like his friends, she doubted him. Had no faith in his abilities.

Disaster laughed with undiluted glee, at last appeased.

"I want you to leave this realm," she said with a tremor. "Tonight. Now."

Kane was a man well acquainted with pain. At least, he'd thought so. Now, he learned the error of his ways. *This* was true pain. Rejection from the female he craved.

He'd gotten good at building walls inside himself, and used the skill now. Expression even, giving nothing away, he said, "Very well," with all the calm of a man discussing the weather. "I won't bother you any longer." He turned from her and stalked out of the enclosure.

As he stormed down the hall, he ran into William.

"The problem?" William asked after taking one look at him.

"Doesn't concern you," he said. "Just keep your boys away from Tink. I won't be around to protect her."

"Hell-ooo. We've talked about this. She's yours and I won't let them—"

"She's not mine," he interjected harshly. "And keep your boys away from me, too. They come near me, and I won't be responsible for my actions."

He stalked away from William, grabbed the first drink he found, then another and another, and nearly drowned himself. He danced with Synda, twirling her across the floor. He danced with her friends. They put their hands all over him and he had to swallow back vomit time and time again. Then he danced with Synda again while the king nodded his approval.

"I have to have you, Lord Kane," Synda whispered,

warm breath fanning against his ear. "Let me. Please. You won't regret it. I'll do anything you ask."

He opened his mouth to refuse her, locked gazes with Tink, who was watching him with guarded eyes as she cleaned a table, and said, "Yeah, let's go."

CHAPTER TWENTY-THREE

The Realm of Blood and Shadows

TORIN SAT AT his desk, fingers pounding at the computer keyboard with so much force he cracked the outer shell. Again. With a curse, he tossed the thing aside and grabbed a new one from his box of spare parts.

There were disturbances all over the world. People were fighting, rioting and looting. For no reason! Cameo and Viola were still missing, and he'd failed to find a single trail to lead him to their whereabouts. They were out there, possibly hurt.

He had no idea what kind of defensive skills Viola possessed. Cameo, on the other hand, was a warrior to her soul and could take care of herself. He knew that. Had seen her fight. Girl had a wicked habit of slitting throats. But she wasn't infallible.

An unfamiliar sound caught his attention and he spun in his chair, cocking the gun he always kept in his lap.

A young girl stood there, holding her palms up, all innocence. "Please," she said in a strained whisper. Color drained from her cheeks.

"Who are you and how did you get in here?" he demanded, even as he looked her over.

She had dirty hair, at one time it might have been blond, the strands tangled and knotted and hanging limply to her elbows. A stained and ripped nightgown bagged over her too-thin body, the material falling all the way to the ground.

"You are Torin, correct?"

"I'm Death, if you don't answer my questions."

"I'm not willing to share my name, and I flashed." Still she whispered. Why?

"Well, then, I'll call you Crazy, because only a crazy person would come here without an invite."

She nodded, no inflection of emotion darkening her features. "You may call me whatever you wish."

Very accommodating, wasn't she? "Why are you here, female?"

She ignored him, saying, "Please, may I lower my hands?"

"No."

"My arms are shaking, and I can't…I'm not strong enough…" Her arms lowered slowly, as if heavy weights had been tied to her wrists and pulled. "I'm sorry. Please don't shoot me. That's not the way I want to die."

"You're lucky I don't like blood in my room." He lowered the gun as well, placing it on his thigh, making sure to keep the barrel aimed at her stomach. "I don't like it—but I'll deal with it. This is the last time I'm going to ask. Why are you here?"

Nervous, she twisted the fabric of her gown. "Cronus came to me several weeks ago and told me I was to grant you twenty-four hours of my time."

Still. Whispering. He didn't like it. He was reminded of all the nights he'd spent with his friends, on the road, when they'd found women and brought them back to the tent—but he never had. The couples had tried to be quiet, but they'd always failed.

I want you, the females had whispered. *I need you.*

This girl—

Her claim finally registered. Cronus was the former king of the Titans. Sienna, Paris's girl, had killed him, and taken over the Titan realm of the skies. But just before his death, Cronus had made a bargain with Torin. In exchange for guarding the All-key—a spiritual relic capable of freeing the possessor from any lock—Torin would be granted an entire day with a woman he would be able to touch without causing a plague.

Despite the king's death, the bargain must still stand.

And that might explain why the Paring Rod hadn't sucked him up. Because of the All-key, it couldn't hold him. A startling realization—one that suddenly paled in comparison to the knowledge that he could…*touch her...*

The moisture in his mouth dried as he narrowed his study of her, taking in smaller details. Despite her disheveled state, she was pretty in a subtle, understated way. Her eyes were large and brown…and haunted. There were secrets inside her. Dark secrets. Her nose was small and rounded cutely at the end. Her upper lip was plumper than her bottom lip, and shaped into a heart.

Her hands were scabbed over and streaked with dirt. There was a bruise on the side of her neck—and it wasn't a hickey. It was too long, too thin, and extended under the fabric of her gown.

She stood utterly still, quiet, allowing him to scrutinize her at his leisure. Her gaze remained averted, glued to the side of the wall. It had taken a warrior's courage to come, and yet she couldn't face him head-on while he looked his fill?

Touch her, he thought again.

"Who are you?" Torin asked more gently. "Please. I have to know."

"I told you. I won't offer my name."

Why? What reason could she have to deny him? "Will you tell me why you're whispering?" he asked—in a whisper.

Bright red spots grew on her cheeks. "This is my voice. I can't talk with any other or any louder."

Why? And how many more times would he be forced to ask that question?

"May I…sit?" she asked.

His eyes roved over the bedroom so few people had ever entered. His dirty clothes were on the floor. His bed was unmade. Empty beer bottles littered the night-stand and desk.

He hopped to his feet and raced around the spacious enclosure, gathering clothes, tossing out bottles. He also made the bed.

"Yes," he said. "Sit. Are you hungry? Thirsty?"

Hesitant, she eased onto the floor instead of any of the chairs or the bed. "I… Yes," she replied. "Please."

He couldn't bring himself to leave her, so, he did something he'd never done before. He withdrew his cell and phoned Reyes, the keeper of Pain, saying, "Bring me a couple of sandwiches. And chips. And brownies. And sodas. And anything else we have. All right?"

"I'm glad you called," the warrior said. "Danika has—"

"And hurry." He hung up before Reyes could reply.

"You have servants?" the girl asked, finally meeting his gaze.

His hands began to sweat. Ugh. He couldn't touch her with sweaty hands. "I have friends." He motioned to the bed, his arm trembling. "Wouldn't you rather sit somewhere more comfortable?"

"Here's fine. I'm so dirty. And I know I must smell, and—"

"Honey, you're good just the way you are."

She peered down at her hands, once again wringing the fabric of her gown. "You are Disease, I'm told."

"I'm not Disease. I just host him." And he wanted the demon out. So much so, he'd even spent a little time with the angels. Or rather, the Sent Ones led by the cold-as-ice Zacharel. He'd learned that demons could enter a body, create a stronghold and produce a terrible toxin that destroyed the possessor from the inside out. Fear strengthened the toxin—and thereby the demon—and joy weakened it.

But he'd had no reason to entertain joy. Until now.

"Why are you in this condition?" he asked gently.

"I'd…rather not discuss that, either."

So many secrets. "How did Cronus get you to agree to this?"

"I'd rather not—"

"Never mind. I get it." No personal information was to be shared. He didn't like it, but he wasn't going to push. She could flash away, and he would be unable to chase her down. "You know my name, and you know about the demon, but do you know anything else about me?"

She thought for a moment, shook her head.

"Well, I hope you've figured out by now that I'm not going to hurt you." Despite his threats.

A knock sounded at the door.

"That's the food." Torin rushed to open up and came face-to-face with a scowling Reyes. The warrior was tall and dark and intense, and holding a sack of goodies in one hand and a small painting in the other. "Thanks, man. I owe you. Just leave everything on the floor."

"What's going on?" Reyes demanded. "You've never—" He was in the process of straightening, his gaze sweeping through the room out of habit. A warrior knew to check his surroundings. He spotted the girl and did a double take. "You have a female in here?"

The muscles in his jaw tightened. "It's not what you think."

Brown eyes found him and pleaded. "Torin, man. Cameo and Viola are missing. We don't need a plague on our hands, too."

"I haven't touched her, but even if I had, you wouldn't need to worry. She's immune."

"Good, that's good, but she could still become a carrier, right? Let me escort her out of the fortress before any damage is done. She's—"

"Fine. She's fine." *Could* she become a carrier? Cronus hadn't said.

"She's at risk right—"

"Just trust me, okay?" Torin bent down, grabbed the bags.

"Wait." Reyes thrust the painting at him, forcing him to take it.

He did. Reluctantly. He didn't want to know the future. He didn't want to know if only doom awaited him.

Reyes rubbed two fingers across his stubbled chin, and said, "Danika painted the canvas last night, and I thought you'd find the finished product interesting. You'll want to take a look. Trust *me*." The warrior turned on his booted heel and stomped away. No doubt to inform the rest of the gang what was going on.

Gossips!

Torin shouldered the door closed and faced the girl. Her gaze was latched on the bags.

How long since she'd eaten?

He set the painting down and turned it around, facing the colored side toward the wall. One day, he'd look. But not today. He'd been waiting for this day forever it seemed.

He moved forward, crouched in front of the girl, and set a feast before her. She didn't react immediately, was too busy taking everything in. "Go ahead," he said. "It's yours. Whatever you want."

She reached out with a trembling hand and took one of the sandwiches. Her eyes closed as she bit into the bread, and she chewed slowly, as if relishing the flavors. Then, driven by a need she couldn't control, she tore into the food with abandon.

"Slow down," he said. "I don't want you to get sick."

She acted as if she hadn't heard him, devouring every crumb, draining every drop of soda. He could only watch, fascinated. And spectacularly angry. Clearly, she had been starved.

"Where are you staying?" he asked. What he really wanted to know: Who was responsible for this?

"I don't want to talk about it."

"At least tell me you're over the age of eighteen." She looked so young.

"I'm…not, I'm sorry. I'm seventeen."

Disappointment hit him, and hit him hard.

She flattened her hand over her middle, those ocean blue eyes going wide. A moan of pain escaped her.

He arched a brow. "Too much too fast?"

She leaped to her feet, gasping out, "Help."

"Bathroom is to the left."

She raced into the small enclosure, and Torin stayed

right on her heels. When she hunched over the toilet, he did something he'd never before done, even though, like now, he always wore gloves. He grabbed her hair and held it back. And just in time as she heaved the contents of her stomach.

When she finished, he released her and stepped back. "Why don't you take a shower? Everything you need is in this room, even a change of clothes." He kept a few shirts and sweatpants in here. He kept shirts and sweatpants everywhere, actually, always wanting to be covered, never wanting to risk exposing his skin to another's touch.

A female had never worn his clothing before, and he kind of liked the idea.

But she's only seventeen, and you aren't a cradle robber.

Stupid Cronus, finding him a girl too young to touch.

At least, for now.

She remained slumped on the floor and wouldn't look up at him.

"You'll feel better, and then you can try eating again."

"All right."

"Do you need my help?"

"No. No," she reiterated.

Thank the Most High. He wasn't sure how he would have reacted. "When you're done, we'll talk, all right?" He shut the door, sealing her inside.

Several minutes passed before he heard the water switch on. While she showered, he paced, waiting. Thinking. Twenty-four hours, she'd said. That's how long he had with her. That wasn't long enough.

He wanted to ask when she would turn eighteen. He

wanted to drop to his knees and pray it happened during their time together.

Creepy much?

Surely she would not become a carrier of his disease. Cronus wouldn't have sent him a carrier. The moment she was an adult, Torin could allow himself to touch her. It didn't have to be sexual, either. They could hold hands.

To experience the warmth of another's skin, the softness, the sense of connection, the tactile knowledge that he wasn't alone…

He moaned at the heady thought.

A long while later, she emerged, a cloud of steam following her. Wet, her hair was dark, almost brown. She'd brushed it, but the strands had decided to curl. With the dirt scrubbed off her face, he could see the purity of her skin. Pale, like porcelain, with a slight tracery of veins. Flawless.

She wore his clothing, the material so loose it bagged on her.

"Thank you," she said in that whispery voice.

"You're welcome."

He watched as she shifted uncomfortably, still not looking at him.

"I know I get twenty-four hours with you," he said, "but I'd rather not take them consecutively. I'd rather spread them out. One hour a day, for twenty-four days. Would you be okay with that?" He could use the time to earn her trust, to get her talking and relaxed. Happy to see him. And maybe, if his luck was holding, she would want to keep seeing him.

Surprised baby blues landed on him. "But I thought…"

"What?"

"Never mind." She bit her bottom lip, nodded. "Conditions allow for it, so, yes, I would prefer to come an hour a day for twenty-four days."

His knees almost buckled. "Thank you."

She nodded, saying, "Until tomorrow." In a blink, she was gone.

CHAPTER TWENTY-FOUR

JOSEPHINA HURRIEDLY STUFFED her meager possessions in a bag. A wad of cash she'd saved. A change of clothing. Her mother's locket—one she never wore, too afraid someone would rip it from her neck.

Kane hadn't left. His wedding was today, and she wasn't going to stick around to watch. Maybe he'd go through with it. Maybe he wouldn't. She had a feeling she would wonder for the rest of her life—and cry.

As she tied the bag closed, her stomach clenched. Tears beaded in her eyes, and she sniffed with frustration. Stupid tears! They came so often now. Ever since she'd met Kane.

I shouldn't have kissed him that last time.

But she'd lost herself in the pleasure and the riotous sensations and the heat and the pressure and the need…everything. The past had fallen away. The desire to die, muted as it had become, had breathed its last. Kane had become her world, and she hadn't wanted to ever be found.

And he'd wanted to stay with her, too. But…yeah. But: the word that had ruined everything. She'd had a choice. Be with him, risking the wrath of the king, or be without him, protecting him.

Protecting him had seemed more important than her desire—but only by the slightest degree.

One day, Kane might even thank her. Heck, he was

already happy without her. He'd left the ball with Synda and though Josephina had looked for him, she hadn't seen him since. She had no idea what had happened between the pair, but rumors were rampant. Kane had spent the night in her bedroom.

One of the tears spilled over, and she wiped it away with the back of her hand.

Whatever. Alone in the servant's wing, Josephina tiptoed down the hall and peeked out the window overlooking the driveway. A line of carriages stretched down the road; each contained an Opulen probably bursting with eagerness to reach the royal gate. The wedding was set to begin any minute.

There was no better time for escape. The servants were busy below. The king and queen were distracted. The guards had to watch the grounds to make sure the Phoenix stayed away.

"Seriously?" a voice said from behind her. "You're actually running from me?"

She spun around and came face-to-face with a very angry Kane. He wasn't wearing wedding finery. In fact, he looked…slovenly. He wore a wrinkled T-shirt that read Honey Badger Don't Care, whatever that meant, and his pants were ripped in several places. His eyes were bloodshot, and thick lines of tension branched from his mouth.

"Why aren't you in the human realm, or better yet, downstairs preparing for your nuptials?" she demanded, hating him, hating herself.

"You're *that* eager to marry me off?"

She raised her chin, refusing to reveal the turmoil inside her. "You bedded the princess, didn't you? I think you've got enough eagerness for the both of us."

His features softened, making him appear boyish

and hopeful and so lovely her chest hurt. “Do I detect a note of jealousy, Tink?”

“You certainly don’t! I don’t care what you do or what skank you do it with.”

A lie. She hated lies. What was wrong with her? Since meeting him, she’d become more than a crybaby. She’d become a shrew.

The softness vanished in a blink, and his eyes narrowed. “All right. Yeah. I slept with her. I also slept with a boatload of women before I even reached Séduire. But you know what? Synda was the best I’ve ever had.”

It was like a punch to the gut, a blow so low she wasn’t sure she would ever recover. Humiliation burned in her cheeks, and maybe it was fused with disappointment and fury. How could he! How could he go from Josephina’s kisses to Synda’s bed, and then brag about it?

The fury suddenly overshadowed every other emotion.

“Congratulations,” she said as drily as she was able. “You’re officially like every other man in this realm.” She had saved his life, and he had saved hers. Circumstances hadn’t allowed them to be lovers, but they could have been friends. She’d always wanted to be his friend. Yet he’d just ruined any hope for such an outcome. “I wish you’d stayed away from me. I wish I’d never met you.”

His features didn’t change, not this time, but his voice went low and quiet, dripping with disdain. “Too bad. I didn’t, and you did, and you have no one but yourself to blame. You should have left me in hell.”

“Oh, don’t worry. I’m about to do just that.” She tried to step around him.

He moved with her, blocking her. “You’re not going

anywhere. Synda got into trouble last night and she's earned another punishment."

Josephina froze. "What did she do?"

"Does it matter?"

It had to do with him, didn't it?

"You're to be whipped."

"No, no, no." That would mean the king was searching for Josephina. She knew him. Knew he would actually postpone the wedding ceremony to find her, wanting the situation dealt with before placing Synda—and thereby Josephina—into another man's care. And if he discovered she'd planned an escape… How could Kane be so cavalier about it? Shaking her head, she backed away from him. "How could you do this to me?"

"I didn't want any of this to happen, Tink."

"Don't call me that! You don't get to call me by a cutesy nickname when you just ruined my only chance for freedom."

"You want freedom?" His volume increased with every word. "Well, then, I'll get your freedom. Right now. Then, I'll be leaving the realm, and so will you. But don't worry. I won't be with you, so you won't have to fear my inability to protect you." He extended his arm, intending to grab her.

She jolted out of reach. "I believe you can protect me, idiot, I just don't want you hurt doing it. And if you do this, you'll be hurt. They'll hunt you. Forever."

The sharpest edge of his intensity dulled. "Being hunted was something you were willing to risk, obviously. Do me a favor and allow me the same choice."

She…had no response to that.

"I've thought about this, and thought about this, and I've nearly given myself a brain aneurism from thinking some more, and this morning I finally picked a plan and decided to stick with it. You're not going to like it, but honestly? I don't really care. I don't like you within these walls, and I can't deal with the demon any longer. I have to get out of here, and I have to kill him or I'm going to start hurting people, maybe even you. Again."

He was rambling, without giving her any useful information. "You can't just—"

"I can." He lunged for her, latching onto her before she could get away, and draping her over his shoulder. A favorite position of his. At the moment of contact, breath exploded from her lungs. She kicked and hit at him, but he sped into motion without missing a beat. "Every woman I come across throws herself at me, but not you. You keep fighting me."

"I'll never stop!"

"That's probably wise." He took her through secret passages he shouldn't have known about, up several flights of stairs, and into the daylight. "Why are you still wearing gloves? You know you can control your ability now."

"Because my hands are ugly." People had begun staring.

"Listen to *me*. Believe *me*. They're not."

She caught the scent of freshly cut grass and flowers, and the sound of murmuring voices…voices tapering to a quiet. Shock bombarded her, and she stilled. He wasn't sneaking out. He was walking through the crowd of wedding guests. How could he…the courage such an act required…the utter stupidity!

"I told you I'd marry your daughter, and I will," Kane called to the king. "That's not going to change. But I want this one."

What! Marry…*Josephina?* Despite their discord? No, that couldn't be right.

"There's two ways this can go down. You'll either gain a connection to my family by giving Josephina to me—in marriage—or I'll kill you here and now. Pick."

Yes. Her. But…but…

I won't let him. I'll put a stop to it.

"No," Leopold, standing behind the sputtering king, snarled. "You can't—"

"Go with option two," a male said with a laugh, interrupting him. "I'll finally get to put my pimp hand to good use."

She turned her head and watched as William, Red, Black, White and Green stepped into the gazebo where the royal family awaited the bride and groom. All five warriors were armed for war. Swords peeked over their shoulders. Guns were sheathed at their waists. And there were more men behind them! Men she recognized from the picture books the scribes had commissioned.

Oh, sweet lightning. The Lords of the Underworld were here. The frightful males were loaded with even more weapons than William and his crew. There was the scarred Lucien, the dark Reyes, the scary Sabin and the irreverent Strider.

Her heart sped into a faster rhythm. "Hi," she called, and waved at Lucien. "I can't believe this is happening. I've dreamed of this day all my life."

His scarred features were pale, and there were bruises under his eyes. He looked as if he'd been without sleep for several centuries. "Your wedding?" he asked her.

"No, I'm not getting married. I've been waiting to meet you," she said, her voice fluttering.

"All right, calm yourself," Kane muttered. "And yes, you're getting married."

"Kane—"

He continued. "I didn't want help, but I realized I needed it. There was no other way. But don't you ever trust the Rainbow Rejects. They're only aiding me now so they'll have an easier shot at you later."

"William, my darkling," the queen gasped out. "What are you doing? You're to be my protector."

The king roared, "Darkling? You're calling another male by *my* pet name?"

"Shut it, both of you," William snapped, all humor gone. "We've heard enough out of you."

The queen's mouth floundered open and closed, but she never made another sound.

Leopold stepped forward, but Red reached out and grabbed him by the neck, jerking him backward. In the next blink, a blade was poised at the prince's hammering pulse and he was gurgling in pain, a bead of blood leaking to the fluffy collar of his dress shirt. He tried to speak, but the weapon prevented any sound from forming.

"But what about me?" Synda called, racing up behind Kane, her wedding dress not quite fastened. She had to hold up the beautiful Fae lace with her hands. And her veil was askew, about to fall out of her pale curls.

"Shut it, woman," Kane snapped, mimicking William. "If I have to listen to one more bit of cruel, inane chatter from you, I'll remove your tongue. I swear I will."

Synda stopped, just stopped. No one had ever rejected her before—well, not for long. Bewilderment and hurt danced in her eyes, and Josephina almost felt sorry for her. Almost. She was too busy reeling. Kane had just put the girl in her place.

Red bloomed in the princess's eyes as she marched

through the sea of guests, throwing people out of their chairs.

The king blustered, saying, "This isn't the way of things, Lord Kane. We should—"

"Pick," Kane shouted. "I didn't ask for commentary."

Silence rolled through the masses, every gaze on Tiberius. The king switched his attention between Kane and his friends.

"Very well," he finally gritted.

"Good choice." Kane placed Josephina on her feet and glared down at her.

"Should I curtsy to your friends?" she asked to hide her nervousness. "I feel like I should curtsy."

He leaned in until they were nose-to-nose. "You'll accept this. Whatever you feel about me, whatever you believe about me, this is the best choice for you right now."

A wave of dizziness struck her. "I can't let you do this." She needed to tell him something else, but…what? She couldn't recall.

"Unlike your father, I'm not giving you a choice." He turned to the male officiating the ceremony. "What are you waiting for? Begin."

The priest obeyed him, but she didn't hear a word he said. Her thoughts were too loud. Surely she couldn't marry the very warrior that had slept with her half sister only last night. Surely she couldn't allow him to welcome a lifelong war. Surely she wouldn't bind her life to his, giving herself to him, while wearing a maid's uniform, looking her worst.

Even if he was the most incredible man she'd ever met…even if every inch of her body screamed, *yes!*

But would he ever be faithful?

Did he even want her or was he just trying to protect her, as he felt he owed her?

Her gaze strayed to Kane's friends. What had they thought of her at first glance? She'd been slung over Kane's shoulder so…probably not much.

"I'm really quite wonderful," she muttered.

"I know. You've told me," Kane said. "Now answer the priest."

"I will, just as soon as you tell me what he asked me."

The same murderous red she'd just seen in Synda's eyes pulsed from Kane's. "Just say yes," he snapped.

A beam in the canopy above them snapped and fell, and Kane had to drag her out of harm's way.

"Say it," he commanded.

"I will if the question was, does Kane annoy you? Because yes, he does," she said, attention returning to the other lords.

"Tell me the answer to that question again," Kane demanded, but he didn't sound offended.

"Yes," she threw at him.

He nodded, satisfied.

Lucien winked at her and she couldn't help but offer him as big of a smile as she could manage at the moment. Reyes nodded in acknowledgment. Strider gave her a thumbs-up. Sabin continued to glare. She wanted Kane's friends to like her—even though she didn't currently like Kane.

"This is a mistake," she whispered. Yes! Those were the words she'd wanted to give him. "We shouldn't do this. Let's stop before it's too late."

He squeezed her hand so tightly she whimpered, but even then, he didn't loosen his grip. He slid a ring on her finger, the metal heavy, with a huge stone glittering in the center. A stone she didn't recognize. The color hovered somewhere between ruby-red and sapphire-blue.

"It's already too late. Don't ever take this off, understand?" Kane said.

Too late? They were…they were…no way.

Still. Eyes wide, she nodded.

"Oh, and here's the big guy's ring," William said, handing her a plain, over-warm band that was vibrating.

Trembling, she slid the thing onto Kane's finger, and finally he released her.

"It's done," he said, and there was a wealth of satisfaction in his voice.

Josephina could only nod, dazed.

A scream nearly split the daylight. "You're not taking her away from me!"

Not Synda. But…the Phoenix?

Definitely. The entire back end of the garden burst into flames.

Kane threw Josephina over his shoulder.

"Not again," she gritted out.

Lucien held out his arms. "I'll take her now. And I'll take good care of her, you have my word."

"Change of plan," Kane said. "She's going with me. At least for now. Get the others to safety. And thanks for coming, my man." He took off in a dead run. Smoke wafted to her nose, making her cough. Shouts of fear erupted through the crowd.

"How do you propose to leave the realm?" she asked, trying not to panic. Only a select group of Fae possessed a key between the human realm and this one. Kane wasn't select, nor was he Fae. She had planned to steal Leopold's for her own escape, but that was now an impossibility.

"Like this." Kane withdrew a flesh-colored glove

from his pocket—a key. "Before you ask, I stole it. And no, I'm not ashamed and I won't return it."

"I don't want to chastise you, you silly man. I want to pat you on the back. Now, do you know how to use it?"

"Yeah." He quickened his pace.

She expected some of the guards to chase him, no matter what her father had said, and she expected guests to try and pass him, desperate to get away from the fires, but he was moving too fast for anyone to catch. Within seconds, he was at the front gate and he wasn't even winded.

He fit the glove over his hand and waved from high to low, side to side, in the shape of a door. A sheet of the landscape fell away from every place he touched, leaving a black hole.

"Think about where you want to go, and step through," she hurried to explain, even though he'd claimed to know what to do.

He stalked into the darkness, and then, suddenly, they were out of the realm of the Fae and in the realm of the humans. Tall buildings knifed on both of her sides. Harried people strode along narrow sidewalks. The scent of coffee and car exhaust and even urine filled her nose.

"Close the door," she said, and he obeyed, once again waving his hand through the air.

He set her on her feet, took her by the wrist, and tugged her forward. "Let's go. The door might be closed, but I want you as far away from it as possible."

"Where are we?"

"New York. I want you masked by the crowd."

Should have guessed, she thought. She'd been here before, and there was no place like it.

"What about your friends?" she asked.

"They'll be fine."

"You were going to leave me in their keeping?"

"For a while, yes."

A while. How long was a while? *Probably better not to know.*

They walked for hours, and the more they walked, the busier the streets and sidewalks became. Any other time, the crowd would have bothered her, but just then her mind was too busy reeling. She was out of the Fae realm. She was with Kane. Maybe even married to him—had they truly finished the ceremony? They'd never kissed.

Didn't matter, she supposed. For a little while, she would be safe from her family. She wouldn't have to worry about being punished. She wouldn't have to worry about the king hunting her down for a few days, at the very least. He would need time to plan a strategy against a man like Kane.

For the first time in her life, she was free.

Joy burst through her, and with the joy came an unquenchable desire to truly live. To do all the things she'd never dreamed possible. To fall in love, get married and—wait. She was already married. Maybe. She would have to talk to Kane about that. He probably hadn't meant his vows. If he'd spoken any vows, that is. She could have slapped herself for not paying attention. For all she knew, she'd pledged to be his slave.

Whatever. It still didn't matter. With this first taste of freedom, her entire world had changed. She'd already decided she was done accepting the abuse thrown her way. But now, she was done allowing fear to hold her captive. The future was hers to embrace, and she would hold on as tightly as she could.

Kane flicked a glance in her direction, did a double take. He stopped, and his eyes widened.

"What?" she asked, nearly bumping into him.

"You're smiling." There was a reverent tone to his voice, one he'd never used before.

"I am?" She reached up and patted her lips, and yes, she *was* smiling.

For the second time that day, his features softened. "You're happy, and you wear it well." But a second later, his cheeks blushed, and he turned away. "Come on. I haven't slept in days and I'm about to crash. We need a place to stay."

CHAPTER TWENTY-FIVE

New York

WIFE.

The word echoed through Kane's mind all through the night. He toyed with the ring William had given him, a simple gold band that should have been cool to the touch but wasn't; the metal burned him and he wasn't sure why.

Wife.

He had a wife. A woman forever bound to his side. She was his, and he was hers. Not just instinctively, but legally. The knowledge did something to him. Something powerful. Before, he'd only scratched the surface of possessive. Now, the sensation dominated. Tink. Was. His.

Want and need combined, creating a combustible fire. He burned. He ached. He yearned.

Finally, he would have.

His hand shook as he reached out and smoothed a lock of hair from her cheek. The long, thick length of her eyelashes fluttered open, and he found himself peering into beautiful baby blues.

After renting the room, he'd climbed into bed and tucked her into the curve of his body. She hadn't protested. He'd left the lamps on, and now, golden light cascaded over her. She was curled on her side, facing him. Locks of dark hair spilled over the pillow and sheets.

He should have given her to Lucien, as planned. The warrior would have taken her to the Realm of Blood and Shadows, and Kane would have gone about the business of finding a way to kill the demon. But the arrival of the Phoenix had changed everything. He'd wanted—needed—Tink within his sights, his to protect from the flames.

Even though she hadn't wanted to marry him.

Now, it was done, and there was nothing she could do about it.

"I'm your husband," he said, almost angrily. He didn't pull his hand away.

"Maybe," she whispered.

"What do you mean, maybe?"

She traced a fingertip along the shape of her lips, as if remembering something—or yearning for it. "Well, I don't exactly remember what vows were exchanged."

"You agreed to be my wife, and I agreed to be your husband. That's enough. It's done. There's no changing it."

"We could, I don't know…get an annulment maybe. We've both been prisoners, Kane, and I'm not going to be your new cage."

"You aren't a cage. You're my everything." Moving with a speed he usually reserved for the battlefield, he cupped the back of her neck and dragged her against him. The softness of her body collided with the hardness of his, and he had to grind his teeth to silence a hiss of pleasure. "No annulment. Later, no divorce. Death is the only thing that will part us."

Her eyes flared with hope, only to quickly narrow

with suspicion. "Are you going to be with other women while we're together?"

"No." And that was the truth. "I didn't sleep with Synda. I shouldn't have lied. I'm not a liar, and I won't do it again. Not for any reason. I was hurt by what you said, and lashing out."

A pause, as if she didn't dare hope he'd spoken honestly. "Really?" Her eyes narrowed slightly. "That's pretty low."

"I know. But not as low as actually sleeping with her would have been," he added, hoping she'd agree.

Slowly, she nodded. "All right. I'll give you that."

He'd been *devastated* by her rejection, and he'd wanted out of that ballroom so badly he'd leaped at the first opportunity. Sleeping with Synda had never been a consideration. "I tucked her in to bed, then sat on the couch in the adjacent room most of the night, making sure she stayed put and out of trouble. At least, I thought I was making sure. She used a secret passage I didn't know about and snuck out to have sex with Red in the garden."

Tink slid her hand across the small space between them and traced her fingers over the center of his chest, where the dragon brand had been. The pleasure…it was too much, not enough. He hooked one of her legs over his waist, twining their bodies as much as possible while they were still clothed.

He could barely breathe, but he could do nothing until he'd told her the truth about him. He'd made too many mistakes with her to make another. She would think less of him, yes. How could she not? But he was going to be with her. Here. Tonight. He wanted this marriage cemented. And if he had a negative reaction to something she did, he didn't want her worried about the reason or thinking he didn't want her.

"The other women I mentioned…I told the truth. I was with them before I found you. I thought sex with them would make me forget what had happened in hell, that I'd forget about being helpless, but it only made me feel worse. Memories taunted me and I…vomited after every encounter."

"Oh, Kane," she said, shifting her fingers through his hair. "I'm sorry."

No judgment. Just compassion.

Once he had thought he hated compassion, the cousin to pity. Not today. "You make me crave things I never thought I'd crave again." He nuzzled the side of her neck. "I want to be with you, Tinker Bell." Wanted everything she had to give.

"I…I…want to be with you, too. I want to smother your bad memories with good. I want to be all you know, all you see." So softly admitted. "What I said at the ball, in the secret room…Kane, I believe in you. I really do. You are the strongest, bravest male I know, but I couldn't bear the thought of being the reason your life was thrown into another war."

Any remaining hurt was soothed.

War. Disaster laughed. *I'll give her war. I'll make sure you break her heart before I kill her.*

He wouldn't break her heart. He wouldn't let her be hurt…ever.

"Some things are worth fighting for, Tink, and I'll prove it. Give me a minute." Kane left her in bed and prowled through the room, stacking all lamps and wall hangings in the bathroom, then shutting the door and rigging the lock. Soft moonlight drifted into the space as he crawled back into bed.

Tink softened against him, warm and welcoming.

Now…now he was finally going to have her.

"I want you," he said, the hunger gnawing at him now. "All of you."

A moment passed before she nodded.

"Roll over."

This time, there was no hesitation. She obeyed.

"I want to be everything you need," she said, "the way you're everything I need."

A heart he'd thought hardened beyond redemption thrilled. "You already are." He rose on an elbow and unbuttoned the back of her uniform. As the material parted, his eyes adjusted to the dark and he was able to see the plain white undergarments she wore. Lovely. Pure.

Every inch his.

"All right. On your back."

Again she obeyed.

As he eased the gown from her shoulders, down her waist, and over her feet, she shivered. The undergarments and then her ring and gloves received the same treatment, at last leaving her bare. Beautifully, exquisitely bare.

He looked her over more leisurely. She lay utterly still, allowing him to drink his fill. He could only marvel. Every inch of her had been made for his specific tastes. Lush, yet slender. Ripe for plucking, yet delightfully innocent. She undid him. Destroyed him. Ruined him for all other females.

My woman is perfect.

"Wait, my ring," she said, trying to swipe it out of his hold.

He held it back, out of reach. "Not until you promise the gloves are gone for good."

"I don't know why it's so important to you, but all right."

"We're going to be what's known as a disgustingly lovey-dovey couple. I want skin, not leather."

As her features softened, she said, "I promise."

He slid the ring back on her finger.

Her lips lifted in a *slooow* grin. A vixen's grin. "Now, it's time for *you* to take something off. It's only fair."

"I do want to be fair." A dark fever drove him as he ripped off his clothing. Tink's eyes devoured with the same greed he had displayed. He wished he had the patience to let her study as he had studied, but need could no longer be denied. He stretched on top of her, remembering at the last second to brace his weight on his elbows, and oh, the agony. The agony of being this close to her and not being inside her.

Have to get inside her.

"Spread your legs," he demanded, and she obeyed.

Suddenly he could feel her against him, the most intimate part of her, all barriers gone; the exquisite, moist heat nearly pushed him over the edge.

"Oh, Kane. It's…it's…" With her nails in his back, she arched against him.

As he swooped in to kiss her, the bed began to shake, stopping him even while grinding him against her with far more force.

He hissed. She cried out.

"Silly demon," she said on a moan. "This is actually…oh…*oh!* Don't stop, Kane. Please, don't stop."

Disaster cursed. The bed ceased moving.

Growling, Kane smashed his mouth into her. He'd meant to proceed gently, but…screw gentleness. She hadn't wanted it any time before.

She opened for him immediately, welcoming him,

moaning with her pleasure; he swallowed the sound. He kissed her, kissed her harder, kissed her deeper, every second wrought with more tension than the last. As his hands moved on her breasts, her stomach, between her legs, she came alive.

A crack echoed. He caught the scent of plaster in the air. The wall was taking the brunt of the demon's fury.

Tink started.

"Forget him," Kane said. He fit his hand between her lower back and the mattress, and lifted her, drawing her more firmly against him, fitting them together until not even a whisper separated them.

She gasped. Her fingers shifted through his hair, tugging the strands. "Already done. Now give me more."

"Always." His lips returned to hers in a fierce meeting of mouths, dueling tongues, and nipping teeth. The passion…the utter rapture. The ecstasy.

"I want to touch you, too."

"Yes."

Her hands roamed over him, exploring him, learning him, fisting his length, and that should have bothered him, but he was too relieved to be with her to entertain even a glimmer of reservation. The past fell away. There was only Tink and this moment and the pleasure and the light. Here, in her arms, surrounded by her, accepted by her, needed by her, the wounds inside his soul finally began to heal. Strength infused his bones, plumped his muscles. The blood in his veins became molten, his need for her too intense to ever again deny.

"I like this," she said on a groan.

"Glad."

"I want…the rest…" The words ended on a groan. "Do the rest."

"Soon." He took over completely. Awed by her—

mine, she's mine, and I can have her, can have this, *as many times as I desire*—he did everything in his power to prepare her for his invasion. His mouth, on her body. All over it, lingering. Her taste, down his throat. Like honey. His fingers, between her legs. Rubbing, playing. She moaned, again and again, and the sounds were like music.

He *liiicked*. Sucked. Kneaded. Played again. Worked his fingers in *slllowly*…picking up speed…faster and faster…all while he whispered to her, praising her sweetness.

"I'm going to…something's happening…"

"Let go, sweetheart. I've got you."

She erupted, the pleasure hitting her, making her spasm and gasp. And when she came back down to earth a few minutes later, he started up all over again.

Panting, she said, "That was…that was…"

"Next time I'll be in you, and it'll be even better."

"Yes," she said, a plea, barely discernable. "Please. If you don't…I'm going to…oh, I need that again… *please*."

Yes. Now. No more waiting. She was his. He needed to claim her. Brand her from the inside out.

He donned a condom and moved into position, settling between her eagerly opened thighs. Concern for her was the only power strong enough to stop him from immediately thrusting home. "It's going to hurt at first. There's nothing I can do about that, but it'll get better. I promise it'll get better. But I'll stay still until you're ready, okay?"

"Hurts *now*. Just. Do. Something."

He surged inside her, roaring, the reins of his control instantly shredded, the power of the joining utterly overwhelming him.

She cried out, the sound laced with pleasure and pain.

Mine. She's all mine now. Claimed. Possessed.

He remained still, as promised. Sweat poured from him. His heart thundered at the incredible pressure inside him. Pressure he resisted with all of his might.

Any second, he would break apart.

"Want me to…pull out?" he panted. *Please, don't want me to pull out.*

"No. Go! Finally doing…what I…need."

He almost laughed. Almost.

He slid backward, and she squeezed at him, trying to hold him inside. Then, he slammed forward, giving her more, giving her harder, all hope of regaining control gone. He utterly ravaged her. His need for her was too great, and she liked it, was still grasping at him, once again begging for more, and more, and more.

"You feel so good," he moaned. He told her how much he wanted her, needed her, had to have her, and she responded with soft mewls. "Don't think I'll ever get enough."

"Kane."

"Tink, my Tink."

His already frenzied rhythm quickened, and when she gave another cry, this one high-pitched and broken, a testament of her release, the pleasure utterly consumed him. He roared with the sublime satisfaction of his.

When the last of his shudders subsided, he collapsed on top of her. Drained. Sated.

Awed.

Panting, she said, "That was…that was…"

"Awesome and wonderful." He rolled onto his side, freeing her from his weight. "Like you."

She kissed the hammering pulse at the base of his

neck. “No wonder you did it so many times before coming after me.”

No condemnation. Still no judgment. Was there any woman like her? “Sweetheart, nothing has ever compared to this.”

She snuggled against him, a content little kitten, rubbing her cheek against his chest. “Husband?”

Oh, he liked the sound of that. “Yes. Wife.”

“Let’s do it again.”

WHEN MORNING DAWNED, Josephina was once again snuggled against the warmth of Kane’s body. She hadn’t slept, had been too busy marveling. The man wanted by all others wanted her. The man who couldn’t tolerate the touch of others had yearned for hers. Now, he held on to her as if he couldn’t bear to let her go. As if she meant something to him.

What a wonderful life she suddenly lived.

And what a wonderful man at her side. He’d experienced the worst life had to offer, was still hurting inside, might always carry the scars, but he’d turned to her. He’d found a measure of peace with her; she would cherish him all the days of her life.

A strange vibration tickled the skin of her cheek, and she frowned. “What’s happening—”

“It’s from my ring,” Kane said with a sleep-rich rumble. “It’s been bugging me all night, shaking my arm, creating some kind of heat.”

“That’s not exactly normal ring behavior.”

“I know. Apparently, William is some kind of collector, and he was willing to trade this one for a bag of Skittles. Don’t ask me where he found it. I don’t know.”

“Hmm, Skittles,” she said with a moan of longing.

He snorted. “You’d trade your rock for the candy,

wouldn't you? Never mind. Don't tell me. I'll only want to Super Glue the thing to your finger."

She held the ring to the light, the jewel sparkling majestically. "Even though it's size giant, I won't take it off." It was a symbol of their commitment to each other.

He kissed her temple, gentle and sweet and almost boyish. "Are you hungry, wife?"

Wife. Was there a more beautiful word? "I'm starved, actually. Husband." Oh, yes. That one. She might never get tired of saying it.

"Me, too," he said, his voice going low, "but I doubt we're talking about the same thing."

"Well, are we talking about sex?"

He gave a bark of laughter. "Yeah, but your body needs to heal before that particular appetite can be sated. A fourth time." He hugged her tight and rolled, then rose from the bed. "Cover those dangerous curves, woman, and I'll take you to the diner next door."

"Yes, sir." Long locks of hair tumbled down her shoulders as she sat up. Her body still ached, and her heart…well, her heart had yet to calm down. In all the futures she'd imagined for herself, she'd never seen one like *this*.

Muscles flexed as Kane gathered his weapons, his underwear, slacks, and a shirt. His hair was rumpled, his gaze heavy-lidded and sexy. Naked, barefoot, he padded into the bathroom and showered with the door open.

When he emerged on a cloud of steam, wearing the very clothing he'd gathered, he crooked his finger at her. "Your turn."

The tension he'd sported all these weeks was completely gone.

Smiling, Josephina walked past him—naked. He

moaned, his eyes locked on her, as if in pain. She brushed her teeth and showered, then dressed in the hated maid uniform. "I'd rather wear the curtains," she grumbled as she joined him by the door.

"We'll go shopping after we eat."

A short time later, she was sliding into a booth in the back of the diner, Kane across from her. The place was packed with old school charm, the tiled floor black and white, the walls covered with fifties memorabilia.

"Do you have enough money to pay for your breakfast?" Kane asked as he studied the menu.

"No." He'd left her bag in Séduire.

"I guess you'll have to find a way to pay me back. Waffles aren't free."

"Hey. We're married. You insisted. That means whatever you have is mine."

His lips twitched at the corners. "So you now agree that we're married?"

"Answer a question for me first," she said, wanting to tease him the way he teased her. "Are you loaded? I mean, the stories say you are, but I just want to be sure before I pledge my life to yours."

"I'm more than loaded. Torin could turn anyone into a billionaire."

"I knew there was a reason I liked him. But to answer your question, yes, I agree. Your money and I are one."

He stopped trying to hide his grin and dazzled her with a display of pearly whites.

I'm so *falling for this man.*

A waitress wearing a poodle skirt approached their table, making Josephina feel less conspicuous in her gown. The woman had a notepad and pen at the ready.

"Can I take your…uh…" She locked eyes with Kane

and her words tapered off. She fluffed her hair. "Hi. I'm Claudia. My friends call me Claude."

Uncomfortable, he tugged at the collar of his shirt. "We'd like—"

The building began to shake and the patrons to gasp. The ketchup bottle resting on the side of the table shattered, every glass shard arrowing toward Josephina, several even slicing into her arm. Blood beaded over the wounds.

Kane muttered a curse, threw down his menu and stood, pulling Josephina to her feet. "Come on. We need to leave."

"Disaster?" she asked.

"Yeah."

"Wait," the waitress called.

He ignored her. The moment they stepped outside, a car slammed into another car directly in front of them. Impact tore a scrap of metal from the wreckage, tossing it at Josephina's head. Had Kane not jerked her to the ground, she would have been decapitated. But he did, and the piece cut through the diner window.

Glass shattered. Cars honked. People shouted obscenities. Footsteps pounded as bystanders raced away.

Forcing her to stand, Kane's grip tightened on her, the pressure almost enough to snap her bones.

"What do you need?" she asked. "How can I help you?"

Silent, he led her inside their hotel. The building was tall and well kept, with plush carpets and pretty paintings on the walls. There was a chandelier overhead, though nothing as grand as those in the Fae palace.

"Kane?"

He remained silent as they stepped into the elevator, strode down the hall and finally entered their room.

"Talk to me, Kane. Please."

"You're going to stay here." There was a grim quality to his voice, and he wouldn't meet her eyes. "Leave and you'll regret it. And don't open the door to anyone. In fact," he said, withdrawing a gun from the waist of his pants, "do you know how to use one of these?"

"No. Fae women are forbidden from learning how to defend themselves."

His features darkened. "I should have started training you, as promised, and I'm sorry I didn't. But don't worry. The gun is ready to go, complete with silencer. All you have to do is point and squeeze the trigger." He set the weapon on the nightstand, his hand trembling.

"Where are you going?"

A moment passed in silence. "I plan to feed the demon so he'll stop trying to hurt you. At least for a little while."

CHAPTER TWENTY-SIX

JOSEPHINA PACED IN front of the massive bed she'd shared with her husband only an hour ago, her hands wringing together. The change in Kane had startled her. In seconds, he'd gone from affable and flirty to downright mean. And there'd been guilt in his eyes…so much guilt, made all the worse because it had been ringed by a toxic mix of self-disgust and shame.

Just how did he plan to feed such a terrible demon? If he placed himself in danger…

Having trouble catching her breath, she eased onto the bed, propped against the pillows and closed her eyes. She had only ever projected her image into other people's minds; never had she attempted to see the world through another's eyes. Here, now, she had to try.

Kane needed her, whether he knew it or not. If she could figure out where he was, she could race to the rescue. No longer did he have to fight against the evil on his own, and she would prove it.

"YOU WANT A disaster," Kane muttered, "I'll give you a disaster."

Want the girl dead was the demon's snarled reply. *Dead, dead, dead.*

"Well, you're not getting that one." He would die first. But then, that wouldn't help, either, would it.

He would distance himself from Tink, go so far away

from her the demon wouldn't be able to reach her. After seeing those cuts on her arm…the drip of crimson…yeah, distance was what was needed.

Where could he go?

No. Not him, he realized. Her. She had to go. He would call Lucien. He would send the warrior to pick her up, and have her escorted to the fortress in the Realm of Blood and Shadows, as he'd originally planned. Kane would stay away from her, and she would be safe.

The demon would be satisfied.

He pressed his thumb against his wedding ring, spun the metal. Soon, the band would be his only connection to Tink. He punched the building beside him, and the brick cracked. He never should have tried to create a normal life with her. Not until the demon was dead.

Disaster growled.

Kane turned the corner of the sidewalk. A window shattered as he passed. People shouted with fright and scrambled away from the sea of glass. "What are you doing now?" he gritted. "I'm giving you what you want."

You give, even while you plot my demise. Perhaps it's time I ended you, and freed myself.

"You'll be crazed, mindless."

Aren't I already?

He wouldn't panic.

An SUV slammed into a lamppost. A biker swerved, hit a curb. The bike flipped end over end and crashed into Kane.

Teeth grinding, Kane kept going. "You're hurting innocents."

I know. Isn't it great?

"Stop."

Let's bargain. I won't try to kill you, or others—if.

"If?"

See that woman over there? I want her. Give her to me.

Across the street, a pretty woman stood outside a shop, watching the chaos down the way.

"No," Kane snapped.

The water main broke, liquid suddenly shooting into the sky. Two cars collided.

"No," he repeated, wiping cold droplets from his brow.

A black bird careened from the sky, slammed into Kane's chest before falling to the ground. There was a pained squawk as feathers rained in every direction. Struggling to breathe, he bent down to check the damage to the bird.

It died before contact was made.

The girl. Give me the girl.

Kane straightened, closed his eyes for a moment. He knew what Disaster really wanted—for Kane to betray his wife, ruin the trust they'd only just managed to build and destroy any hope for a future. Then, when Lucien carried Tink away, the distance between husband and wife would be more than physical. It would be mental, emotional. And it wouldn't matter if Disaster died or not. The damage would have been done, all hope torched, Kane's life ruined.

What better catastrophe was there than that?

I can't do it, Kane thought. *I won't do it.*

And yet, a second later, when a billboard fell from the side of the building, and humans rushed away to avoid being crushed, the word *apocalypse* reverberated in his head and he found himself crossing the street, approaching the woman.

Maybe your Fae will never find out, Disaster said, glee in his tone. *It can be our little secret.*

No. There were no secrets. Truth had ways of seeping out. More than that, he would never keep something like this secret from her.

In the back of his mind, he suddenly thought he felt another presence. Someone soft and gentle, sweet and innocent. Someone who smelled like fresh-baked bread.

Tink?

He frowned, searching the area for any sign of her, finding none. His guilt must be playing tricks on him. Either that, or Disaster was.

"I'm not going to do what you want," he said.

Kiss this woman, and I'll leave your Josephina alone.

Tink. Safe. "Ma'am," he said, acid burning a path up his throat.

The woman looked up at him. Fear glazed her eyes. "What's happening out there?"

"A whole lot of dangerous," he said. "Why don't I escort you somewhere safe?"

The window behind her shattered. Screaming, she threw herself into his arms.

A hand here...a mouth there...so helpless...

Memories hit him, swift and hard. As he fought the urge to jerk away from the woman, the past, to scrub himself from head to toe with steel wool, he gently detached himself from her grip.

KISS HER!

Sweat beaded on his brow. Behind him, the roof of a building caved in.

The woman trembled. "It's the end of the world," she whispered.

Like…an apocalypse.

Urgency rushed through him, joining forces with

fear and panic. "Swear it," he said to Disaster. "Swear you'll leave Tink alone."

"Who?" the woman asked.

I swear it.

Before he could talk himself out of it, Kane leaned down and kissed her. She stiffened, but she didn't push him away; the urge to vomit hit him, and he straightened.

In a snap, the presence left him.

Disaster laughed. *I was lying, of course. How foolish of you to trust me.*

Kane punched the brick wall, uncaring when his knuckles broke upon impact. He should have known. The demon would do anything to ruin his most prized relationship—and had probably succeeded. *And I went along with it, all for a lie.* He punched the wall again.

"I-is everything okay?" the woman stuttered.

"I've been looking for you," a male voice interjected from behind him.

The power that wafted from that voice startled him. Disaster, too. The demon yelped in sudden fear and hid in a far corner of his mind. Kane spun and met the gaze of a Sent One. The warrior wasn't anyone he knew personally, but he recognized the green fauxhawk, the Asian features, the gleaming white robe and oh, yeah, the impressive white-and-gold wings arching over wide, muscled shoulders, sweeping all the way to the floor.

"Who are you and why are you here?" Kane liked the Sent Ones. He did. They'd helped his friend Amun, the keeper of Secrets, at the worst hour of his life. They were training Paris's wife to lead the Titans out of darkness and into light. They hadn't killed Aeron—not permanently, at least—when he married into the family. But now wasn't a good time.

"Uh, who are you talking to?" the woman asked.

"I'm Malcolm," the warrior said, acting as if she wasn't there. "I'm here to check on you. We knew you were in hell, but heard you had escaped. I was told to find you and verify that you were indeed alive and well."

"I'm alive." But far from well. "Is that all?"

"O-kay," the woman said. "I don't care if you can save me from the end of the world or not. I'm out of here."

Footsteps sounded but Kane never diverted his eyes from the Sent One before him.

Malcolm crossed his arms over his massive chest. "No, that's not all. Six demons killed Deity, our king, and those demons are now living on earth, desperate to possess as many humans as possible. If you're well, you are to help us find them."

Yeah. He'd heard about the king's death, and knew there'd been a change of management in the skies. "I can't help you right now. Sorry. Look around. You'll realize I've got too many problems of my own."

A pause. Then, "I just came from the realm of the Fae. Where you were married?"

"Yeah." Kane held up his left hand and wiggled his fingers, shamefully making light of a symbol he cherished. "So."

"So, the woman you were kissing was human." The warrior's gaze moved away—only to return in a snap and latch onto the ring. "Where did you get that?" The question was uttered quietly, yet lashed like a whip.

Nerve-endings raw, Kane snapped, "What business is it of yours?"

Something dark crossed over the male's features. He

ignored the question, demanding, "What are you doing out here, without your woman?"

Destroying my life. He closed his eyes for a moment, desperate to escape the harsh reality of those words. "Watch me as I don't discuss that with you."

The warrior tapped two incisors together as he looked at the ring, then Kane, then the ring, then, finally, Kane. "I can guess. You carry Disaster, and you're trying to feed the beast to keep him calm."

Hearing it stated so plainly irritated him. "If you knew, why'd you ask?"

"I wondered if you knew."

"Well, now that we're clear, you can go."

Malcolm tilted his head to the side. "Do you plan to kill the demon?"

"Yes."

"You'll die, too."

"Maybe not. Aeron used to be keeper of Wrath, but he's now demon-free and living large."

"Aeron was given a new body."

"So I'll get a new body, too," Kane said. Maybe there was a store somewhere.

"That's not how it works."

"Look. The demon left me before—" when Tink had sucked him out "—and I did just fine."

"You were only alone for a short period of time."

And he knew that, how? "Yeah. So?"

"So, the creature's departure emptied you out. Eventually you *would* have died."

Disbelief would have wasted time. Sent Ones couldn't lie. Frustrated, Kane scrubbed a hand down his face. "Explain."

"Think of a cup filled with oil. When the cup is

tipped over, the oil spills out. Soon there is nothing left but emptiness."

And Kane's body was the cup.

"Man cannot live on empty." Malcolm paused, said, "Tell me. Do you hate your wife?"

The moment of camaraderie was ruined. He stilled, preparing to attack. "Back off, warrior. I won't hesitate to snuff you out."

"I'll take that as a no, you don't hate her. Then why were you kissing another woman to calm the demon? That wasn't necessary."

Kane palmed a dagger. How dare this piece of— The words *that wasn't necessary* registered, and he stilled. "What do you mean, that wasn't necessary?"

"You Lords of the Underworld," Malcolm said with a shake of his head. "You've been dealing with the evil for so long, you've simply accepted it. You've stopped fighting it."

"I fight it every day."

"Do you?"

He sucked in a breath. "You're on dangerous ground again, my friend."

Unaffected, Malcolm gazed down at the ring. "What you feed grows stronger. What you starve eventually dies."

O-kay. "You've lost me."

"Are you always this obtuse?"

"Are you always this rude?"

"Yes."

Sent Ones and their honesty, man. "I'm feeding the demon to calm him. He's acting up and putting my woman in danger."

"No, *feeding* the demon is what's putting your woman in danger."

"I don't get what you're saying. Help me understand." He would do anything to walk away from this day with Tink at his side. "If I starve the demon, he'll throw a tantrum."

Malcolm leaned back and crossed his arms over his chest. "So what. When you deprive your body of food, your stomach begins to hurt and grumble loudly in protest. The demon is the same. When it becomes hungry, it acts up. Deny him satisfaction, and his power to throw tantrums will weaken."

Feeding, and starving. Life, and death. "I can kill the demon this way," Kane said, a light dawning in his mind. "I can starve him to death."

"Exactly."

"Emptying me out."

The Sent One shrugged. "Yes, that, too."

Killing Kane, as well.

Realization slammed hard, but true. To keep Tink safe, forever, he had to die. And if he died, he would never have his revenge against Disaster. How could he? They would meet the same fate.

There would be no happily ever after for him.

He wanted to protest. To fight *this*. There had to be another way. A way that would allow him to live with his wife for an eternity, to watch Disaster perish and finally have the last laugh. But just then, with the Sent One watching him with the barest measure of pity, he knew there wasn't. And in the end, he would rather die, knowing Tink was safe, than live, knowing he was putting her in danger.

She was more important to him than…anything. Even vengeance.

Heart racing, Kane said, "I have to go." But he paused a few feet away, a memory sliding into place.

"I don't know how to help you with your demon problem, but I do know you have a friend that disappeared," he said, remembering what he'd heard about the Sent One, Thane, from Taliyah. Malcolm stiffened. "I heard he appeared in one of the Phoenix camps. The one with a new king. I believe they're holding him captive."

Hope flared in Malcolm's eyes.

Kane leaped back into motion. He would do this. He would starve and kill the demon, and then die himself. He wasn't sure how long it would take. It would be best to call Lucien, and have Tink whisked to a safe zone now, before Disaster began to act out from hunger pains, but he wanted to spend every one of his remaining seconds with her.

When the demon acted up again—and he would—Kane would just have to find a way to shield her. Because if he was going to die with a smile on his face, he needed her by his side.

CHAPTER TWENTY-SEVEN

THE MOMENT KANE burst into the hotel room, Josephina launched a pillow at his head. He stopped in his tracks, and she launched another.

"You snake!" she shouted. "You horrible, despicable snake!"

The door shut with a loud thud. He held up his hands, all innocence. As if he wasn't a lying, cheating scum who'd betrayed her the day after their wedding.

"Tink, it's just me."

"I know!" She jerked the ring from her finger and threw it at him. The monstrosity slammed into his chest before thumping to the floor. Angry beyond measure, she picked up the gun he'd given her and pointed the barrel at his chest. Her hands were shaking, her blood as hot as fire. "I said no, just to save you, but you *insisted* I marry you."

Darkness descended over his expression. "You plan to murder me to get free of me?" So softly asked.

Tearing her up inside.

Tears welled in her eyes. His hair was tangled, his eyes bloodshot, and his skin pallid. Obviously, too much pleasure with the blonde from the sidewalk had drained him. His clothing was wrinkled and torn—had the female gotten rough with him? Her stomach heaved.

"Yes! I saw you with her," she croaked. "Saw you kiss her. *After* you'd had sex with me and promised to be faithful." A few hours ago, she would have called it making love.

But never again.

A muscle ticked in his jaw, the catalyst to a deep, dark coldness that began to fall over his features. "You invaded my mind."

Planting her feet on the floor, she raised her chin. "I sure did." At first, she'd been so excited by her success. She was bound to Kane in a way she'd never been bound to another, so, of course she could reach him the way she'd never reached another. But then she'd realized there was a pretty female standing in front of him, and he couldn't take his eyes off of her lips.

Josephina had wanted to die.

She'd also wanted to kill!

"Tink," he said.

"Don't Tink me! I'm not your Tink. Not anymore."

"Put the gun down, and I'll explain everything that happened."

"I don't want the gory details."

He raked a hand through his hair, causing the strands to stand on end. "Give me a chance. Please."

"I did! And you betrayed me at the first opportunity."

"I hated every moment of it, I promise you. Disaster wanted her, I didn't. He was destroying everything around me. I wanted to calm him down, that was all. He promised to leave you alone if I kissed her, and I wanted so badly for him to leave you alone."

She hadn't been able to hear Disaster while in his mind, but she'd certainly heard Kane. *Swear it,* she remembered him saying. *Swear you'll leave Tink alone.*

One of the tears escaped, slid down her cheek. "What would you do if the situation were reversed, and I smashed my mouth against some strange man, just to save you?"

His eyes narrowed. "I would have ripped him to pieces, put him back together and then ripped him apart again." He approached her, aggression in every step. "I made a terrible mistake. But I promise you, I wouldn't have done anything more."

"It doesn't matter. It still hurt."

"I'll never do it again, you have my word." Another step closer. "A Sent One came—"

"Sent One? And stay where you are!"

He froze, his mouth curved in a tortured frown. "A Sent One is a winged warrior tasked with fighting evil, like an angel, only…not. He told me to starve the demon, no matter what Disaster does, and eventually you'll be safe."

"Oh, I'll be safe all right," she said quietly. "I'll be safe away from you."

"Tink." He took another step toward her.

"I said stay back!"

He didn't. He increased his speed. Instinct kicked in, and her finger flexed on the trigger. *Pop.* The gun recoiled, smoke curling from the barrel. Horror filled her.

Kane was in front of her a second later, swiping the gun out of her hand and tossing her on top of the bed. Before she finished bouncing, his weight slammed into her, pinning her down.

"We'll work on your aim. Later."

"Let me go!" Josephina fought against him with all of her might, beating her fists into his face, his chest, trying to buck him off with her body. Not once did he try and deflect her blows.

"I'm sorry," he rasped. "I'm so sorry. I didn't want to do it. I hated myself. I hated being there. I hated the woman. I was sick about it. I just didn't see another way, but I should have done something, anything else."

"Get off me! Let me go!"

"I can't. I can't let you go. I don't know how much time we'll have together, and I want to savor every single second."

She stilled long enough to glare up at him and pant, "Do you have any idea what it feels like to see your husband kissing another woman?"

Silence drenched with shame.

Silence that drove her into a deeper madness. She erupted, beating at him until her hands were throbbing and her lungs were burning from the forcefulness of her pants…until all she could do was collapse on the mattress and sob for the precious trust he'd torn to shreds.

Kane rolled onto his side and gathered her close. He cooed to her, smoothing the hair from her face. His breath fanned over her cheek, and she hated the sensation—because she loved it.

Finally, the sobs quieted. Her eyes were nearly swollen shut, and her nose was stuffed up. Every ounce of energy she possessed had drained from her, and yet still she tried to sit up. "I don't want to—"

"Just let me hold you," he beseeched. "Please."

She relaxed against him because she had no other choice. Dizziness had taken root, and refused to leave.

His hands lowered to her neck and massaged, and she thought he was…trembling? "I hurt you, and I dishonored you, and I am so sorry, Tink. I'm so sorry. I was stupid."

She wasn't going to respond. She wasn't. But the words, "Why did you pick her?" slipped from her, and she cringed. The woman had been everything Josephina was not: blonde, as delicate as the Fae royal family, with smooth hands and pale skin.

He buried his face in the hollow of Josephina's neck, saying, "I didn't. Disaster did."

That shouldn't have made her feel better. Nothing should have made her feel better. But…it did, she realized.

"I know you're sorry, Kane. I do. I believe you weren't acting from a place of desire. But I can't do this. I can't live like this, always wondering what you'll have to do with other women to satisfy the demon."

"I'm going to starve the demon. I won't do anything to satisfy him ever again."

"You say that now. But what happens when his hunger becomes too much to bear? How can I trust you?"

"What are you trying to say?" he croaked.

She steeled herself. "I had no idea I was such a jealous person, but I am, and I don't think that's going to change, and I don't think I can forget what I witnessed. So…I'm…leaving you, Kane. I don't want to be with you anymore."

Warm liquid trickled down her skin, as if…as if… Kane were crying. "Please, don't leave me. I need you. I'll make it up to you, I swear. I'll never even look at another woman, Tink. I'll cut out my eyes first. I'll never touch another woman. I'll cut off my hands first." His arms tightened around her. "Please. Please. I need you. I'll be in hell without you."

Right now, she was in hell *with* him.

"You won't have to put up with me for long, I promise. Please, Tink. Please."

He kissed her nape. He kissed her jawline. He kissed her ear and her cheek and her brow, her eyes and the tip of her nose. Her mind tried to compute what he'd just said. Something about his words bothered her. Something about not having to put up with him…for…*oh, my…* He licked the seam of her lips, and she opened automatically, her newly awakened body craving what only he could give. Their tongues brushed together, and she tasted…salt. He *had* been crying. Because he couldn't stand the thought of being without her.

Desire bloomed, urgent, insistent, traitorous. Her blood heated, and it had nothing to do with rage. She tried to remain quiet and still, but the more he kissed her, the deeper he kissed her, and the deeper he kissed her, the more she moaned and groaned and writhed against him, desperate for more.

As she tried to fight her body's response, he peeled her clothing away, then his own, but somehow his lips never left her, never gave her a moment to think past the pleasure. He stole the air from her lungs, provided her with air from his own. Without him, she couldn't breathe. Didn't want to breathe.

Skin against skin. Heat against heat. Softness against the most rigid steel. He surrounded her. He was hard, fully aroused, and hyper-focused on her. His gaze watched her, gauging her every reaction, his mind calculating his next play. His fingers moved on her, in her, stoking her need higher. His mouth followed.

"Let me show you how much you mean to me," he pleaded as he rose up, placed himself at her core. "Let me make love to you."

"A-all right," she managed to say. "One last time."

His gaze met hers, and oh, the hurt she saw was devastating. She wanted to snatch back her words, but her own hurt choked them before they could form.

"I *will* win you back, Tink. I will earn your trust, and you'll want to stay with me."

He covered his massive length with a condom and sank inside her.

She cried out, arching to take him deeper.

He didn't move for a long while, just remained in her to the hilt, filling her, making her grow more desperate by the second. Her breasts ached, so needy. The crevice between her legs throbbed, practically weeping. Her skin burned, so feverish. Her body was the war zone, and he was the soldier determined to win it.

"Kane," she said on a moan. "I want…I need…"

"Me, Tink. You need me." He slid out…out…then back inside her, and this time, he slammed hard, making her see stars. "I'll give you everything."

JOSEPHINA CAME AWAKE gradually, slowly becoming aware of the warm pool surrounding her. Warm pool?

She blinked open her eyes, wallpapered walls coming into view. She was in the hotel room she shared with Kane, she realized, and in bed. Kane was behind her, his arms wrapped tightly around her as if he feared she would run away. After lovemak—uh, having sex, they must have fallen asleep. How many hours had passed?

Gingerly she sat up, and, body aching from the passion of the night, turned to face her hus—the guy she was sleeping with. Horror filled her. "Kane. You're bleeding." His poor shoulder…there was an open wound, exposing muscle, maybe even bone, and a flow of crimson raining to the sheet.

"What's wrong?" he asked sleepily, groggily.

"You're bleeding. I shot you, and we both thought I missed, but we were wrong, because now you're bleeding."

Like her, he blinked open his eyes. A slow grin lifted the corners of his mouth.

"You spent the entire night with me."

"Listen to me. You're injured. I shot you."

"No, you did miss. Disaster somehow drew the bullet out of the wall and gave it another try. He succeeded. Thankfully, the thing went all the way through. Now, did you hear the part about spending the entire night with me?"

"You were shot while I was sleeping, and you failed to wake me up?"

"You needed to rest. Like I was going to disturb you."

How could he act so casual while *bleeding to death?* She hopped from the bed and raced to the bathroom to gather a cup of water and clean rags. By the time she returned, he had rolled onto his back and lay propped against the pillows, the very picture of male satisfaction. She cleaned him up as best she could and applied pressure to stop the bleeding.

"You should have told me," she chided.

"I was content and didn't want anything to change."

"Yeah, well. I'm sorry I tried to kill you," she said on a sigh.

"Don't be. I deserved it."

"No, you didn't." She cut up the clean end of the sheet and wrapped the material around his shoulder, using it as a bandage. "What you did with that woman, Kane…"

"I know, Tinky Dink," he said sadly. "I know."

Tinky Dink. A new nickname. Her heart constricted painfully. "You did it for me, and I get that, but it still hurts."

"It will never happen again, I vow it, no matter what Disaster does or says. You're the only one I want, the only one I'll have." A heavy pause. "Will you stay with me?" he asked quietly.

Would she? Hurt still swam through her veins. Kane had been hers. He'd chosen her above all others. Finally, she'd mattered to someone other than her mother. No longer had she been a nothing. A servant and blood slave had become the envy of every Fae female and probably even some of the men. But who would envy a cuckold?

He said he wasn't going to do it again, like thousands of men had said to thousands of women throughout the years.

Maybe, last night, she could have walked away from him. But what the demon had meant as harmful—the bullet—had actually softened her. Seeing Kane in a small pool of blood, realizing how close she'd come to losing him…

I'm not ready to lose him.

If—when—the demon acted up again, they could revisit this topic. Until then…

"I'll stay."

CHAPTER TWENTY-EIGHT

KANE ORDERED ROOM service. After he and Tink had eaten their weight in hamburgers and fries, he spent the rest of the day teaching her how to fight the biggest and the baddest of threats with her fists, blades and bullets. His shoulder gave him a little trouble, but he pushed through. She was an excellent student, a natural—unsurprising, considering she fought her way out of hell with no training whatsoever. She listened intently, put her whole heart into practicing, and what she lacked in strength she made up for in speed and cunning.

He was glad. He wanted her prepared for life without him.

Just how long would it take to starve Disaster to death?

You'll change your mind, the demon said, but he was no longer laughing.

Disaster couldn't imagine starving because he'd never experienced it; even now, his appetite was sated. Seeing the sharp edge of hurt still hanging in Tink's eyes…yeah, Disaster had feasted. But that wouldn't last. Kane wasn't going to let it.

Whatever the demon threw at him, whatever danger he encountered, he was done acting the fool and catering to the very nature he despised. Tink was getting his best, and nothing less.

When he felt like he'd pushed her hard enough for

one day, he gave her a gentle nudge forward. "Take a shower. We need to leave. I don't want to stay in the same location much longer."

"All right." Panting, damp with perspiration, she disappeared inside the bathroom.

He wanted to join her, but didn't dare. Not until she invited him.

She emerged a short while later, a towel wrapped around her luscious little body. Hair as black as night dripped at the ends. "Your turn."

He halfway expected her to be gone by the time he finished, which is why he rushed, and yet he found her standing in front of the bed, looking shockingly sweet in a black leather corset top with purple ties at the bottom and a long, puffy skirt with dark lace.

"Where'd you get the clothes?" He cursed himself for not yet taking her shopping, as promised.

She shifted uncomfortably. "Some guy with wings and a spike of green hair down the middle of his head stepped into view, dropped a bag, winked at me and stepped back out of view."

Malcolm, the Sent One, he realized with a bead of annoyance. He'd stepped from the spirit realm into the natural, clearly. "You should have called for me." The moment his snippy tone registered, he cringed. *Dial back the anger.* She was in a fragile state where he was concerned, and he had to tread carefully.

Her eyes narrowed. "There wasn't time."

At least she hadn't yelled. Very gently he said, "Next time, if someone appears, no matter who or what they are, no matter how fast they appear and disappear, or if you think they're my best friend, call for me. Okay? Please. Just in case I need to intervene."

She nodded stiffly.

"Thank you." He dug through the bag and found a plain T-shirt and pants, dropped his towel and dressed.

Tink turned away, and he had to brush flickers of sadness aside. Things wouldn't always be this strained.

"Let's take off," he said. "We've got a long journey ahead."

"Where are we going?"

"You've always wanted to spend time with the Lords of the Underworld, and I want to—"

"Drop me off?" she interjected tersely.

"No. I'm staying with you."

He got her outside, in the heat and light of the day, and scanned the crowds and buildings, searching for anything suspicious. This close to Times Square, there were flashing lights and stores everywhere, both offering great cover.

He dialed Lucien, but it went to voice mail. Next, he tried Torin. The warrior answered on the third ring with a curt, "What?"

O-kay. A very un-Torin-like greeting. As Kane led Tink around a corner and up to a coffee cart, he said, "I'm in Manhattan. I need Lucien to pick me up." Lucien could flash from one location to another with only a thought, even between realms. "Me and my wife."

At the counter, he held up two fingers.

Torin sputtered out a very undignified, "Wife?"

"Didn't the boys tell you? Lucien, Reyes, Strider and Sabin were at the wedding."

"They've been a little busy thinking up ways to find Viola and Cameo."

"Cameo?" He tensed. "What happened to her?"

"The same thing that happened to Viola. She touched the Paring Rod and vanished."

An instant flood of worry threatened to drown him. "What's being done?"

"Anya talked to some guy she met while in prison," Torin said. "He helped create the Rod, and he assured her the females were still alive. Just trapped."

He pushed out a relieved breath.

"Give me the deets about your girl."

"Her name's Tink—"

"Josephina," she interjected loudly.

"—and she's half Fae. A royal, a daughter of their king. Wait till you see her. She's the most beautiful woman ever created. But she has as many enemies as us."

"Hey," she said. "I don't have that many, and only one is my fault. Actually, no. The Phoenix is your fault, too. But thank you for saying I'm beautiful."

Two steaming cups were set before him. He stepped aside to doctor both with cream and sugar, then gave one to Tink. He remembered the longing looks she'd given the coffeepot during his breakfast with the royal family.

He watched as she sipped, closing her eyes to savor, and his chest constricted with a longing of his own.

"—time and place," Torin was saying.

"Wait. Sorry. What was that?"

"Stop lusting after the ball and chain and pick a time and place to meet," the warrior repeated. "I'll make sure Lucien is there."

"Two hours. Sabin's old apartment."

"Consider it done."

He severed the connection. Then, seizing any excuse to touch his woman, he slipped the phone into a pocket of her skirt. "Guard this for me," he said.

"Will your friends like me, do you think?" she asked,

and nibbled on her bottom lip. "The few I've actually met have only seen me at my worst."

He heard the uncertainty in her tone. "The wedding was your worst? Honey, your worst is most people's best. My friends will love you." If not, Kane would hand out some serious beatings. "They'll guard you with their lives."

"Yeah, but what if they think I'm all wrong for you?"

"Impossible. You're perfect for me. Besides, wait till you meet *their* wives. Or have you already heard stories?"

She shook her head. "New reports of your most recent exploits haven't yet come in to the masses."

It was humiliating to know they'd never realized they were being spied on. "Well, Sabin and Strider are consorts to bloodthirsty Harpies. Lucien is engaged to Anarchy. All three females are annoying, always stealing weapons out of my room, but as they would say, they're simply amazeballs—and so are you."

A smile—small, but there. "Thank you."

He soared. "Is there anything you'd like to purchase before I take you out of the city? Anything at all. I plan to get you some clothes, but we can also get shoes, purses, jewelry, whatever you'd like." If he had to buy her affections, he would. He didn't care how pathetic that made him. He just wanted her happy.

"No. Really, I'm good."

The vibrations in his wedding ring intensified significantly, startling him. Frowning, he held the metal band to the light. In the center, as if the band were a movie screen, he watched Red shove his way through a crowd.

Kane glanced up—and spotted Red, shoving his way through the crowd, closing in on him. The ring had known, had…warned him?

"Is something wrong?" Tink asked.

"Yeah. We've picked up a tail." He trashed his coffee, did the same to Tink's.

"Hey," she grouched. "I wasn't done with that."

"Sorry. Don't want you to burn yourself." He launched forward, barreling past oncoming humans, dragging Tink with him. With his free hand, he withdrew a dagger.

"Who's the tail?"

"One of William's kids." No. Scratch that. All of William's kids were probably here. Those four were like ants: never alone.

"What are they, anyway?"

"Trouble." And they weren't coming near Tink. He would kill them first.

Yeah. It was time to kill, he decided. He'd warned the Rainbow Rejects about what would happen if they came after Tink. The warning had been a courtesy to William. His last courtesy. The boys hadn't listened. Now, Kane would follow through.

"I'm going to hide you in one of the shops, okay? I need to have a chat with the boys, and I don't want you to—"

"Kane!" Tink vanished.

No, not Tink. *Kane*. No longer was he racing down the sidewalk with his woman behind him. He was standing in a narrow hallway, white fog wafting all around him. A shout of denial split his lips as he turned left, right, searching for Tink.

He clawed through the mist, only to discover—more mist. He checked his ring, but there was no longer a reflection. Panic set in. Where was he? What had happened? Not many beings had the power to flash another without contact. Only Greek and Titan royalty, and—

The Moirai, he realized with sickening dread. They'd used their powers to transport him from New York to their home in the lower level of the skies.

He sped down the hall. He'd been here before, knew the way, and didn't need to look to know the walls were comprised of thousands upon thousands of braided threads. Those threads vibrated, coming alive, playing scenes from his life—past, present, and maybe even future—but he didn't allow himself to stop and study.

He was careful to breathe as little as possible. The air was laced with some kind of drug, something to keep him pliant, and maybe even susceptible to suggestion. Tink thought the Moirai operated that way, that they weren't really controllers of fate, but rather massagers of it, pushing and kneading, tricking, until their victims were putty in their hands, blindly following wherever they led.

Not me. Not any longer.

He reached the end of the hall and entered the weaving room. The three hags sat on wooden stools, each female hunched over the loom, with her long, white hair frizzing over her shoulders.

Klotho had spotted hands and spun the threads.

Lachesis had gnarled fingers and wove those threads together.

Atropos had pupil-less eyes and snipped the ends of the locks.

"Send me back. Now." The last time he was here, he'd shown the utmost respect. He'd kept his tone level, his gaze averted. This time he whipped out his demands, his gaze direct. The outcome was too important.

"You made a wrong turn." Klotho cackled.

"Such a bad wrong turn," Lachesis reiterated.

"Bad turns lead to bad ends," Atropos said without any inflection. "You should have married the other one. Or two."

No. No, he wouldn't believe it. Tink belonged to him, and he belonged to her. He wanted no one else—would have no one else.

"There's still time to change directions," Klotho added.

"Oh, yes, there's still time," Lachesis reiterated.

"That's the only way you'll survive the pain," Atropos said.

Kane came forward, with every intention of shaking the females into submission. "Send. Me. Back."

Klotho looked up and frowned. "You're ruining our tapestry, warrior. The scenes you're creating aren't as colorful as the ones we wish to create."

They'd predicted his future for the *colors* his actions would lend to their *blanket?* Inconceivable!

Roaring, Kane slashed his dagger through the threads closest to him. Moved forward, slashed through more. All three hags gasped with horror.

"You're going to send me back to my wife, or your throats are next."

"You wouldn't!" the one in the middle gasped.

"If you've seen my past, and gotten a glimpse of my future, you know I'll do much worse than that." Determined, he stalked forward.

ONE SECOND JOSEPHINA was being dragged by Kane, the next she was on her own in the middle of a crowded sidewalk. Shock had her stumbling to a halt, but she quickly righted herself. Where had he gone?

She spun, searching the area, trying not to panic. People, people, so many people, each on a mission, marching in every direction. A building here, a building there. Birds on the sidewalk, pecking at trash.

"Kane," she shouted.

The lady next to her jolted back, as if she'd gone insane.

"Kane," she shouted again. There was no response.

He'd…abandoned her? Decided she was too much trouble?

"Someone must have flashed him away," a voice said from behind her. "How perfect. We've been looking for you, female."

Trying not to cry out, she whipped around and faced the male from her nightmares. The handsome Red, capable of morphing into the monster she'd drawn into herself.

First rule of fighting, she thought, recalling Kane's rules. *Act casual.* "I don't know why. I want nothing to do with you."

"We wish to spend time with you."

Anger burned through her. "I advise you to reconsider. I'm a biter."

His brothers stepped up beside him, flanking him, and all three stared at her with rapt fascination.

"For you, I won't mind teeth marks," Black replied.

Humans continued to walk around her, the females stopping to give the warriors a second and third glance, as if interested in exchanging numbers, before realizing the males weren't the type to be played with and hurrying away.

Refusing to back down, she said, "I know what you really want, and my answer is no. My ability only works with my consent."

Red offered her a slow smile. "Getting your consent won't be a problem."

If he'd hoped to intimidate her, well, he'd just done a great job. She was certain there had never been a colder smile.

Second rule of fighting. Don't be afraid to show off your weapons. Sometimes fear will drive people away. "I'm willing to fight for my freedom," she said, proud of her lack of quivering. She withdrew the blade Kane had given her. Where *was* he?

"You'll lose," Red replied matter-of-factly. "But don't worry. We'll be careful with you."

Black and Green nodded.

Dread nearly knocked her off her feet.

They approached.

KANE APPEARED IN the exact spot he'd left. Only, Tink wasn't there. He rushed to Sabin's apartment, gaze constantly scanning, searching for any sign of her. Every second was agony. When he reached his destination, he burst through the doors.

Lucien jumped up from the couch, frowned. "Where's the girl?"

"I don't know." About to hyperventilate, Kane plowed a hand through his hair. "I have to find her."

The Rainbow Rejects wouldn't kill her, he knew that much, but oh, she might want to die when they finished with her. She could be in pain, right that very moment, and the thought tortured him.

"Get Torin on the phone," he croaked. "I need to know what happened, and I don't care how many databases and security systems he has to hack into to find out."

CHAPTER TWENTY-NINE

The Realm of Blood and Shadows

IT DIDN'T TAKE Torin long to dig up the video Lucien had requested for Kane. "I'm sorry. Just one second longer," he said, then messaged the footage to the pair. That done, he swiveled his chair around.

First, his gaze hit the painting still resting beside his door. He hadn't peeked.

Second, the female sitting at the edge of his bed.

The mystery of her name had not yet been solved, even though she'd come every day, as promised. In an effort to relax her, he hadn't pressed her for information, but had allowed her to watch him as he researched the Paring Rod, looking for answers about Cameo and Viola, all the while getting to know his mannerisms, his habits. He'd fed her. He'd allowed her to wander around the confines of the room.

What would crack her hard shell?

"You're very good to your friends," she said.

"They're very good to me right back."

"You love them."

"Very much."

She nibbled on the end of a strawberry he'd given her, licked the juice from her fingers. "I have a friend." A beat of silence. "I miss her."

Finally. Personal information. *Easy. Don't push too hard, too fast.* "She's…gone?"

"No. I see her every day, and I speak to her, but there are always prying eyes and ears, so our conversations are limited."

"Who pries?" he asked, treading lightly.

"The others."

That told him nothing—but it was a start. "The others listen to you and your friend…." He propped his elbows on his knees, trying to appear relaxed rather than foaming-at-the-mouth eager. "What's her name?"

"It'd probably be better if you didn't know," she said. "But…I'll tell you mine."

"Please," he rushed out.

"I'm…Mari."

Excitement at learning this new detail nearly shot him out of his chair to fist bump the ceiling. "Where do you come from, Mari?"

"The…past," she whispered, looking down at her bare feet.

"I don't understand. The past?"

"Cronus plucked me from long ago and imprisoned me in one of his homes. I don't know how many years passed before my friend was placed in the cell across from mine. I can't visit her, and she can't visit me. We can only talk to each other through the bars."

A prison? He withdrew the mental files he'd kept on her, and compared those with what he saw now. Her pale hair was tangled each new day, her skin streaked with dirt, despite the showers she'd taken here. But the fear had slowly faded from her eyes, and the food she'd eaten had caused her cheeks to fill out.

"Cronus is dead," he said. "You don't have to return. You can stay here without fear."

"You still don't understand. We're stuck there, tethered somehow. We have no water, no food and have only managed to survive…I'm not sure how. He must have done something to us."

Yeah. There were ways to keep prisoners nourished without actually feeding them. Ways that kept the prisoners docile and weak.

"We've tried to dig our way free, but so far, we've had no luck. I can flash in and out to meet with you, because Cronus made the allowance before he died, but no one else can leave, even through a flash."

Rage started little fires in his bloodstream. He still had no idea what "from the past" meant—actual time travel? Or was she an immortal Cronus had found in, say, the Middle Ages, and the monarch had kept her imprisoned all these centuries?

"You should have told me sooner," he said, still trying for a gentle tone.

"I didn't know you. I didn't know what I…wanted from this."

"I can help you. Cronus's homes were given to one of my friends—Sienna Blackstone. This friend also has the former Titan king's abilities and powers." Most of them, anyway. "If you'll tell her everything you know about the home, she'll find it and release you and your friend."

Hope glistened in eyes gone dark. "Really?"

"Really." *And then you can stay with me.*

Hand fluttering over her heart, she hopped to her feet. "I don't know what to say."

"Say thank you." For now, that would be enough.

"Thank you, thank you, a thousand times thank you," she said with a grin.

"You're welcome."

He stood. "I'll call Sienna." She split her time between training with the Sent Ones and hunting the Unspoken Ones, monsters now on the loose. "She'll come and meet you, and we can get started on our quest. Agreed?" He held out his hand.

She looked at the glove, then his eyes, then the glove. Slowly she removed the material, and…he let her. He couldn't bring himself to stop her. Then, she studied the hand that hadn't seen the sun in decades and gulped.

"Mari?"

"I agree." She placed her palm against his, twined their fingers, and shook.

His response embarrassed him. His body instantly reacted, as if preparing for the dirtiest kind of sex. His skin tingled as if brushed by living flame, and his blood turned molten.

Must. Have. More.

CAMEO PACED THE confines of the office. It was weird. Visually, no part of the room was off-limits. She could see everything. The desk, the chair, the bookcases, the glass shelves. But she couldn't *walk* everywhere.

Anytime she approached the shelves, she would experience a moment of vertigo, blink and find her nose in the far corner of the room.

The same had happened to Lazarus, but only once. After that, he'd given up. Now he reclined against the far wall, watching her with sardonic amusement.

"Is the guy still there?" she asked. "And you never told me who he is."

"Yes, he's still there. But he's more of a monster than a guy. And his name? No. I won't give it."

Why not? "What's he doing?"

"Watching you."

The thought irritated her on every level. "Why can't I see him? Why can't I get to him?" And where was Viola? What had happened to her? Was she still trapped inside the Rod? "You led me to believe I would be involved in a dangerous battle."

He waved her words away. "I was wrong. It's happened once before."

"Well, stop lazing around, and help me figure out a solution."

"No. I understand why the monster is having so much fun. Watching you use the same methods every time, and failing the same way, just to try to reach him is highly amusing."

So. Irritating. "I hope you choke on your own tongue."

"Why, so you can dig it out with your own?"

Argh! "Are you flirting with me?"

"How cute." He looked past her. "Pretty warrior woman doesn't know the difference between an informed question and flirting."

Was he speaking to the invisible beast? His supposed enemy?

She marched to the wall where he sat and sank beside him. "I'm done being the night's entertainment."

"Too bad." His dark gaze swept over her at a leisurely pace. "You're quite attractive, female, but your voice needs work. A lot of work."

"Insults from *you?*" She drummed her nails against her thighs. "I remember you, you know. A few months back, you attended the Harpy Games with Strider and Sabin. You're the consort of the Harpy in charge."

Fire crackled in his eyes—literal fire. "I am no one's consort."

Hit a nerve, had she? "I wonder what your consort

would say about that. I met her. Juliette was her name, yes?"

His nostrils flared, a testament to the fury brewing inside him. "When I get out of this office, and I will, she'll be too busy being dead to say anything."

"Because you plan to kill her?"

"Yes." Simply stated, leaving no doubt he meant what he said. "I once chose death over her companionship. I will again, no problem—only this time, I'll do it in reverse."

"Maybe I'll kill you and gift her with your head," she replied pleasantly.

"Maybe I'll cut out your tongue and do the world a favor."

She gritted her teeth. "Maybe I'll gut you just for giggles."

"Maybe I'll stab the life out of you and do *myself* a favor."

Enough! Cameo jumped to her feet and motioned him over. "You want to do this, warrior? Because I'm ready. Anytime. Anyplace."

Lazarus unfolded his big body and straightened. "You don't want to take me on, little girl. You'll lose."

She went chest to chest with him. "I think differently. On both counts."

He squared the wide width of his shoulders, standing his ground, not the least bit intimidated. A mistake many men had made. "Do your worst then. But have no doubts, I'll then do mine."

No. She wouldn't do her worst. That's what he expected, maybe even wanted. She'd just have to go another route and surprise him.

Like a child, she shoved him with all her might. His

startled expression was priceless as he stumbled backward and into the wall—no, *through* the wall?

Gasping, Cameo rushed to the space he'd last occupied. One second she stood inside the office, the next she was outside. Trees swayed in a gentle breeze. A river rushed and trickled over smooth rocks. Birds sang as they flew across the sunny skyline. White clouds drifted past, serene and flawless.

"What did you do to me?" Lazarus demanded, striding from the shade of one of the trees to get in her face.

"Me? You went through the wall, and I must have followed."

He spun, seeming to take everything in at once. He stiffened. "I think we're moving between the dimensions," he muttered, clearly talking to himself. "That would mean the Rod spit us out in another dimension, the office was another, and *this* is yet another."

This was the first she'd ever heard of different dimensions. "Care to explain what you mean to the rest of the class?"

He scrubbed a hand down his face. "There are two realms. Natural and spiritual. Between the realms are dimensions—pockets of life caught between the natural and the spiritual."

Dread wrapped hard fingers around her heart. "What does that mean for us?"

His eyes were dead as he said, "We'll never go home."

CHAPTER THIRTY

New York

KANE'S FURY PROVED limitless. Tink's abduction had been caught on a nearby security camera, allowing him to watch the way Red, Black and Green had cornered and grabbed her. She'd put up a fight, the way Kane had taught her, and she'd even managed to bust Red in the eye, but she'd been no match for the strength of the immortals, and they'd put her to sleep with pressure on her carotid and carried her away, soon disappearing from view. He'd hunted as if his life depended on success—worse, Tink's life—but the three had covered their tracks too well.

I should have killed those hellhounds when I had the chance.

Kane tossed and turned on the lumpy motel bed. He needed to relax, and concentrate. He planned to summon Tink, somehow, through their link, and force her to project her image into his mind. They would talk. She would tell him where she was.

He forced himself to close his eyes. Lucien had refused to leave his side, and was now resting comfortably on the other bed, Anya draped across his body. "I'm a living tramp stamp," she'd said laughingly before drifting off.

Lucien hadn't wanted to spend the night without her.

Actually, Lucien couldn't function a few hours without her. It was disgusting. It was embarrassing.

That's what I feel with Tink.

Disaster chuckled. *Too bad you'll never see her again.*

The fiend was in the best mood of his existence. Though Kane had hoped to provide zero nourishment, he'd unwittingly prepared another feast—and was still serving seconds. The darkness of his emotions had become an internal IV for the demon, offering strength and contentedness, no matter what happened around him.

"Tink," Kane inwardly shouted. "Tink, I need you. Need you so much." Even when she'd been ticked at him, she'd never been able to resist aiding him.

There was no response.

Time for another tactic… "Tinker Bell. Josephina. Wife! You have five seconds to appear or the next time I see you I will put you over my knee."

Still no response.

"One. Two. I'm serious, I mean it. Three. Four. Last chance to save yourself from the humiliation of my wrath. Fi—"

Fog rolled in, surrounding his bed. Then Tink was standing over him. "You will not put me over your knee, you…you…caveman!"

Every cell in his body cried out in relief. It had worked. "Are you okay?" he demanded. "Have the warriors hurt you?" There were no bruises on her skin, and the clothes Malcolm had given her were still intact, without a single tear.

If Lucien and Anya heard him, they ignored him.

"I'm good," she said. "The guys have actually been kind of nice, doing their best to romance me so that I'll decide to live with them forever and, I'm just guessing here, make them my brother husbands." She looked Kane over, and what remained of the ambivalence left her in a snap. "What about you? You said you needed me. Is something wrong?"

"Of course something's wrong. You're not at my side. And what do you mean you heard me? Why didn't you reply right away?" he demanded, but he already knew the answer. He was still in the doghouse.

Chin trembling, as if she were suddenly fighting tears, she said, "I'm not helpless. Not anymore. I'm handling things."

"I know, Tinky Dink. I do. But I miss you. I want you with me for all the days of my life. I'm not complete without you. Let me come for you."

JOSEPHINA PEERED AT Kane, his sweet words echoing in her mind. *I'm not complete without you.* She had to forgive him for the kiss, didn't she? She had to torch the bitterness trying so diligently to grow roots deep in her heart, or she'd be trapped in this state for the rest of her life. He'd done what he'd done out of desperation and a desire to protect her. He'd promised never to do it again, and she believed him.

He wanted to make things right between them, but so far, she hadn't given him a chance. He'd called for her, his voice whisking through a doorway they'd somehow opened between their minds—*I need you*—and though her heart had sped into a wild beat of excitement, she'd ignored the urge to respond to him. For a little while, at least.

She just…she hadn't wanted him to see her like this. Defeated. Not again. Unlike the Fae, he prized strength in a female. So, she'd wanted to prove herself worthy and free herself, surprising him.

She would be all, *Ta da! Here I am. Look at what I did all by myself. Aren't I spectacular?*

He would never again think to kiss another woman just to protect her.

But, at this rate, Josephina may not ever get free.

So, she had a few choices to make. Either she believed Kane would want her, no matter what, or she had to let him go. Either she forgave him completely, and stayed with him, or held on to her hurt and bitterness and remained alone. She couldn't have both. If she couldn't trust him, if she couldn't forgive, but stayed with him anyway, she would continue to lash out at him, and she knew very well what such cruel treatment could do to a person.

"Kane," she said.

He looked away from her. "Yes, Tink."

He thought she meant to reject him, she realized. "Project to me."

He knew what she meant, and a second later, he was standing before her, gazing at her with hope.

Her chest constricted as she wrapped her arms around his neck and held on tight. "I'm really glad you called me."

He buried his face in the hollow of her neck. "You are?"

"I am." The tears returned, but this time, they sprang from a well of joy. "Can I ask you something?"

"Anything. Anytime. Always." He straightened, brushed the corners of her eyes with his thumbs.

She gulped, almost unable to bear his tenderness. "Would you have picked me above all women? If you hadn't been forced to marry me, I mean."

"I would. I do. And I was never forced, Tinker Bell. I wanted you, and I would have found a way to have you. Your father just made things easier for me."

Her mouth curved upward of its own accord. "So… you think I'm special."

"The specialest."

A laugh bubbled over. "I know it didn't seem like it at the time, but I would have picked you above all men."

"Even Torin and Paris?"

"Especially Torin and Paris. You are, without a doubt, the sexiest man ever created. I just didn't want you to regret what we were doing."

"I'll never regret my time with you." He kissed her, a sweet meeting of lips more about comfort than passion. But oh, the passion was there, too. Always it was there. "What you said…thank you, Tink. I was always the warrior left behind. My friends didn't want to risk the trouble Disaster would cause and I couldn't blame them. It's nice to be wanted."

He understood her pain, she realized. Their circumstances might have been different, but the outcome had been the same: a deep sense of rejection. He'd probably longed for acceptance all the days of his life. He'd probably hoped and dreamed of helping his friends, only to be crushed time and time again when they overlooked his amazing battle skills.

"There's no one else I'd rather have fight for me," she said truthfully.

He graced her with another kiss. "You are a treasure. I hope you know that."

She beamed at him. A compliment she hadn't had to give to herself. Was there anything sweeter? "Where did you go when we were running from the Brother Husbands?"

"The Moirai summoned me."

"Oh." Oh, no. "What happened?"

"I did what was necessary, and it might take the witches a few years to recover," he said flatly. "Where are the Brother Husbands—is that what we're calling them now? Where are they keeping you?"

"I don't know," she said.

"What do you remember seeing?"

"Well, I remember being on the street, then engaging the boys, then…nothing until I woke up inside a tent. I don't know what's outside it—I would have looked, but I'm bound to a post."

He arched a brow. "You consider their binding you to a post doing their best to romance you?"

"They only bound me after I threw Green's specially prepared food in his face—a fourth time. Anyway. The air is hot and smells of patchouli. There are four fur beds on the ground, and I think I hear screams in the background."

A dark curtain fell over Kane's features. "I know where you are. I'll be there before sunrise."

HE HAD TO return to hell.

The moment the fog disappeared, taking Tink with it, Kane stopped projecting his image and rose from the bed. His legs shook. His stomach twisted.

A hand here...a mouth there...so helpless...

A whip across his legs. A dagger along his ribs.

Hot breath on his wounded skin...kisses...

Panic threatened to fell him. He wouldn't let it. Whatever his body's reaction, he had to do this. He couldn't leave Tink in hell. *Wouldn't* leave her. He knew the things that happened there. Oh, yes, he knew, and now had to race to the bathroom to empty the contents of his stomach.

He rinsed out his mouth and stared at his haunted reflection. Tink could be stolen from the Rainbow Rejects and tortured by minions. If that happened, she would stop wanting to live and once again start wanting to die. She would never smile or laugh again. He couldn't fathom a life without her smile. She needed him, and he'd vowed to protect her, no matter what, even if he had to face his worst nightmare to do it.

He forced himself to stalk to the side of Lucien's bed, and, with a trembling hand, shook the warrior awake. "I need you to flash me to…hell." He described the camp Lucien was to find, doing his best not to vomit. This had to be done.

The pair asked no questions. They stood. Lucien tucked Anya in his right side, and wrapped his left arm around Kane's shoulders. Used to be, he could only flash one person at a time, but his power was increasing.

Kane fought the urge to jerk away. Ignored the thought that he'd rather die than return. For Tink, he would suffer anything.

Lucien flashed to the rocky entrance. Then deeper inside. Screams of agony filled the hot, sulfur-scented air. Disaster hummed with approval, loving how close he was to his minions.

Kane almost fought his way out of his friend's hold. The worst of his memories played through his mind, picture stills, a flash of one, then another, images of pain and suffering, somehow all the worse because he now saw them in black-and-white—except for the blood. Scarlet dripped from his many wounds.

Deeper inside the cave. Deeper still…

The next time Lucien paused, Kane hunched over

and dry heaved. The warrior didn't release him—perhaps he knew Kane would have bolted. When he finished, he straightened and wiped the moisture from his mouth with the back of his hand.

"Just a little farther, I think," Lucien said, and flashed again.

"I can make it." Maybe.

At last the warrior stopped at the top of a smoky cliff.

Kane croaked out, "Here." Patchouli saturated the air, a scent he knew far too well.

Still battling the urge to run, he crouched and peered down at a land littered with jagged rocks and black dirt. There were trees, but they were gnarled and without any sign of life. In the center was the tent Tink had mentioned, big and flesh-colored—Kane knew the Rainbow Rejects had skinned people to make it.

Tink was inside. Bound to a post. Helpless.

Fury overshadowed the worst of his revulsion. The men themselves sat around a fire pit, roasting marshmallows, utterly at ease. Probably strategizing the best way to "romance" Tink.

My Tink. No one romances her but me.

"What are you guys doing here?" a familiar voice demanded from behind.

Kane twisted while palming a dagger. He came face-to-face with William.

"Willy Willy Boo Bear!" Anya said with a grin. Her beautiful face lit with delight. "I've missed you like crazy."

"Well, I haven't missed you, brat."

"Have, too."

"Have not."

A slap fight broke out.

Normally Kane would have been amused. Now? His nerves were too frayed.

"Enough," Lucien said, and the ridiculous fight of the she-cats stopped.

"I'm going to kill your boys," Kane said. And fast. He wanted out of this place.

"Funny, but *I'm* going to kill my boys," William gritted, taking the spot beside him. "They actually left me for dead in Séduire. And good thing, too, because the Phoenix burned down the king's gardens, and someone has to face punishment. He's picked your Tinker Hell, because, apparently, she's to blame for everything. He'll be sending a contingent of soldiers after her."

Kane studied the area, plotting the best course of action against the Rainbow Rejects, saying distractedly, "Too bad she belongs to me now, not him." If he climbed down the cliff, he would be easily spotted. The Rainbow Rejects would be distracted, would leave their posts to fight him. Lucien could flash into the tent, and whisk Tink to safety.

"He's certain you're tired of your Tink by now. He's expecting a thank-you hug."

That was because, to Tiberius, she had no worth.

The man needed to be taught better.

"Forget the Fae. Where's White?" he asked. If necessary, he would fight her, too.

"She helped her brothers ambush me, but at least she came back to doctor me," William said. "Therefore, I only put her in time-out."

William had once put a Hunter in time-out. The male had chewed through his own wrists in an attempt to escape the pain the warrior had unleashed.

"By the way," the warrior added. "Have you noticed anything unusual about your wedding ring? I'd always heard it had strange powers, but I never wanted to risk my precious life by putting it on."

Kane judged the distance from the bottom of the cliff to the campfire. "So you risked my precious life instead?" If the Rainbow Rejects opted not to fight him, they might have enough time to get to Tink before Lucien could flash in and free her.

It was a chance he'd have to take.

"Uh, yeah," William said. "Hello. I'm smart like that."

"The ring shows me when an enemy is near."

"What?" Electric blues narrowed to tiny slits. "Give it back."

Kane ignored him, saying, "I'll take care of the Rainbow Rejects. Lucien, you'll take care of Tink."

"What about me?" Anya demanded.

"You get to cheer us on." Lucien would never forgive him if something happened to his precious.

"Hold up," William said. "If I know my boys, and I do, they've bound your Tinker Hell with special chains. Lucien won't be able to cut her loose, and if he can't cut her loose, he can't flash her. He'll need a key."

A complication, but not one that was insurmountable. "Do you have a key?"

"I do." William offered no more.

Kane massaged the back of his neck. "Get the key and I'll give you the ring."

"I was hoping you'd say that. This is gonna take me a while, so I'll see you when I see you." A grinning William vanished.

Kane wasn't waiting *a while*. Not here. Not with Tink so close. "New plan. You two stay here until William gets back, then swoop in and grab Tink. I'll get the Rainbow Rejects out of the area."

He didn't wait for their reply. And he wasn't going to waste time climbing. His sense of urgency rising, he stood and jumped, falling down…down…down and landing on his feet. Impact split the bones in his shins, but he didn't care, his adrenaline too high to let him feel such pain. A scowl marred his features as he straightened.

The boys glanced up. The moment they spotted him, they leaped to their feet. But they didn't run.

"Must admit, I expected you sooner," Red said, unfazed.

"This is our territory," Black said. "You should have stayed away."

Green rubbed his hands together with glee.

"Tink is mine, and I will never share her."

Kane and the Rainbow Rejects launched toward each other, meeting in the middle. A black mist instantly puffed around them, locking the four of them in a circle of menace. He'd expected it, and was ready to go with a dagger and an ax, hacking at his opponents. The males arched to elude impact, then, as they straightened, slashed at him with their growing claws. Maybe they made contact. Maybe they didn't. Still he felt only the fiery edges of his rage and determination.

He looked at Red, smiled—but launched the ax at Black.

Black wasn't prepared, and had no time to react. The metal embedded in his throat, severing his windpipe. He hit the ground, and stayed down.

Red roared, a testament to his rage. Green bared his teeth in a fearsome scowl filled with fangs. Kane palmed a second dagger, and attacked with more vigor. He remained in constant motion, slashing, ducking, slashing again, cutting the pair to ribbons.

"Kill you," Red snarled, going low and knocking Kane's ankles together.

He hit the ground, but rolled back to a stand before either male could pin him.

Silent, he stalked forward and hit at them with renewed strength, driving the pair backward. But Green worked his way behind him, and struck, probably drilling a hole in the back of his skull with the slam of his fist.

Kane nearly blacked out, but didn't let it slow him. He went low, spinning, kicking out his leg, knocking Green down…rising, nailing Red in the shoulder.

The warriors quickly recovered, swiping at him. He had to crisscross his arms again and again, his body arcing one way then the other, to avoid being pummeled and land other blows.

Realizing this was getting them nowhere, he allowed Red to hit him, because he couldn't sidestep it *and* strike at Green. He pounded his fist into Green's chest, sending the warrior stumbling back. Kane followed. The moment Green righted, Kane performed a hard jab to his jaw, followed by a second kick. This time, the dazed warrior fell. Kane was there when he landed, twisting his neck—breaking his spine.

Green stayed down, too.

Red jumped on Kane's back, wrapped his arms around his neck, and tried to do the same to him, exactly as Kane had hoped. He rolled into the movement and ended up face-to-face with the guy, as if they were hugging. He wasted no time sinking a dagger into Red's side, straight into a kidney.

Grunting, the warrior stumbled away from him. Kane threw the second dagger and cut into the male's thigh, forcing him to his knees. Then, determined to end this once and for all, Kane kicked him in the face, breaking his nose and sending him flying back. He grabbed two more daggers, and, when Red rolled over to push upright, shoved the blades into his shoulders, pinning him down.

Disaster shrieked inside his head, and a second later, a rock fell from the cliff and careened toward Kane. He darted out of the way a split second before contact. Red wasn't so lucky.

The black mist melted away as Kane stood. He felt… ragged, desperate, as he stumbled forward, searching the area, wishing he were anywhere but here, his panic returning now that the fighting was done. He needed to leave. Had to leave. Now. Where was Tink? He needed to grab her and get her out of this hellhole. First, though, he probably needed to breathe. Why couldn't he breathe?

As he patted at his throat, finding no external obstruction, he spotted Lucien, Anya, William and *Tink* sitting in front of the fire. He stopped. Tink's black hair was brushed to a glossy shine, her skin scrubbed clean, and her clothes in perfect condition. She was safe. Relief and joy intermingled, a potent combination that managed to chase away the worst of his panic, opening his lungs and allowing him to suck in a measure of oxygen.

William eyed his boys, who were still lying on the ground. "They're not dead. Only a beheading will kill them."

Kane moved forward, intending to deliver the final blow.

"Don't," William said, stopping him. "I've changed my mind. They've learned their lesson. They'll never approach your woman again. I'll make sure of it."

Very well. Kane didn't need to see them dead—

he just needed the reassurance that his *mine* was safe from them.

He faced Tink.

She stood, wiping her hands against her thighs. Nervous? Or frightened of him? He was covered in blood, after all.

“Kane,” she said.

He took a step toward her. “You’re free. That was fast.”

William shifted. “Yeah, so, I was mistaken about the chain and key. Anya got her out. Go figure.”

“She was bound by rope, nothing more, and I somehow managed to cut her loose,” Anya said drily. “Imagine my surprise.”

William had tried to trick him, just to gain possession of the ring. Kane wanted to care. He didn’t care. His gaze remained locked with Tink’s. She approached him. A second later, they were running at each other. She threw herself in his arms, and he spun her around.

“Told you I’d be here by morning,” he whispered.

“Thank you.”

“Welcome.” Now, he could get her out of here. Couldn’t tolerate another minute inside these jagged walls. “We need to—”

“Disaster,” a female screeched in the distance. “Disaster is here!”

“Where? Where is he? I must have him!”

Every muscle Kane possessed knotted. The minions had sensed him. The minions…the minions who had…had…NO! Sickness returned to his stomach, churning viciously. The females wanted to bind him and cut away his clothing. They wanted to touch him and taste him and steal his seed.

They'll have you, Disaster said with a laugh. *Over and over again.*

Going to vomit.

"And now it's time to bail." William unsheathed a Sig Sauer from the waist of his pants. "I can only flash myself. Lucien, you take care of the others."

Lucien nodded and flashed a protesting Anya to safety. He reappeared a few seconds later, grabbed a now trembling Kane and Tink, and flashed them away, too. The last thing Kane saw was William running forward, grinning with delight. And when he next blinked, he was standing inside the walls of the fortress he'd never thought to revisit, once again barely able to breathe.

CHAPTER THIRTY-ONE

The Realm of Blood and Shadows

JOSEPHINA TOOK IN as much of the fortress as possible as Kane dragged her down a hall and up a flight of stairs. "I almost can't believe I'm in your home. I mean, I'm *actually* in your home. I'm living every Fae woman's dream."

The portraits on the walls caught her attention. Each contained a Lord of the Underworld in the buff, his manhood shielded by something feminine. A ribbon. A teddy bear. A scrap of lace. Then there were the portraits of the delicate blonde, the epitome of what Fae males found attractive. In one, she wore a ball gown. In another, a negligee. In yet another, black leather.

"She's pretty," Josephina said, trying not to compare herself to the beauty. "Does she belong to one of your friends?"

"No."

The sharpness of his tone startled her. She studied the stiffness of his back, the jerkiness of his stride. "Kane? Is everything all right?"

He ignored her. He even ignored the people they passed.

"Kane, is that really you?" said a male with black hair and violet eyes. Josephina recognized the infamous keeper of Violence. He was close enough to touch.

A baby girl was cradled in his arms. Oh, sweet mercy, he had a child? Why had the scribes not delivered such a juicy tidbit?

Silent, Kane dragged her past the pair.

"So wonderful to meet you," she called. "I'm Josephina, and I absolutely love—"

Kane jerked her around the corner.

"What are you doing here? I thought you were on your honeymoon," said Strider, coming out of a bedroom.

"So lovely to see you again," Josephina called.

A petite redheaded lovely moved to his side, and she elbowed him in the stomach.

"What'd I do now, baby doll?" Strider asked with a grimace.

"Honeymoon?" the redhead said with a stomp of her foot. "He got married and you didn't think to tell me?"

"Hey, Paris and Torin wouldn't happen to be here, would they?" Josephina asked Strider. "I might die of a heart attack, but it would be worth it—"

Kane pulled her in front of him, and slapped his hand over her mouth. "That's enough out of you."

He stopped her in front of a door. A bedroom, she realized when he got her inside. He released her and shut them both in. Awed, she drank in every nook and cranny. The chamber was spacious, with distressed walls of stone and a cracked marble floor. The furniture was antique, worn but chic. There were no pictures, though, no personal touches of any kind.

"I need to—" Kane scrubbed a hand down his face. "I…need to go," he said, his gaze anywhere but on her.

She spun to face him. "You're leaving me?"

"I'll be back," he rushed to add. "And I'll introduce

you to everyone. I'll give you a tour. Whatever you want."

"I want…you."

She was no longer the passive girl he'd first met. She'd been through too much, had survived too much. *They'd* survived. She'd decided to stand up for her rights, and that hadn't changed. She would fight for what she wanted, would even fight Kane himself. "What's going on, Kane? What's wrong with you? Tell me. Don't push me aside. Not this time."

"My head's messed up," he said in a tortured voice. "The weeks in hell…the demons…"

"I'm so sorry. I should have realized." She closed the distance between them, placed her palms on his chest. His heart drummed fast and erratic. Being there had reminded him of all he'd endured, and yet still he'd come for her. Such a precious man. *My man.* "Let me help you. Please."

"I… Yes. Okay." He picked her up, carried her to the bed, and laid her across the mattress, then snuggled up beside her.

"Talk to me. Purge the poison."

A moment passed. Then another.

Then, "I don't know if you know this," he said quietly, "but it's possible for a woman to arouse a man's body, even if he doesn't want the woman herself. That's how, when I was trapped in hell, countless minions were able to…do things to me. It was far worse than I led you to believe. It was one female after another, their hands and mouths everywhere, as they tried to steal my seed. They wanted to have my babies, and I was rarely left alone. All the while, Disaster laughed. He's laughing now. He loves every second of my pain and humiliation."

"Oh, Kane." Her poor, poor Kane. "It's not your humiliation, darling. It's Disaster's. It's the minions'. They alone carry the shame."

"I could have fought harder."

"Could you really?" she asked. "When you're already stronger than any man I know?"

"I'm not," he said with a shake of his head.

"Yes, you are, and today proves it. Despite everything you endured, you still came back for me."

Against her cheek, she felt his heart skip a beat. "I did, didn't I? But…when I heard the demons closing in, I felt sick and cowardly. I should have faced them. I should have destroyed them. And one day I will. But today, I only wanted to flee."

And it had embarrassed his warrior soul, she realized. "Oh, Kane. Cowardliness has nothing to do with feeling, and everything to do with action. You acted *despite* everything. You are brave and valiant and worthy, and you had more to think about than vengeance. You had a woman you were trying to protect. You knew what the minions were capable of, and I bet you wanted me as far away from them as you could get me. Am I right?"

Only the slightest hesitation before he admitted, "Yes." Then he rolled onto his side and buried his head into the hollow of her neck. Something warm dripped onto her skin. A…tear? His arms wrapped around her and held on tight, and another droplet splashed, and then another and another. Soon, Kane was sobbing, great, gut-wrenching sobs, tremors racking his entire body.

Her heart breaking for him, Josephina cooed at him and ran her fingers through the silk of his hair. How long had these tears been trapped inside? How long had his inner wounds festered?

A few moments after he quieted, he rolled to the side,

removing his weight from her, and sagged against the mattress. "I'm sorry," he croaked.

"Why?"

"I just acted like a wom—uh, a child."

"Tears aren't childish, silly. And they're not reserved for women, thank you very much. You were wronged, you were hurt and you suffered greatly. You're allowed to react."

His fingers dusted along the line of her jaw. "Your wisdom humbles me."

"I *am* amazingly smart."

He chuckled, only to go quiet a second later. "They didn't succeed, you know. I didn't leave any of the minions pregnant."

She was glad. He wouldn't have survived that kind of connection to the Underworld.

Josephina sat up without ever breaking contact, and peered down at him. Whatever she'd meant to say was superseded by, "No fair. When I cry, I look like a hag who's just left a boxing match. You look as beautiful as always."

He offered her a slow, lazy smile. "You think I'm beautiful?"

"I think I've told you I consider you the incarnation of beautiful." She tugged his shirt over his head.

"No, you told me I'm sexy. There's a difference. And not that I'm complaining, but…what are you doing?"

"Remember when I told you I wanted to smother all your bad memories with good? Well, we're starting today. Now." His boots were the next to go, followed by his pants and underwear, leaving him totally and completely naked.

Josephina perused him unabashedly. Actually, *beautiful* and *sexy* were words too mild for him. He had muscle stacked upon muscle, and flawless bronze skin, all topped off by the butterfly tattoo on his hip.

She traced the jagged edges of the wings. "The artwork catches my attention every time."

"Evil sometimes comes in a very pretty package."

Very true. "You want to be rid of it. Of him."

"More than anything."

"Then we'll find a way to make it happen." She pressed her lips against his, feeding him a soft, sweet kiss. "Together, we can do anything. Now, grip the headboard."

"Tink..." he said.

"I won't do anything you don't like. I promise."

"Whatever you do, trust me, I'll like."

Trembling, he stretched out his arms and did as she'd commanded, and when she next kissed him, he accepted her without reservation, meeting her thrust for gentle thrust, before pressing more firmly, taking more deeply, changing the tone of the kiss. There was passion, yes. There was always passion between them. But he also kissed her with something more heady than reverence, as if she were the most important part of his life. As if he would want and need her always. As if he couldn't bear the thought of ever being without her.

Josephina took her time tasting and laving every inch of his body, learning how to please him as he offered instructions, telling her what he liked, and she obeyed, worshipping him, watching his face for any sign of uncertainty or distress. He never flinched or paled. He appeared undone. He appeared on edge with the force of his desire.

"I'm about to...Tink, you have to stop. I want to touch you, do things to you," he croaked. "Want to have you."

Not just want but needed, she realized. Before, he'd

been bound, had lost all sense of control. He might never be able to fully relinquish power to her, and that was okay. She loved the way he mastered her body.

"I'm yours," she said, "to do with as you please."

He had a condom on in the next instant, and her waist gripped in the one after that. He lifted her, and filled her, and all she could do was dig her nails into his chest and hang on for the wildest ride of her life.

He was untamed, undisciplined. He was savage. He was also brutally sweet. Because, as much as he took, he gave back even more, touching her in all the right places, driving her need higher and higher. And when the pleasure hit its peak, she could only throw back her head, the tips of her hair brushing against his groin. He roared, arching his hips, surging that much deeper, propelling her to a whole new level of satisfaction.

Panting, she collapsed on his chest. His arms wrapped around her and held tightly.

"Don't ever leave me," he said, kissing her sweat-damp temple.

"Never," she vowed.

"It's wrong of me, I know it is, but I need you to stay with me."

"Wrong of you how?"

He cleared his throat. "I…know a way."

It took her a moment to realize he'd returned to their earlier conversation. "The starving thing?"

He nodded. "Things might get rocky for a while, and you'd probably be better off without me, but—"

Ah. That's what he'd meant about asking her to stay being wrong of him. "I'm not going anywhere without you," she said.

He closed his eyes, as if savoring her words. "No, you're not going anywhere without me."

KANE LEANED AGAINST the door frame and grinned as he watched Tink interact with the other women in the fortress. He'd introduced her to everyone just this morning, and she was already a part of the family.

She'd only asked for three autographs.

Everyone had been so busy hunting details about the Paring Rod, and what could have happened to Cameo and Viola, they'd forgotten to rest or eat. They'd needed a break, a distraction, and Tink was now providing both.

The women loved Tink and fawned over her, and sure, that could be because he'd threatened to murder anyone who hurt her feelings, but he didn't think so. There was something so welcoming about her. She smiled, and amusement lit her entire face. She spoke, and the wisdom of multiple lifetimes poured from her lips. She included everyone in her conversation, and showed no partiality. They were all special to her.

"Tell us more about life in the Fae palace," Ashlyn said while rocking her daughter to sleep.

He should leave. He had to talk to his friends about his deal with Taliyah—and they would probably want to wipe the floor with his face for offering up their fortress. It would be best to get that out of the way while Tink was distracted. He turned to walk away.

"Well," Tink said. "I'm now the most envied woman in the land. I married the famed keeper of Disaster."

He heard the pride in her voice, and couldn't help but turn back to her. He saw it in her eyes, too, and his heart soared. His friends could wait.

Anya bounced Urban up and down and patted him on the back, struggling to get him to burp. "I want to hear more about Kane beating up your lecherous half brother. I bet that rocked your panties off! It would have mine, if I ever wore any."

Haidee, Amun's wife, shook her head; a mix of blond and pink hair danced over her shoulders. "You have to forgive her. She's just a little crazy in the head."

"Uh, try a lot crazy in the head," Anya retorted, as if she were complimenting herself. In her mind, she probably was. "I should have been committed centuries ago. Oh, wait. I was!"

"Stop talking, Anarchy. Josephina was just about to tell us if Kane's as much of an animal in bed as I think." Gwen, Sabin's wife, waved to Tink, a silent command to continue.

"I'm pretty sure I wasn't going to talk about that," Tink said, taken aback.

"Oh, yes, you totally were. And while you're at it," said Kaia, Strider's consort, "I'm going to give you one of my galaxies' famous makeovers. Strider told me your family treated you like a servant and I firmly believe the best way to get revenge—besides killing the stupid jerks with a blade…or a hammer…or a saw—is to kill the stupid jerks with jealousy."

Sienna, Paris's wife, snapped her fingers and a rack of dresses and a vanity piled high with makeup appeared. "Ta da! Let the makeover begin."

"Neat trick," Tink said, clapping.

Gilly, William's teenage charge, leaned toward Tink, her expression earnest. "I hear you spent some time with William. Did you happen to notice the kind of women he…you know?"

"My poor ears," Anya said. "They do not need to hear about Willy you-knowing."

"You guys are weird," Scarlet said. "I should kill you all in your sleep. That way, I'd stop stressing about missing friends—because I wouldn't have any friends. It would be win/win." She was the keeper of Nightmares, the wife of Gideon, and there was no one scarier. Most people ran from her at the first opportunity.

But not Tink. Tink patted her on top of the head. “Don’t go near Kane, or I’ll have to hurt you.”

“What about William?” Gilly prompted.

“She can go near him if she wants,” Tink said with a nod.

“No.” Gilly twisted the fabric of her T-shirt. “His women.”

“Can I go to my room now?” Legion, Aeron’s adopted daughter, interrupted. She was pale and withdrawn, and Kane hated the reason why. Like him, she’d spent a little time in hell.

Earlier today, he’d gone to her room to talk with her. She hadn’t responded when he’d knocked, so he’d gone in thinking to leave her a note. He’d found her huddled in the far corner, her knees drawn to her chest as she etched pictures on the wall. Pictures of Galen, once the second in command of the Hunters, now under Sienna’s control.

Galen, who’d once thought to enslave the girl.

“Legion,” he’d said, and she’d stiffened. She had the body of a porn star, and yet, at that moment, she appeared to be nothing more than a child.

With her back to him, she’d said, “I hate that name. I won’t answer to it.”

“What would you like me to call you?” He’d kept his tone gentle.

“Anything but that.”

“All right, then. I’ll call you Honey.”

“Whatever. I want to be left alone.”

His heart broke for her. “I’ll go. I just wanted you to know I’ve been where you are, and I’ve been through what you’ve been through, and if you ever want to talk about it with someone who understands, come find me. It doesn't make you better, but…it helps."

Now, in the present, Olivia, Aeron's wife, wrapped an arm around her shoulders. "Stay with us a little longer. Please."

Legion—Honey—flinched at the contact, but nodded reluctantly.

"Well…" Tink scanned each expectant face, a gleam of awe dawning in those baby blues, as if she couldn't quite believe they were talking to her—and actually liked her. So wise in so many ways, yet so innocent in so many others. "Let me tackle this one at a time. First, the Fae palace is huge and luxurious and filled with treasures, but the people kind of suck."

Gwen and Kaia smiled and nodded.

"I think a treasure hunt is in our future," Kaia said.

"Agreed," Gwen replied.

"Second," Tink continued, "I won't divulge a single detail about what Kane and I do in the bedroom. Except to say that it's awesome. I'm probably the most satisfied woman in the fortress, if not the world."

"No way. I am!" Anya said.

"No, me!" Kaia replied.

"Third, a makeover would be nice. Thank you. Fourth, William…yes. He spent time with a beautiful but very cruel blonde. The queen, who is kind of like my stepmother. I'm sorry."

Gilly nodded, the twinkle fading from her eyes. "A married woman," she said. "He's not the man I thought he was."

Tink reached over and squeezed her hand, a gesture of comfort and understanding. When she realized she wasn't wearing her gloves, she jerked her arm away.

"I'm sorry. I shouldn't have touched—no, wait. I can. Kane made sure."

He grinned—the pride was back.

Hate her! Hate them! Disaster banged against his skull, roaring, growling, threatening.

Beside him, a light bulb shorted out. At his feet, a crack formed in the marble.

Here we go, he thought, fighting a spear of dread. *The hunger pains had begun.*

Every eye darted to him. He ground his molars and nodded in acknowledgment.

A hard hand on his shoulder drew his attention to the male behind him. "You ready?"

Surprised, he said, "William. What are you doing here?"

"That's the welcome I get after everything I've done for you? Thanks a lot, dude."

Kane drew back a fist and let it fly, nailing the warrior in the nose. Blood instantly spurted. "No, that's the thanks you get."

William grinned, his warped sense of humor obviously coming out to play. "Better."

"Next time you try and trick me, I won't stop with one punch."

"I'm sure."

And now that that was settled… "Last I saw you, you were headed into a fight with the minions. What happened?"

"A slaughter, that's what. Those females got what was coming to them, I assure you. And now, you owe me, like, big time." He blew the ladies a kiss and started toward the library. He only looked back at Gilly once.

Kane followed him, and, taking a page from his playbook, threw one last glance at Tink. She smiled at him, so sweet and pretty, and he smiled back.

"I owe you nothing," he said to William. He wasn't sure whether to feel elated his enemy was dead, or ticked that vengeance would never be his.

He'd go with ticked.

"So, where'd you get my ring?" he asked, just to taunt the warrior.

Those electric blues narrowed to tiny slits. "You mean *my* ring."

"That's what I said. My ring."

A pause. A stiff shrug. "Fine. Keep it. I stole it from a woman I bedded and killed. What? Why are you looking at me like that? *Anyway.* The ring's probably cursed, luring you into a false sense of calm."

Another light bulb shorted out, a spray of flames seeking Kane as if he wore a bull's eye. He remained silent as he entered the room. William shut and locked the door, just in case the women decided to come looking for them. Kane swept his gaze over the men scattered throughout the room. Lucien, Sabin, Strider, Amun, Paris, Gideon, Aeron, Reyes, Maddox and Torin, who stood in the far corner. Weeks had passed since they'd all been together like this.

Together, they were a force to be reckoned with.

"So your girl's in trouble, huh?" Strider said. "William told us about her father's plans."

"What can we do to help?" Sabin asked.

Help, he'd said. He wasn't trying to take over, and didn't plan to leave Kane behind. He understood Kane's need to participate in his woman's liberation. Some of the tension left him—

Until another light bulb shorted out.

"First, I have to be straight with you," he said. "I

need you out of the fortress, no questions asked, in a little less than three months."

"What?"

"Why?"

"What's going on?"

Yeah. No questions asked, he thought with a roll of his eyes. Whatever. "To find Tink, I made a bargain with someone. That person gets the fortress."

"Who?" Sabin demanded.

"None of your business. Just do it."

There was grumbling. Of course there was grumbling. But the warriors would have done the same thing for their women, and they knew it. There was no debate in the end—they would leave.

Next, Kane outlined his plan for the Fae king, and all of his friends nodded encouragingly. It was dangerous, and it required a huge sacrifice from every person in the fortress, but it was the fastest way to prove Tink's worth to her father—and all of the Fae.

Then, and only then, would Tiberius understand Kane would never let her go. Hunting her would do no good. She would never again be a blood slave.

When he finished, Sabin stroked his chin and pondered. "Will it hurt?" the warrior asked.

"No," Kane replied.

"Cause any lasting damage?" Reyes demanded.

"No."

"You're sure?" Lucien asked.

"I am."

"Well, you have my agreement," Strider said with a shrug. "Now, you just have to get Kaia's."

Kane nodded. He'd expected that. "I will." He wouldn't fail.

William placed his hand over his heart. "This plan

is *so* devious, it's almost as if I thought of it. I'm quite impressed."

Kane flipped him off, just because. And even as the wall beside him rumbled and shook, as if preparing to collapse on him, he felt lighter than he had in weeks. He felt…free. Free of the past and the pain, the memories and the hate.

Last night, Tink had done something to him. She had soothed the beast inside, perhaps. Or maybe she had cauterized what remained of his wounds.

Now, he would do the same for her.

"We leave in the morning," he said.

CHAPTER THIRTY-TWO

KANE LEFT TINK sleeping in their room, and knocked on Reyes and Danika's door.

"Go away," Reyes shouted, sounding out of breath.

No need to wonder what was going on in there. "I need to speak with Danika. I'm staying put until I do."

Pounding footsteps. The hard twist of a knob. A scowling Reyes appeared. He was shirtless, his pants undone, his hair askew. "You're flirting with death."

"And I'm sure Lucien finds me adorable. The painting," he said, looking past his friend to the beautiful girl strolling toward him, tying a terrycloth robe around her waist. "What can you tell me about it?"

She nodded, saying, "I struggled with the appearance of the female. One second I saw a brunette that could have been Josephina, but I'm not one hundred percent certain about that, and the next I saw the pale-haired female I ended up painting."

When he'd first met her, Tink had changed facades, but the ability of the Phoenix had left her, so she wasn't the pale-haired one in disguise. "The Moirai told me I had two possible mates. William thought one was his daughter White, and I thought one was Tink's half sister, Synda. Both are blondes."

She thought for a moment, sighed. "You should show the artwork to Josephina. If that's her body—"

"It's not."

"—she would recognize herself."

"She won't." He'd seen and kissed and touched every inch of her. "I know her body better than she does."

Danika gave another sigh. "I can believe it. Anyway, there's something strange about that painting. I've never had trouble locking onto an identity, and I've never been wrong."

"Tink's safe." The assurance was for him, not Danika. "I'm not going to let anything happen to her." Even though his plan involved throwing her straight to the wolves. "There's nothing more you can tell me?"

"No, I'm sorry."

"This meeting is over, then." Reyes shut the door in his face.

PANTING AND SWEATING, Josephina peered up at Kane. He hovered over her, panting just as hard, sweating just as badly. She watched a bead trickle from his forehead to his temple and catch in his hair, mesmerized.

"How was that?" she asked.

"Absolutely terrible." His lashes fused, hiding the brilliance of those angry hazel eyes. "The worst."

Brutal honesty sucked sometimes. "I'm sorry."

"You should be."

"I'll do better."

"I'll believe it when I see it."

Hey! "You're seconds away from being slapped!"

"That would be a welcome change."

She shoved him off, and he rolled to a stand. They'd been training for hours, and she was tired. She hadn't slept last night—even after Kane had made love to her and exhausted her—her mind too busy outlining every possible flaw to his crazy plan. The only real fight she'd ever been in had happened in hell, but at the time she'd had the abilities of the Phoenix and had simply burned everything that had approached her. She didn't have that luxury now.

He helped her stand, his calluses tickling her skin. "You have to use every weapon at your disposal. A rock on the ground. Your knees. Whatever. Don't be afraid to get down and dirty, and inflict major damage. If your attacker's face is within striking distance, like mine just was, poke out his eyes. Break his nose with the heel of your hand, sending cartilage into his brain."

Josephina anchored her hands on her hips. "Until now, I haven't wanted to do those things to you, and that's the only reason you've been able to take me down so many times."

"The *only* reason?"

Argh! She ripped off her tennis shoe and tossed it at him.

The heavy heel banged into his shoulder and toppled to the ground.

"Better." He nodded with his first display of pride. "That's a habit that must run in your family."

"Do you want to feel the sting of the other shoe?"

"I *need* to know you can take down an opponent, Tink. I don't know what I'd do if something happened to you."

Okay. All right. That, she could understand. The plan hinged on her, and what she could do. She would be in the thick of danger, and he would be worried.

She would be worried, but she wasn't going to let it stop her. *I'm stronger than I've ever been. I'm determined. I know the stakes.*

I deserve to live and love. And I will.

"Kane," she said, stepping toward him. "You've left me no choice. I have to do this."

She punched him in the mouth. Pain exploded through her knuckles and arm, and his head whipped to the side. Slowly he faced her. A cascade of crimson flowed from the corner of his lip, obscene against the bronze of his skin. He grinned, the blood even staining his teeth.

"Now that's my girl. Good job."

A knock reverberated through the room, saving her from an embarrassing display of self-congratulations.

"We're ready for you," Sabin called.

Kane's grin disappeared. "We'll be down in fifteen minutes."

He tugged Josephina into the bathroom, stripped her, stripped himself and turned on the water for a quick shower. Soapy hands wandered, and once again Josephina found herself panting from exertion. As much touching as they'd done, her body was already primed.

"We only have a few minutes," she said.

"That's all I need."

"Really?" But, every time before had taken hours. "Are you sure I'll enjoy this? I mean, I want you, but I also want to reach the end."

"I consider it a personal mission to ensure that you do." He donned a condom and pushed her against the wall. He was inside her a second later, and oh…oh! The way he moved…hard and fast, nothing held back…he wrung groan after groan from her. He kissed her, a tinge of desperation to every thrust of his tongue.

"I could drain the life out of you in seconds," she rasped. "I could kill you."

He moaned with pleasure-roughened arousal. "Tell me more."

"You'd never know what happened. One moment you would be lucid, the next you would be dead."

He became a wild man, whatever tether he'd had on his control broken. Her thoughts derailed as he hammered at her, the pleasure too much, not enough and... *yes, yes, yes...*

"Kane!" she shouted, her body breaking apart, reforming, every inch of her branded by the man in her arms.

He bit the cord between her neck and shoulder as he shuddered against her, the pressure somehow propelling her into another level of rapture. For a minute... an eternity...black dots flashed behind her eyes and silence cloaked her ears. She was lost to the pleasure.

When she came down, Kane was grinning at her. "Told you," he said, all masculine satisfaction.

The tub shattered beneath their feet. He slipped and caught himself on the curtain rod above their heads. Her legs were still wrapped around Kane's waist, her feet protected from the shards. But not his. Blood welled from several incisions.

"This will pass," she said.

"I know." Scowling now, Kane carried her out of the debris. He set her on her feet, and they dressed as swiftly as possible and rushed to the ballroom to meet with his friends.

The women formed a line in the center, their men behind them.

"I don't like this," she muttered.

"Trust me." He gave her a swift kiss. "Your family will never see you coming."

And she had to do whatever was necessary to defeat them. That way, they would never again think to use her.

"Are you sure you want to do this?" she asked the women. She was to borrow the strength and power of everyone but Scarlet, who was demon-possessed, Ashlyn, a nursing mother, and Danika, whose visions of the future could distract her.

Each female squared her shoulders, raised her chin.

"Very well." Trembling, Josephina reached toward Gwen. She stopped just before contact. "Last chance to back out. When I'm done, you'll be weak. It could last a few hours or a few weeks."

"Weak schmeak. I know the problems dirtbag dads can cause."

"Her father is Galen, keeper of Hope and Jealousy," Kane explained, stepping up beside her to offer moral support. "Though he doesn't carry the kind of hope you might think. It's false hope that Galen offers. Real hope is essential…miraculous." He looked at her, his hazels bright. "The kind that you gave me."

The kind he'd given her.

She melted into him.

"Do it. Drain me. You'll need what I've got," Gwen added as Sabin came to stand behind her. "I'm amazingly strong and faster than light."

Sabin placed his hands on his wife's shoulders. "Just don't hurt my favorite toy, and we'll be fine."

Gwen preened as she tapped her thumb against her chest. "Today I'm his toy." Next, she hitched that thumb in Sabin's direction. "Tomorrow he's mine."

Toy. Yes. The perfect word to describe such a delicate-looking female; Josephina wasn't sure how much strength she would be able to take without putting the girl into a coma.

"I'll be gentle," Josephina promised, wrapping her fingers around Gwen's wrist. "And thank you for this. I don't know how I'll ever be able to repay you."

"I'm sure I'll think of something."

She closed her eyes, flipped the mental switch that

she now knew caused her pores to open and create suction…pulling…pulling on the strength the female possessed.

Energy fizzed in her veins, as potent as if she'd stuck her finger into a light socket, and she reeled at the force, feeling shocked and giddy.

When she released Gwen, the poor girl sagged into her husband's arms. "Wow! That was amazing."

Kane urged her to turn to Kaia.

"You'll want what I've got most of all," Kaia said. "I'm part Phoenix, and I start fires when I'm angry."

The moment they touched, Josephina experienced the same crackling surge of energy, but also a flood of warmth. Heat…so much heat swept through her, and she felt as if her body would erupt into flames at any second. It was a familiar sensation, the same one she'd encountered with the other Phoenix.

With Anya, she felt as if she had been invaded by a mighty wind.

With Haidee, there was freezing cold.

Gilly tried to step up to the line. "My turn," the girl said.

William appeared at her side and tugged her to the far corner of the room, saying, "Not going to happen, Gum Drop." To Josephina, he called, "She's only human."

"Being human isn't synonymous with weakness," the girl said.

"*Synonymous* is a big word for such a small child," he retorted.

"Hey! I'm not a child. I'm old enough to carry my weight around here."

"Well, then, I guess it's a good thing you don't weigh very much."

She pointed a finger in his face. "One day I'm going to show you just how strong I actually am, William the Idiot."

He shrugged, as if he didn't care, but the hard gleam in his eyes said otherwise.

"I don't think I can hold anything else," Josephina said. She could burst at any second. Never had she felt this strong. This…invincible. And…and…she couldn't just stand there. She had to move.

"What are you doing?" Kane asked after she'd leaped into motion.

"Running around the room." She was too hot….too cold…too everything. Could fight any enemy. Conquer the entire world. And she wouldn't even chip a nail, she thought with a maniacal laugh. "Are the women okay? Do you think they're okay? I really hope they're okay." The words poured from her, coming faster and faster. Just like her steps. Soon she was sprinting—and not even winded.

"William," Kane called, watching her. His lips twitched at the corners. "We're ready."

The warrior glanced away from the teenage girl, and said, "Just a sec," before turning back to the girl and getting in her face. "Go to your room and wait for me. We're going to discuss the whole proving-yourself thing and put a stop to it now, before I'm forced to clean up a mess I'll make you wish you hadn't made."

"Stop telling me what to do. You aren't my father."

"How many times do I have to tell you I've never wanted to be your father?" he yelled, raising his voice for the first time since Josephina had met him. "I want you safe, and I'll do whatever is necessary to see to it, even hurt your feelings."

All of the Lords watched with unabashed shock.

Cheeks reddened from the force of her anger, Gilly marched from the room.

William watched her until he could watch her no more. Then he tangled a hand through his hair and faced the men, his expression devoid of emotion.

"Let's do this." He strode to the center of the room and withdrew a few things from his pockets. Pieces of gum?

He held the—no, not gum—*whatever* up, and when he let go, the small, chewy-looking objects actually remained in midair.

"Incoming," he shouted, and everyone in the room turned away.

Kane threw himself at Josephina, knocking her into the ground, absorbing most of the impact. What—

Boom!

A hot gust of air licked over her, then Kane was rolling away from her and helping her to her feet. Or rather, trying to. She accidentally jerked him down beside her, and he hit with so much force he might have punctured a lung.

"Sorry," she said. "Sorry."

He laughed. Actually laughed. "Don't worry about it, sweetheart." He stood and motioned for her to do the same.

She hopped to her feet and saw that William had somehow blasted through the realm to create a doorway into Séduire. Night had fallen—the time for parties. The entire Fae court would be gathered in the throne room. The moon was out, a crimson sliver in the blackness of the sky. A walking path was lit by torches.

"Maybe we should think about this," she said, suddenly nervous.

"No more thinking."

What about stalling? "What happened to the key?"

"Apparently, if you aren't a Fae, they break down and stop working," Kane replied. "Mine stopped working."

"All right. Okay." If she didn't act now, she wasn't going to act at all. "I'm ready." She raced forward.

"Aren't you forgetting something?" Kane called, stopping her.

"What—" Oh, yeah. "Sorry." She backtracked and grabbed Kane's hand. He cringed, and she realized she had to keep her newfound strength in check or she would crush his bones. "Sorry again!"

His grin returned, wide and toothy and full of good humor. "I told you. Don't worry about it. Now do what needs doing."

They marched toward the Fae realm.

"I'll give you thirty minutes, then I'm coming in," William announced.

"We've got this," Kane replied without turning back.

His friends were staying in the Realm of Blood and Shadows to protect their weakened women. William was their backup.

"See you in thirty," William said with a wave.

"I said no."

"Twenty-five, then."

"Frustrating," Kane muttered.

They passed through the doorway, entered the charred remains of her father's garden. Dark smoke still wafted through the air.

Josephina's heart thundered in her chest. What if she failed, like she'd done during much of her training today? What if Kane got hurt? She would forever blame herself—and rightly so.

Yeah, but what if you succeed?

From the corner of her eye, she thought she spotted

the warrior with white-and-gold wings, the one who'd brought her new clothing. But…surely not. That would mean he was following her.

She searched the darkness, but found no other sign of him.

"This way," Kane said.

He led her toward the palace. Whenever a guard passed, he would shield her with his body, doing his best to hide them both. Finally, they reached the door to one of the secret passages.

Inside, Josephina took the lead. Down the hall. Up a flight of steps. Down a flight of steps. Around a corner. Around another corner. Trading one passage for another, moving at such a rapid pace, never giving herself time to think, until they reached their destination.

Her heart drummed as she stopped. Through the two-way mirror, she saw the throne room was as crowded as she'd expected.

"You ready?" Kane asked.

No. Yes. She had better be. "I am."

"You've got this, sweetheart. I believe in you."

Now, to believe in herself. Josephina pushed open the door, and with her head held high, entered the throng.

Two girls spotted her and gasped. They told their friends, and their friends gasped. One set of eyes after another found her.

Josephina walked forward, Kane behind her; the crowd parted, making way. Soon, the royal family came into view, each member perched on a throne.

Leopold spotted her and stood. Synda waved and smiled, as if Josephina hadn't ruined her wedding. The queen scowled.

"Well, well," the king said, rubbing his jaw. "You

have returned." His gaze slid to Kane and filled with satisfaction. "Tired of her already?"

Kane wound his arm around her and kissed her temple. "I'll never be tired of her. She's mine. I chose her then, and I choose her now. I'll choose her tomorrow and every day after."

Sweet heat. No one had ever… He'd just said…

Murmurs swept through the crowd. Josephina turned in a circle, meeting the stunned gazes of the Fae. These people had ignored her and talked down to her and laughed at her pain. No one had ever offered to help her. Now, envy looked back at her.

In a single moment, Kane had undone years of rejection. He'd given worth to the female no one had wanted. This man… He wasn't a disaster. He was a savior.

And he's mine.

King Tiberius frowned. "Then why are you here, Lord Kane?"

Do it. Finish this. "He heard you were looking for me, coming for me," Josephina said. "I decided to save you the trouble and settle things."

"You want to settle things?" The king perked up, motioning to the space at his feet. "Then bow before me. Offer your apologies for the destruction of the garden and accept your sentence when it's pronounced."

"And what, exactly, did I do wrong?" she asked, lifting her chin.

A pause. Then, "Just like your mother…everything."

Anger torched any remorse she might have entertained over this. Bludgeoned any sadness, strangled any guilt.

But then, realization struck her. He blamed her for her mother's decline and death, and always had. Always would.

Had he actually *loved* the woman, in his own warped way?

"I would like to approach you, yes." Eyes narrowing, she moved away from Kane, and every ounce of her new, massive strength was required not to ghost her fingers through his hair, enjoying one last touch before Séduire forever changed. Before *she* changed.

At the dais, the guard backed away, allowing her to draw closer. In front of the king, she bowed her head, presenting the perfect picture of submission. "Majesty," she said with a curtsy.

"Lower."

The command scraped against the piece of her heart that had hoped she would finally, at long last, find favor with him.

"How about this instead?" Quick as a blink, she grabbed him by the throat, lifting him from his seat, startling him—and crushing the pipes beneath her fingers. "You bow before *me*."

CHAPTER THIRTY-THREE

The Realm of Blood and Shadows

FRANTIC, TORIN PACED beside his bed. Mari had arrived a few minutes ago—only to collapse. She was sick. So very sick.

And he was responsible.

He should never have touched her, should never have allowed her to shake his ungloved hand.

He was so worried for her he could barely see straight. She lay on the bed, coughing for the thousandth time. Blood gurgled from the corners of her mouth.

Fury blazed at the edges of Torin's worry, and he punched a hole in the wall, desperate for some type of release. "Why didn't you tell me I could make you sick with my touch?"

"I had…to die."

"You *had* to die?" He stomped to her side. "And you thought I'd be okay with being the weapon responsible?" How was he supposed to live with himself, knowing he'd killed yet another innocent?

"No…worries. No plague. Only me. Never touch…anyone else."

Oh, he knew she was only ever allowed in her prison and his bedroom, but that didn't make this any better. He stalked to his door and locked it, ensuring none of his friends could burst inside for any reason. "You still should have told me," he croaked. "It should have been my choice."

"Sorry. Not want…to die. Resisted. But. No other way. Cronus said…friend would be…freed."

Cronus had also said Torin wouldn't sicken the woman sent to him. Clearly Cronus had lied. "The king of the Titans is dead. Your friend won't be freed."

"Vows last…even after death."

And Torin hadn't been smart enough to obtain a vow, had he.

She had coughed between every word. A hacking cough that had shaken her entire body. "Moment I die… she has freedom."

Mari had given her life for her friend. He understood the desire. He did. But that didn't make this any easier. He returned to her side and peered down at her. Her skin was ghostly white, a blue tracery of veins apparent. There were bruises under her eyes, and her lips were split and scabbed from being chewed. The last time she'd visited, she had looked healthy and whole. Now, twenty-four hours later, she was reduced to *this*.

Death was knocking on her door. Maybe she would answer today. Maybe tomorrow. Either way, she *would* answer. There would be no saving her.

No, he thought next. No. He had to try. Something. Anything. So far, he'd failed to help Cameo and Viola, but he could help this woman.

In the bathroom, he wet a washrag with cold water. He raced back to the girl's side. Gloves covered his hands, so he didn't hesitate to drape the cloth over her forehead. He'd never touched a human twice, and wasn't sure what would happen to Mari if his skin were to brush hers a second time. Would she get sicker faster? Probably.

At his computer, he printed the list he'd recently created. The ones with medicines that might aid humans if ever his plague got out. Then, he called Lucien. "Flash to the States, to a pharmacy. I need a few things." He tossed out the names.

"I won't leave Anya, Tor. She needs me right now."

"I'll put a camera on her. I'll make sure no one approaches her, I swear. Just do what I asked. Please." Torin hung up on him and stuffed the phone in his pocket. He peered down at the girl. "Now you listen to me. You're going to fight this. You're not going to give up and allow yourself to die. You want your friend out, there's another way. I told you about Sienna. Well, she arrived at the fortress just this morning. Give her a chance."

Tears streamed from Mari's eyes and tracked down her cheeks.

"Please," he said.

She gave an almost imperceptible nod. But a nod was a nod.

"People have survived this." Not many, but a few, and no one who'd had direct contact with him. "You can, too." She had to. His heart couldn't take another death.

Bang, bang, bang.

"Leave the stuff and go," Torin called, knowing Lucien was at the door.

"What's going on?" the warrior demanded.

"Just…trust me," he replied as Mari coughed.

Tense silence filled the room.

"Reyes told me about the girl you had in there. Is she sick? Is she the one in need of the medicine?" Lucien's voice was soft, quiet, and yet still managed to cut through the wood of the door.

"Leave the stuff and go," he repeated.

Movement at the corner of his eye. He turned—and there was Lucien, dropping a bag on the floor. The warrior had flashed inside the room. His mismatched eyes scanned the area and landed on the girl.

Accusation tightened his features. "You said she was immune."

"I was wrong. Now get out. I don't want you becoming a carrier."

"You should have told me about this." The accusation in Lucien's expression was like taking a knife to the back. "I need to take everyone to a new location. Especially the women and children."

Yes. Of course. He should have thought of that. How foolish could Torin be?

"I need Sienna's help with something. Freeing another girl. She's in a prison Cronus owned. Tell her to start looking for it. Please."

"What are you going to do?" Lucien asked. "What about this girl?"

"Don't worry about us."

Lucien pinched the bridge of his nose. "I can't believe you did this. I thought you'd learned."

"Not his…fault," Mari croaked.

"Of course it's my fault," Torin snapped, and she flinched.

Lucien looked ready to stomp over to the girl and scoop her into his arms. Instead, he backed away, saying, "Call me if you need anything else." He disappeared.

Torin went through the medication, deciding to administer the antibiotic and cough suppressant. As he waited for any sign of recovery, an idea struck him. He didn't allow himself to consider the many ramifications or the danger to himself. He raced to his closet and grabbed a nylon bag. He stuffed it full of weapons and any other equipment he thought he might need. He covered his hair and forehead with a bandanna, pulled a ski mask over his face to ensure the rest of him was covered, as well. He added the medicine to the bag, wrote a note to his friends, and then did something he'd hoped to circumvent forever.

He looked at Danika's painting, expecting to see this moment, this tragedy—or, maybe, the outcome.

In it, Torin reclined on a black leather couch. He had a glass in one hand, and a cigar in the other—neither hand was gloved. He was grinning, an expression he hadn't donned in a very long time, he didn't think. There were people around him. So many people. Shock had him stumbling backward. Danika had never before shown him a *happy* ending.

Happy.

He could be happy.

The girl coughed, drawing his attention back to her. Hope spread wings and flew through him. Maybe she would survive.

He crouched beside her.

"When you flash back to the prison, I want you to hold on to me and will me to go with you. Okay? Can you do that? I'm covered. Your skin won't ever be in contact with mine, and your condition won't worsen." *Please don't worsen.*

She licked her dry, cracked lips, but left no moisture behind. "Why?"

"I'm not leaving you alone in that cell. I know you have to go back, and there's no way I can stop you, so I'll just have to go with you. I'll be there to doctor you, and maybe you'll get better." *You have to get better.*

"You won't…be able…to leave."

"That's fine. Sienna will find us and I'll introduce you."

Between coughs, she replied, "Can…try."

He stretched out beside her and pressed his mask-covered face against her chest. Her heart was beating too hard and too fast. Heat radiated through the material barriers between them. He draped his arm over her middle and twined his legs through hers.

The position was new to him. One he'd never before experienced. One he was ashamed to admit he liked, despite the circumstances. He'd never been so close to a female. Meanwhile, she was dying.

"I'm here," he cooed. "I'm with you."

"Here we…go."

A second later, the world around him vanished and a new one took shape.

It had worked.

He saw a small cell with crumbling rock walls. There was no window, and barely any light. The only door was made of metal bars. There was no bed, no blankets. The air was cold and damp.

A soft, pained moan left her.

They were on the frigid, hard ground, and it had to be painful to her aching bones. Torin hopped to his feet and tugged the clothes from his bag to create a barrier, a makeshift mattress. Then he picked her up and eased her down.

"Mari?" a pretty voice called from across the way. "Is that you? Are you back?"

In response, Mari coughed.

"Are you okay?" the girl asked, concerned. "And who's in there with you? The shadow I see is too large to be yours."

"My name is Torin," he called. "Mari is sick, and I'm here to help her."

The girl released a string of curses. "You touched her. You touched her, and now she's going to die."

"No," he said. "I won't let her."

Bars rattled. "You better hope she doesn't. She does, and I'll find a way out of here. I'll destroy you and everyone you love."

CAMEO'S PATIENCE RAN out as she shoved past another tangle of thorn bushes. Her skin was sliced in too many places to count, her feet were throbbing, and she was pretty sure there were bugs in her hair.

She'd been so close to Pandora's box, was now so far away.

"I want out of this dimension, like, yesterday," she said.

"I'm looking for the doorway into the next." Lazarus paused to move a branch out of her way. "Impatient much?"

"A girl I know could be trapped in another dimension, too, and I want to find her. So yes, I'm impatient." She stomped past him. He released the branch and laughed when the thorns slapped her. Whirling around, she pointed a finger in his face. "I'm going to hang your balls in my trophy case if you do that again."

"Good. Hold on to your anger. Your voice is unbearable when you're complaining." He stepped around her and resumed his journey.

"I never complain," she muttered. "I'm a warrior. I'm strong. Tough. Unbeatable." She'd fought in wars, saved her friends. Battled her way out of enemy territory. "Besides, it's impolite to point out my only flaw."

"Only?" Lazarus pushed another limb out of his way—only to let this one swing back and slap her in the face. "Oops. My bad."

She snapped her teeth at his back.

"I saw that."

"After I remove your balls, I'll strap you to a slab of concrete and force you to listen while I sing."

"Now that actually scares me." He chuckled. "You amuse me, female."

She *amused* him? "That's a first."

"But true nonetheless. Unlike the woman who tried to enslave me—a name you will not speak again or you will finally see my dark side—you aren't the type to hurt an innocent man."

"You aren't innocent."

"Have I harmed you?"

"No," she grudgingly admitted.

"Then with you, I'm innocent." He flicked her a glance, lingered. "You are so tiny, and so sad, and yet you consider yourself fierce."

"I *am* fierce!" And if she hadn't needed him so much, she would have shown him.

"Of course you are," he said, and if he'd been facing her, she was certain he would have been patting her on top of the head.

Her gaze drilled into his back. His wide, muscular back. Because of the heat, he'd removed his shirt. Sweat ran down in rivulets. His skin was gorgeously bronzed, inked with the most vibrant tattoos, and—

"Do you ever laugh?" he asked, tugging her from her inspection before her knees could start knocking.

"I've been told I have."

"You don't remember?"

"No. Joy isn't something that sticks."

A loud roar reverberated behind her.

Lazarus stopped and twisted, a strange amber light shining in his eyes. She bumped into him, and his arms wrapped around her, holding her steady. He was strong. Amazingly strong. *And I shouldn't find that attractive,* she thought. *I should be immune. I've spent centuries with men just like him.*

"Be still and quiet," he whispered, his gaze searching the trees.

Well, maybe not just like him. Her friends would have asked nicely.

Her ears twitched as she, too, listened. In the distance, she could hear the swish of tree limbs shaking through the air, the clap of leaves banging together.

"Run," Lazarus said, and broke into top speed, dragging her along with him.

"What is it?"

"You don't want to know."

A hideous creature broke through the line of trees behind them. The…whatever it was had the body of a wild hog and the face of a dragon. Gnarled wings stretched from its back, and long saber teeth extended from between its lips.

She'd never seen anything like it. "It's closing in." And she was the closest target, so she would be the first meal.

"So am I." Lazarus picked up speed. "I've found the doorway."

After another few steps, he leaped through the air, dragging Cameo with him. They flew toward a wall of leaves. She expected to feel the brush of limbs against her skin, but there was only a rush of cold air. Then, the forest vanished, and a new scene took shape around her.

Cameo crashed into a cold metal ground. When she caught her breath and stood, she looked around—and kind of wished they'd remained in the forest and faced the beast.

CHAPTER THIRTY-FOUR

Séduire

As Leopold backed away, and Synda cheered, and the queen slid to the floor to crab-walk away from her, Josephina tossed her wheezing father over her shoulder. He was a big man, and yet, he felt as light as a feather. He skidded across the floor, slamming into Fae after Fae before hitting the back wall. He was the bowling ball; they were the pins.

Rage and fear darkened his eyes as he jumped to his feet. "You…you…" he snarled.

"Yes. Me."

Kane rushed through the room, shutting every door, rigging every lock, sealing everyone inside. He looked to Josephina, smiled proudly, then nodded to the area just behind her. "Incoming."

She turned and saw a contingent of guards racing toward her. Adrenaline surged inside her, fizzing in her veins, amping her up. The moment the males reached her, she erupted into a flurry of movement, breaking noses with the heel of her hand, snapping arms in two, kneeing men in the groin, punching, punching, punching just as she'd been taught. Impact should have stung, but she felt no pain.

No one could latch onto her. Her limbs and body simply moved too swiftly.

Moaning and groaning, the men dropped around her, and when there was no one left to challenge her, she maneuvered over the mound of bodies, triumphant, intending to face her father once and for all.

While the queen and Leopold banged at the doors, trying to beat their way out of the room, and Synda cowered behind a throne, Tiberius watched her, waiting.

“You won’t win this,” he said.

“Agree to disagree.” A violent wind shot from her, arching her back, lifting her off her feet, shoving the rest of the bodies out of her way and into the walls, clearing her path before setting her down.

Gasps sounded from the Opulens. Kane was keeping them in the back of the room, but the ground was cracking under his feet, and little flames were being sucked from the wall torches and into his hair. He had to pat the fires out while keeping his attention on the crowd.

Must hurry, she thought. Eyes on her target: her father. Feet: moving forward.

“How are you doing this?” Tiberius demanded.

“You’re not the only one able to use your gifts to your advantage.”

She threw a punch. The king ducked and her hand went through the door behind him. Wood shards rained. She jerked with all her might and took a chunk of wood with her, leaving a hole. But just before she gained her freedom, Tiberius kicked her in the stomach. She propelled backward, skidding across the floor.

Kane’s bellow of fury bounced off the walls.

She held out her injured hand, a silent command for him to stay back. She had this.

The king cracked his knuckles and grinned. Josephina stood, and returned his grin, her amusement wiping his away.

"I won't go easy on you," he said.

"You never have." She raced forward, her feet carrying her across the room in less than a blink, the objects at her side blurring.

Grin widening, the king held out his hands as she threw another punch.

Thud.

Her bones vibrated from the force of collision, but she never made contact with him. The king had used one of his abilities, erecting an invisible shield, protecting himself.

"I'm unbeatable," he said, smug.

No! She hadn't come this far to fail. There had to be a way to reach him.

Anger rising, she beat her fists against the barrier. It was solid. The king laughed. The anger inside her rose…and rose…burning through her veins, singeing muscle and bone. Sweat began to pour out of her, the heat unbearable. Surely she was melting.

"Poor Josephina." Tiberius tsked. "You've already lost, you're just unaware."

Strong arms banded around her, surprising her. The dank, musty scents of the dungeon enveloped her, and she knew the culprit was Leopold.

"I can't let you do this," he growled into her ear.

"You can't stop me." She banged the back of her head into his nose. Yelping, he released her. She turned and punched him in the chest with so much force he flew back and slammed into the throne, where Synda was hiding.

The sound of cracking bone echoed. Leopold slumped to the floor, his eyes closed, his body limp. There was a ring in the center of his shirt, the material singed at the edges. He'd been…burned?

Josephina whipped back to the king—only to take a blow to the jaw. Sharp pain exploded through her head. The new abilities and strength must be fading, dang it. She hit the floor, her brain banging against her skull. Tiberius struck again, kicking her in the stomach.

Bye bye, oxygen. Even as she wheezed, she straightened, not wanting to give him another chance to launch a sneak attack.

"Ready to give up?" he asked. "You'll never be able to bypass my defenses. No one will."

She reached up to wipe the warm trickle of blood from her face and realized one of the king's rings had left a jagged gash on her cheek.

She looked for Kane, and found him fending off the rest of the guards. Soldier after soldier attempted to evade him to get to her, determined to protect the king, but Kane remained in a constant state of motion, stopping them. Finally, the soldiers accepted they'd have to take him out. Evasion became a full-fledged attack, daggers and swords swiping.

Hurry, hurry.

"I'm more than a no one." Ears ringing, she moved slowly, purposefully, and flattened her hands against the invisible barrier.

He kicked her, his leg penetrating the shield no problem, and she stumbled back—but still she came back for more. "Give up, Josephina. You can't win. I've fought opponents far stronger than you. Far faster. Far smarter. And you…you're weak. Disposable."

"I'm not! I'm worth something." Fury stopped rising and simply exploded. She hit the shield, and flames shot from her, dancing together, growing stronger, hotter, until the air began to sizzle, creating a hole in the barrier big enough for her fist.

Tiberius paled. “How did you—”

Josephina punched through the opening once, twice, three times, moving so swiftly he couldn’t dodge, breaking his nose, knocking out two of his teeth, dislocating his jaw. Blood sprayed against what remained of the shield, blending with the flames.

“That’s for my mother,” she said, hitting him again. “That’s for Kane. That’s for me. That’s for having a black heart. That’s for…my mother again.”

His knees buckled. By the time he hit the ground, he was out.

Panting, she peered down at him. She’d done it. She’d defeated him.

She should have felt more triumphant, but the sadness she’d denied had found new life, filling her, spilling out. But that wasn’t going to stop her. She grabbed the king by the hair and dragged him to Leopold. Then, she searched the room for the queen…there! She was still prying at the seam in the doors, desperate to escape.

Josephina simply stepped up behind her, joined her fists, and struck. The woman fell to her side and stayed down.

William appeared just in front of the unconscious body. Red, Green, Black and White appeared just behind him, completely healed.

“Looks like we arrived just in time, gang,” William said with a grin.

The group rushed into the thick of battle, unsheathing swords along the way.

“No!” Josephina cried out.

But they didn’t attack Kane; they attacked the people around him.

The black mist that usually accompanied the Rainbow Rejects remained at bay. Maybe it wasn’t needed.

The boys never mutated into their other forms, and with only a few minutes of hacking at the opposition, William and his children had the rest of the crowd backing away in fear.

"Knew you'd need us," William said with a pat on Kane's shoulder.

A winded, blood-splattered Kane snapped his teeth. "I had the army right where I wanted it and was about to make my final move."

"Please. You were at the cliff, about to be kicked over."

"Whatever." Kane stalked to Josephina's side. Gently he cupped her jaw and tilted her head to the left, allowing light to fall over her wound. "That's going to scar."

"Yes." Unlike full-blooded immortals, she wore her injuries forever. "I'll still be beautiful to you." After everything this man had done for her, she wasn't ever going to doubt his attraction to her.

"More than beautiful. Exquisite." He kissed her, soft and sweet. "I'm so proud of you."

"And I'm proud of you."

Black hoisted the queen over his shoulder, then wrapped an arm under Synda's stomach and hung her at his side. "I'll take these two." His gaze moved to William and narrowed. "I deserve some sort of reward for vowing never to touch Kane or his woman."

"That vow saved you from my deathblow. That was reward enough. Now, you'll put the females in the dungeon, or else," William commanded.

Kane grinned. To Josephina, he said, "I have a need to help take out the trash. There are a few words I'd like to say to your father. You're good?"

"I am."

Kane kissed the tip of her nose. "I'll be right back."

He flung the prince over his shoulder, then grabbed the king by the hair. He motioned to Black with a nod of his chin. "Lead the way."

Black didn't bother trying to open a door but crashed through, using the queen as a battering ram.

Licking her lips, Josephina faced the crowd. Every eye was glued to her, wide, expectant and angry.

"All right," she called. "You saw my strength, my skill. You saw the strength and skill of my friends." As she spoke, she could feel the rest of the energy leaving her, and within a few seconds, a strange heaviness was settling over her limbs. To mask the oncoming weakness, she eased onto the king's throne and continued her speech. "There's more where that came from if—"

A shadow dropped from the ceiling, snagging her attention as it landed on White's shoulders. The girl had no time to react. One second she stood proud, the next her head was on the floor—without her body.

Josephina screamed.

As the girl's body flopped to the floor lifelessly, blood pouring from her severed neck, the person responsible landed on her feet and straightened.

"I told you that you'd regret what you did to me," the Phoenix said with a grin.

Red realized what had happened to his sister and fell to his knees.

Green released an agonized "Nooo!" The first word he'd ever spoken in Josephina's presence.

A pallid William clutched his heart.

Shock slammed through Josephina. The horrific nature of what had just happened—

Wasn't even the worst part.

As she reeled, White's entire body changed. Her skin darkened, blackened…cracked, leaving thousands of tiny round pieces. Those pieces sprouted legs and broke away from each other. Bugs, she thought with a wave of revulsion. The creepy crawlers sped into action, sweeping through the room, covering the floor, the walls, chasing the Fae and trying to burrow under their skin.

Shrieks and panicked footfalls erupted. Fists banged at the closed doors. People were stampeded as others struggled to push their way out of the only opening. Someone must have found a key to another realm, because a new doorway was created at the back of the room. A few of the Fae managed to race through it—but so did some of the bugs.

The bugs. Oh, sweet mercy.

Where were they headed?

Amid the chaos, the Phoenix circled Josephina. "You have only yourself to blame for this. Well, yourself and your man. He crossed the Moirai. They said he changed their fate, and so, they changed his. They were only too happy to use me to punish him—and what better way to punish him than to destroy his darling wife?"

"Leave Kane out of this. It's between you and me."

"The Moirai dropped me in your life at the perfect time. You're finally without your protector—and I'm without patience. This battle has been too long coming."

The Phoenix launched at her.

Josephina spun out of the way, and the girl soared past her, dang it. Instincts, she thought—she needed to override them. She *needed* contact, even if it hurt.

The Phoenix quickly gained her footing and turned, swiping out a hand covered with metal claws. Josephina twisted to the side, taking the nails in her forearm, even while sucking a little of the girl's strength. The Phoenix didn't seem to notice—yet. As warm blood trickled down Josephina's arm, the girl came at her again, and this time, her thigh took the brunt of the abuse. This injury proved worse, but she was able to suck in even more strength.

A fist into her heart. Hissing, Josephina wrapped her fingers around the girl's wrists at the moment of contact. She was swept forward as the girl drew back for another strike, but managed to hold on, taking more and more energy.

Strengthening.

The Phoenix weakening.

Realizing what she was doing, the girl jerked away, out of reach. "You dare try to thieve from me again!"

"Try?" She forced a laugh.

Growling, the Phoenix dove at her. Her arms crisscrossed as she attempted to slice Josephina into pieces, without allowing any prolonged contact. Josephina dodged, moving faster than she had a few minutes ago.

"Someone's been practicing. So, how about we take this up a notch?" Grinning now, the Phoenix walked a wide circle around her, flames shooting from her fingertips and onto the ground. Those flames grew, reaching toward the ceiling. Smoke billowed, making Josephina cough.

Beyond the circle, she could hear Red cursing. What William and Green were doing, she wasn't sure. The panicked murmurs and frantic footfalls of the Opulens had faded, but anyone remaining was still in danger. They were her people now, she thought. She'd left them without a leader, and they needed her. They were hers to protect.

"Very well, then," she said with a nod. "Let's finish this."

Ding, ding.

Josephina threw herself into round two, managing to

land just as many blows as she took. When the Phoenix tripped over one of the cracks Kane had left behind, Josephina raced forward, dropped to her knees and skidded across the floor, stopping at the girl's feet. She grabbed her ankle and jerked her legs out from under her. As soon as the girl hit, she reached out to squeeze her arm, absorbing several more streams of energy.

The Phoenix pushed her away, and jumped to her feet—only to stumble with weakness.

"Kill you," she gasped.

Knowing she had to act now, even at the expense of her own life, Josephina barreled into her. They fell and smacked into the floor, the Phoenix taking the brunt of the impact—but not all of it. Though dizziness swamped her, she crawled up the girl's body, straddled her waist and gripped her by the neck. Another stream of energy entered Josephina. Another and another. The Phoenix tried to bat her away, failed.

"Tink!" she heard Kane shout, just before he ran through the flames.

As he crouched beside her, blisters popped up on his face, arms and hands. The ends of his hair smoked. He didn't waste time asking questions, but slammed his fist into the girl's temple, knocking her out.

Buzzing with energy and heat, so much heat, Josephina scooted away.

He picked the girl up and tossed her out of the fiery circle, calling, "She's all yours, William."

Even though she was overcome by a deluge of emotions—grief, relief, sadness, joy, fear, heartache—Josephina pushed to her feet. "I've got to put out the fire."

"Let me. I—"

"No. It's calling to me," she interjected, and it was. She felt…connected to it, its warmth her warmth. "It wants to be with me." She reached out and the flames instantly leaned in her direction. The moment the tips brushed against her skin, her pores opened up, as if she was drawing power from another person, and the flames were sucked into her body.

"Tell me you're okay," Kane said, gathering her in his arms. He hissed, as if she was burning him, but didn't release her.

"I'm…uninjured. You?"

"Same."

She scanned the throne room. Bodies littered the floor. Most were dead, some were writhing in pain. William, Red, Green and Black were gone—and so was the Phoenix.

"What happened?" Kane croaked. "I came in, and William and Red were nutcases, muttering about defeat and death and destruction. As I jumped through the flames, William demanded I give him the Phoenix."

Tears welled in her eyes, and she explained as best she could about White. Kane paled, released her and fell back on his haunches.

"I did it. My actions, my decisions, killed her. Unleashed her destruction. In this realm. In another realm. An apocalypse has come. And it's my fault," he said.

"No, the Moirai are at fault. They sent the Phoenix."

"Because of me. Because I failed to heed their prediction. Because I attacked them in their home."

"Kane, no. The only reason the Phoenix came here in the first place was to get back at me. If you want to blame someone besides the Moirai, blame me."

"No," he said with a shake of his head. "Never you. Petra's hatred first brought her here. Her stubbornness."

"Well, then, you see. You're not to blame."

His eyes narrowed. "And you're not, either."

She patted his knee. “Okay, then. We’re agreed. The Moirai and Petra will carry this shame.”

A pained look passed over his face, and she knew he wanted to agree with her, but was struggling with his acceptance. And she understood. The Moirai’s predictions had haunted him for so long, he’d just *expected* to carry the guilt.

“Something will have to be done,” he said. “The threat will have to be contained.”

“I happen to know the Lords of the Underworld are up for the challenge.”

He nodded. “You’re right.”

“Always.” If anyone could fight this new threat, it was the Lords—and one day, it *would* be contained.

Kane placed a swift kiss on her lips, and the pain was still there, deep in his eyes, but now, there was also a measure of resolve. “I think you just manipulated me.”

“Me?” she said innocently. “Never.”

Another kiss. “Don’t ever change.”

CHAPTER THIRTY-FIVE

JOSEPHINA AND KANE spent the rest of the night seeing to the defenses of the palace. The bugs had spread throughout the land, and the people were in revolt, fighting each other over the silliest things even while they attempted to storm the outer wall to get to Josephina.

When the two of them finished, when they finally got everyone calm and the wounded tended, she was so exhausted she could barely hold up her head. So much blood…so much violence…

Kane swept her into his arms and carried her to his old bedroom. "I'm sorry about what your father said to you. He was wrong, you know."

"I know that. Now."

"He never saw your worth, and that's his disgrace, not yours."

Similar to the words she'd given him earlier. Smart man, using her methods against her, stopping her argument in its tracks.

He kissed her temple. "You need a nap."

"Do not."

"Well, then, I need to clean up your wounds and I don't want you aware of the pain."

"I'll clean them."

"And you would still feel the pain. That's what I'm trying to avoid."

"I can handle pain."

"But you shouldn't have to." He set her on her feet and pinched the artery running up her neck.

"Don't you dare—" Glaring, she collapsed on a cushioned settee.

His determined face was the last thing she saw.

When she came to however long later, he was still with her. He had a phone pressed to his ear. "Now you know as much as I do. And I'm sorry, man. I'm sorry this happened." A pause. "I'd still really like you to come. The circumstances are the same in both realms, so the women won't be in any more danger here."

"Kane," she rasped.

He spun to face her. "For me," he said, and disconnected the call. Those hazel eyes filled with guilt. "I was just talking to Lucien. William and his children are unreachable. The bugs reached the human realm. No one knows exactly what harm they'll cause."

As he spoke, he walked toward her and discarded his shirt. "The doors are locked. The soldiers I'm willing to trust are doing patrol." He reached down to unbutton her shirt. "Are you mad at me?"

"Yes."

"Do you want me to stop?"

"No." A little mad would never mask the intensity of her desire for him.

Pupils expanding, he eased on top of her. Warm skin and against warm skin, driving her wild.

"Kane, I have a confession to make. I think I…love you," she said, tangling her hands in his hair. "How do you feel about that?"

He closed his eyes for a moment, a look of utter bliss consuming his beautiful features. "I don't know how to express the pleasure the thought of your love gives me, but sweetheart, I want you sure. It's wrong of me, but—"

"Wrong of you how? We're married."

A dark look shuttered over his features. Silent now, he bent his head and kissed the pulse hammering at the base of her neck, a strategic move meant to distract her from her question, but she…wouldn't…*oh!*

His tongue stroked over her collarbone, before delving lower and playing at her breasts. All the while, his hands expertly shucked the rest of her clothing, leaving her completely bare. And then, his hands were free to dabble elsewhere…everywhere.

Every silken touch and wanton caress, soft here, harder there, reminded her of his inexorable power over her. He could take her to heights she'd never dreamed possible.

"I won't show you any mercy," he vowed.

"I don't want your mercy."

"What do you want?"

"You. Only you."

He was in the process of kissing her inner thigh. At her words, he looked up at her. Heat filled his eyes. "You have me." He swooped back up, meshing his mouth into hers, his tongue sweeping inside, claiming, dominating. "I'm yours."

After that, he lost his leisurely pace. He lost his gentleness, too.

He fumbled with the waist of his pants; the very second the material gaped open, he was inside her, her back arching as pleasure speared her.

"Tell me," he commanded as he moved, lines of tension branching from his eyes.

She knew what he wanted. "I love you."

"Sure?"

"So sure."

"Again."

"Love you."

Her words were like fuel to an already raging fire. He became a man possessed by need, only need, rough and wonderful, driving her higher and higher, until all she could do was scream her pleasure.

He roared with his.

But even after he'd collapsed on top of her, he still wasn't done with her. He rose up on his elbows and peered down at her. Need still blazed in his eyes. Panting, she watched as sweat trickled from his temples.

"More," he said, and stoked her desire all over again.

"I FOUND YOU a dress," Kane said a long while later. He tugged on his pants. "Will you wear it for me?"

Josephina watched him, her sated body still humming with pleasure. "Of course."

"Good. Meet me in the throne room in an hour." He blew her a kiss before leaving her alone.

Only then did she realize he'd never offered his own declaration of love. He loved her, though. She knew he did.

But she wanted his admission. *I'll have to step up my game.*

Draped over the corner chair, she found a beautiful ball gown made of the most delicate blue fabric. Not even Synda had ever worn anything so fine. Josephina showered and brushed her teeth, then trembled as she dressed. She took special care with her hair, pinning the sides at the crown of her head.

The only flaw to her appearance was the gash in her cheek. Kane had knocked her out and sewn it up himself, and though he'd placed a flesh-colored bandage over it, it was noticeable.

Down the stairs she went, no guards or servants in sight. Only the leaders had been imprisoned in the dungeon with the royal family. The rest of the army and staff had sworn allegiance to Josephina last night.

She reached the throne room and found Kane waiting for her just outside the doors. He'd changed his clothes, and now wore a clean, pressed white shirt and black slacks. His hair was brushed, the wounds he'd received during battle already healing.

He smiled when he spotted her. A real smile, full of light and heat. "You look beautiful."

"Thank you. But why—"

He pushed open the doors. "Your coronation. And wedding. It's two-for-one day at Chez Fae."

The remaining members of the high and low court had been gathered together and bound at the wrists and ankles. Though many looked as if they wanted to shout at her, all remained silent. Had they been threatened by Kane?

Her gaze skidded back to him. "Wait. Did you say wedding? Because we're already married."

"It wasn't a ceremony you remember or even liked. So, I'm giving you another." He offered her the hook of his elbow. "Ready?"

This man *had* to love her. Trembling, she accepted, and he led her forward.

That's when she saw…*oh, my, but I married a darling man.* There was Maddox, with the beautiful Ashlyn. The babies were…nowhere that she could see. There was Lucien, with the vivacious Anya. Reyes, with the talented Danika. The young Gilly was at Danika's side. Sabin, with the pint-size Gwen. Aeron, with the angelic Olivia and bombshell Legion. There was Gideon, with the fierce Scarlet. Amun, with the glowing Haidee. Strider, with the fiery Kaia. Paris, though he was minus the powerful Sienna.

Each warrior nodded at her encouragingly. Each female smiled at her. Joy broke through a dam erected in her childhood, flooding her.

"Don't worry about the Opulens," Kane said. "Their knowledge of my past is actually quite handy. They fear what will happen if I'm upset."

"Well, they hate me."

"They'll grow to adore you. They won't be able to help themselves."

Kane stopped in front of the king's throne and faced Josephina. He cupped her cheeks. He wasted no time, saying, "I, Kane, promise to take care of you for as long as I live. I promise to put your needs above my own, and compliment you every chance I get. I promise to make you smile at least once a day. And I promise to be yours. Only ever yours."

This is really happening. Light-headed, she managed to squeak out, "I, Josephina—Tink—Aisling, promise to take care of *you*. I promise to weather any storms the demon causes, to always value your strength. Anytime I decide to go to war, you'll be the first person I call." She stuck her tongue out at his friends, and each of the warriors grinned. "Now and forever, I belong to you."

Kane leaned down and kissed her, and it wasn't the sweet kiss she'd been expecting. He gave her tongue and heat and passion, taking and giving, pouring desire into her, drinking desire from her.

The world faded away—until the loud cheers of his friends jolted her back to awareness. Kane lifted his head, and grinned down at her.

"You're still sure about how you feel?" he asked.

"Always."

He peered into her eyes. "Good. Because you're it for me, Tinker Bell, Tink, Tinky Dink. My one. My only. My everything. My mine." He rubbed the tip of his nose against hers. "And guess what?"

"What?" Any more goodness, and she would burst.

"The magnitude of what I feel for you has drained the fight right out of the demon. He's gone quiet."

Her heart soared at the thought—Kane was finally free. They both were. "Oh, Kane. That's so wonderful."

"It is," he said, though he smiled sadly. He stepped to the side before she could question him.

Someone moved in behind her and settled something heavy on her head. She almost looked up. Almost. But realization struck and she managed to remain perfectly still. The royal crown was now upon her head, a symbol of power and position. And now, now she was to be ruler of these people, the driving force of an entire race.

She wasn't strong enough on her own. She wasn't wise enough. What if she made the wrong decision? Lives could be lost. Sickness churned in her stomach, and she fought the urge to run away. She hadn't been made for this kind of responsibility. Wasn't sure she could carry it…

"Your queen," Kane announced.

But she had to do it, didn't she?

KANE TOOK A moment to look past the negative he'd caused and focus on the positive. He'd fallen in love. He'd married the finest woman in creation. He'd helped her claim her rightful place.

He'd finally defeated Disaster. Soon, the demon would die.

And soon after that, Kane would follow.

Danika had finally gotten something wrong. Her painting wasn't going to be an issue. White—if White had been the blonde, and he thought now that she had been—was dead.

That meant the Moirai had been wrong, too, just as Tink had predicted. White wasn't going to end up with the man who would start the apocalypse. She wasn't going to end up with anyone at all.

All of their choices had changed the course of their lives.

But he wasn't going to think about any of that right now. Nothing mattered but Tink. Twice he'd taken her without a condom. She could be pregnant, even now.

Longing made him ache—the best kind of ache. He wanted to have children with her. He wanted to be around to raise them.

Another impossible dream.

He had to make sure she was prepared for anything. Everything.

The Opulens had been ushered outside the palace, promised death if they so much as thought to form another revolt. Tink sat on the center throne, her faux smile still frozen in place. He saw the terror in her eyes, and knew the weight of her new responsibilities was only beginning to become clear. She would triumph, however; he had no doubts. She was finally beginning to realize her worth.

Anya and the other women raced up to speak with her. His friends approached him, and formed a circle around him.

"My queen is better than your queen," Paris said, punching him in the arm good-naturedly.

Kane rolled his eyes. "There's no queen better than mine."

"Want to bet?"

"Yeah. I do." Kane liked and respected Sienna—she'd done good things for the Titans since taking the throne, and she was helping Torin out of a bind as they spoke—but she was no Tink.

"Loser has to wear a dress to Anya's wedding."

I'll most likely be dead. Still he said, "You've got a deal."

Maddox nudged him. "You're going to stay here, aren't you?"

The group went quiet.

Kane nodded. "I'm staying. Tink's needed here, and I'm going to help her settle in." It would be his last work on this earth.

He hated that he would be leaving her to deal with the war he'd helped ignite. He hated that he would be leaving his friends all over again. He told himself they would all be better off without him—but that didn't make the goodbyes any easier.

Reyes pushed out a heavy breath. "It's good that you're helping her. Family comes first."

Kane nodded in agreement. "Thank you for understanding."

"Hey, understanding is what the bro code is for," Strider said. "Just keep a room ready for me. I'll be visiting. Count on it."

"We all might," Sabin said. "We're about to be homeless."

He gave each warrior a hug, and wished Cameo and Torin were here. Even Viola.

The females would be found, alive and well. These men would make sure of it. And whatever was going on with Torin would be resolved. Kane wouldn't believe otherwise.

He glanced over at Tink, his gaze always drawn to her. He spotted Malcolm, the green-haired Sent One standing behind her, his arms crossed over his middle as he listened to her conversation with the other females. None of the women seemed to notice him.

Apparently, he'd wanted Tink to see him in the hotel room, but Kane to see him now. What was his game?

Anger sprouted from roots that had yet to wither. "You," Kane shouted. "What do you think you're doing, hanging around here?"

Malcolm met his glare, and vanished.

"I'm not going to ask who you were talking to," Maddox said. "I'm just going to go. Ashlyn and I must return to our babies. They are with the Sent One Lysander, and he had better be doing a good job or he will find himself without a head."

Lysander, one of the seven leaders of the seven armies of Sent Ones. Married to Bianka, Kaia's twin sister. Perhaps Zacharel, Lysander's friend, had sent Malcolm, Zacharel's soldier, to guard Tink?

Perhaps I should have been nicer.

Kane slapped Maddox on the shoulder. "I'll miss you guys."

"If ever you need anything," Sabin said.

"We're only a phone call away," Strider finished.

"When we find Pandora's box, we'll let you know," Reyes said.

Kane had spent centuries of his life searching for that box. To know he wouldn't be alive when it was finally found and destroyed was a terrible blow. But whatever. He'd rather take out Disaster now, while the creature was too weak to fight back.

The men gathered their women, and Lucien flashed them away two at a time.

Kane strode over to Tink. "Well," he said.

"Well," she said.

"You're officially the most powerful person in this realm."

"No, that would be you, the new king."

King? Him? He was her man, and that was enough. "The kingdom is yours. The people are yours. You'll always be the final authority."

Instantly, the terror returned to her eyes. "I don't think I can do it," she whispered.

"Tell me those words didn't just spring from the girl who put the former king and queen in their place—the dungeon."

"Yeah, but I did it with help," she said. "Yours, the girls who fed me their strengths, William's. The Rainbow Rejects." Her chin trembled. "I couldn't have done it on my own."

He wanted to tell her she would never be on her own. Yeah. He wanted to. "You can do this, Tink. I have faith in you."

"And I have faith in myself—sometimes."

"That'll increase."

"You're sure?"

"I am."

"Because you believe in me. And you love me," she said. "I know you do, whether you've said the actual words or not."

"You, Tinker Bell, own me. There's nothing I wouldn't do for you. No line I wouldn't cross. I love you so much I can barely see straight. I'm obsessed with you, addicted to you. I respect you, and I revere you, and a thousand other words I'm not eloquent enough to express."

Tears welled in her eyes. "Well, you did a great job just now. I think that's the sweetest thing anyone has ever said to me."

"Then everyone else is foolish."

"Oh, Kane…I shouldn't let you give up your home to stay with me. I should force you to leave. I'm finally in control of my own destiny, and you should be in control of yours."

"I am in control." He planted his palms on the arms of the throne, and leaned into her face. "My place is with you. I choose you. I'll always choose you. But go ahead. Try to force me to leave. I dare you."

She gazed up at him with luminous eyes. "Thank you."

"Like I said. You've got me, all the days of my life."

CHAPTER THIRTY-SIX

KANE STOOD BESIDE Tink's throne, and watched as she resolved disputes between the Opulens and poor alike. She had settled into her new role quite nicely, having taken charge of the palace staff and tasked the high and low court with the reconstruction of the garden. There had been several riots, and one male had even snuck into the palace and tried to assassinate the new queen.

Kane and the guard now under his command had quelled the riots, and killed the male. He had not died easily—because Kane hadn't let him.

Word of Tink's feats the day she'd fought her father had spread, gaining her more and more notoriety and support. These people had grown up on the exploits of Lords versus Hunters. They prized cunning, and she'd displayed ample.

Now, only a few weeks into the new regime, the people were beginning to prize Tink.

"Next," the guard manning the line shouted.

Two Opulens stepped to the bottom step of the dais.

Tink shifted uncomfortably in the throne. How beautiful she looked. She wore a new gown of pink silk, with pearls falling over her shoulders, and velvet rose vines hanging from her waist.

The same roses were woven through her dark hair, making her look as if she'd just stepped from a magical forest. Even her makeup added to the illusion. Bold, glittery eye shadow formed catlike points at her temples. Her cheeks were bright with color, and her lips bloodred.

"Tell me your problem," she said to the pair.

The woman on the left raised her chin. "No. I won't do it. It's bad enough I was dragged here, but you're nothing more than a servant. I don't care that you're married to a Lord. There's no reason I should have to abide by your judgments."

It wasn't the first time words like those had been spoken to her, but suddenly Kane was determined that it would be the last. He marched forward, only to stop when Tink held up her hand. She stood, a study of elegance, and glided down the marble steps until she stood in front of the fuming female.

He doubted anyone could see the slight tremor in her limbs, but he could. He knew her—every luscious inch of her—and watched her more intensely than most. She was nervous, but angry. Sad, but determined.

The guards stealthily closed in. They'd been warned. If anything happened to Tink while they were near, they would die. Painfully. No questions would be asked. No excuses would be heard. And yet, Kane struggled to remain in place. He wanted to be down there, by her side, protecting her as instinct demanded. He was her man. But he'd taught her to look after herself, and now she was queen of an entire nation. He couldn't swoop to the rescue without damaging her credibility.

Any other time, that might not have stopped him. He would have killed anyone who questioned her credibility, and that would have been that. But this time, he had to know. *Could* she survive without him?

Every day, Disaster weakened a little more.

Every day, a single fact became clearer. For Kane, the end was near.

Tink lifted her ungloved hands and cupped the offender's cheeks.

The woman gasped, tried to pull away, but failed. Her skin grew pale. Her mouth floundered open and closed. Then, her knees buckled and she hit the ground, unconscious.

"I'm no servant," Tink called loudly. "I'm queen, and I will be obeyed."

Head held high, she strode from the room. Kane followed after her, the Opulen lucky he didn't stomp on her as he passed. He didn't say a word as he sidled up to her, and she didn't, either. They made it into their room, and Kane shut the door.

"I shouldn't have done that," she choked out. "I was angry and I overreacted and I could have seriously hurt her."

"You left her alive, and taught her a valuable lesson in the process. That's more than she deserved." More than he would have done.

"All I taught her was to fear me. And that would be wonderful if I wanted her fear. I don't. That's what my father had." She wrung her hands together and paced in front of the bed. "I should have done to her what I'd done to the others. Sent her away without a verdict. One day she would have come back and she would have been willing to listen to anyone to settle the dispute. Even me."

He shrugged. "Maybe you're right."

She stopped and peered over at him. "Wait. You're not going to defend my actions, no matter how foolish I was?"

Can't grin. "Cut yourself some slack. You're new to

this. And you're doing better than I would have done. If I were queen, everyone would have received a death sentence at minute one."

She rolled her eyes. "While you would make a very sexy queen, I know you're just saying that to be nice."

Her definition of "nice" was a bit skewed. Adorable, but skewed. "Sweetheart, when have you ever known me to be nice?"

She thought for a moment, nodded. "That's true. You're the meanest man I know. I'll probably be known as the Mad—but Wonderful—Queen in all the history books, just for staying with you."

Won't laugh. "Well, well. Someone has a smart mouth today," he said, stalking forward. "And that someone is getting a spanking."

She yelped and darted around the bed. "Kane!"

"Silly Fae. You can't get away from me."

"But I can try." She quickened her pace, and the chase was on.

She ran around the dresser, the vanity, through the bathroom, the closet, and anytime he would get his hands on her, she'd manage to wiggle free. Soon they were both laughing, out of breath, but he wasn't one to give up—not when she was the prize.

He caught her, and they tumbled to the floor in a tangle of limbs. Her laughter died as he pressed his lips to hers.

"Kane," she breathed, melting against him.

"My Tinker Bell. I'm going to have you."

"Yes. Hurry. I want you."

"No, I'm going to savor you." He took his time undressing her, every moment a new revelation of his feelings for her—because he loved every inch of her. Every curve. Every hollow. Every scar.

He kissed his way down her body, treasuring her breathy sighs, her heated touches, the languorous way she moved, clutching at him, as if touching him was something she'd been born to do.

He would never get enough of her.

And he would never forget her, not even in death.

In a way, they'd grown up together. When they'd met, they'd both been in a very dark place. They'd lacked hope. Their fears had overwhelmed them. Together, they'd climbed out of the depths of hell—literally and figuratively. They'd found reasons to laugh. They'd let go of hate and embraced love. The weaknesses they'd had had been blasted by fire and were now strengthened with steel. They hadn't broken. They wouldn't break.

He couldn't even imagine what would have happened to him if he'd never gone back for her. Disaster had tried to stop him, and maybe the Moirai had even tried to stop him, but there was something in him that was greater than both. Love. And love couldn't ever be stopped.

Kane parted her legs and slid inside her—home, this was his home—then set out to slowly drive them both insane. She writhed against him, losing herself to the pleasure, the passion, the moment, the inexorable connection.

He was the one to beg for more. He couldn't get enough.

His control began to fray. Always she had that effect on him. His motions came quicker, harder. And when he began to surge so forcefully her head banged into the wall, her lips parted on a scream of pleasure. She arched her back, taking him even deeper, and he found himself following her over the edge, growling and shuddering with the force of his release.

He wasn't sure how much time passed before he recovered enough to pick her up and carry her to the bed. He only knew he didn't want to let her go. Touching her was a need, a requirement. And not knowing how much longer he would be with her made the thought of separation so much more difficult.

But he had to go. She needed sleep, and if he stayed, he would take her again.

She snuggled under the covers and gazed up at him sleepily.

"Do you still love me?" he asked.

"Always."

"I love you, too." He kissed her brow. "So much. You're my number one."

"Number one," she said on a contented sigh. "What I've always wanted to be."

By the time he straightened, she was already asleep. He dressed, stepped into the hall. When he stepped forward, intending to return to the throne room, Malcolm appeared just in front of him, stopping him.

Startled, he furrowed his brow. "You want to tell me what's going on and why I keep seeing you?"

"Want? No. Will I?" Malcolm shrugged. "In a moment. First, tell me why you're so unhappy."

"Unhappy? When I've done everything I set out to do, giving Tink a new life, a reason to live?" He tried to scoff. He failed.

"Yes," the Sent One said.

"Why do you care?"

"We will get to that, as well."

He popped his jaw, and admitted, "I don't want to ever leave my wife. I'd return to the way things were, with Disaster, but I also don't want the demon able to hurt her. Basically, I'm damned if I do and damned if I don't."

"And that is the crux of a curse such as yours. But perhaps I can soften the blow."

"What do you mean?" Kane demanded.

You'll never be rid of me, Disaster said, his low, whispery voice wafting through Kane's mind. Determined as he was to survive, the demon had lost his fear of Malcolm.

Kane's hands fisted.

"I will kill Disaster, once and for all," Malcolm said. "I will burn the evil out of you. No demon can withstand the sword of fire. The problem is, this will—"

"Kill me, too," Kane said hollowly. Everything always came back to that. "How does that help me get what I want most? A demon-free future with my wife?"

"It doesn't. But at least your spirit will live on."

"That's exactly what would happen without your sword of fire."

"Yes, but without the fire, the essence of the demon's evil will remain inside you, and when you die, your spirit will go down rather than up."

Meaning, if he died the way he'd intended, his spirit would go to hell. For all eternity. Trapped with more demons. Suddenly Kane had to fight to breathe. He hadn't considered such a consequence. "My friend Baden was beheaded while he was possessed. He went to another realm."

"Yes, and that realm is located in a corridor of hell. The people there don't know it yet, but they will. Every day the walls thin a little more."

Kane tangled a hand in his hair. Poor Baden.

"If I do this," Malcolm continued, "I could be kicked from the skies. Killing a man is against the rules."

"I'm not exactly a man."

"Close enough. Probably."

“So what do you want in return?” he asked again.

“Your wedding ring.”

“My ring?”

The Sent One gave a single, stiff nod. “You heard correctly. And keep in mind, Disaster is about to take a final stand. He’s weak, but he won’t die calmly. I have a feeling the chaos he caused in New York will seem like child’s play.”

And Tink would be at the center of it.

“So do we have a deal?” Malcolm asked. “You will give me the ring, and I will kill you and your demon before he has a chance to act out one last time.”

If he said no, Tink could lose her kingdom amid the chaos Disaster caused. She could be hurt. Or worse.

Was there really a choice here?

“Give me one more night with my wife. I’ll meet you in the garden at dawn. So, yes, we have a deal.”

JOSEPHINA LOST COUNT of the number of times Kane made love to her that night, before he fell into an exhausted sleep, but she never grew tired of his advances—because she knew what he was planning to do. Connected to him as she was, she had been waking up inside his head. She didn’t even have to try anymore. This time, she’d overheard his conversation with the Sent One.

She’d thought she’d known just how badly her husband wanted Disaster killed. But she hadn’t. He was willing to die himself.

Die.

Tears filled her eyes, and her chin trembled. Did he not understand she would be lost without him? That she would be right back where she’d started—praying for death?

I can’t let him do it.

But…more than she yearned to have him at her side, she yearned to see him happy. To know he was living the life he'd always dreamed.

She couldn't have both. Not as long as the demon was inside him. Because, the only way to keep him here, with the demon, was to guilt him, and that she wouldn't do. She wouldn't trap him with her emotions the way the minions had once trapped him with their chains.

She had to let him go, didn't she?

Her heart drummed into a too-fast beat. No. She didn't have to let him go, she realized. Not when she could save him and finally set him free, giving a life for a life.

Her life for his.

Almost every day of her existence, she had been punished for other people's crimes. The past few weeks, she'd done what she'd done to stop that from ever happening again. She'd planned and she'd fought and she'd conquered. But now, she had a chance to end Kane's pain once and for all.

If *she* took the demon inside herself…if *she* met with the Sent One…

She could receive the final blow, saving Kane.

She would die. Once, a part of her had been resigned to such a fate. Now? All of her rebelled. But for Kane, she would do it. She would act as a blood slave was meant, and willingly take the punishment of another.

He deserved a chance to be the man he'd always dreamed of being. He could rule these people better than she ever could. And he would. He wouldn't shrink from the duty just because she wasn't here. He had too much honor.

I have to act now. What had her mother used to say? A horse had to be saddled before it could be ridden.

Knowing she only had a few hours until morning dawned and he would be expected in the garden, she slipped from the bed to quietly dress. Then, using the secret passageways her father had been so fond of, she made her way to the dungeon. Two guards stood sentry at the entrance. They nodded when they spotted her, and moved their crisscrossing swords out of the way. She soared past.

She had examined the cases of the men and women her father had kept down here, and had found out that most had done nothing more serious than annoy him… or have something he'd wanted. So, she'd released the "offenders" and given them bags of gold from the royal treasury. The money couldn't make up for the pain they'd endured, and the years they'd lost, but it was a start.

Rather than keep the remaining prisoners out front, their arms shackled above their heads for all to come and view, she'd placed each individual in a cage, and she'd made sure they were far enough away from each other that they couldn't talk and plan an escape.

The first cage belonged to her father.

She peered through the bars. He paced at the far wall, muttering to himself about the injustice of his circumstances. His clothes were ripped, dirty, and his hair tangled.

He spotted her and froze. "You," he said on a sizzle of breath. "Let me out. Now."

"No." She shook her head. "You earned your place down here. I'm still trying to fix the messes you created for an entire race of people."

"People that belong to me. I can do whatever I choose with them."

"Not anymore."

His eyes narrowed to tiny slits. “Did you come down here hoping to buy my love? To taunt me with what I lost, and promise to give it back if only I’ll acknowledge you?”

She laughed without humor, and he blinked in confusion. “The time for that passed long ago. And no, I didn’t come down here to taunt you.”

“Whatever your reason, it was a mistake.” He raced to the bars and reached through, wrapping his fingers around her neck. She could have avoided contact—but she hadn’t wanted to.

As he squeezed, she curled her ungloved hands around his wrist and drew from him. Strength. The abilities he possessed.

He tried to sever the connection, but the suction was simply too powerful.

When finally she released him, his knees collapsed and he toppled to the floor.

“Thanks for that,” she said. Her muscles buzzed with energy. Her blood crackled. “It’s why I came. You see, I’m not going to survive the morning, and I’m hoping your abilities will die with me, leaving you as helpless as the people you’ve hurt.”

As he roared a denial, she moved on to the next hall of cells and came to the queen’s personal quarters. The female was just as dirty as the king, but she turned her back on Josephina, as if she still couldn’t bear to speak with her.

“I’m proof of his infidelity. You hate me. I get it.”

Silence. Not even the rasp of breath.

“I was an innocent party in all of this,” Josephina added, determined to say her piece. “I was a child. I was lonely and scared, and desperately wanted someone to love me. My mother was a woman trapped by circumstance. No one in this realm said no to the king, and you know that. She didn't want a married man, but rather than help her escape his notice, you shunned her."

Annnd, still nothing.

In a secret place in her heart, she had wanted an apology. An acknowledgment. She would never get it, though, and wouldn't spend another second hoping for it, wasting this precious energy.

Sighing, she moved on to Synda's cell. The girl had heard her and was waiting for her, fingers twined around the bars.

"Let me out," the princess begged. "Please."

Josephina opened her mouth to pour out every hurt this girl had caused, to voice every wrong she'd had to endure, but she stopped herself. Synda would listen, but she wouldn't hear. She would nod, but she wouldn't truly understand. She would tell Josephina everything she longed to be told, Josephina would free her, and Synda would forget what she'd promised. Unlike Kane, the girl had never fought the evil inside her.

"I'll let Kane decide what to do with you." She reached through the bars and cupped her sister's cheeks. "You need help. I don't know who you are without the demon, and maybe you don't, either, but it *is* possible to fight the demon's whims."

Tears cascaded from the corners of Synda's eyes. "I know. I just don't know how to do that."

"Talk to Kane. He may not like you at first, but if you're honest with him, if you're sincere about wanting help, he'll come around. Goodbye, Synda." With that, Josephina released her and walked to her brother's cell.

He was sitting in the corner, close to the bars, and facing her. His knees were drawn up, and his head propped against the wall.

"You look well," he said.

She ignored the compliment, saying, "You aren't going to beg me to free you?"

"Why should I? For the first time, I'm not looking over my shoulder, expecting death."

"Oh, please." He'd had the pampered, privileged life she'd always envied.

"It's true, Josephina. Every day I expected death to come for me."

"I don't see why…unless you treated other girls the way you treated me. You should have been my friend."

He shrugged. "I wanted to be more. I still do."

"You're my brother."

"I'm not."

She frowned. "Of course you are."

He laughed bitterly. "You think you were the only child born out of wedlock? You think the king was the only one to have affairs in the years of his marriage? He let me know in no uncertain terms that I wasn't his child, I was the queen's, but that he was keeping me because he needed an heir."

She…actually believed him, little facts sitting up in her mind. He looked nothing like Tiberius and never had. The king had always been distant with him. Had always chosen Synda over him. Why had she never suspected?

Shock rattled her knees. "Why didn't you tell me?"

"Had anyone found out, I would have been killed." Another bitter laugh. "Actually, if any of his women had ever had a boy, I would have been killed. I lived day by day. I knew you understood that, and thought it bonded us."

It would have. If she'd known. "I would have kept

your secret, if only you'd been my friend. I needed your support, not your lust."

He traced a symbol on the floor. "Does your…husband treat you well?"

"He does."

"And you like him?"

"I love him."

Sadness darkened his features. "If you ever want him killed, come see me. I'll take care of it for you."

She stood there for a moment, thinking about what could have been between them. Not romance. Never that, even without the blood tie. But companionship. Affection. Support. "Tell Kane what you told me. I'm not sure he'll show you mercy. You forced your attentions on me, after all, but he might let you live. A part of me likes the thought of you finally finding peace."

He smiled sadly. "I never would have forced you, you know. I just wanted the chance to prove how good we could be, despite what you believed about us."

Maybe it was naive of her, but she believed that, too. "Goodbye, Leopold."

He shouted as she walked away, his voice dripping with concern—*that sounded like a permanent goodbye, Josephina*—but she kept going.

Back in her bedroom, she found Kane sleeping soundly on the bed. She reached out and removed the ring from his finger, the key to his future, then smoothed her hands over his brow, the need to touch him too strong to ignore. He leaned into her, his lips curling at the corners.

Goodbye, my love.

As if he'd heard the heart-wrenching cry inside her, he cracked open his eyelids. "Tink. Get back in bed, sweetheart. Let me hold you."

"Sleep, darling," she said.

"Hmm."

To ensure he stayed down, she used the same move he'd used on her, squeezing his carotid until he returned to his dreams.

Then, she wrapped her fingers around his wrist, closed her eyes and drew the darkness out of him and into her, just like she'd done that night in the forest. Before, the demon had entered her with a vengeance. This time, he was too weak to scream obscenities. He was merely a heavy weight inside her, a presence in the back of her mind.

She released Kane the moment she knew the demon was with her, not wanting to take his strength, too.

His features smoothed out, and he smiled again, so peaceful her chest ached. He must have sensed, on some level, that he was now alone.

No question, she'd made the right decision.

"I love you," she said, and kissed his temple. "Never forget."

CHAPTER THIRTY-SEVEN

KANE AWOKE AS sunlight poured through the open curtains. He sat up with a jolt.

Morning.

He jumped out of bed, then cringed, hoping his abruptness hadn't woken Tink. But she wasn't in the bed, he realized. He quickly dressed and left the room. She was probably in the breakfast nook.

It was better this way, he thought. He'd already said goodbye the only way he could. If he were to see her now, he might change his mind. He might break down and cry. If he told her the truth—and she would insist on the truth, and he would give it because he was unable to deny her anything—she would try and stop him. He might let her. Anything for more time with her.

To avoid the guards and servants, he used the secret passageway to get to the garden, and why was his torso burning? He stopped long enough to look under his clothes, and blinked. The butterfly tattoo had faded significantly. Because the demon was dying?

In the warmth and light of the new day, he felt strangely calm and burden free, considering he was about to die. He felt…lighter.

When he turned the corner, he saw Malcolm and Tink standing several yards away. Shock stopped him in his tracks.

"—the ring, just like you wanted," Tink said, placing something in the warrior's hand.

Malcolm looked down at her. "As thrilled as I am to have it, my deal was with Kane."

"And now it's with me. I absorbed the demon and now carry him in *my* body."

The Sent One frowned. "You don't look as if you carry the demon."

"That's because he's too weak to cause any trouble."

The conversation confused Kane. He fingered the ring on his—bare skin, he realized. The ring was gone.

Dread slithered through him.

"Without the demon, Kane is going to die, anyway," Malcolm said. "Why should I help you achieve the same fate?"

"He's going to… No! I won't believe that."

"Nevertheless, it's true."

"But…but…." She went still, as if she couldn't even bare to breathe. "He never experienced the life he dreamed of…a life free of Disaster. He should know how it feels to be at peace before he dies, and I can give him that chance, even if only for a little while."

"And you're willing to give your life for that chance? Take a moment. Think about this. Once it's done, it cannot be undone."

"I have thought about it. I want to do it here, now."

Malcolm nodded. "Very well. My bargain is now with you." He held out his hand and a sword of fire appeared.

In that moment, a sickening realization dawned. Tink had taken the ring, and she'd taken the demon, and she now planned to take Kane's place.

She was going to die in his stead, simply to give him a few days, maybe a few weeks, without the demon.

"No!" Kane screamed. "No! Don't you dare!"

But it was too late.

Malcolm had already been in the process of striking. The fire pierced her chest, and her scream of pain shattered every corridor of his heart.

"No!" he cried. "No!"

The sword slid out of her and Kane saw a gap the size of his fist.

Tink collapsed. And Malcolm vanished.

Kane dropped to his knees and roared up at the sky.

In a daze, when the shock of what he'd witnessed had worn off, but not the horror, never the horror, Kane crawled to his wife, gathered her in his arms and cradled her precious body against his chest. He held her for what seemed an eternity, but it couldn't have been more than an hour.

There was no blood on her or him. The sword had cauterized the wound, and it wasn't right. He should be covered in her blood, should have tangible evidence of the pain she had endured. He should have to wear it, a constant reminder of the disaster he had allowed—even without the demon living inside him. He *needed* to see his shame. His grief. His failure. Something, anything, but this…nothingness.

Nothingness. Yes. That's all he had now.

His wife, his love, was gone. For nothing! Didn't she know he could not have peace without her?

Tears must have been brewing at the back of his eyes because they suddenly spouted out, like rivers of anguish. He sobbed like a baby, and he didn't care who saw him. Guards and Opulens came up to him and tried to talk to him, to learn what had happened, but he snarled and sent them running away.

"How could you do this?" he demanded of Tink. But he already knew the answer, didn't he. She'd loved his life more than her own. "How?"

He brushed his fingers through the softness of her hair—her *blond* hair? Yes. Blond. Even her features had changed. She looked like Petra, and he had a moment of hope, thinking Petra had died and not his wife. But then her hair and features changed again, and he found himself peering down at someone he didn't recognize.

When she changed a third time, and the strange image remained for an hour, then another, realization hit him and all hope withered. This was Tink, the blonde in the painting, and she was dead.

She had drained the Phoenix, acquiring the girl's ability to shift identities, that was all. Because, now that the shifting had stopped, whatever spark had tried to ignite had been extinguished.

His Tink was dead, and she wasn't ever coming back.

He howled up at the sky.

He had his freedom now, but the price had been too high.

He wanted to lash out, to kill someone, destroy something, but he couldn't bear to release his Tink. So he sat there, even as the sun disappeared behind clouds and rain poured. He sat there as day turned to night.

Malcolm appeared a few feet away, his skin pallid, his lips compressed into a hard line.

A growl rose in Kane's throat.

"I know I'm the last person you wish to see right now, but I must tell you what I've learned. I…went to my leader, told him what I'd done. He has assured me you will survive the removal of your demon, just as the girl wished."

Well, what do you know? Kane could release his

wife, after all. He stood, his hands fisted. "I might survive, but you won't."

The Sent One raised his chin. "Hear me out, warrior."

"How could you kill her? You are forbidden from taking human life, and she was half human."

"The moment she accepted your demon, I stopped seeing her that way."

"That doesn't change your rules."

"No, nor does it change my circumstances. I was going to be punished either way."

Will...kill...

But the warrior wasn't finished. "I was wrong when I told you that you would be emptied out. Your cup wasn't spilled over. Water was poured inside, slowly displacing the oil. Now, you're filled with the water…with love. I'm…sorry for your wife's death."

"Doesn't matter now." He withdrew two daggers.

The Sent One sighed. "You don't want to fight me."

"You're right. I want to murder you." He launched one of the daggers, aiming for Malcolm's neck, but he vanished, and the weapon soared past him, embedding in a tree. Then, he reappeared.

Kane threw the other dagger, and the Sent One performed the same move.

He advanced. They'd settle this with their hands, then.

"Your woman." Frowning, Malcolm tilted his head to the side as he looked beyond Kane's shoulder. "She's on fire."

Kane spun, seeing flames dance at the end of her big toes. Once again, hope ignited as he realized what was happening. If she had retained Petra's abilities, she could rise from her own ashes.

But what if Petra had been close to the final death?

He watched, desperate, as the flame spread to Tink's other toes…to her ankles. Her knees. Her waist. Her shoulders…her head. Until she was engulfed.

She began to wither. A pile of ashes formed.

Then, nothing. The flames vanished.

Another hope destroyed.

Kane erupted.

He tore out hunks of earth. He kicked and punched trees. He—

Was blown backward by an intense wave of heat. He rolled to a stop and jumped to his feet. Beside him, Malcolm did the same. Another fire now raged, this one crackling over the ashes, lifting them, swirling them together.

Please, he thought. *Please.*

A female form came into view, floating in the center of the flames. Tink's face took shape, then her hair, and body, and his heart nearly burst from his chest.

She opened her eyes, and the flames died in an instant. Her naked form fell to the ground, and she hmphed, losing her breath.

Breath. She had breath.

It had worked!

Kane dropped to his knees, the rush of relief too much for him.

She held up a trembling arm, twisted it in the light, then held up the other. "I'm really here." Her eyes widened. "Kane, I'm really here!"

He lumbered to his feet, staggered over to her. He needed to touch her. Like, now. Emotion clogged his throat as he fell at her feet and gathered her in his arms. "I've never been so glad to watch someone catch fire," he said, squeezing her tight. "You reformed, sweetheart. You reformed."

"But only the Phoenix can do—" Realization dawned on her beautiful face. "The Phoenix! I took from her."

"Yes." A miracle of perfect timing. A choice…and a destiny.

"William must have killed her," Malcolm said. "That's the only way Josephina would have retained the ability. Which means, it hasn't faded and it won't. She's no longer half human. She's fully immortal, though it appears her ability is weaker than that of other Phoenix. They usually catch fire moments after the deathblow is struck."

Kane had thought his tear ducts had dried, and yet, droplets rained down his cheeks. Tink. Fully immortal. His forever. "Thank you," he said, the words for Tink, for Malcolm and his leader. "Thank you so much."

Malcolm looked to the sky, paused and might even have smiled. "I have been told to tell you the baby reformed with his mother. Though he is only a few days old, he is specially gifted, and very strong." After dropping that bombshell, he vanished.

A baby. A boy.

To know this soon…

Kane almost couldn't process the news. Reverently his hand moved to his wife's still-flat stomach.

Her eyes were wide and luminous. Then she laughed, joyous. "A baby, Kane."

"Are you happy?"

"More than I ever thought possible. I always thought my gift and my circumstances were a blessing and a curse, but all along they've been a blessing, never a curse. I'm alive, and we're going to have a baby, a baby that will be free—and you're free, Kane. You're free! The demon is dead. He's no longer a part of you or me."

He buried his face in the hollow of her neck, breathed

her in. "What you did for me…I'll never be able to repay you. The price you paid…the pain you just endured…" He shuddered. "Don't you ever do anything like that again. I need you. You're mine. We belong together."

"Now and forever."

He pulled back to peer into her eyes. The stitches had burned from her cheek and the swelling had gone down, but even still, a jagged six-inch line stretched over her skin. The hole in her chest had been filled, but there was a big, puckered scar.

"The injuries happened before you were fully immortal, so the evidence of them will never go away, I bet," he said.

"Are they bad?" she asked, rubbing the scar on her chest.

"Bad? They're amazing. Like you. Badges of courage—of your love for me." He searched the rest of her, groaned. "We need to cover you up." He tore off his shirt and tugged it over her head, concealing her bare breasts. He removed his pants and handed the material to her, leaving him in his underwear.

She smiled, a big happy smile. "The women are going to be drooling over you."

"They can drool, but they can't touch."

"Because you're mine," she said, "just like I'm yours."

"Forever," he said.

"Forever," she agreed.

A forever that would be very busy. "I want this kingdom at peace before our son arrives. I want Cameo and Viola found, and my debt to the Sent Ones paid. I'll have to help them find the demons that killed their king."

"Together, we can do anything."

He kissed her, soft and sweet. "For now, I'm only interested in holding you, feeling your heart beat against mine, and proving you really are alive."

"I think you want to remove my clothes," she replied huskily.

He kissed her again, this time strong and sure. "Yes, but the removal of clothing is only step one."

"And step two?"

"Come. I'll show you."

* * * * *

Lords of the Underworld
Glossary of Characters and Terms

Aeron—Lord of the Underworld; former keeper of Wrath

All-key—a spiritual relic capable of freeing the possessor from any lock

All-Seeing Eye—human with the power to see into heaven and hell, past and future; Danika Ford

Amun—Lord of the Underworld; keeper of Secrets

Anya—(minor) goddess of Anarchy; beloved of Lucien

Ashlyn—human female with supernatural ability; wife of Maddox

Atropos—a Moirai

Baden—former Lord of the Underworld; keeper of Distrust (deceased)

Bianka Skyhawk—Harpy; sister of Kaia, Gwen and Taliyah; consort of Lysander

Black—one of the four shadow warriors; famine

Cage of Compulsion—artifact with the power to enslave anyone trapped inside

Cameo—Lord of the Underworld; keeper of Misery

Cloak of Invisibility—artifact with the power to shield its wearer from prying eyes

Cronus—former ruler of the Titans

Danika Ford—human female; girlfriend of Reyes; known as the All-Seeing Eye

Deity—former king of the Sent Ones (deceased)

Ever—daughter of Maddox and Ashlyn

Fae—race of immortals that descends from Titans

Flashing—transporting oneself with just a thought

Galen—former second-in-command of the Hunters; keeper of Hope and Jealousy

Gideon—Lord of the Underworld; keeper of Lies

Gilly—human female

Glorika Aisling—mother of Josephina

Gorgon—immortal creature able to turn any living being into stone

Greeks—former rulers of Olympus before Titans

Green—one of four shadow warriors; death

Gwen Skyhawk—Harpy; sister of Kaia, Bianka and Taliyah; wife and consort of Sabin

Haidee—former Hunter; Amun's wife

Hunters—mortal enemies of the Lords of the Underworld

Josephina Aisling—half human, half Fae; aka Tinker Bell, Tinker Hell, Tink, Tinky Dink

Juliette—a Harpy

Kaia Skyhawk—part Harpy, part Phoenix; aka the Wing Shredder; sister of Gwen, Taliyah and Bianka; consort of Strider

Kane—Lord of the Underworld; keeper of Disaster

Klotho—a Moirai

Lachesis—a Moirai

Lazarus—an immortal warrior; only son of Typhon and an unnamed gorgon

Legion—demon minion in a human body; adopted daughter of Aeron and Olivia

Leopold—only Fae prince

Lords of the Underworld—exiled immortal warriors now hosting the demons once locked inside Pandora's box

Lucien—coleader of the Lords of the Underworld; keeper of Death

Lysander—elite Sent One

Maddox—Lord of the Underworld; keeper of Violence

Malcolm—a Sent One; member of Zacharel's army

Marigold—a female from the past

Moirai—three immortal witches who weave destiny; aka "The Three Fates," "hobags"

Neeka—deaf Harpy; prisoner of the Phoenix

Never-ending—a portal into hell

Olivia—an angel; beloved of Aeron

Olympus—former city of the gods; now known as Titania

Opulens—the Fae upper class

Pandora's Box—made of the bones from the goddess of Oppression; once housed demon high lords, now missing

Paring Rod—artifact with ability to rend soul from body

Paris—Lord of the Underworld; keeper of Promiscuity

Penelope—queen of the Fae

Petra—female Phoenix

Phoenix—fire-thriving immortals descended from Greeks

Princess Fluffykans—Viola's pet Tasmanian devil

Realm of Blood and Shadows—location of the Lords of the Underworld's current fortress

Red—one of four shadow warriors; war

Reyes—Lord of the Underworld; keeper of Pain

Sabin—coleader of the Lords of the Underworld; keeper of Doubt

Scarlet—keeper of Nightmares; wife of Gideon

Sent Ones—winged warriors that fight evil

Séduire—the realm of the Fae

Sienna Blackstone—ruler of the Titans; beloved of Paris

Strider—Lord of the Underworld; keeper of Defeat

Synda—Fae princess; keeper of Irresponsibility

Taliyah Skyhawk—Harpy; sister of Bianka, Gwen and Kaia

Tartarus—an underground holding cell for immortals

Tiberius—king of the Fae

Titania—the city of the gods; formerly known as Olympus

Titans—rulers of Titania; children of fallen angels and humans

Torin—Lord of the Underworld; keeper of Disease

Typhon—an immortal creature with the head of a dragon and the body of a snake

Urban—son of Maddox and Ashlyn

Viola—minor goddess; keeper of Narcissism

White—one of four shadow warriors; conquest

William the Ever Randy—immortal warrior of questionable origins; aka the Panty Melter

Zacharel—elite Sent One; leader of the Army of Disgrace

Zeus—king of the Greeks